Lucretia Gray Noble

A Reverend Idol

A novel. Fifteenth Edition

Lucretia Gray Noble

A Reverend Idol
A novel. Fifteenth Edition

ISBN/EAN: 9783337000097

Printed in Europe, USA, Canada, Australia, Japan

Cover: Foto ©Andreas Hilbeck / pixelio.de

More available books at **www.hansebooks.com**

A REVEREND IDOL

A NOVEL

FIFTEENTH ‘EDITION

BOSTON
TICKNOR AND COMPANY
211 Tremont Street

Franklin Press:

RAND, AVERY, AND COMPANY,

BOSTON.

CONTENTS.

A REVEREND IDOL.

CHAPTER. I.

THE great preacher of St. Ancient's had just arrived
at his summer lodgings. These were a front chamber and a back one, under the roof of Mistress Doane,
widow of Capt. Azariah Doane, drowned mariner of
Cape Cod. As the new-comer disappeared up stairs,
his landlady remarked that "he didn't exactly look like
a minister; but 'twas certain he was a regular high-born
gentleman, because he stepped right into things just as
he found them, putting on no airs at all." And black
Susannah, the only audience which the widow had for
her comments, replying with whatsoever comments of her
own on the stranger, forthwith alluded to him as his
Honor. Nor could any instructions about the proper
distributing of titles among the professions ever after
prevail on her to drop this fashion of designating the
Rev. Kenyon Leigh.

"His Honor" (he had, by the way, this approximate
claim to Susannah's peculiar term of distinction, that he
was the son of a judge) was stepping meanwhile from
one to another of his chamber-windows to see the wide
view therefrom, which nothing intercepted, save, at one
window, the overshadowing boughs of a Balm-of-Gilead
tree, which had grown to quite an imposing size for a
Cape-Cod tree.

1

Mrs. Doane was right.   Although there was nothing in
the stranger's mien or dress which jarred on your idea of
a minister, when you found that he was one, still you
would never have taken him at first sight for a minister,
even of the Muscular Saint variety.   No : while he was
a most uncommonly tall, powerfully-built man, the very
last of characters which he suggested was the type popu-
larly known as the athletic clergyman.   Intellectuality
predominated in him rather than animal spirits.

Just now he had the look of a man glad, for some
reason, to reach the desert; and a desert it was which
stretched before him.   The vast sweep of the open
Atlantic, its shore scarcely more than half a mile distant
from the front of the house, bounded the horizon ; while
away to one side, the gray tower and fantastic arms of
a windmill, a few weather-beaten roofs of the little village
of Lonewater, to which the widow Doane's house nomi-
nally belonged, but from which it was quite outlying, —
these were the sole signs of human life in the landscape.
All else was a strange, rolling waste of sand-hills, only
broken here and there by little belts of pine-trees and
shrub-oaks, which with the golden masses of the poverty-
grass, still in bloom, touched the sand-heaps and their
hollows with some hues not wholly unbeautiful to the eye,
however little they might promise of harvest.

All this lonely scene being apparently just what the
present spectator had desired to find, he took up his portmanteau with a well-pleased look, and descended from his
grand front apartment with upright walls, into the back
bedroom with walls at every angle, which completed his
suite.   This second chamber was entered going down by
a step ; for the house, a double one, and two-storied in
front, apparently had several fractions of stories behind,
descending, by gradations, under the long back roof,

sloping slowly to the earth. It was an architectural style marked by a decided originality in windows, which, punched in all sizes and at all levels of distribution through the sides of the house, made an effect without rather unique.

The insane windows, however, freely admitted air, and all things were of spotless neatness; and the traveller, as if reminded to make himself so, directly proceeded to wash the dust of a July journey from his face. During this ceremony he wound up the looking-glass a couple of feet or so, whereby a great bunch of peacock's tail-feathers, which had ornamented its top, went flying into the water-basin below. Considerately fishing out these plumes, he wandered back with them into the front apart-ment, where he stuck them, dripping, over a brazen image of the god Brahma, which was the centre-piece of the mantel there, rich with other such heathen trophies, brought by the departed Capt. Azariah from over the sea.

Having laid about him with a few more of these initial strokes of re-arrangement, such as are wont to characterize a man's entrance upon feminine premises, he seemed to consider himself quite domiciled, and returned to the front windows, again to revel in the delightful solitariness of the prospect. And, lo! the fair Sahara had contracted a blot. One would have said, from the change in the man's face, that that brazen Fate on the mantel suddenly con-fronted him in some spectacle without. This was singu-lar, for the new object in the landscape would generally have been considered a charming one. It was an uncom-monly pretty girl, uncommonly the centre of masculine admiration; and she was making straight for the house. There was, in fact, a group of three maidens, all more or less pretty, escorted by three young men; but *the* pretty girl, whom they called by the boarding-school-romance name of Monny Rivers, seemed to require some *quantum* of attention from all the beaux, and to receive it, by whatever mysterious charm, without alienating her fair companions.

The six creatures were all dressed in perfect style for the occasion. They were undeniably urban carpet-baggers to this world's end which their disgusted observer from the chamber-window had intended solely to carpet-bag himself. Whatever nonsense the belle was uttering as the laughing group came on, there was plainly no end to it; and, as the rest of the party strolled slowly along to a vehicle which Mr. Leigh now perceived was in waiting for them at the head of the lane which led towards the sea, who but she opened the gate, clearly as an *habituée* of the place, and ran up the walk into the house? Yea, up to the very chamber opposite his own, he heard her tripping feet ascend, whence, securing some matter of extra wraps for her friends, she presently returned to her attendant cavalier at the door, who, taking the shawls, escorted the young lady back to rejoin the others.

They were scarcely clear of the house when the minister went down stairs with an immediate word which he had to say to his landlady. In her neat sitting-room he found the pleasant-faced dame (approaching sixty) who had received him on his arrival, and put to her the directest questions as to the number of her family.

"Perfectly quiet," replied Mrs. Doane. "No family but myself and one boarder; and she the loveliest young lady from the city, as is the greatest favorite with everybody, and is going to stay here all the summer through now. And she was in the house a moment ago, but is gone away riding a while with her friends."

"Yes, I saw her," said the minister, with a certain simplicity he had of speaking the truth; and, turning abruptly, he vanished at once from the room, leaving his landlady to lift astonished hands that ever a man, even a minister, who had seen Monny Rivers's face, should not be pleased with the idea of having her round. For plainly she had discerned that the new boarder was *not* pleased with that prospect.

Deeply pondering the mystery, she concluded, at last, that he must be apprehensive lest the whole six whom he had seen together would be haunting the house, to the making of more stir than he desired. So she resolved to take up-stairs a little pitcher of root-beer as a good sedative for the ruffled nerves of a weary traveller, and improve this errand to inform him incidentally that her young lady's friends were only very transient visitors at the Cape. Two of the young men, indeed, in the trio who escorted the belle, had each respectively a sister in the two young ladies accompanying her. It was in pretended devotion to these relatives, that the brothers had included Lone-water in their summer touring; but in truth the latter had exhausted all the arts known to fraternal cajolery to persuade their sisters, school-friends of Miss Monny, to set foot in the dull hamlet for an hour. As for the third admirer, he pursued this worshipped maid with no subterfuge of a sister to sustain him. But for no one of the three rivals who had met so unexpectedly in the village on the same errand, had Miss Monny any preference which would encourage a prolonging of their stay.

Of all this Mrs. Doane was well aware, as she had much more than a summer landlady's acquaintance with her young boarder; for the latter had had as nurse, 'through several years of her childhood, a poor cousin of Mrs. Doane's, through which lowly relation the Cape-Cod widow's house had come to be, from time to time, a summer resort of Miss Rivers ever since.

So, now, the good woman, gathering herself up, made ready her innocent stratagem of beer, and ascended to the presence of the distinguished new arrival to offer the same, and drop the renewed assurance that Lonewater was the most retired place in the world, and that Miss Rivers's friends were all to leave in a day or two, when the young lady would be perfectly quiet and alone. This promise of having the society of the belle solely to himself did but add another shade to the already shadowed clerical brow, as Mrs. Doane failed not to observe. And although the minister politely accepted, whether he drank of the jorum or not, her pitcher of refreshment, she had scarce regained her room when she saw him go forth for a walk, not seaward, but straight back towards the village. Whoever had followed him would have seen that his private errand was to seek there a rather ample-looking house, abode of one Capt. Gawthrop; which house, he had incidentally learned during his ride from the village, had accommodations for boarders. It was, in fact, the place where Miss Rivers's admirers, enduring each other under the same roof as best they could, were at present quartered; and the inquiries which Mr. Leigh now hastened to make at this door suggested a possible change of his own lodgings thither when the rooms should be vacant.

In explanation of this mysterious behavior of the Rev. Kenyon Leigh, who was an unmarried man of thirty-four, it must be said that he was — adored of women. There had been a good many years now of his single estate to attract these adorations in; and the tragical thing was, that, as he grew older, young girls worshipped him all the same and a good deal more, while the maturer maidens and young widows naturally put more personal hope into their devotions: so time brought to this suffocated idol no relief, but an ever-widening circle of the incense-burners. This pernicious atmosphere, however, had not quite spoilt our hero into that most intolerable of cox-combs, the man who fancies every woman must be in love with him, although his apprehensions at sight of a pretty girl so far his junior, and surrounded by her beaux, might seem to imply something very absurd in that direc-tion. The best of men will have moments which by no means represent their normal mood and character; and we beg that Mr. Leigh's proceedings be not prematurely judged; although he did so prolong his ramble as to return late enough to take tea alone, and then requested break-fast to be served to him next morning in his own apart-ment. At dinner and tea of that day, as it chanced, Miss Rivers was herself absent: so he escaped for four meals the pretty girl of whom he made such an extraor-dinary *bête noir*.

But on the second day, as the young lady returned home a little before bedtime, the motherly Mrs. Doane came to her chamber with some good-night gossip, and a kero-sene lamp to aid the dim candle which was winking there. In these lights one saw a rounded girlish figure, of aver-age height, but more than the average vitality of young American maidens. As Monny exchanged her costume of the day for a loose dressing-sack, there were revealed arms and shoulders moulded like those of some sculptured goddess: the exceeding beauty of the girl's hands, in-deed, had cost her dearly in one adventure of her life, whose consequences were not yet past. Her face might not have been considered to possess the ideal perfection of her figure, as the features were irregular; but it was still a very lovely and charming head, — eyes of the darkest brown, and hair of the lightest hue that could be called brown at all; not auburn, but golden in its high lights, and with just a hint of warm brown in the shadows. She had cheeks that dimpled as she smiled, very white and perfect teeth, and a complexion like morning light The rare-hued hair curled naturally; not in tight ringlets, but in large, loose, rolling twines, that lent themselves readily to any style of coiffure: as they were all shaken down now in complete dishevelment, the girl looked fair as a vision. It was a picture in which wealth of color and expression atoned for the want of classic features.

Mrs. Doane, thinking, as she had often done before, that her young boarder was the prettiest girl alive, was led on in these leisurely moments to talk of the masculine new-comer who so strangely saw in this radiant inmate a drawback to her house. The latter, I should here remark, not having heard of everybody in her young life, had never distinctly heard of the illustrious Kenyon Leigh, until she had heard that a New-York preacher of that name was coming to board at Mrs. Doane's. The girl's home was not in New York. The preacher's fame was too utterly removed from the sensational to be as yet noisy (he had been out of the country for the past year); and Miss Monny, moreover, had been brought up to attend the Unitarian Church with one set of her relations, and the Orthodox with another. She was an orphan, having lost both parents by a peculiar fatality when she was scarce a twelvemonth old.

Ere going out in the morning to-day, she had had a mere passing introduction to the new boarder, and had observed, with disapproval, that he was not an aged man; her ideal of the proper clergyman being a very old man with white hair. Where the clergy were to stay while their hairs were whitening was probably a question that she had left unsettled: at all events, mademoiselle decidedly regarded any man at all young as an impertinence in the ministerial office, and certainly as the most unpleasant of beings in any sentimental attitude.

With this predisposition as to clergymen, she now heard the confidences which Mrs. Doane commenced slowly to impart, beginning by mentioning Mr. Leigh's request to have breakfast served in his own room that morning

"Well, for a minister, and a son of Goliath, isn't he a poor fussy worm of the dust?" idly commented Miss Monny, carrying to the fireplace the boots which she had just taken off, and knocking their little heels together to shake out the sand they had gathered.

"I think, dear," pursued the matron, opening further a subject which would have been hard to introduce if the girl had been of a less amiable disposition, — "I think he didn't quite like the idea of your being here. He said nothing direct, of course ; but I saw he wasn't pleased at there being another boarder in the house."

The belle widened her brown eyes a little at this, her first experience of being regarded as a nuisance by the other sex, but stood in a silent attitude of waiting to hear more. And Mrs. Doane went on : —

"The fact is, he's been to Cap'n Gawthrop's to ask about board there when your friends are gone. He didn't really engage himself, but made inquiries, as if he might be going to move, maybe. You see, Susannah had just gone over there to take Mis' Gawthrop that receipt for tomato-soup that she wanted of me, and heard, unbeknown (the kitchen-door being open), every word he said ; and 'twas, that, if he came, he'd pay them to take no boarders but himself. I thought he was going to be such a splendid boarder to suit," sighed the matron : "he stepped right into the house so hearty and at home when he first came."

"Very much at home indeed, I should say," satirically replied Miss Monny, "to be wanting a whole house to himself when he only lives in two rooms of it, and ordering breakfasts up and down as if he were in a hotel," said the maiden, seating herself emphatically on the side of the bed, her long regard for the widow making her quite personally indignant at the particularly able-bodied boarder who thus inconvenienced her.

"Perhaps he won't go away, after all. I don't believe he will," presently added the girl, seeing the matron's anxious face. "When he has taken a second look at the Gawthrops, he'll see that it's a thousand times nicer here; and he'll stay for his own selfish sake, since that's all he thinks of," pronounced Miss Rivers. "So I wouldn't worry, aunt Persy," she said with affectionate cheeriness, calling the widow by the name she had used in childhood, Mrs. Doane's baptismal appellation being the scriptural name of Persis. "And if he *is* so unprincipled as to go," continued the young lady, tugging vainly at a velvet ribbon that was knotted round her full throat, and pausing in her words a moment to seek a pair of scissors, — "if he *does* break his engagements that way, and he a minister," resumed Miss Monny, having chopped herself out of her necklace, and made a nip or two in the air with her scissors, as if at the derelict divine, "why — I'll pay more for *my* board," simply concluded the girl, seating herself again on the edge of the bed. "I have two rooms, you know, this summer; and it's fair I should pay more, if he leaves on my account."

"No, Miss Monny," said the matron decisively. "You've done nothing awares to be in the way, but always kindness to me and mine; and you pay me now all that I should feel it right to charge any young lady for country board. I've no use for the rooms, seeing, from one cause and another, none of the children are coming home this year with their families; which was why it seemed just the providential time for me to take this minister, and so make a little money to help keep things along. And he agreed perfectly obliging to have dinner between one and two o'clock, which I was afraid he wouldn't be willing to give up the New-York fashion of dinner at night, and supper turned about into luncheon in the middle of the day," rambled on the housekeeper; "which was a great relief to me, as dinner is a meal that I want to have the freshness of the day to get up in. No, there was nothing else in the world he was difficult about," murmured the matron, musing on the one strange exception to the new-comer's amiability. "And it seems he is a very famous man in New York," she added more aloud to the girl. "Mis' Gawthrop's son's wife's cousin was to New York visiting a little over a year ago; and her friends, taking her round to see the lions, took her once to hear Mr. Leigh preach, she said; but they were too late to get in. The church was crammed and over-flowin'; and she said 'twas always so, and that all the ladies in New York were after him."

Monny received this last announcement with a little shriek of merriment. "The idea of anybody's being after that enormous! Any woman who wasn't a horrid giraffe would have to stand up on stilts to marry him. Or she might have a strap put through his arm to reach up and hold on by, the way they do in the horse-cars," said the girl, twisting her pocket-handkerchief into a loop with a peculiarity she had of losing herself for the moment in any passing fancy. "Graceful, to come down the aisle leaning on your bridegroom this way," she said, suggesting, with a single upward thrust of her white arm, the tableau of an average woman clutching at the noosed elbow of a Titan about fifteen feet high.

"Law, how you do make pictures out of the air!" exclaimed Mrs. Doane, impressed, even in her present pre-occupation, with the dramatic power of the girl.

"Why hasn't he a wife?" asked Monny severely, dropping the presentation of Mr. Leigh's wedding-group, and sitting up against the tall, old-fashioned bed-post, to consider his case in its actuality. "Of course he stays unmarried on purpose to have all the ladies after him, and so get up a great name for popularity, and have his church crammed. It isn't likely that there is any thing particular in his brains. He's too big. I've read somewhere that the most talented men are generally small."

"As to that," rejoined the widow, "the Lord has put the remarkable souls of this world into all sorts of bodies, first and last, as if to show us that none of his human temples are to be despised. Great men have been handsome, and they've been homely; they've been small, and sickly, and nothing to look at; and they've been strong, and fine, and grand to look at, as this minister is, certain," broke off Mrs. Doane. "And, considering how women will run after any tolerable kind of a minister," she went on, but neglected to finish audibly her sentence, being lost in meditation over that violence of feminine onslaught which this very superior specimen of a minister had doubtless suffered, that he had come to flee appalled at the bare sight of a young lady. For Mrs. Doane's secret conviction was a very firm one as to what was the minister's real objection to her house.

The fair objection, meanwhile, was so little aware of where her objectionable character came in, that she still fancied the difficult New-York clergyman merely wanted to steep himself in some supernal quiet which he feared she or her visitors might disturb. So her mind was quite free to consider philosophically that mysterious infatuation of her sex for ministers, suggested by Mrs. Doane's unfinished remark; and, striving charitably to construe a mania so unshared by herself, she said, —

"It's all because a minister is a kind of general person to tell troubles to. Women are full of troubles that they want to pour out, and have some man say, 'I'm sorry, and you'll be appreciated in heaven.' Lucy Snowe wasn't silly, and she hadn't committed any crimes; and in the long vacation she went and confessed to a Romish priest in his box. She wasn't a Catholic, and she wasn't in love with the priest, · — she wanted to pour out."

"Lucy Snowe? — A friend of yours did such a thing as that?" inquired in rather a scandalized voice the Puritan matron.

"Lucy Snowe in Charlotte Brontë's novel, you know," explained Monny; "and she was a very serious character indeed."

"Well, howsoever they may fix it up in novels," rejoined Mrs. Doane decidedly, "I don't believe all the live women who run after ministers are very serious characters, and I guess some of their troubles would keep. In a great city like New York, now, I reckon there's a gathering of idle, romantic ladies after a famous preacher, much as there is after a play-actor, or a forrin prince that comes visiting. Only they throw bouquets to one kind of star, and go to see the other about their souls; and since a minister can't well ask a lady whether it's heaven she's seeking, or only to flirt with heaven's ambassador, I think a truly high-minded one must feel sometimes as if his business was considerable mixed."

"H'm!" said Monny. "Isn't everybody's business mixed in this world? And a minister shouldn't preach that there's a way to get through all your snarls pious and patient and .proper, if he can't get through his own so."

"Well," answered the matron meditatively, "it looks as if this minister had made up his mind that the only way to avoid snarls with ladies was to keep as far away from the whole race of 'em as possible."

Monny, who, weary with the junketings of the day, had gone idly on with this conversation as she loitered through the process of preparing for her slumbers, here started with that sudden flash and widening of her brown eyes which denoted a discovery. "Oh! you mean that he fancies I—*I* will be laying snares for his attentions?" cried the astonished belle; and the idea was so completely ludicrous to her she laughed herself out of breath.

She sobered presently, however, with a rising of maiden resentment, as she said, "The first man in this world who ever insulted me with having such thoughts."

"Now, my child, you see this stranger knows nothing about you, except that you are a young lady with a face of your own; and as he hasn't studied the difference between you and a regular flirt, and he can't help seeing the string of beaux that are after you"—

"Now, Mrs. Persis, you know I never asked them to come here,—no, nor wanted them. I've had all the riding and hops and nonsense I wished for this summer; and so I came away from aunt Helen and the fashionable places, down here, on purpose to stay alone, alone, alone with you in this dear old house, that is the only place I have to go to in the world where I can get serious enough to work with all my might at what I want to."

"Yes, dear, I know; and if this minister could have the least idea of what kind of girl you really are—but he couldn't imagine it: I believe no man would ever imagine it," murmured the elder woman, speaking with the emphasis of some thought in her mind as she gazed at the beautiful young face before her.

The owner of that face was not listening just then: she was trying to realize that it was seriously possible for this preposterous minister to leave Mrs. Doane's house on her account, and wondering what she could do about it, with so concerned a look on her speaking face, the widow said, —

"Really, my child, I don't know how I came to let this all out to you. But, now I've said it, what was in my head was, that maybe, if you kept out of his way a little for a day or two — you're always open-minded, dear, to understand things just as they're meant: so you won't take offence at my asking you, for instance, to have your breakfast to-morrow morning by yourself. You see, then, if he should ask again to have breakfast in his own room, I could mention that 'twas served down stairs for him alone. I don't mind any thing about the work, only I can't get things hot way up in the west chamber; and I know gentlemen do like to have their meals hot."

"He may burn himself up with his meals, for all me!" declared Monny indignantly. "And I will have my breakfast anywhere and any time that will be easiest for you, aunt Persy," she added with immediate good nature towards the blameless woman who had this intolerable boarder to manage.

"Thank you, dear," said Mrs. Doane, taking up her candle. "I thought, maybe, if he was suited for a day or two, he might settle to stay after all, as he didn't positively engage to go to Cap'n Gawthrop's. I wouldn't wish to remember my own profit before my neighbor's, only so far as I may have some claim, having laid out money in expectation of his being here."

"How much do kitchen ranges cost?" suddenly asked the young lady, remembering that Mrs. Doane had imported such an article in the past week, because of the com'ng gentleman boarder. The new apparatus which thus graced the kitchen on Mr. Leigh's account had been an outlay which quite alarmed the widow now to think of ; but she would not accept advances of money from the impulsive girl on this bill. So she replied, in general terms, that she had long wanted the range, as her old stove was small and worn out, and that Mr. Leigh set his own price, when he wrote to her, for his board, at so great a figure, she felt she must have the best conveniences for preparing meals. He paid more money than anybody could have thought of asking for board in a plain old house like hers.

"Money doesn't pay for bad manners; and he has the worst manners I ever heard of," pronounced Monny, thumping her pretty head into her pillow with the energy of her condemnation.

But, when Mrs. Doane was gone, she began to consider very seriously whether any thing could be done to make this abominably mannered but pecuniarily profitable boarder stay where he was due. For the girl was quite unselfish enough to put her own inclinations out of the case in regard for the widow, whose thrifty struggles to keep the old place — so dear to her as an independent little home for herself and a summer retreat for her children, whose means were all very moderate — Monny was well acquainted with.

She pondered, — whether one could reason with the renegade minister, of righteousness, and a judgment to come for those who devoured widows' houses, letting them buy kitchen-ranges in vain ; whether to send him a certificate in writing that she would stay in he. own rooms, and not cross his sacred vision for the season (these steps seemed hardly feasible) ; whether to go away herself. That, too, would be a loss to Mrs. Doane ;

besides, she had made a very especial effort to come and spend the rest of the summer just where she was. The case was involved. A masculine boarder who was going to leave a house for fear a young lady there would find him too agreeable; the young lady really finding him as intolerable as he could possibly desire, yet forced to wish for his stay, lest a widow should be defrauded; the young lady prevented by the conventions of society from informing him of her sentiments, viz., that personally she so desired his departure, he would be profoundly safe to stay, and she would hate him to his heart's content, if he would only remain for the landlady's good.

Opening and shutting her sleepy eyes on this remarkable muddle of conditions in a vain effort to see through it some clear line of action, Miss Rivers went at last to the land of dreams, leaving the minister undisposed of.

CHAPTER II.

THE Rev. Kenyon Leigh fell so far short of the wickedness expected of him as to make no second demand for a private breakfast; but wholly unaware of the excitement caused by his first one, and his discovered call at Capt. Gawthrop's, he descended innocently next morning to seat himself wherever Mrs. Doane's usual breakfast-table might be spread, and with whomsoever might be wont to gather round it. Only the widow gathered there, no other mortal appearing save Susannah to wait on the table.

Peacefully alone with his landlady then, the minister partook the morning meal, going out directly thereafter for a ramble down the lane and a short walk on the beach. It is doubtful if the young lady boarder was at all in his absorbed mind this morning, save as some unconscious touch of satisfaction may have been there that her languidly fashionable habits apparently prevented her from getting up to breakfast, as her pleasure-roving habits did from ever appearing at the regular hour for any of her other meals. The absorbed mind was turning back to long intermitted tasks; for, instead of being at the beginning of his vacation this midsummer morning, the minister considered himself rather at its end. So far from having come to this retreat to rest, he had come there with peculiarly vigorous intentions of work.

He had been a minister never before given to long vacations; but he had been silent, and absent from his pulpit, now, for nearly a year past, journeying in Europe and in the East, from which travels he had landed in New York only a few days back. He had intended, indeed, to remain abroad yet two or three months longer, but had returned home thus in advance of the time set for him to occupy again his city pulpit, because his foreign trip had not brought him the restoration which he had hoped to find in it. The malady which had sent him abroad to try the cure of a complete change was no physical one, only a secret sense which had come to him, even while his popularity was brilliantly on the increase, of the failure of his first enthusiasm in his work.

The first enthusiasm in all work, in mere aims of living, is fed more or less by illusion; and whether there will be power to go on with the work, with the high purposes, when the illusion begins to vanish, is one of the great tests of a life. One sees many men go down at this point; apparently established lives make intellectual or moral decline, or both, when age is yet very far from touching the faculties, and when, if it be a moral falling-off, it would seem that the mere strength of previously correct habits should have insured them: it is experience that has withered the young dream under which their good forces triumphed.

Kenyon Leigh's work happened to be preaching; and, however little the clerical mark was on him to the eye, he had attained to a breadth of success in the pulpit which proved that he was pre-eminently born for his calling. Whenever and wherever he spoke, the Puritans flocked to hear him, though he preached in a gown; and the radicals, though he preached the strait gospel. This singular light which had always been in his interpretations to the most widely different classes of minds burned yet

in his own soul : his present depression did not arise from
what could properly be called a failure of religious faith.
No : while he was eminently a thinker himself, and given
to constant and candid study of the scientific and critical
thought of the day, some insight of a poetic soul had so
enabled him to pierce to the eternal heart of truth in the
Christian creed, that he could preach still, as an honest
man, the old religior.

Nevertheless, there were problems in his profession
which weighed on him in proportion to the breadth of
the man ; and he had reached now, as we have implied,
that critical period in life, which, as to mere years, may
come earlier or later than it had done to Kenyon Leigh,
when, with every faculty ripe for the best action, energy
is paralyzed by a loss of the early sanguine belief in the
results of action.   He did not regret his choice of a life-
work : he only wanted to get a new start in it, — that
courage of the actual, faith to go on working with all
one's might in the knowledge of things just as they really
are.   It had seemed to him that he might best win this
new courage by a complete dropping and forgetting, for
a time, of all his labors : for this prime end he went to
Europe.   He had spent several years of his student life
in a foreign university : for this and other reasons the
Old World was peculiarly attractive to him, and he had
certainly enjoyed his trip.

Still the chief hope in which it had been undertaken
was not fulfilled : that precious inward spring of the
early enthusiasm in his work did not rise again.   On
the contrary, the longer he staid abroad at this time,
the longer he wanted to stay.   Discovering this fact in
himself, he faced suddenly about with characteristic resolution, and came home, to seek out for a time such a
seclusion as this of Cape Cod, and see if he could lay

hold of the primal forces there by buckling straight down to the writing of new sermons.

Now, in one direction the weary minister had not had a vacation : respite from adoring women had been denied him. They had gone out with him on the English steamer, and come home with him on the French one ; and it was astonishing by what conjunctions they had crossed his track all over Europe, and even in Palestine and among the Pyramids. He could swear, as did Sir Launcelot, "by truth and knighthood," that he "gave no cause, not willingly, for such a love," being a man who never, in any profession, would have gone sprinkling thin and wide the vapory shower of his affections, as doth the ladies' man ; and clerical philandering was forever impossible to him.

Lest it should be imagined, however, that this hero is intended to add his note to the prolonged ululations of these latter days over the ministerial perils, it may be necessary solemnly to state the fact, that, in all his adored existence, he had never found any thing worse than weakness, the very innocentest silliness, in the ladies who thus hunted him.

But just now he was quite abnormally sensitive to all the pains of life, adoring women especially ; and when, into that solitary cave by the sea which he fancied he had secured out of reach of all such, there marched at the first breath that particularly twinkling damsel, why, he felt the longed-for peace of that widow's house most darkly threatened. For, so far as he had attained to any philosophy concerning this species of charmer, he con cluded that the talent for enslaving men, when it existed in this supreme perfection, exercised itself like an instinct upon whatever subject came to hand. He did not wish to be that subject at hand ; and, in short, he behaved in an hour of weakness as we have recorded. This morning, however, his soul was stronger: he had descended manfully, as we have seen, expecting to meet the enemy at the family board. And now, although he had no revelation of the ties between himself and Mrs. Doane's new cooking-stove, yet, as a man really considerate of widows expectant of boarders, he had, perhaps, begun to fear that the bonus which he proposed to give on departure might not solace the matron. Then, the apprehended flirt having been thus far so mercifully taken up with other men as not to be even visible in the house, which without her was completely satisfactory to him, altogether, it is probable that his plan of removal was considerably in abeyance just now. Certainly, as he walked down the lane, he was not on his way to Capt. Gawthrop's; and he proposed returning, after a brief ramble, to his rooms at Mrs. Doane's, for a long morning's study.

Going swiftly down the lane now, and crossing some intervening barrens, he came out upon the high bluff-like bank of the ocean, far below which was the beach, conveniently reached, however, by the hollows which at various intervals intersected the undulating bank. Presently descending the latter by one of these openings to the lower promenade of the beach, he had scarcely reached it, when he heard mingled with the sound of the retiring waves (the tide was going out) other music, — a girl's laughter, a big dog's bark, and the racing feet of both. Scamper they came, or rather, went; for they were running from Mr. Leigh when he first caught sight of them. Facing about, however, at the farther goal, which was a stake standing aslant in the sands, the maiden solemnly counted, "One, two, three!" catching back the dog, over and over, as he showed a disposition to bound incontinently away before the proper moment. Then, when he manifested at last a due respect for figures, on they came like the wind.

In this race, the dog being perhaps demoralized by his mathematical effort, the girl actually came out a pace ahead, whereat she clasped her shaggy competitor round the neck with such an exultant little cry, the looker-on could but laugh in sympathy with the triumph of his species. Miss Rivers, abashed to have been discovered by anybody in her frisky gambols, straightened herself in a breath, and beheld — whom but that imposition of a minister, as he strode into view from the overarching of the huge sand-bank!

That frank, cordial laugh of Mr. Leigh's might have re-assured even a young woman ashamed of being caught indulging the frolic glee of a child, if she had heard it with an unprejudiced ear. But, as it was, this untimely ecclesiastical mirth, "which any decent being would have suppressed, coming upon people so unexpectedly," thought the indignant racer, — this merriment was received as a fresh outrage by the much-outraged Miss Monny. And when the minister added to his "good-morning" the interrogatory whether she was getting up an appetite for breakfast, it was a little too much.

"I had my breakfast an hour and a half ago," tersely replied Miss Rivers, remembering how she had eaten it on a corner of the table-cloth, abject, and like a Pariah, to have the board cleared for this New-York Brahmin.

"Indeed!" said the unconscious Brahmin, getting a rather new view of the languid young lady who break-fasted at sunrise, and ran like Atalanta on the beach. "Do you breakfast so early every morning?"

Atalanta was getting her courage up. Here was her opportunity. Swallowing timidity, and helped by her preciously small opinion of the stately Samson before her, she said steadily, "I never breakfasted so early before you came. I have something to say to you," she added, indicating a suitable seat for the audience on a pile of driftwood not far away.

The minister, rather surprised, nevertheless obeyed the imperious little wave of the feminine hand, and bestowed himself on the driftwood, waiting for young mistress Rivers to go on ; and thus she went : —

" I breakfast so early because you dislike young ladies, and because — the reasons which make all other women like clergymen do not take effect on me."

The gentleman thus addressed looked blank for a moment, and then — he was too radically truthful a man for some hint of that confusion which attends on being "found out" not to touch visibly his face. How on earth he had been found out was a riddle to him ; but such was his doom, and he met it by saying, — a half smile stealing involuntarily round his lips as he surveyed more attentively the frolicsome sprite of a moment ago transformed into the grave young person who had seated herself on a rock at the severest distance at all compatible with conversation, — " Pray. what are some of those universal feminine reasons for liking clergymen which do not influence you, since you feel obliged to put so politely your side of the dislike?"

" Well," returned the calm reasoner on the rock, " the devotion of women to clergymen is, of course, not a tribute to personal qualities at all; because any one can see that very inferior men, if they happen to be clergymen, are still highly honored by women. It is a party duty, and I do not have a very strong feeling of my party duty?"

" Party duty? " repeated Mr. Leigh, somewhat puzzled.

"Certainly. Women, you know, are not considered to have much influence in this world, except a moral influence, to be of much consequence, except to practise virtues. So the man whose business it is to proclaim the importance of virtues is the magnifier of their office; he declares the dignity of their existence; he may be called the spokesman of their side. And to honor your spokesman, and set him before all other men, is no more than what self-respect requires, I suppose," meditated Miss Monny, rather impressed with her own discovery that there was really something to say for this minister-adoring weakness of her sex.

"And you confess yourself to be wanting in this grave matter of self-respect?" returned the clergyman.

"Yes: I do not realize myself enough as a general creature, as a piece of woman in the lump, to feel bound up with what is called woman's cause in that way. Though sometimes I do," subjoined the girl, again with her *naive* air of half abstraction, as if she were settling things with herself, as well as settling the clergyman. But, recalling the latter business, she added, —

"And as a conceited minister might imagine that it was because he was personally more admirable than other men that he received so much attention from women, and as, in any case, there is an unpleasant effect in seeing so many women devoted to one man, it is not an order of things that I should wish to help on."

"And how about the sight of so many men devoted to one young woman?" rejoined Mr. Leigh, not particularly given to this kind of bantering, but really not knowing what else to say in this most extraordinary dialogue.

"That is the proper order," returned the belle with dignity, and without the shadow of a smile.

Something in the girl's manner indefinably removing

all her remarks from the daring of native impudence, her listener still remained attentive on his log, awaiting further communications. And the maiden who had this unique task before her, of making a man perfectly at ease by convincing him of his total unpleasantness, went on with it as she might by saying, —

"Mr. Leigh, as you disliked the idea of my being here when you knew nothing about me but that I was a young lady, and as I had my feeling about your being here when I knew nothing about you but that you were a clergyman, there is nothing personal in any thing that is necessary to be said in order to come to an understanding. It is a class that happens to be disliked on both sides."

"Certainly it is a class," replied the minister, imitating the girl's gravity of tone. "And I will therefore consider that there is no personality in whatever may still be on your mind to say."

"What is on my mind to say," returned Miss Rivers, "is that Mrs. Doane needs both her boarders, and that, if you leave her house, I shall feel that I have done her a harm. I would stay out of your way, if I could, at all times ; but, as at meal-times it will not be possible for me to do so much longer, I thought if you could understand that I shall consider it perfectly fair for you to remain here and take no notice of me as a class that you dislike " — said Monny, pausing a little to steady her voice, for this manner of speech was too unwonted to her to be maintained without some inward effort.

"I perceive," said Mr. Leigh, with his penetrating glance reading the face of the girl who had succeeded in adding a new variety to his extremely large experience of feminine interviews, — "I perceive that you have a very brave and unselfish regard for Mrs. Doane ; and I hereby

agree to continue to represent in her house the class that
you dislike," he said, with a humorous sparkle in his eye.
Then rising from his log, he bowed good-morning with
the amused tolerance of a man taken to task by a child
(he had lost all impression of his fellow-boarder as a
young lady), and went on his way. In a moment more
the sea and sky, and the gathering shape of a new sermon,
quite absorbed his thoughts, to the exclusion of all ladies,
— young or old. Save, perhaps, as he looked out on
the wide sweep of the Atlantic, there may have come
some passing thought of a certain lady on the other side
of it who would be coming home ere long, — Mrs. Van
Cortlandt, a widow of thirty-five, belonging to his own
church in New York. . He had had passing thoughts of
that lady for four years.

On the very first sabbath of his preaching as installed
rector of St. Ancient's, glancing over his new flock while
the choir chanted the opening anthem of the service, his
eyes fell on a most queenly lady, whose face, with its luminous pale complexion, jet-black hair, long-fringed gray
eyes, and incomparably beautiful curves of lip and cheek
and chin, was indeed a face to stand out from all others,
and one which brought instantly into Kenyon Leigh's
mind the lines of Michael Angelo's sonnet to Vittoria
Colonna : —

> " If it be true that any beauteous thing
>   Raises the pure and just desire of man
>   From earth to God, the eternal Fount of all,
>   Such I believe my love " —

This " beauteous thing," whose type of loveliness
stirred emotions which rose so accordant with the chants
of the temple, was, in reality, one of the very worldliest of
mortals: But the minister had never discovered this in
all his after-knowledge of Mrs. Van Cortlandt. he had

found many things in her, on personal acquaintance, which distinctly pleased him, besides her peerless face. If her elegant manners, for instance, were somewhat cold, a touch of the frosty Caucasus was not without its charm to a man who had had rather too abundant experience of feminine gushing.

Nevertheless, after four years time, Mr. Leigh had still only passing thoughts of Mrs. Van Cortlandt; for, finally, she had only pleased his taste. But she had gone on pleasing his taste now for four years, and he had never been in love in his life. All the ordinary triflings with sentiment, his profession and his peculiarly flattered position in it had utterly deterred him from and given him a distaste for; and a serious passion had never befallen him. So that, without belonging by nature among those defective beings — more or less defective, and below the highest type of humanity, however wide a name some of them may have left on the earth — whose sympathies flow warmly only in some universal channels, whose affections are all satisfied with the diffusive benevolence of a philanthropy, a reform, a religious mission, — without being originally one of these men to whom marriage is intrinsically a mistake and a burden, Kenyon Leigh had yet grown into such a relation to his work, that it had been quite possible that he might come among these characters at last. Just now, however, it was more possible, it was even highly probable, that he would do far worse. The woman to whom he stood uncommitted as yet by word or deed, or even look, was, nevertheless, subtly and steadily drawing him in.

Thackeray makes an assertion somewhere in one of his famous novels, to the effect that any woman who has not a positive hump can marry any man, let her have oppor tunity enough to meet him, and devote herself to her end with sufficient strategy and determination. With no humps, and with infinite opportunity, strategy, and resolve, the beautiful Mrs. Van Cortlandt had pursued the famous preacher as a husband (by no means in that crowd of poor simple ladies who pursued him openly) for the last four years. And this likely-to-be-successful pursuer was the one woman in all the train who was so far from truly loving Kenyon Leigh that she did not even believe in him.

Mrs. Van Cortlandt had brought out of her former married experience — it had been an experience of ten years, long enough to frame comprehensive theories in — a thorough disbelief in all men. And not only her minister made no exception to her general unfaith in his sex, but she disbelieved in him even more than in the average of men. Not that she in the least suspected the Rev. Kenyon Leigh of hypocrisy, — of leading, or of ever having led, any life but that which he seemed to lead. Just the life which he really led, precisely the man that he was and seemed to be, had irritated, nay, angered her, scores of times. Mrs. Van Cortlandt's disbelief in men was a disbelief in them as husbands. She held a fixed creed that all men were too supremely absorbed in something else ever to be absorbed in a wife beyond some briefest little time of courtship and early marriage. Her first husband had been absorbed in her for just that short space, and no more. Then had appeared the fundamental masculine nature, — a nature whose interests, comforts, pleasures, were all in things which women cared little or nothing about, — a surprisingly alien, fickle, selfish, unsatisfactory genus.

Mr. Van Cortlandt had, in truth, been very much in love with his wife when he married her, thinking her beauty divine, as indeed it was. Her beauty had never

faded, but his affection undeniably had. She had not
poisoned him : he had had the best medica. care in his
last illness, which was malarial fever, of which he had
died at Rome, a perfectly natural death, about a year
before Mrs. Van Cortlandt first beheld the famous new
rector of St. Ancient's.

A being who has lost capacity to live by the heart and
its simple joys may be all the more prone to live by the
fancy and its most fantastic caprice ; and the widow took
so strong a caprice for this invulnerable minister as to
set up an establishment in New York, to the abandonment
of all her previous plans for existence.   These had been,
to make her permanent residence abroad, where she had
brilliant social introductions, and where, with her unworn
beauty and the large wealth left her by her incompatible
first husband, she was quite in a position to marry a title.
Mrs. Van Cortlandt was a denationalized American whom
it would scarcely be correct to speak of as aping the
style of the European nobility, so perfectly had she
assimilated, as the natural food of her pride, whatever
was external in the tastes and habits of the titled circles
that she had long moved in abroad.   But being learned
in life now, — life with husbands, — she decided, for a
strange jumble of reasons, to marry Kenyon Leigh before
any other man in the two hemispheres; and for a man of
the Western Hemisphere, she reasoned, his ancestry on
both sides was as nearly noble as possible.   The man
himself took the proud woman's fancy as a kind of mon-
arch : what she herself would have styled a true imperial
sway, she saw that he exercised over most men who came
in contact with him.

It was true, indeed, that Kenyon Leigh had a great
personal power, — a power, too, which was quite separable
from his moral excellence, or even his intellectual gifts. .

For he gave some impression as of an instinctive un ler-
standing of all human experience, joined with a certain
invincible calm which is the mood of the highest courage;
and such men, whether they be good or bad, seem always
to draw human beings to themselves as with a kind of
enchanter's spell. There is something, perhaps, in the
calm of these wide-seeing natures, which acts re-assuringly
on the general human heart. One feels that they have
looked on all the terror of existence, and yet live; and
mortals follow them as if to learn their secret; and this
when the Olympic tranquillity which so fascinates may be
that of fatalism rather than of faith, and their intuitive
knowledge of all that mortal spirits bear, not of the true
strain of sympathy. Thus one or two of the great con-
querors of the world — men pitiless in their ambitions,
and largely material in their aims — appear certainly to
have had some form of this strange personal power.
They compelled all creatures to their will, not so much by
outward violence as by a mysterious inward force, a
something which invincibly *attached* men to their fortunes; and this by a bond which was not one of interest,
nor yet of what we ordinarily call love or fear. The old
stories always current — of the invulnerability of these
heroes, that they bore charmed lives which bullets could
not touch — seem to point to this same impression which
they diffused, — of being masters of fate itself; and all
weaker spirits gathered to them perforce, as if to share
in· that great conquering.

.Never was a more unconscious possessor of this personal power than Kenyon Leigh: we should say a more
unwilling possessor of it, if he had been at all aware of
the gift. He was no demigod of war, seeking to draw
the strength of a million men to strike through his single
arm : he was a preacher who wanted people to see the

truth, and not himself. For, of all kinds of hero-worship,
that most abhorrent to him to be the object of was min-
ister-worship. The absolutely delicate and generous spirit
has always an especial sense of confusion in receiving
adulation for any thing in the line of what can be called
moral services. The truly benevolent man does not like
to be praised for his charitable gifts ; still less the truly
religious man, for his piety or pious eloquence. Thus in
his private intercourse this minister would sometimes turn
on an indiscreet flatterer such an icily cold shoulder as
only outraged shyness can do. He had the sensitive personal reserve which belongs to most fine natures, and
this, joined with an intense manliness, made something
extreme in his recoil from that position of a pet which
there is some disposition to place an admired minister in.
And Mrs. Van Cortlandt saw this most simple-hearted of
men as a personage who sat solitary on a throne, at once
attracting general worship, and profoundly scorning the
worshippers. It was her very *beau ideal* of a superior
being.

If Mr. Leigh's independence of all men took her fancy,
still more did his even greater independence of all women.
It is not necessary for us to look closely into any such
line of questions as whether Mr. Van Cortlandt (this gentleman had inherited his wealth, and had spent most of
his married life in European capitals and in very elegant
leisure) had amused himself unlawfully with other fair
female society when his wife's had quite ceased to amuse
him. It is sufficient for our tale to note that it was in
the nature of Mrs. Van Cortlandt, and in all her modes
of belief, to be intensely jealous of the man over whose
heart she had lost power, whether he gave her this cause
or not. So it was a matter of great account with her, that,
in marrying Mr. Leigh, she would be forever guaranteed

from rivals in other women, both by his profession and his extreme non-susceptibility to feminine attractions. This latter trait in the man she recognized well, and that his total escape from all entanglements in the flatteries of women was due quite as much to his idiosyncrasies as to his prudence.

The widow had studied all his idiosyncrasies for years, and she believed that she knew Kenyon Leigh by heart: in fact, she knew him every way *but* by heart. It is only some outward husk and rind of the truth that the keenest unsympathetic search into a human soul ever attains to.

The lady over the water was not in the minister's thoughts, as we have said, this morning, save for a passing moment as he looked over the sea, because those thoughts were engrossed with a new sermon. He woke out of it for a moment, however, as springing up the high bank again, after a half-mile or more on the beach to return to his lodgings by another way than that he had come, he recognized Capt. Gawthrop. This retired salt, living in a good-sized house, being somewhat impecunious, a great gossip, and knowing the Cape withal from end to end, was extremely fond of taking metropolitan boarders, and was naturally hoping this morning to secure the new arrival from New York, who had made those inquiries at his house the night before. But this hope was doomed to disappointment; for Mr. Leigh walked up to him with the announcement that he should remain through the season at Mrs. Doane's.

CHAPTER III.

"THAT minister is going to stay. I've had a talk
with him down on the beach, and it's settled,"
cried Monny, who with her companion, Duke George, —
an immense Newfoundland dog of a breed brought home
long years before by Capt. Doane, — had rushed directly
for Mrs. Doane's house, after her rencounter with Mr.
Leigh, to relieve the anxiety there with this announcement.

"Bless you, child!" said the pleased widow, who was
found in the young lady's own chamber, bestowing fresh
towels on the rack. "I knew he would like you as soon
as he got the least acquainted with you."

"Like me! He has the worst opinion of me, and I
have the worst opinion of him, — the very worst; and
that's the contract," declared the maiden, bringing down
her pink palm on the pate of Duke George, who having
placed himself upright on his haunches, close to her chair,
held his nose aloft with the air of a witness ready to
testify to all points.

"You needn't worry, aunt Persy, thinking he was
dissatisfied with the house, or with you, — not a bit. I
was really the whole trouble: I saw it the moment I
accused him. And of all the spoilt, spoilt peacocks, even
among popular ministers, he must be the crown," cried
the belle, emphasizing this time on Duke George's crown
with a fervor which she atoned for by sundry softer pats
and pulling of the ears, which caresses he laid his head in
her lap the more deeply to enjoy.

"Why, what ever have you accused him of, child?" asked Mrs. Doane, aghast. "Truly, my dear, although he has been rather strange about this, I do think he is a very uncommon, grand kind of a man, — I mean a good one, as well as a famous."

Miss Rivers, who had not the least respect at present for the New-York minister's fame, and who had very decided views as to his goodness, here made a sudden move, out of the chair into which she had dropped, to the next room, calling the widow, as if to show her something there. For naturally she did not wish the latter to know what argument she had made with the clerical boarder for her sake. Mrs. Doane, believing from the girl's habitual politeness that she could have said nothing amiss to Mr. Leigh, accordingly put away her surplus towels, and, dropping the ministerial question, followed Miss Rivers into the east chamber, as the square front room on this side of the house was especially called. There was no bed in this apartment at present; but paintings in oil and water-colors, and drawings in every thing, in all stages of completion, figures rather than landscapes, filled the room.

"It's a born miracle, like all your pictures!" exclaimed the widow, surveying the canvas on the easel, to which Monny had called her attention merely to divert it from closer inquiry into her conversation with Mr. Leigh. "How long are you going on, dear, doing these wonderful things, and letting nobody know but your aunt and uncle, and forbidding even them to show your pictures to anybody?" said Mrs. Doane.

"Till I get a little surer that I am truly fit to paint pictures," replied the girl.

"As if the Lord didn't make you fit to paint pictures when you came into the world! for I've always heard

Mary Ann tell of your drawing pictures all over the walls, and everywhere, before you could talk plain; and now, when with half a dozen strokes you can make the perfectest likeness of any face you see!"

"O aunt Persis! that isn't painting true pictures at all. I can make a likeness of a wooden kind, without thinking a thought. That comes natural to me. I could always do that. Besides, old Monsieur Durocher that I've told you of, who was so poor and discouraged that he came to be drawing-master in my boarding-school, — he was a thoroughly trained French artist; and he taught me like a faithful, furious angel two whole years. It was he, I suppose, who first got me in the way of hiding my work so; that is, he kept me always doing hard studies, never letting me finish any thing like a picture fit to show. He said I would be praised too soon, and spoilt.

"You see, he beat into me, when I was very young, all his own ideas about art, which were very high and true ones; and he used to scare me so with scoldings, and praise me so beautifully in streaks, I could not help learning true drawing and color, just like a man. Yes, he said that he taught me as thoroughly as if I was a man, and that it was a thousand shames that I wasn't one. You see, even he seemed to think it the most unaccountable strange mixture that I should be a girl, just like other girls, and yet serious in trying to paint pictures. But, if it is my nature to be so mixed, how am I going to get away from my nature?" asked Monny, looking up with a childlike appeal to this old woman, with whom she talked much in her mere young need of utterance.

"Seeing, child, that it has pleased Heaven to mix your nature of very uncommon gifts, I should say 'twas one to be very thankful for. And your pictures would certain be taken the greatest notice of in these days, when there's so much said about women's talents and their rights."

"Why, that's just my worst trouble," quickly replied the girl, — "all that I read about woman's sphere, etc. You see, to tell the truth, I have painted so many years now, I have really been thinking lately, especially this summer, that I would finish up two or three of my pictures that I am the least dissatisfied with, and send them somewhere to be exhibited, — without my real name, you know. And when I began to think about this, I began to read every thing I saw on what is called the 'Woman Question.' I had never noticed such articles much before ; for they did not look very interesting, and I thought they were all about women's voting, — and I've never wanted to vote, — or about their being lawyers and doctors and ministers ; which I'm sure I don't want to be. But I read all women's-rights articles, whether for or against, very carefully indeed now ; and the whole subject grows a great trouble to me," said the maiden pensively. "For men that I can see are truly able men, who have studied and thought a great deal, and who seem to wish the world to go right, and not wrong, yet say things about women and their place which discourage me dreadfully about painting pictures.

"You know, aunt Persy," Monny went on, laying down her palette-knife, "in order to do your best at any thing, you want to feel, first, that the work is worthy to be done ; and, second, that it is a worthy, a right thing in yourself to try to do it. Now, that last point is where I get no assurance from literature ; and literature is the only means I have by which to find out what the serious minds of the world, the minds that I should wish to be approved of, think about things. So far as I can make

out their sentiments, it appears that most of them would
not believe in women's painting pictures at all; that is,
they lay down such and such qualities as the proper
feminine nature, which, they say, are not the qualities
to make good artists, poets, etc.   So you see, a woman
is placed in this dreadful strait, that, if by any chance she
should do what was confessed to be a really good work
of art, her very success would imply that she was somehow out of the proper feminine nature.   That is, your
picture must be poor, because you are a woman; or you
are a very poor kind of woman, if it is good."

"Bless you, child!" said the matron, surveying in her
manifold feminine charm the maiden who thus summed
up her "dreadful strait,"—"nobody would ever think
of calling you a poor kind of a woman.   And seeing you
care so much, as is right you should do, for the opinions
of serious minds, if you would only let me show your
pictures to this famous minister"—

"Mercy! I don't mean *minister* seriousness," cried
Monny.   "I mean the men who write the solid reviews
and essays,—the men who have deep knowledge about
this world, and what is right and true to do in it."

"Indeed!" said the pious Orthodox woman, with some
admonition in her voice.   "And what is the whole calling of ministers but to tell us what is right and true to
do?"

"Oh, y-e-s!" assented Monny rather slowly, being
infected, young as she was, with so much of our day's
distrust of the institutional as to look even for her chief
ethical guidance elsewhere than to the pulpit, although
its ministrations had her regular Sunday attendance.
"Yes.   But perhaps the way of the world has changed
since the way of sermons began, that mostly I seem to
get more practical light from the men of thought and high

principle who write about subjects of this earth, that you haven't got to die in order to find out the truth of."

"Well, my dear, we shall want something for a dying hour too; and since, for all your gay life, Miss Monny, I have always found you to be a very conscientious girl, and one showing a proper respect to holy things and ministers"—

"This minister isn't a holy thing!" cried Miss Monny with disdain. "He is one of those preachers, who, what with his size, can lead captive silly women, of course, as was said of some famous preacher, if he only says 'Mesopotamia.' He can't have any true eloquence, because he's a humbug himself. Oh, yes, he is!" insisted Monny, as the matron showed signs of expostulating. "A light-minded man in a serious profession is a humbug; and no talents can make him otherwise. And if it isn't light-minded for a man to be so outrageously vain as to suppose that a girl can't eat breakfast with him without falling in love with him, and he an old bachelor minister"—

"Now, now, my dear, nobody would call Mr. Leigh an old bachelor."

"Why, he is as much as thirty," rejoined Monny, surveying that period of life from her decade on the sunny side of it. "Not as old as he *ought* to be, of course," she pronounced, with her views as to the duty of ministers to be venerable, "but old enough, and I should *think big* enough, to be sober-minded; which he isn't. And as for letting him see my pictures, he is the very last being in the universe that I would allow to see them, and I shall keep the door of this room fast locked every minute while he stays here. And I shall wish you to be very careful, aunt Persy, not to drop a syllable to let him know that I have ever touched a paint-brush in my life."

"Oh, there's the butcher's bells!" exclaimed Mrs. Doane, — for a string of bells round · his horse's neck heralds the Cape-Cod butcher; and, trusting to time to reconcile her boarders, the matron rushed down stairs to provide for dinner.

The young artist thus left alone set seriously to work. This old house having been a kind of deposit for years of her efforts in art, there were many big canvases in the room, crowded with conceptions daringly impossible for so young a hand and brain to execute, fettered, too, by all those innumerable hamperings incident to the secrecy with which she pursued her art. There were elaborate groups out of poet and romancer, and the girl's own wild head ; but through all these prodigal attempts — sketched, half painted, and abandoned — could be traced a steady growth of power, and of wisdom, at last, to choose the simpler theme. Thus the picture at present on her easel, which she was working up from a smaller sketch made from the life, and evidently the life of this region, had but a single figure, — merely an infirm old fisherman pulling up a boat before a threatening storm. Yet the strip of lone marshy shore, the rising wind in the sky, the passion of the far-struggling sea, with the worn-out old mariner pausing in his broken strength to look out upon it, and realize that he could cope with sea and storm no more, — these simple elements were not only rendered with rare technical skill, but so rendered, that the mystery of Nature's eternal energy, and the ephemeral life of man, brooded solemn and pathetic over all the canvas.

The girl who could do these things had toiled with the tireless patience of true genius ; and, if she had had no one to encourage her among her natural protectors, she had had the next best thing, — no one to interfere. Her father, Endicott Rivers, came of one of the oldest, and, in former generations, most illustrious, of New-England families; and in young Endicott himself the original vigor of the stock, which had somewhat lapsed in his immediate ancestors, gave marked promise of return. His brilliantly opening life, however, was cut tragically short when he was scarce twenty-five years old, by a sudden explosion in a Western mine, into which he had descended from a traveller's curiosity; and his young wife had died a few months after from the anguish of this bereavement, leaving baby Anemone — which romantic name became Monny, for short — scarcely a year old. The child thus orphaned had been reared in the home of her father's sister, Mrs. Helen Rivers Slabwell. This lady (she was more than a dozen years older than her lost brother, Endicott) had not inherited very strongly herself from the intellectual side of her distinguished forefathers. But, if she had very little force of brain or character, she had a radical refinement of feeling and habit, a grace of gentle breeding, which never forsook her, although she had been considered to take a very long step downward in her marriage. The Slabwell *mésalliance* had proved, however, a truly happy union on both sides. Indeed, as observers will have noted, in marriages where there is some superiority on the side of the wife, if she has the tact to prevent this from becoming the ugliest of situations, there often resides a peculiarily enduring element of charm. King Cophetua may grow remiss in attentions to his beggar-maid; but the page who marries the princess is likely to hold out in the spirit of consideration.

The princess in this case, Miss Helen Rivers, had been extremely short of revenues when the plebeian John Slabwell, whose revenues were rapidly rising through shrewd investments in lumber, first beheld the lady, and decided,

that, unless he could spend on her the money which it had
thus far been the sole object of his existence to make,
that existence would be to him thenceforth and forever
a futile and disgusting rack.   There was an objecting
father, and the lady herself at first objected; but finally
the sheer infatuation of the suitor, who had schemed day
and night, raised heaven and earth, to devise orderly
means whereby to pursue the mere chance acquaintance
which some little accident of travel had given him with
the lady born so far out of his circle, — this infatuation
touched the feminine heart.   For among the men of her
own circle (although she had not been wholly neglected by
them) Miss Helen had never had a truly infatuated lover,
as she had nothing in herself which the general masculine
verdict would have pronounced striking attractions of
either person or mind, and she had lost all the prestige
of surroundings by the nearly total ruin of her father's
fortunes just as she was entering on young womanhood.
In short, she decided to marry this one adorer, who was
an adorer indeed (the objecting father being finally reduced), and she never regretted the step.

Mr. John Slabwell was an American citizen whom
re-action from the grim Puritan theology had left with no
religion ; large disbelief in the politicians of his own party,
and total disbelief in those ᶜf the other, with no patri-
otism ; conviction that there was a native and ineradicable
tendency in a certain class of human beings to dirt, rags,
and six families in a room, with no social science ; narrow
early education, and life engrossed thereafter in money-
making, with no taste for reading any thing but newspapers.   There was but one spiritual pole to his being;
viz., a very especial consideration for women.   This saving trait had kept remarkably upright in various directions
a moral constitution which might not otherwise have been

very strongly based. Thus he was as severe as any Puritan on all masculine vices and dissipations, as having a very direct tendency to make women unhappy. One vital objection he still saw to men's going to the devil, — the wrecks of women that would strew their way. To the man with this soft chivalric spot in his hard Yankee composition, his lady-wife was just helpless enough to be endearing. Then the repose which there had been no space for in his own life, the leisure which he would not have known what to do with personally, he had a delightful sense of drinking in, ready sublimated, as it were, in the atmosphere of a woman whose graceful step very few earthly occurrences could hasten, whose very words came forth with a gentle slowness which might have wrought on some husbands, in impetuous moments, with any thing but soothing effect. As for the lady, however unlike she always remained to her husband in outward style and bearing, she never assumed the remotest air of a porcelain vase swimming down the stream with an iron pot. Having once decided to become Mrs. Slabwell, her very respect for traditions made her loyal to the doctrine, as decidedly one of the oldest of traditions, that the husband is the head of the wife. She dropped all her old social affiliations with her marriage; which she did the more easily as her early married home was set up, not in the city, but at just that suburban distance from it which seems to enable one to arrange life without any dependence on society at all. At least, Mrs. Slabwell found sufficient variety for her tranquil tastes in the daily going and coming of her husband to and from town, in superintending her servants, watching her babies grow, and the flowers in her conservatory, during his absence, and driving with him, on his return, behind the pair of high-conditioned horses that he always kept, softly swallowing her impulse to shriek when they went at their most sp.nning pace, reflecting that death or mutilation was the worst that could happen, — mere trifles to the rudeness of showing a contrarious hostility to the pleasures of one's husband. In this amiable content Mrs. Slabwell reared her four children to young manhood and young womanhood; and the last of these was married, and settled in life, just before the niece Monny, who had been educated at a New-York boarding-school, came home (the Slabwells had at this date a fine residence in the city proper) to make her *début* as a young lady.

This event caused an immediate enlargement of the Slabwell circle. Certain especial circumstances gave the young girl some favorable introductions at the outset; and then on such occasions, for instance, as the grand charitable balls and bazaars of the city furnish for showing off the fair of one circle to the brave of another, the distinctively fashionable young men walked promptly over whatever line separated their set from that of the Slabwells, to pay their court to the charming young ward of the lumber-merchant. And when the feminine fashionables, those more watchful keepers of the social gates, discovered that the young stranger came of the old Rivers family, they immediately recognized that there was nothing more to be said. For the old Rivers family (it had softened into Unitarianism in its later generations) had been among the earliest founders of this representative Puritan city of Moralmount: the family had been conspicuous, indeed, in Puritan annals, on the old soil, as far back as the English struggle between Crown and Parliament. And although Monny's own grandfather Rivers (he had died shortly after his son Endicott's marriage) had been chiefly illustrious for the skill with which he had scattered a large inherited fortune without being at all dissipated, — being, on the contrary, a most spotless and high-minded gentleman, — the shining ability, as well as the virtue, of the early house of Rivers, was still suf-ficiently historic among the old families of Moralmount for this fair young orphan of the line to be welcomed among them with no snubbing.

Mrs. Slabwell herself might perhaps, ere this, have so far recalled the claims of her maiden name as to upbear her married one, if she had had less pride, and more ambition ; if it had not been both beneath her dignity, and above a certain little indolence which characterized her, to push in the least for social honors.   But when, without any vulgarity of pushing, Miss Monny blossomed out into a decided belle in Moralmount best society, — those younger and gayer circles of it into which the girl naturally fell, — aunt Helen was quietly gratified to chaperon her.

Nevertheless, to the chaperon's gathering alarm at last, the belle took no marrying interest in any of her numerous train of would-be suitors.   No : she did not even senti-mentalize with her adorers.   Whatever nonsense her nim-ble fancy and merry tongue charmed them with, it was not tender nonsense.   One single experience, very early, very rash, comprised all her sentimental histories.   The girl was not cold-hearted, but deep-hearted ; and " ce besoin d'affection qui devore la jeunesse" had its imper-sonal stay in the art which both absorbed and regulated the intense susceptibilities of a poetic nature.

This present summer, Monny's running away from Newport (where aunt Helen took a cottage solely on her account) to bury herself in her favorite hiding-place at Cape Cod, with her old nurse's relations, had been a par-ticularly severe trial to the amiable Mrs. Slabwell.

" Her bloom will be over very soon now : she is almost twenty-one," that lady had lamented to her husband.

"Now, Helen, the child grows more and more of a rose every day of her life."

"Still, that peculiarly fair complexion is at its best but a very little while," said the lady, with grave anxiety.

"Now, Helen, do you suppose men marry a skin? Really we are not quite so bad as that, — not when we see something choicer," said the present elderly husband, remembering how the ladylike grace of Miss Helen Rivers, who had only a pleasing face, had been more fascinating to him than all the pink cheeks in the world. "A girl," declared Mr. Slabwell, "who is more company than a roomful, whom nobody ever gets tired of, morning, noon, nor night, can take her time about marrying, — take her time. There's plenty of men that'll want her — a long while yet. And you know she likes to go down to that lonesome place just because she can paint pictures there all day long. Let her have her own way."

"I wonder sometimes," said the wife, "if we have ever done right to let her have her own way so, in painting pictures all her life, and shutting them up where nobody can see them; though, to be sure, I should hardly wish her to be known as an artist. It is true, that foreigner who gave her lessons at school so long told me that she had a very great genius; and it's perfectly astonishing, of course, to see the pictures she paints, especially since her trip to Europe with Harry and his wife. But," continued aunt Helen doubtfully, "the young women whom I see occasionally at watering-places, sitting round on camp-stools, sketching, seem to me extremely forward, eccentric young persons, fantastically dressed; and apt to fall into conversation with men to whom they have not been formally introduced; intending no ill, doubtless," said the lady, "but really not persons whom we should wish to hear Monny mentioned with at all."

Thus spoke Mrs. Slabwell, recalling some of those crude dabblers in literature and art, which the necessities of our time, and its liberties, have made so numerous among women; certain specimens of which flighty sisterhood, ubiquitous at summer hotels, had crossed aunt Helen's path. "If only," she resumed, imagining with a shudder a niece of hers joined to those unconventional rovers with the camp-stools, who represented to her woman as an artist, — "if only Monny had taken more to music, like her mother! Her mother played and sang beautifully, although she had only the advantages of that country-town where she belonged." (Young Endicott Rivers had so far followed his sister's example as to marry into a family less ancient than his own.)

"She wrote verses, too, that Endicott said were beautiful," continued Mrs. Slabwell, "although she never cared to print any thing. Nobody knows, however, what she might have done, if she had not been so bound up in him, and broken her heart at his death."

"Wasn't your brother given to drawing too?" asked Mr. Slabwell, in some endeavor to reconcile his wife to Monny's sad propensity.

"Not faces," said Mrs. Slabwell; "only bridges and such things. He was so talented he could have been any thing. But what he really fancied was to be a civil engineer; although, to please father, he studied law, you know. He was a great reader, too, just like Monny. But still he liked to be out of doors as well, studying the elevations of the land, and the construction of things," said Mrs. Helen, her ideas being rather confused just here. "It was some curiosity of that sort which led him to go down into that mine. He was adventurous, dreadfully adventurous, for a young man who was never wild in his habits," sighed the sister.

"Well," replied Mr. Slabwell profoundly, "as a girl wouldn't be likely to take to civil engineering, and planning bridges, and as the mother wrote poetry, the father's talents might come out in the child in this poetical way of drawing faces. At any rate, it's certain nobody ever put such a taste into the child's head: so it must have been born there. And seeing it has always given her something to take up her mind, so that you never hear her asking, in the dullest of times, what she shall do with herself, let her have her own way," said uncle Slabwell, administering his invariable recipe. "Let her go down to that old place and finish out her summer, if she wants to. Good healthy air down there. She'll come back in the fall fresher than ever." So uncle John had begged Monny off for her visit.

Mrs. Slabwell was by no means a match-making guardian of the unseemly eager sort. She merely felt that a girl whom it had pleased Heaven to make a universal attraction to mankind should improve her high privileges of selecting a husband while they were at their best. There were no jealousies in the Slabwell family; and it had not at all disturbed aunt Helen that her niece should have a social success which her own daughters had never had. Her own children, the loyal wife never forgot, were as near to their father as to herself: so she deemed it fortunate that the marriages which their personal choice had made, among the newer gentry of the city and suburbs, had not been such as to remove them to any chilling height above the paternal ways. But there was still a lingering sentiment in the calmly contented breast of Mrs. Helen Rivers Slabwell which would be gratified to see some member of the present generation of her family married into that circle of more traditions where the Rivers family had an original right to stand.

Also it would be highly convenient if Monny should marry wealth as well as station; so that the girl's own fortune, which was very moderate, need not be too largely increased by dowry gifts from her uncle, thought Mrs. Slabwell, not loving her niece less, but her own babes more. These babes had grown up, very pleasant but expensive creatures, likely to find ultimate use in their new households, reflected the maternal mind, for all that Mr. Slabwell would have to bequeathe. He would provide, of course, for orphaned Monny, as for his own child, if need were. But why should need be? thought aunt Helen, when her niece was a girl whom men sought, utterly regardless of the question whether she owned a pin.

Yet here was this belle, with such brilliant opportunities, encouraging none of her suitors, and taking the most unpractical flights into the desert, as if maidens were young forever.

Aunt Helen could but sigh a little, in spite of her natural serenity of temper and the marital efforts at con-solation.

CHAPTER IV.

THE minister was soon deeply at work in the seclusion of his Cape-Cod lodgings. Contrary to his usual practice when sojourning in such by-places, he declined to deliver any sermons at present. It was a very peculiar period with him ; and he chose to be a private hearer, for a while, in the little Orthodox Church of the region, which duly invited the famous Episcopalian to its pulpit.

So Monny did not hear the preacher, and she had judged the man. As for whatever great things she heard of him in the former capacity, they were, like his fine and superior presence, absolutely nothing to this young seeker after the sincerities, since she believed that his character did not correspond. She remained in a very poor opinion of that character. To begin with, it decidedly cheapened any man in mademoiselle's eyes to have the reputation of being pursued by ladies : he was the occasion of this unbeautiful reverse of "the proper order." Altogether, she avoided his presence to the utmost degree possible in the case of two beings boarding in a simple house like Mrs. Doane's. She esteemed it to be only in her bargain that she should do this, and it certainly was in her inclination.

So, being conveniently fond of bread and milk and fruits, — edibles that required no hot serving, — she continued to take breakfast and tea everywhere but with the ꓕister : even at dinner she contrived in many ways not ꙍ sit the meal out with him. And on all other occasions, although her behavior had no overt incivility, her genuine indifference to the man's existence made her pass him by as if he were a post.

A man who is regarded as a post by a young woman has this advantage, that he can study the genus *femina* in such a specimen with a calm security, not · always vouchsafed a man in these delicate studies, of having nothing to pay for his lessons.

It certainly behooved a reverend idol to come to what coherent knowledge he could of that mysterious sex with which he inevitably had so much to do ; and a pair of young feminine eyes in which he was so shorn of his beams that plainly a more rayless object in the shape of man had never crossed their vision, — this was certainly the providential pair of eyes into which he should look to post himself up in the abstract science of womankind. Doubtless some such conviction of valuable opportunity not to be lost moved Mrs. Doane's clerical boarder in those moments of relaxation when he emerged from his studies, to turn, as he began to, an occasional glance, which had a certain light of curiosity in it, upon the elusive young lady boarder, if by any chance she paused a moment in his atmosphere.

Such a chance occurred, for instance, one warm afternoon, as the minister was inhaling what breeze there was upon a shed-like piazza built out on one side of the Doane house, and styled by the family, the "porch." The porch was curtained with a variety of twining annuals climbing vigorously to the roof on strings, and was altogether a cosey bower to read an English review in, of a drowsy hour, as Mr. Leigh was doing, when Miss Rivers came slowly up from some point without the house. In her hand was a small paper parcel which had just come to her from Boston by the railroad express-wagon as she was walking in the yard; and, sitting absently down now on the edge of the porch, she opened the little package on the spot. It contained a long mane of nearly black-brown hair, being that appendage to the feminine toilet known as — a switch; and the girl, having compared it approvingly with what seemed a sample lock of hair enclosed, lifted up her fair arms, and coiled the thing twice about her head, as if to test its length.

The minister regarded this frank operation over the top of his magazine with a puzzled smile, and then remarked aloud, as the first intimation to the absorbed maiden of his presence, "I should say it was not the proper color."

"Indeed it's a perfect match," answered Monny roundly, facing about to behold this ministerial spy and critic making unasked observations from the other end of the porch. "It is for Clara Macey, who plays the organ in the village church here, and whose *head* ought to be brought out," added Miss Rivers, turning back to her switch, which she had begun to comb out with her fingers, braid up, and test the capacities of generally.

"And the rest of her left in?" asked the gentleman, mystified at this peculiar accenting of words.

"Certainly — subordinated," replied the young lady gravely. "Her head is her point; and it is all lost so with her hair," she lamented, more to herself than to the reverend inquirer.

If, by the way, the sober-minded are distressed to find a clergyman indulging in this trivial talk, they must remember that he could only investigate the laws of this young lady's being by taking her on her own plane. Moreover, as Tertullian's liberty of discourse on the feminine toilet is somewhat curtailed to the modern clergyman, so that really he cannot quite inform his lady-hearers from the pulpit that they "have learned their artifices from the demon," it may be that this New-York minister, who certainly had a world of beswitched heads to preach to, had a distinct professional anxiety to ascertain just how Satanic these arts were. At all events, he still plied his interrogatories.

"What! she has lost all her own hair, and her head too?"

"Lost her own hair!" repeated Monny, still busy with her disentangling. "She has plenty of hair; too much, in fact, and very nice. Her hair is pretty, but she isn't pretty in her hair."

"Oh!" exclaimed Mr. Leigh, filling out for the present with that monosyllable the complete blank which this last deliverance left in his understanding.

But, after taking breath a little, he returned to the charge, obliged to address, however, the young lady's profile, and mostly the back of her head; Miss Rivers being much too deeply absorbed with her switch to take any notice of the bass voice talking away at the other end of the stoop, save to throw it answers, when she must, in the most absent manner.

"A young person," persisted, under this snubbing, the inquiring mind which had forgotten the state of Turkey, and whatsoever else was discussed in the English review, — "a young person who suffers under the disadvantage of too much hair, and that misfortune is to be remedied by piling on more hair" —

"Too much hair for the way she wears it, all hanging loose, a style not becoming to her," said Monny, with an effort to see if a thoroughly categorical account would appease this tiresome questioner. "So nobody knows that she has any beauty at all, and she does not know it herself. But the shape of her head is perfectly beautiful, which is a very rare beauty indeed, and its poise on ner throat; and she has the loveliest little ears," pursued the artist, forgetting in her own enthusiasm the inappreciative audience. "And when her hair is all done up in simple, severe coils, that I am going to make her a little present of this switch to wind solid on, then," pronounced Miss Rivers gravely, "although people may never call her exactly handsome, she will yet be admired for a refined, distinguished air, and it will be a great help to her without and within."

"Within!" repeated the minister, surveying yet more curiously, as this exposition went on, the pretty curled creature who made herself a missionary of false hair to others, since she was denied the bliss of wearing any herself. "It is of the nature of a *moral* support, then, to a young woman to know that she has — what is it? — ears of a superior style, and a head remarkably joined on?"

"Certainly," returned Miss Monny, not desiring any conversation at all with the Rev. Mr. Leigh; but, if he would persist in talking, she was not to be put down by his flippancies, — "certainly it is a moral support to a young woman, and every human creature, to be conscious of some good points. That may be a reason," suddenly added mademoiselle, as a new illustrative idea here popped into her head, "why boys in their early growing-up are generally so much more awkward and distressed in company than girls are. Girls at that age are praised just for their looks. But boys' looks are at their worst when they are growing up (and nobody cares for boys' looks anyway), and they have no gowns to show them off, and they have not yet come to their brains, and so they are abashed and ill at ease till they are old enough to develop values after their kind, and then they come out comfortable and self-possessed, and enjoy society themselves, and make it enjoyable for other people; which shows," concluded the young logician, "that men, as well as women, in order to do their best, have a necessity to be what you may call admired, if anybody insists on that word, and chooses to give it a silly meaning," said the maiden with a slight toss of her curls. "I mean the men who are not vain," added this paradoxical young person. "Of course perfectly conceited people (such as the Rev. Kenyon Leigh, was the speaker's secret thought) do not need to be sustained by any approval but their own. But the truly fine souls, — yes," repeated Miss Monny with a deeply reflective air, "I should suppose the very finest souls among men might often suffer most from bashfulness in their early youth; because, of course, they would be more sensitive than other men, more alive to the ideal, and so more aware of their own crudities."

Now, as it happened, the very gentleman present could have taken out a first-class brevet as "a fine soul," according to this theory; since, however little it might appear at this period of his life, Kenyon Leigh had been, in spite of the high social advantages in which he had been reared, a quite morbidly bashful youth. So this young damsel's speeches had some curious touches of reminiscence for him, which made him rather wish to hear her go on a while longer; and he was a little disappointed, when, bringing that important cue to an end with these last words, she arose, and whisked into the house.

A day or two later it chanced that Mr. Leigh was again sitting on the stoop a little while after dinner, opening his mail, when he heard Monny's clear voice calling within the house to Susannah, —

"There's Clara Macey coming along the road. Please ask her to come in. I want to see her a moment."

It was one of those days, perhaps, when there was nothing in the papers; for this name pierced to the minister's consciousness, through the newspaper paragraphs he was reading, as that of the young woman whose *head* was to be brought out. And, as Miss Macey presently came up the yard, he lifted his eyes, and discreetly, through the vines, took a critical look at the maiden's possibilities of beauty, and really beheld none.

A slight girl, whose pale, small-featured face looked thin and insignificant, lost as it was in a mass of unconfined dark hair, which, slightly crimped, hung from the head in what a man would probably call the mop style of coiffure. This young person, disappearing within the house, re-appeared, after the lapse of some twenty minutes, accompanied by Miss Rivers; the young villager holding her wide hat in her hand, conscious, perhaps, of a new grace to display, as indeed she had. Miss Rivers had dressed her hair; and, behold, her head, which was small, was really of the perfect classic mould, and, with her hair deftly coiled in a manner to bring out its beautiful arches, she was quite another being. The low brow and finely-pencilled eyebrows had a decided beauty; the pale complexion, which was yet pure, harmonized well with the type of face, which, now that the bushy hair was so arranged as to be a grace instead of a drawback, had verily that delicate, distinguished air which the gospeller of vanity beside her had averred to be its quality. Really, as the two maidens moved about among the flower-beds, Monny cutting a bouquet for the caller, it struck the observing minister as rather a pretty deed, for a foolish one, that the girl on whom Nature had lavished so much should take such pains to bring out the quieter charm of her less fortunate sister. So, when the latter had departed, what did the clergyman do but make a remark to

Miss Rivers as she came up the walk, congratulating her on her success.

The young lady, lifting her eyes to behold Mr. Leigh again behind the curtaining vines, minding things so far from his proper business, replied gravely, "Yes: I have studied the modes of hair."

"Has it not cost much time to gain such a high mastery of modes?" asked the minister, his eye unconsciously straying over Miss Monny's toilet, a simple white one; but the man recognized in it, as a man might, some mysterious felicity of arrangement.

"Time?" repeated Monny: "that is according to how much force you put into the time. For myself, I put my soul to the fashions." With which calm declaration in the face of a clergyman, the butterfly vanished.

"What have you been saying to the minister?" asked Mrs. Doane within the house.

"H—m! He volunteered some weary old suggestion about the time women waste on dress. And I told him that the way not to waste time on dress was to give your whole mind and strength to it for just a day or two, spring and fall, when the new fashions come, and then shake your soul clear of the whole subject till the next season," said Monny, whose habit of bestowing on the clergyman only the briefest verbal droppings from her inward processes of mind made her words often convey to his brain any thing but her real meaning.

"By the way, aunt Persy," continued the girl, "it really seems to me that women themselves — those who write on dress-reform, I mean — help to belittle their sex, although, of course, they don't intend it, by their everlasting harangues on dress. It does give such an imbecile impression of women to hear, that, after so many thousand years, they haven't got the first rag of their

garments right yet. My women's-rights books up stairs
are full of assertions that the present style of feminine
dress absolutely necessitates endless worry and waste of
time and every thing. Now, any observer knows that
the world of difference there is in different women in their
faculty of dressing well on small means is not nearly so
much in the quantity of time they spend as in their quali.y
of *sense* about clothes ; that is, taste in choosing what .s
pretty, and prudence in buying what will wear well."

"I think you're quite right, my dear," said the old
lady. "I find myself that these women's-rights talkers
stretch things terribly. But then it's always more striking
to propose some entirely new order of things than to consider whether the fault with the old order isn't merely an
abuse of it by a foolish class who would abuse any thing."

"Of course," rejoined Monny. And, the outer air
being now cleared of the minister (he was just heard
going up the front stairs), the girl sauntered back into it
again, by a side door, to regain, in a few moments' solitary stroll under the open sky, her mood of work, after
the little interruption of her hair-dressing benevolence.
There was an apple-orchard which came well up in range
of the house on one side, the low Cape-Cod trees branch-
ing too near the ground for even Monny to walk upright
under them ; but the straight outer line of the orchard
was a favorite little promenade with her when the bosky
tops of the trees just shadowed her head with the wester-
ing sun. As she paced there now, her fair musing face
a little bent, the minister, seating himself at his study-
table up-stairs, glanced down, all unobserved, through
the white fringes of his festooned cotton window-curtains,
and smiled to himself, thinking how much like a serious
being that young girl looked, if one did not know that
she was merely putting her soul to the fashions.

Probably, indeed, the universal attention which this girl's face was wont to draw among far more perfect ones was because even the casual eye was surprised by it somewhat in the same way as was the minister; that is, the life of thought in Monny rayed out through a style of face not currently supposed to belong to the thoughtful woman. So the quality of expression which would have made a plain woman called intellectual looking was chiefly recognized in this pretty creature as giving some peculiar light to her beauty. Strangers would turn in a crowd for a second glance at this vivid young face, to find, on such glance, that it was not so perfectly handsome as it had seemed, but was even more striking.

The minister certainly did not ascribe unusual mental activity to his fellow-boarder; for she seemed the very idlest of all young human flowers, folding her fair leaves for a while in this Cape-Cod retirement, he concluded, in order to re-open more freshly for the season of city gayeties. Her convoy of elegant youth had disappeared; and she had, as sole company, the oddest variety of local visitors, whom she would entertain in her rooms through all the long morning hours, — half-grown girls from the village, with some points of picturesque beauty in their faces; little boys rather extravagantly ragged and bare-legged for this tidy region; and, above all, one strange, gaunt old fisherman and his old wife, living several miles away in a wild solitude of the seashore on the back side of the Cape. This aged son of the sea was known by the sole name of Isry-Chris, which was short for his full baptismal name of Israel Christopher. Whatever the family name was to which this superior appellation, recalling at once the head of the chosen race and of navigators, had been prefixed, it was entirely obsolete by some exaggeration of a custom, peculiar to the re-

moter regions of the Cape, of calling all individuals
blessed with a double baptismal by that as by their full
name.   As for the old wife, she had lost her name, bap-
tismals and all ; but she had a special piece of her husband's name assigned to her whenever it was necessary
to speak of the pair separately ; thus she was invariably
Aunt Isry, and he Uncle Chris.

The Isry-Chrisses — this was the name always used to
denote the family as a unit — carried on quite a commerce
with Mrs. Doane, especially during the time of her summer boarders, as Uncle Chris raised certain delicate
varieties of fish out of the waters on the back side of
the Cape, while Aunt Isry raised particularly fat chickens
on the land ; likewise they peddled all manner of berries
in their season.   But, whatever relations of trade they
had with Mrs. Doane, they had apparently intimate relations of friendship with her young lady boarder, who not
only had them up in her rooms by the hour, but once or
twice the kind of wagon-cart in which the Isry-Chrisses
made their journeys had arrived, beautifully swept and
garnished, with an extra seat inserted, upon which Miss
Rivers rode away in state to make a visit of days at
the fisherman's cottage across the Cape.   The minister
rather missed her in these absences ; for the girl had
some effect of a sunbeam on his present grave mood, —
an idle, tricksy flash, that he turned to catch sometimes
in a passing humor of the moment, to see how insub-
stantial the airy brightness was.   So he found it cheery
one day, after such an absence of Miss Monny, to hear,
as he came in from his afternoon rambles, her young
voice again in the family sitting-room as she was dancing
about there with her blithe queries after the household.

" Where's Popo ? " he heard her ask ; and, supposing
this to be one of her innumerable appellations for Duke

George, he pushed the unlatched door, made his proper greetings to the newly-returned, and kindly informed her in what direction he had last seen the quadruped.

Monny bowed silently, with some kind of suppression in her face, which was presently interpreted to Mr. Leigh by overhearing her, before he reached his study, run after Mrs. Doane, crying in the resonant *sotto voce* of a child bursting with restrained laughter, "*Did* you hear the minister tell me where Popo was? 'Is thy servant a dog?' I meant Popo for himself, — short for Popocata-petl, highest peak of the Rockys!" And the all-adored preacher of St. Ancient's, reduced to having his health inquired after by a young lady as the Rev. Popocatapetl's, attained his apartments.

Nevertheless, whatever whim it was which made the busy minister wont to break out of his pre-occupations with some word to stay this ever-flitting girl when he could catch her, seized him just as often after he knew that she called him names as before. There were curious touches of mystery about her. For instance, on those long solitary rambles which she took daily, she was sure to have on her arm an angular, frame-like thing, loosely wrapped in a shawl (it was her sketching-apparatus, which, since Mr. Leigh's advent, Monny kept thus con-cealed).

"What is that square bundle that you carry about so much?" he asked her bluntly one morning in the porch, as she came in glowing from her early walk, just as he was going out.

"It's a mirror," shortly answered Monny, entering the house.

"What do you say such things to the minister for?" asked Mrs. Doane within doors, as Mr. Leigh went beyond hearing.

" To strike him dumb," laughed Monny, remembering the amaze on Mr. Leigh's face; for he gave this young lady such credit for candor, he had accepted her statement as the literal truth.

" You should have seen his eyes," the girl went on, half laughing, and half indignant. " It was a little more than he expected, and he expects a good deal in the way of idiocy in women. Oh, yes! he does. I know him. And you needn't always stand up for him so, aunt Persy," said the maid, shaking her head at the matron with affectionate sauciness.

" It *is* a mirror, — mirror of nature," repeated Monny, sitting down, and making good her asseveration to Mr. Leigh by writing the above title in her sketchbook on the spot, affixing the date of month and year with a great flourish.

" Does he deserve the truth," demanded Miss Monny, shutting her book thus christened, with a bang, " when he actually swallowed what I told him as a fact? A man capable of believing that a girl tugs a looking-glass two feet square all over these sands! — and he preaches to women, great, crammed churchfuls of them, (more fools they!) and tells them they have immortal souls, of course; and all the while, down at the bottom, he has such an opinion of them as that. If a girl must admire her own face out on a morning walk, as if she couldn't find a pool, like Narcissus! "

" Narcissus? " queried Mrs. Doane rather blankly.

" The vainest man that ever lived — except a spoilt minister," explained the damsel.

" Now, Miss Monny, when there could never be a gentleman of more simple, unpretending ways than Mr. Leigh."

" H—m! " rejoined Miss Rivers. " I never said he

strutted visibly, — that he had any cheap, parading ways
of vanity. The man has a good outward style, of course,
just by being brought up in good society; but down in his
soul he's a lordly, woman-despising, domineering " —

Any further expense of adjectives on Mr. Leigh's
account was here cut short by Monny's running to the
front door, which opened at the moment to admit her
model for the day. It was her habit to spend the morning hours in painting from the life; her models, of course,
being that queer train of visitors which the minister had
remarked. But the afternoon hours, when she painted
without her models, she spent in her closest and most
exhausting work; and, from the silence which prevailed
in her apartments, the minister concluded that she devoted this part of the day to solid sleep. Yes: he would
see her come down and walk under the lee of the orchard
at its close, with eyes in which dreams seemed still lingering. Sometimes, however, she looked strangely weary
(the lonely artist had many misgivings this summer,
although she toiled more consecutive hours at her easel
than she had ever done before) ; there was a languor in
her girlish step, something like dejection in all her young
movements, which made her silent observer from the
upper windows wonder if some mysterious malady was
preying on this radiant girl; and he began to soften his
substantial tread when he passed her door in those silent
afternoon hours, lest the frail sleeper should be awakened.

Monny's being one of those high nervous organizations
to which a wink of sleep by daylight is a constitutional
impossibility, she considered the minister's view of her
capacity as a sleeper (revealed to her by Susannah, who
had observed the bated step with which the considerate
Hercules stole through the upper entry of afternoons) to
be only one more proof of his contemptuous estimate of

young ladies; and she kept stiller than ever in her apartments to confirm him in his precious idea of the way in
which she passed her time.

It was perhaps in this idea of Monny's fragility, that
one moonlight night Mr. Leigh woke out of the revery
in which he was pacing up and down before the house
to observe that the young lady was sitting bareheaded on
a wayside rock at a little distance in the quiet road. She
so grew on his mind at every turn in his walk, that finally
he went into the house and rummaged in the entry to find
some shawl belonging to her, but could lay hands on
nothing but a broad-leafed straw hat, armed with which
wrap he presented himself to the maiden.

"Miss Rivers, you should not be sitting so long out in
the night air without any protection," he said.

The young lady slowly turned her head, and surveyed
the intrusive gallant with so distant a gaze he might as
well have proposed to put a jacket on the moon which
she had been contemplating. Dropping, at last, her
gradual eyes to the object in his hand, with a look
which expressed both her sense of the man's audacity
in meddling with the articles of her wardrobe, and of the
absurdity of his selection therefrom, she said, "Thank
you, I am not particularly subject to colds in the *head —
myself.*" The minister had at this moment some remains
of such a cold which he had taken a few days previous.

"The night air seems to be very full of other people,"
she added dryly; for not only the minister was abroad
without a vestige of a hat on his own head, — the day had
been intensely hot, — but Mrs. Doane was visible by the
moonlight taking the air among her flower-beds; and
Susannah, also, was discerned at the moment spreading
linen to bleach on the grass. "Every member of the
household is forth," said Miss Monny.

"The rest are stirring about," replied Mr. Leigh:"
"you alone are sitting here perfectly still. There is a
very great difference."

"Yes: those who stir about make a wind round them,
—all the wind there is to-night: so they are in draughts,
which I am not. They are in a way to take cold, and
not I."

The reason-defying nonsense which mademoiselle thus
coolly babbled did not prevent her from looking extremely
lovely as she sat there in the moonlight: so the minister
was not disgusted enough to say any thing more severe
than —

"Miss Rivers, you must be aware that what it pleases
you to say is — contrary to all experience."

"This will be found contrary to all experience, yet it is
true," quoted Monny loftily. "I read that in a book as
having been said by some great man when announcing the
laws of a new discovery he had just made. It was pronounced a sublime saying."

"It was certainly a bold one," answered Mr. Leigh.

"All great things have the quality of boldness," pronounced Monny magisterially. "The philosopher knew,
of course, that the large mind and the mean mind have
not the same experiences; that they are impressed by
precisely the same fact in an entirely different way."

"But since the large mind and the mean mind are alike
enclosed in physical tissues on which the fact of night
dews makes very much the same impression, your illustra-
tion is hardly in point."

"Many other things are not in point, — not in point at
all," retorted Monny, wishing to make this intruder understand that his presence was not in point, and wondering
how much flaring impertinence and absurdity it would take
to convince him of it.

Apparently it would take a good deal while the maiden sat there unshawled. He stood stolidly immovable, although allowing the hat, which Monny's eyes had scanned so satirically, to drop stealthily on the ground. The belle, of course, made him aware, by an infinitesimal movement of her eyelids, that she saw this, and that it was still another infelicity. But just here, before he had committed any thing else, a more fortunate beau appeared on the scene. This was a fisherman of the region, who came driving up the moonlit lane in a wagon, from which he jumped to announce to Miss Monny that there was such a rare fine sight off the pier in the village, he was sure she would like to see it, and so druv up to tell her, — a big excursion-party from somewhere, with music, and lights dancing over the water, making a perfect picture for her. The young artist's pursuits were well known through the neighborhood, exciting much admiring awe, and a zeal to provide her with subjects, which was apt to be more devoted than intelligent.

Just now, however, Miss Monny welcomed eagerly the proffered opportunity to see the picturesque. She replied to the skipper that she should be delighted to go with him as soon as she could run to the house and get some wraps.

He could take her off in his boat on the water: the boat would carry several, the sailor said, meaning to indicate that there would be room on the present excursion for the distinguished gentleman boarder who was standing by, but leaving it to the lady, of course, directly to select the company.

The lady had not the slightest idea of selecting the Rev. Kenyon Leigh to be of the company: so, without a word, she started at once for the house. The skipper obediently followed her lead, stopping only to pick up the neglected hat which he spied on the ground. This he neatly dusted, and, with the native gallantry of the Jack tar, presented to the young lady; she putting on at once, and with the most smiling thanks, the head-covering which she had so scornfully rejected at Mr. Leigh's hands.

Then, leading his animal and the attached wagon with his off hand, the sailor walked beside Miss Monny up to the house-gate, paying all his *devoirs* to the belle with a manner, which in its felicitous mingling of respect as to a superior, and *naive* eagerness to serve the fair maiden, no art could have improved on.

Mrs. Doane declined the invitation extended her to be of this impromptu party, but Susannah was eager to go; and the sailor soon drove away with Miss Monny and the black woman.

The omitted gentleman boarder had seen a great many of the most brilliant sights of earth; but he stood looking after the retreating wagon with a curious, disappointed longing to see whatever trumpery spectacle might be off the Lonewater coast this evening. He had a vision of a boat rocking on the moonlit waves, and that rash girl needing some one to take care that her shawl was well wrapped about her.

CHAPTER V.

" IN the midst of this Pagan tumultucus live there sweetly and piously dreams a mystic of ancient days, — Fra Angelico da Fiesole. . . . He never took up his brushes without kneeling in prayer, and never painted a Christ on the cross without his eyes being filled with tears. It was his custom not to retouch or recast any of his pictures, but to let them remain as they first left his hand, believing that they were as they were through the will of God."

Over these words Monny had paused one summer day ere her coming to the Cape, as she sat reading Taine's "Italy;" feeling her own self in "a Pagan tumultuous hive," in the fashionable hotel where she was staying with her uncle and aunt, keeping, between dancing and driving, some remnant of her soul to art by devouring *in toto* the books of the brilliant French critic. Need enough felt this lonely, toiling girl to kneel in prayer before ever taking up her brushes, and, in her many misgivings over her dreadfully mixed-up nature and surroundings, to lay hold of the assurance that she was as she was by the will of God. So those far-off Catholic saints struck her as men that she would like to read more about, beings who spent their lives in reaching out after the unseen, in strivings which had no earthly reward. These, she fancied, must be the lives to quicken hers; and accordingly, when she came through Boston, *en route* for Mrs. Doane's retreat, she went into an antiquarian

bookstore there, as the supposed proper place for such
lore, and bought of a boy, the chief antiquary having
gone out to his dinner, some Holy Fathers. The boy,
being of a sufficient age to think how pretty this pious
young customer was, ransacked his unlearned best; and
a precious collection the innocent pair got together.

Ardent girls who ever plunged into the writings of the
old Catholic celibates, dreaming to find there "the innocence of the calm spirit preserved in the cloister, the
rapture of the blessed spirit that sees God," have found,
for one thing, such a portion meted out to their sex as
would indeed prove, in the words of Oliver Wendell
Holmes, that "the priest has had for woman but a curse
and a command." Such books had this unguided girl
gathered, seeking the brethren of the gentle Fra Angelico, — books whose perusal would certainly have caused
her some darker pain of bewilderment over the "woman
question" than any of the latter-day writings on that
subject which had so perplexed her. The absent-minded
Monny, however, forgot her antiquarian purchase in the
Boston depot, and again forgot to send back from the
Cape to have it expressed to her, until the package,
handed about from one depot official to another, was so
slow in being found, that it did not come through to the
house of Mrs. Doane until Mr. Leigh had been there
some weeks.

There, as it chanced, it was handed up by the express-
man over the familiar porch, one August day, just as
Monny was going out equipped for a walk, and Mr.
Leigh was coming in.

"Oh, my saints have come at last, I hope!" said Miss
Rivers, beginning to pull at the twine string of the
package, in her eagerness; whereat Mr. Leigh, stopping
to produce his pocket-knife, cut the same, and, the

wrapping-paper being torn off, the lost books were dis
closed.

"Do not trouble yourself to go up-stairs again for
those," said the minister, as Monny was turning back to
carry her books to her room. "I am going up-stairs
directly. Allow me to take them, and leave them at your
door."

This very small attention Monny could but accept; and,
saying a brief "Thank you!" she transferred her books
to Mr. Leigh, and went on her way. The minister,
going up-stairs with the books piled loosely on his arm,
turned them up for a moment, and ran his eye carelessly
over the names on their backs, finding it not at all new
in his experience of young ladies, that the very giddiest
of them should be given to some pious reading of the
tenderly sentimental sort.

It required but a glance at Monny's ignorantly chosen
volumes for Mr. Leigh to know that the kind of lore
which they contained was not desirable reading for any
girl; and the idea of these pages falling under the childlike eyes of this particular girl, so indefinably annoyed
him as a man and a minister, that, instead of depositing
the books at their owner's door, he marched them forthwith into his own rooms, and stowed them away in complete hiding there.

So Monny did not find her books; but being a forgetful
maiden, and absorbed at her easel, she did not remember
to inquire for them until the next afternoon, when she
went down to the stoop at the minister's usual hour of
reading there, and said to him, "If you please, Mr
Leigh, I did not find my saints yesterday."

Mr. Leigh looked up. His impulse to confiscate those
Holy Fathers had not waited on the question whether it
would be easy to account for the proceeding or not; and

he was only more in the same mind now, as the girl
stood in the open porch, looking like the creature of light,
which she always did when the full day shone on her.
So he answered deliberately, —

"No. I carried them into my own room."

Monny waited silently to be informed when her property would.be handed out from that apartment; but she
was only met with the decree : —

"Those books are not the best reading for you. Perfect moral action," continued the divine, casting about
in his mind for any explanation possible to make to this
young maiden, and inspired to nothing more skilful than
to proceed thus sermonically, — "perfect moral action
being perfect obedience to what we know of right, the
struggles of honest souls in any age to attain that obedience, according to their own standard, may be a useful
study for the disciplined mind. But the very young and
inexperienced need to seek their models in lives not too
far removed from the conditions of their own. Latin
monks and American young ladies are very utterly removed beings."

Mr. Leigh being much too delicate minded a man to
betray, even by a conscious look, the particular line in
which the Romish volumes offended, Monny could imagine
nothing in this censorship over her reading, but a last
impertinence of the "woman-despising" minister, — an
insinuation that young ladies could not be trusted to
read Popish books, lest they should become enamoured of
Popish practices ; and she burst out indignantly, —

"I think I should have sense enough to know that
what is to be imitated in good men is their spirit, and not
their literal doings, and that I need not put ashes on my
head, nor peas in my shoes, because the saints did : and I
don't know of anybody to study in American conditious

but George Washington, and I've got sick of him. As
for saints," added the girl, with a sudden threatening
flash in her eye, demurely turned to the horizon, " there's
nothing to stand for them in a Protestant country but
ministers ; and their personal goodness, which is the only
goodness I have any respect for, is of course dreadfully
exposed to be all drained away by their profession of
preaching; for some writer says, 'Every time a man
speaks of fine purposes, especially if he does it with eloquence, the less likely he is to accomplish them himself.' "

" Carlyle," said the minister, meekly furnishing the
authority for the quotation that smashed him.

" Well, he is one of the greatest of writers, and of
course he had observed truly." And, tossing her nose in
the air, Miss Anemone Rivers, having propounded these
sayings by no means with the slightest touch of jesting,
but as one who launched incontrovertible propositions into
space, that might hit where they would, swept into the
house.

The minister's eyes remained at gaze for a long moment
on the spot where his young castigator had vanished, some
singular light playing over his face. One would have
said that he was hoping she would re-appear ; but, as there
was certainly no chance of that, he rose at length, and
walked slowly up to his study.

As for Monny, she went surging into Mrs. Doane's
bedroom, on the other side of the house, shutting the
door vigorously behind her, and dropping on a low stool
in the midst of a heap of bright-colored rags which Mrs.
Doane, at work on a fancy rug, was cutting there to avoid
disturbing the shining order of the sitting-room.

"*Now* what do you think that minister has done?" was
Monny's first word ; and she floridly related the seizure of

her books. "Does an Episcopal minister think himself Pope?" she cried at the end of her story. "He isn't Pope of me! I come of the Puritans, the English Puritans, way back on the Rivers side, I do,—the regular old rampageous sort, that wouldn't pay the ship-money, nor bow down to the bishops"—

"Now, my dear child," calmly interposed the matron, "the minister, not imagining how much you know about books yourself, only meant to advise you a little, as a young girl, about your reading. He could never have intended really to keep your books," said Mrs. Doane, considering herself that this would be a rather high-handed proceeding. "What did you say to him?"

"I answered him back," said the girl, with a naughty shake of her head. "He is spoiling my manners, and making me impudent and horrid. But why can't he keep to himself? That was the bargain," cried injured Monny, with an allusion which the widow did not understand. "I don't like him, but I'm willing to let him civilly alone. Why can't he let me alone? Isn't he always asking me questions?—perfectly needless ones, and uncommonly stupid," pronounced the maid, with big scornful eyes.

There was no manner of doubt that the remarks which Mrs. Doane's clerical boarder had grown more and more addicted to bestowing on the young lady boarder were perfectly needless; and, as to their quality of stupidity, it must be confessed that Mr. Leigh had not exerted himself in the least to shine in conversational brilliancy to this maiden, the sole end and aim of all the speeches which he addressed to her being to draw out her own. As he was wont, however, to make these tentative remarks to Monny when no third person was present, Mrs. Doane had not had opportunity to judge of their superfluous and imbecile nature. And, as the reverend churchman had

grown this long while into his landlady's most exalted
esteem and veneration, she only sat thinking now how she
should disabuse Monny of her false notions regarding
him, as the vexed girl went on, —

"What does he mean? I suppose a popular minister
gets to be a kind of holy Turk. He is so used to having
the whole female household of faith bow down to him,
that, even although he despises women, he thinks he
owns them, and expects them to consult him as their lord
and master. Think of a man," cried Monny, reviewing
her wrongs, "who first puts the imposition on a peaceable
girl of objecting to board in the house where she is, for
fear she will trouble him with attentions, and next puts
on her the imposition of troubling her himself with curious,
meddlesome, gratuitous" —

"Now, now, my dear," interposed again the remon-
strant widow, "whatever made the minister think of going
away from here for the first day or two, it's certain that
he has staid ever since as satisfied and pleased as can be
with the house, and " — Mrs. Doane was going to say,
"with you." But she checked herself, and merely resumed, "it's very certain, Miss Monny, that Mr. Leigh
never could have meant any thing so rude as to keep
your books. You say they are Roman-Catholic books;
and, so many girls think there's something romantic about
being a nun, he was going to warn you a little against
those superstitions, since, according to your own account,
the amount of what he said was that those kind of writings were safer for older people to read than for the
young. Of course, as I've said, he doesn't guess how
wise you are in books yourself, and too steadfast in
common sense to be blown round in any such way. But,
my dear, he wouldn't have made such a mistake, if you
ever showed him your serious side."

"I don't want to show him any sides," pouted disdain ful Monny.

".But at least," persisted the matron, "as the fair-minded girl I've always known you to be before, you would wish to see *his* true side; and that's what I think you don't at all do justice to."

"Yes, I do, plenty of justice," declared Monny, who had her own private memory of that conference by the seashore in which she had set the minister's duty in order before him as to his landlady: so all the spontaneity was gone, to her eyes, from his subsequent virtuous behavior in that line.

"His true side is shown," she burst out afresh, "by his engaging a boarding-place, and making all the trouble of getting ready for him, and then preparing to leave it for no cause at all. That's what he calls perfect moral actions!" cried this practical young hearer, to whom the fine discourse on the stoop had gone for mere sounding brass. "He'd better go home to his big church in New York, and hire him a seat in the pews, and get himself soundly preached to one solid year. Only preaching wouldn't do him any good; he knows the trick of it too well: it would be like two Roman augurs winking at each other on the sly, while they humbugged the people with their signs and wonders."

Who the Roman augurs were good Mistress Doane did not know; but what she did know was that the clergy were being spoken of, and by her well-beloved young lady, in a style which seemed bordering on the sacrilegious, and she broke in with a more gravely admonitory tone than she had used before, —

"Miss Monny, Miss Monny, you was speaking a few moments ago of those righteous old forefathers of yours way back in England; and I used to think that something of those far-off ancestors had come down to you to make you strong in the days of your youth, to be so in the gay world, and yet not of it, in your way of being so earnest to know and see into the rights of things. But, certain, you are getting out of that way about this minister, my dear. Mr. Leigh is something more than just a famous preacher for show: for all our people whom he meets here round in his walks take to him wonderful, down to the little children; and, as there's no more chance of ever setting up an Episcopal church here than there is of a Mohammedan mosque, he can't have any proselyting views. Indeed, he looked into our own Orthodox Sunday-school library soon after he came here, to see what books were in it; and he's made them a present of a great box of new ones, as the superintendent told me came a day or two ago on the cars; so that, with my two boarders, this parish will be quite set up for a library," said the widow with pride. For Monny, to whose young life books had been so much, often made her little presents of a few volumes at a time to this only public library which Lonewater possessed. Monny's gifts were not of the tract order of literature. She was not very strong in the line of tracts: but with her own discursive reading she had managed to make a pretty shrewd choice of books that could be squeezed into a Sunday-school library, and yet were not the pseudo-pious trash usually considered the proper thing for such collections; and the liberal-minded clergyman, in his examination of the store in the little Orthodox vestry, had paused over more than one well-thumbed volume of Monny's bestowing, a little wondering what enlightened sense had put it on those shelves.

"I have never told you before," the widow continued, "about Mr. Leigh's good deeds in this village, seeing plainly that he wouldn't like to have them paraded

But I know he has had poor widow Cottrell's house shingled for her, and bought her biggest boy, that's just getting old enough to go on the mackerel-fishing, a new dory for his own, and helped Skipper Saunders, that's had a long sickness, and owns nothing but his schooner, to get it new rigged and furnished, as 'twas all out of repair. It isn't his being so generous with his money in all this that I look at; for being born of wealthy parents, as I hear he is on both sides, and already come into a large fortune on his mother's side, by reason of her death, I dare say, with all this riches, and being open-handed by nature, it's nothing at all to him to give money. But his looking so considerate into the wants of people he'll never see again after a few weeks, and having the gift to help them that have never been used to take regular charity, without hurting their feelings, — that shows what a very rare spirit is in him ; and it is the more beautiful to see in a gentleman that's been brought up in a way never to know any thing about privations himself."

Monny, being sufficiently a Unitarian to have a great respect for good works, had become an attentive listener to Mrs. Doane : so the latter went on, while still braiding her rags : —

"I remember saying to you, my dear, when Mr. Leigh first came here, that I thought women ran into foolishness sometimes, in their over-devotion to ministers. But I should be very sorry if by any careless speaking, and to a girl so young as yourself, I should have seemed to slur over the fact that women have very particular cause to honor ministers as the men whose set calling it is to bring the reign of virtue on the earth. For the reign of evil on the earth will always bear hardest on women and the little children, and all the interests that are naturally most dear and close to us. So, the profession of ministers being what it is, there's been many a just reason, first and last, why women should stand by them. Not that I would say," continued the matron, as her young hearer still sat silent, — "not that I would say ministers, or even their ways of thinking, are the only standard of goodness. I know my own husband, who was as honest a man as ever sailed the seas, — what with roaming so over the world, and seeing so many men and nations, — I know he came to take a very different view of many of the provisions of the gospel from what I did; but, though 'twas natural to me to cleave to the old way of believing, I could see that he was sincere and God-fearing in his way too. And so I reckon the apostle's saying, ' How knowest thou, O wife, but thou shalt save thy husband?' may not mean that she shall keep worrying him all the time to believe just as she does, when maybe it isn't in the nature of his mind to do so, especially in these days, when the foundations of every thing seem to be so questioned into and shaken up.

"But there is one truth that will never be shaken, Miss Monny; and that is, there's an everlasting difference between a bad life and a good one. And if women couldn't rely on the virtue of men, as well as on their strength and wisdom; if we couldn't feel sure that a certain proportion of them can be counted on to stand for the right in managing all the world's large affairs, — we women could never feel at peace going about our more private affairs, knowing well that we should suffer sooner or later, and most helplessly, in all our quiet places, for whatever bad and false doings went on abroad. So, if good men· should be honored by mankind, they should especially be by womankind," solemnly concluded the widow. "And a girl like you, my dear, who I truly believe have a reverent mind for whatever is good and high, — I could wish you would consider a little if you haven't taken an unfair prejudice against Mr. Leigh because he is an Episcopal minister."

"Oh! I don't object to the Episcopal: indeed, I like the Episcopal Church best of any church in the world, and I almost always went to it when I was away at school. Although at first," added the girl, wishing to be strictly accurate in reporting her sentiments, — "at first the order for morning prayer seemed to me so long and circumstantial, the end of Socrates' little prayer used to come into my head, — 'Do we need any thing else, Phædrus? for myself, I have prayed enough.'"

The Orthodox dame was not sure whether a little admonition was not needed here again; but remembering that Monny's vivacity of impressions was quite removed from levity of character, and feeling, moreover, almost equally in the dark as to Episcopalian prayers and those of Socrates, she said nothing. And the maiden added seriously, "But the whole Episcopal service, besides being truly like a religious worship, in having all the people join in it, is so reverential and beautiful throughout, it would seem a pity to cut any of it out for good; only I should suppose they might print the prayer-book, 'Then *may* be read the first, second lesson,' etc., instead of *shall* be; so that, when the preacher had a particularly good sermon, he could omit some of the service to give himself more time — Oh, how black the clouds are growing!" Monny broke off, probably realizing that her suggestions for the improvement of the prayer-book had not much chance of affecting the next church council.

"Yes, the wind has been rising steady ever since noon. I shouldn't wonder if there was a great blow before midnight," said the Cape-Cod woman.

"The rain will not come at present. I believe I want

to run down to the beach, and see the surf," said Monny,
rising; for on this Atlantic side of the Cape a very moderate wind rolled great waves on the shore.

"Take a warm shawl with you, dear, it will be chilly
on the beach, and come back and take tea nicely now
with Mr. Leigh, and you'll see he hadn't the least idea
of keeping your books," coaxed the matron, who, through
the humble but tender relation which her cousin had
held t） this fair girl's childhood, had come to regard her
as a kind of foster-child to herself, — a brilliant young
creature whom she both looked up to and advised.

Monny, who was very easy to be entreated of affection,
and who had been sufficiently impressed by what Mrs.
Doane had said of Mr. Leigh a little to reconsider that
obnoxious man, went towards her room half sorry for
her "answering back."

Yes, turning at the top of the staircase, she took a
sudden resolve to make so much of an apology to Mr.
Leigh as to go forthwith, and ask him with exceeding
polite amiability for her books.

So presently there was a low knock at the minister's
study-door by a hand that had never knocked there before. · Mr. Leigh opened it, to behold — Miss Monny, —
meekness round her red lips, but a glint of the rampageous Puritan ancestry in her eye, as she said in a voice
very low and sweet and obstinate, an accent inimitably
mixed of penitence and persistence, " I'll take my saints,
if you please."

The man mentally thrust " my saints " deeper down
into their hiding-place, took a renewed grip of the Holy
Fathers, as the maiden turned slowly up to him her large
open gaze. Under the influence of Mrs. Doane's words
she was looking at him for the first time, as it were —
this clerical lady-killer, who considered himself mortal at

sight. She was wondering if that conception of hers had really done him injustice ; and, lost in this inquiry, she did not at once take in the words of his reply : —

"Really, Miss Rivers, I have put the books quite away. I can make a much better selection for you of the Catholic writers, if you wish to read them ; and I shall be very happy to do so the next time I go up to Boston. Meanwhile, if you are in want of reading, any thing among such few books as I have here is at your service. You are very welcome to come in whenever you like, and take any of my books or papers that may please you."

By this time Mr. Leigh's words had sensibly penetrated to Monny's understanding, and what with their cool assumption of authority over her, and yet some indefinable impression that came to her with that long, searching look into the face of the speaker, that contradicted the character she had always ascribed to him, and which his present extraordinary proceeding certainly seemed to justify, — what with all these conflicting sensations, she stood quite speechless ; then making a slow, profound bow, still without a syllable, she turned abruptly, and retired to collect her wits.

She retired down-stairs to collect them with Mrs. Doane, not staying even to prepare for her walk. Bursting into that bedroom again, she confounded Mr. Leigh's advocate there by proving to her how entirely deliberate and intentional his confiscating proceeding had been.

"He has put my books quite away, quite!" mocked Monny, but in a merry key, all her wrathful mood of a few moments before seeming to have melted away in her sense of the comicalities of the affair. "He proposes to make a square bundle of my property, and send it back to Boston."

"Well, to be sure!" exclaimed the astonished widow.

"Why, it is a larceny within the law," laughed the girl. "I could have a sheriff to search the Rev. Apostolical Succession's premises for stolen goods. And he would stand up and look at that officer," continued Monny, dimpling merrily as the imposing image of Mr. Leigh denying her her books at his door vividly recurred to her, — "he would just stand up in all his feet and furlongs, and look down at him, and say, still as a lamb and stiff-willed as a lion, 'Really, Mr. Constable, I have put the goods quite away. I have made a square bundle of the plunder, which it doth not please me to untie.' What is the man anyway?" cried the girl, with an emphasis in her voice and a wondering speculation in her eyes, which showed that the minister at last really stirred her curiosity.

Mrs. Doane, feeling that Monny had now some just cause to be vexed with Mr. Leigh, was a little surprised at the mood in which she took this last aggression of his; but she said nothing as the laughing maid, with a few more jests in the same vein, ran up stairs again to equip for her ramble to the beach. As the widow saw her presently tripping away thither with Duke George, the good soul communed with herself a little whether she had not better go and inform the minister that Miss Rivers was a highly learned and sensible young personage, who could be perfectly trusted to read the most beguiling of Popish books. She revolved this plan a few moments; but feeling a decided mystification about this particular affair, and a general uncertainty about Mr. Leigh's whole state of mind towards her young lady, she wisely concluded to hold her peace, and meddle not a word.

As for Monny, roaming off to the beach to find the waves rising high under the darkening sky, the sea-

birds wheeling and whirling already, as with the passion
of the coming tempest throbbing under their wings, —
such a fascination and a study was the sea to the girl's
artist soul at a time like this, only the night and the instant threatening rain brought her blowing home, obliged
to race with the wind at last; for the thunder was rolling
in long peals, and the big drops beginning to fall. However, Duke George bounded on the porch, with his young
mistress close behind him, just as the floods descended;
and the watching Mrs. Doane drew the girl, breathless
but glowing, into the house.

"The minister has just gone up-stairs since we saw
you coming," said the matron. "He couldn't eat his
supper for worrying about you, and he was just coming
out to bring you home."

"Supposing, of course, that I was that proverbial
person that doesn't know enough to come in when it
rains," panted Monny; but even this reply was made not
quite in her old tone of flouting Mr. Leigh. In fact,
some impression from that long, serious look of hers into
his face, so remained to her, that as she sat down to the
tea-table, with Mrs. Doane sitting down again for company, she made no reference to the affair of the books,
and chatted about every thing but the minister.

But when she went up-stairs to her studio, where Mrs.
Doane had kindled on the open hearth the first fire of the
season there, expecting Monny to come home drenched,
as she had done more than once after such rambles, — as
the maiden sat down with a book before the bright blaze,
which the evening was chilly enough to make very pleasant, although she had escaped a wetting, a smile floated
over her speaking face as she thought of the man who
had sequestrated the last addition to her library, — flashes
of merriment sobering into an expression of that thought-

ful, puzzled wonder which had come over her regarding
Mr. Leigh. There was a moment of this revery, then,
opening her book, she was lost in its pages till bedtime.
But again at that hour, as she ended her reading, and sat
idly pulling down her hair as she gazed into the dying
fire, in these dreamy moments the old smile dimp'ed her
face again, and, giving an interrogatory poke to the
paling embers, she murmured half aloud, "What *is* the
man anyway?"

Then Mrs. Doane coming in, candle in hand, as she
often came at this hour, to take a good-night look at
Monny, diverted the girl's thoughts to another channel.

"O aunt Persy! isn't this going to be a dreadful
night for the sailors? The waves were just boiling over
the bar three hours ago, and what a hurricane the wind
blows now!"

"Yes, dear," said the widow, going round to put pegs
in the rattling window-sashes: "it's a hard blow, besides
all the driving rain, and thunder and lightning coming by
spells. But a sailor's eye could have seen this threatening all day, though the sun has shone bright enough off
and on: so any vessels dangerously near the shore have
had time to run into harbor. Sailors know too well what
this coast is in a storm to risk driving on it: so I'm not
so worried as in the gales that come up more sudden.
Though none can ever tell the chances of the sea," sighed
the widow; for Capt. Azariah's ship had gone down of a
still night in mid-ocean, struck in the fog by an iceberg.

The girl to whom was no memory of either parent's
living face, for the deadly accident that had smitten her
young father in a moment from the earth, had always a
special sense of nearness to these mariner's homes, which
had most of them their tale to tell of the men who went
forth, and came back no more; and she reached her hand

with a loving gesture to the matron, as the latter came
and sat down by her chair. Neither the widow, who had
learned these long years now to live bravely and cheerfully
in what was left to her, nor the orphan, whose was that
pathetic loss which can never measure itself with possession, save in fancy, — neither the elder nor the younger
heart was given to morbid repinings ; but still there were
lonely chords in both which made them sit and talk with
peculiar sympathy on a night like this. And when the
girl's head was at last laid on her pillow, the wild wind,
and the fancies which it brought, still kept her waking.
Monny's power of sleep indeed, in spite of youth and
health, was wont, from the extreme sensitiveness of her
organization, to be very easily lost ; and now, as the
hours deepened to midnight, and all the rest of the house
was wrapped in slumber, her senses grew only more pre-
ternaturally active with the fever of the blast. Then,
soon after the old clock in the entry down-stairs struck
twelve, a cloud still charged with electricity rolled up on
the wind, and a fresh thunder-shower, only not so severe
as the one at nightfall, added its tumult to the gale.
Somewhere between the long peals, the wakeful girl suddenly started up at a new sound, which seemed scarce of
thunder, or wind, or rain, — a sound like the faint, far
report of a gun. She listened with throbbing heart to
hear it again, said to herself that it was but the thunder,
and yet could not forget its peculiar echo.

The white heads of the furious waves, as she had seen
them on her walk, rushed on the darkness of her chamber
like spectres : she could not get over that haunting terror
of a ship in distress, and at last, rising up, she thrust her
feet into slippers, and, in a dressing-gown and shawl,
softly opened her door, resolved at least to go down and
speak to Mrs. Doane. A mysterious gust of wind from

some quarter drawing the door violently from her hand,
and sending it to again with a resounding bang, Susannah, who slept in a back-chamber on this floor, woke up at
that noise within the house, more potent to disturb her
than any amount of thunder without; and so, by the time
Monny was telling her fear in Mrs. Doane's bedroom
below, the black handmaid appeared on the scene to
know what was the matter.

Mrs. Doane, who was assuring Monny that she had
heard only the thunder, and endeavoring to persuade her
to share her room for the rest of the night, briefly explained to Susannah, and sent her back to bed again,
adding, "And look to the garret-door, Susannah. The
catch is loose; and it must have blown open to make the
draught that slammed Miss Monny's door, and it will be
swinging all night, and keep the minister awake maybe."
So Susannah went up to fasten the garret-door. But
meanwhile, with the various commotion, Mr. Leigh was
well awake, and called from his room to Susannah, as she
tinkered at the garret-door, to know if any one was ill.

"No, your Honor, nobody sick; only Miss Monny she
git nervous, and tink she hear a gun from de sea, — de
voice of a ship cast away, an' cryin' for help."

Yet a moment more, and the minister too sprang up,
and struck a light in a breath; for faint, and broken by
the wind, but clearly to be distinguished from the artillery
of the skies, came again the dread sound that had started
Monny from her bed, — indeed a gun from that midnight
raging sea, the voice of a ship cast away, and crying for
help.

CHAPTER VI.

MR. LEIGH was out of the house in a very few moments, snatching, as he went, the only rope Mrs. Doane had at hand to give him ; and the three women proceeded to dress more thoroughly. When Monny came down, however, fully equipped in her waterproof cloak for going forth, Mrs. Doane cried out in remonstrance.

"Why, of course I'm going, aunt Persy!" said the girl, pulling the hood of her cloak up over her head. "You know there's but very few men at home in the village at this time, and perhaps even women can help a little."

"Dear child, if there were men enough to line the shore, there's little the strongest of 'em could do to help, if the vessel is where she seemed to be from her guns, — not very far up above us. Right off our beach here, it's almost impossible, you know, to launch a boat, even in fair weather, because of the breakers curving over so, and filling a boat with water, or turning it bottom upwards, before ever it can be got off ; and in a gale like this the best lifeboat that ever was manned would be of no more account than an egg-shell. No : if there's a vessel on the bar, and she can't hold out till morning, till they can get off to her with boats from farther up the shore, there's no hope for them on board of her, except as some poor soul may be washed ashore, and pulled in over the undertow by flinging him a rope. There's always possible some chance like that," said the widow, who all this time had been swiftly filling a basket with bottles and small packages. "So I'm going down with this basket to that little house of Billy Hines, that's so near the beach, you know. They are poor folks, and won't have things to do with, and there may be want of stimulants; and Susannah will stay with you."

"O aunt Persy, Susannah wants to go too!" cried Monny, as she saw the excited eyes of the black woman. "We all want to go, and help carry the basket.

"There's some one at the door now!" exclaimed the girl, and ran to open it. There she found Dick Hines, a stout lad of sixteen, whom Mr. Leigh had met on the way with tidings of the disaster, and had sent on to Mrs. Doane for a coil of cable-rope that was in the old sea-captain's attic. The boy, who was breathless with running through the night storm, panted out what he knew to Monny, while Mrs. Doane and Susannah brought down the knotted pile of rope from the garret; and as the girl knelt on the floor, and helped disentangle the stout cable with her deft fingers, the matron finally allowed Susannah to put on her things, and the three women were to go. Monny, however, could not wait for the lantern of the other two; and, calling Duke George, she ran away on her young feet through the wild night, with the messenger and the ropes, the thunder rolling distantly now, but its accompanying flashes of lightning still showed at intervals the road.

Far down the lane a man with a bright lantern came running diagonally across the sand-hills, and joined them, lifting his light, as Duke George's well-known bass growled inquiry into the character of the new-comer, to disclose the face of Skipper Brickett, an old sailor whom Monny knew.

"Lord bless you! be it you, Miss Rivers?" he exclaimed, with that beaming loyalty with which men of

whatsoever degree were wont to salute fair Monny.
"You'm going to see the wreck? Well now, if you'll
do me the honor to go right along with me. I've got a
good ship's-light here;" and Monny was glad to cling
tightly to the stout sailor's arm, as they came out now
on the sea-banks, where her very senses whirled with
the violence of the gale and the deafening thunder of the
breakers. They kept their way on the bank: as for the
beach below, on which Monny often rambled, even at
high tide, it was wholly swallowed now by the great
waves; and, drawn blindly on by her escort, she scarcely
raised her head, bowed before the driving rain and the
buffeting wind, blowing straight on shore, till, coming
over an unusual elevation of the undulating bank, she
was aware of other lanterns gathering, and dark moving
forms of men; and the skipper suddenly held her tighter,
with, "Stand fast now, my young lady, and look off.
There she is!"

Monny looked off through the bewilderment of storm
and darkness, and that awful roar of the breakers, to see
what seemed a single, dimly lurid light, wildly plunging
and tossing in a world of inky blackness, haunted only by
an endless glimmer of white wraiths rushing tumultuous —
it was the last light of the doomed ship. The vessel had
been driven sheer over the outer bars of the coast, to
strike on the inner one, where, aground, with the waves
beating it to pieces, it had fired the signals of distress
that Monny had heard on her pillow. But, wrenched off
now by the great rollers of water, it was driven, utterly
helpless, at their will, until, even as those on the shore
gazed, a mountainous wave first lifted the wreck on its
crest, then dashed it on the bar again to its last destruction. Monny heard Capt. Brickett say, "There she
strikes!" while as yet her eyes, spell-bound on the phan-

tom light, had scarce discerned any outline of the dark
mass moving with it, until suddenly a long bright glare of
lightning made clearer than day the whole awful scene, —

The disabled hulk of a brig, with a chaos of broken
masts and tangled rigging; a dozen men or more; one
woman, with a child clasped to her breast, outlined against
her dark figure as she stood: the men had dropped their
axes, or whatever they had been striving to cut away all
that dragging ruin with, and float the broken shell of
their vessel a few moments longer: their attitude showed
that they knew the end had come; and the lightning
flashed out, as if to make a spectacle of them a moment
ere their death.

Monny turned sick with horror. The distance between
these hapless victims and the land was so short, yet the
thundering surges that filled it were such as to beat the
life out of any swimmer's breast. Even Monny had been
enough by these waters to know that; and the brief, deep
intonation with which the old sailor by her side, recognizing the dismantled wreck in that great glare of light said,
" It's ' The Rattler ' ! " had in it no touch of hope.

" You'd best come away from this, my young lady,"
he said, trying to lead off the shuddering girl; but at that
moment Monny was aware of Mr. Leigh, who towered
head and shoulders above all the other men, — of this
strong figure moving alert, intense. She paused to see
what his action meant, so unlike the blank despair of the
rest, as he dashed up to an old flagstaff that was on the
edge of the high sea-bank where all the group were standing, having caught up Skipper Brickett's lantern, the
most powerful light which had been brought to the shore.
The minister snatched this lantern from the ground with
the intent to run it up the high pole. Skipper Brickett
with the rest of the little group stepped mechanically for-

ward to aid ; and the flagstaff having an arrangement of sliding cords, as it was still used for some local signalling concerning the arrival of packets, the lantern was readily swung up by the Cape-Cod men to such height as would throw its beams farthest over the water. Evidently, however, this operation was wholly at the will of Mr. Leigh : plainly no other man saw any real purpose in casting this faint ray over that hopeless abyss.

He nevertheless, stretching far over the sea-bank, seemed to study every foot of the waters by its light, and by those intermittent flashes from the thunder-cloud, which still, by seconds, made their ghastly revealing of the sinking wreck. Every thing passed in seconds. Monny saw the coil of rope that had come from Mrs. Doane's flash all its length through Mr. Leigh's testing hand, as the men helped him piece it out with other ropes. She could hear no syllable for the thunder of the surge ; but apparently he put to them some rapid questions concerning the mad currents that he leaned over and watched so intently. But when, springing up from the bank and throwing off coat and waistcoat, he began to knot one end of the completed line about his waist, the men, who had thus far seemed magnetized to do his bidding, broke out in cries that Monny drew nigh to hear : —

"For God's sake, sir, what are you thinking to do? There's no mortal man can go through that sea alive ! There's more than one of us would be ready to swim off to her with a line if there was the least chance ; but we knew, with the first sight of 'em there, they were all dead men."

The minister seemed to hear nothing : he was trying the strength of the knot with which he had fastened the rope about him ; and there was that in his movements which made Skipper Brickett step quickly up to him with, —

"I tell you, sir, it's not for you to throw away your life for such as them fellows there! It seems hard on 'em to say it now in their extremity, and I wouldn't do it if it wasn't for your rushing into death to save 'em; but they tempted just this fate that's come upon 'em. It's 'The Rattler:' I knew the craft the minute the lightning showed her. They're a set of dare-devils, in the carrying-trade from New Orleans. Spoke 'em out to sea two or three days ago, and saw 'em again this noon, when I run into harbor myself, and come home by the cars. They were either drunk or mad to risk this gale along shore."

The minister answered not a syllable as all this was poured rapidly forth: he had no time for words, watching to snatch that fitful torch of the lightning to see how those raging mountains of water rose and fell. And the skipper, looking for a silent moment, as none could help looking who saw, at the face and figure stretching far over the surf in that wild leaping light, turned and took noiselessly up the rope at a few yards' distance.

The brave mariners of these Cape-Cod shores were no respecters of persons when they plunged into the ocean, whose perils they knew so well, to save the drowning. But, when they saw no chance of saving, they could but set the life of this man, who in the few weeks he had been in the village had so won their homage, against that of some careless, drunken wretches, and hold him back from sharing their death as a too costly offering.

So quietly, as Skipper Brickett turned and signalled them, the other men, too, laid hold of the line, forcibly to restrain the minister, who, wheresoever he had learned to splice ropes like a sailor, was yet a landsman, who, in pity of the awful sight before them, had lost his reason.

Kenyon Leigh perceived nothing of these movements:

he was too intent on what he had to do, for he had not lost his reason. No: daring to the last limit of earthly daring, there was yet this difference between a rash man and a brave one, that he had counted the chances, and found one, against the ninety-nine, for him to reach the wreck. He knew that he had at the very outset to leap so far over into the breakers from the high bank as to clear the undertow; and the only possibility of achieving this was to seize that greater wave which ever and anon came rolling in a little nearer than the rest, and go out on its return. If he could accomplish this, then, for the perils beyond, his power to hold his breath a little longer under water than a slighter man, to struggle a little stronger over it, was his chance, — a fearfully dangerous one, but still a chance, and he intended to take it.

All these things, so long in describing, were crowded in the doing as thought and action crowd in such straits of death; and it was not until, seeing afar his oncoming wave, he drew back with one swift, all-gathering glance, for that rushing leap into the flood, that Mr. Leigh saw those who grasped the line, and their purpose. More thunderous than surge or sounding hurricane rose his voice, — the shout of a man who is trifled with in the one possible moment when the impossible can be done, — "Let go the rope!" And, as if literally stricken off by that mighty will, every hand fell from it for an instant; and the next instant — ah! what was there to do but still to let go the rope? For with that Titanic rush and bound he was gone — he was battling with the flood. It rolled him under, but it cast him up again; far the mountain-wave whose crest he had caught swept him beyond the undertow; and, seeing this great escape, the men on the bank threw themselves down, and with breathless watching gave out the rope to the swimmer. The deep gulfs of the monstrous billows hid him, and the awful night; but when he went into it, beyond that faint, shifting penumbra made by the high, wind-blown lantern, he was alive, and struggling onward still, and in dead silence they on the shore still gave out the rope.

For the girl who watched among them with dilating eyes and panting breast, the question she had asked a few hours before swallowed her whole being now : "What *is* the man?"

Utterly superhuman he had seemed to her from the first moment of his rushing up to the old flagstaff, not alone in his great daring, but in that transcendent power to sweep every faculty into service at once, whereby the man of great brain who has any gifts for action can rise superior in a moment to all experience, and "mighty to save," she could only murmur in her hushed heart, remembering every idle jest she had ever made on that Herculean frame which could so second now the heroic will.

Would it bear him through? Once, twice, the black night into which he had passed was pierced for an instant by those sharp lances from the thunder-cloud. The first time, an awful dread froze every soul, for nothing was to be seen but the white heads of the breakers in their savage might; but the next — "*They* see him!" cried the girl — "they see him!" For those human forms on the perishing wreck were straining out over the sea in a new attitude. Surely it was a living man they caught sight of, bringing hope of life to them. The swift darkness fell again, — the moments seemed ages, — but at last, at last, came some tightening thrill on the rope, whereat the sailors on the bank sprang up with a shout; and a wild, wild shout had gone up ere this at the other end of the line, for out of the floods they had drawn their deliverer.

Yea, head and shoulders above the rest, the watchers on the bank could see him stand with those forms on the shattered hulk, when the next lightning-glare revealed them ; and swiftly enough they drew the slack line tense, and made it fast to the high bank, whose height was an advantage now, bringing the rope so far above the general sweep of the waves, that the men who began to pull themselves hand over hand all its length to the shore were immersed only now and then, and by the mere tops of the breakers, when they were well off from the wreck.

A desperate enough feat such a passage — over that wild gulf, through the whirling storm and darkness, and anon the strangling rush of the waters — would seem to ordinary mortals ; but to sailors accustomed to stand on nothing, and reef topsails in a gale, it was practicable : the desperate question was whether the wreck, which was the only pier of that frail bridge in the boiling sea, would hold out till they were all over, when among them was a woman with a child, and one helpless man, " The Rattler's " captain, who had been knocked down and disabled by one of the falling masts of the vessel.

To improvise a car out of a box and pieces of rope, that will draw human beings over such a chasm, has been done before in shipwreck ; and such an achievement would have seemed nothing now, after the miracle of swimming the breakers, save for the fearful straitness of the time, with every moment beating the death-knell of the dissolving vessel ; while to work by, there was only the dim light of the one or two shattered lanterns that they had been able to restore.

But the sailors escaping over the rope brought with them to the shore, attached to their persons, the lines to draw such a machine by ; and, when it was got ready, the poor woman on the wreck was naturally the first to be brought off. She was a Creole Spaniard whom the American captain had taken to wife, and not having the slightest doubt in her Catholic soul that the man who had risen up, plainly divine, out of that impassable flood, was the patron-saint to whom she had been praying in her long agony of terror, — with this faith, and her being a lithe, active creature, wonted to rough ways, she managed, with her child lashed securely about her, so to aid herself at any obstructions in the passage, that she was safely pulled through, and drawn up the high bank by the strong hands of the Cape-Cod men, drenched and gasping, but still alive, with her child.

That young member of her sex who received her there, blessed to have one being among these sufferers whose neck she could properly fall on and cry, of course sobbed over her, and hugged the baby, and stripped off her long cloak to wrap the pair in, all in a breath. And the poor woman, apparently taking the sympathetic girl for another messenger straight from the Queen of Heaven, adjured her to see that *il capitano* was brought over in safety, with which charge the half-fainting mother suffered herself, for the sake of her child, to be carried away to the little house of the Hines family.

Susannah was very glad by this time to go away out of the storm with this *cortége;* and her mistress had not come beyond the little Hines house at all. So Monny was now left alone on the bank with the men, kneeling on its edge, straining her eyes to see into that black night, where the desperate struggle for life still went on. Desperate indeed it was growing to the three men, all that were left now on the wreck; viz., Mr. Leigh, the disabled captain, and a single sailor, a young Portuguese. All the rest had escaped over the rope while the preparations went on to carry over the helpless ones.

How the last of these men came, bringing word that the captain was got ready, and that the lines must be drawn in with all speed, as the wreck was half under water, and could give a foothold but a few moments more; how, drawing in those lines, there came, when but half their length was in, some obstruction, a dead lock out there in the darkness which no eye could pierce, the deafening roar of the surge through which no voice could call; how there were moments of dread waiting, and then a great vibration, a sudden dragging fall of the rope, whereat the men who held it sprang up, and began drawing it in — the very bridge, — how these things passed Monny knew not: a terror more ghastly than had been before in this terrible night seemed to suspend her very breath.

It was indeed the acme of its perils. The two men on the other side could half see and guess the rest of what had happened; viz., that a great wave, the rope-bridge swaying always lower with the sinking wreck, had so whirled and tossed the rude car in which they had bound the disabled captain, as to entangle hopelessly the lines; while, still worse, the swooning, half-drowned man was clutching them fast in his convulsive stupor. In this appalling strait, with the last planks going beneath their feet, there was nothing to do but for both the remaining men to climb out at once by the rope as far as might be, and then cut it away behind them, trusting to be hauled in through the breakers.

The one sailor left by his side being a small, agile man, Mr. Leigh sent him on in advance; then, the rope swaying so low now, that his own weight was chiefly sustained by the waters, he climbed out to where the helpless body of the captain swung, and, grasping the rope with one iron hand, cut it away with the other, and the three men were in the sea

In the annihilating rush that came then through the
waters, Mr. Leigh, at least, had power to remember that
the weight now on the rope would fearfully overstrain it
when the three of them came to be drawn up the high
bank; and drawn they all must be, because of that fatal
current of the shore made by the undertow, against which
the strongest swimmer could avail nothing, but would be
swept along in a line with the shore, unable to make an
inch towards it.

Knowing well these perils, Mr. Leigh decided to lighten
the over-weighted line by throwing himself off it when
it was drawn close in, and trust for his own life to the
chance of seizing some fresh rope that might be thrown
out to him from the bank. Such a chance, indeed, saved
him; for, all the time the sailors had been crawling over
the line from the wreck, the watchful mariners on the bank
had held ready to throw out, in case any of them should
be washed off by the breakers in their transit, a rope with
an iron so attached to its end that it could be aimed with
precision. So now, in these last dread moments, which
might bring forth none knew what, Skipper Brickett
stood waiting with this barbed rope; and, discerning the
heads of the struggling men as they came within the
faint circle of light that rayed from the shore, he hurled
it with such skill Mr. Leigh soon laid hold of it, and,
drawn safely through the surf, he was on the bank even
before the other rope was in.

The men whom he had saved fell at his feet. As for
Monny, as soon as she knew that Mr. Leigh was verily
brought alive again out of the deep, she kept aloof,
hanging over the rope by which those other lives were
suspended. Thus it chanced that as the poor young Portuguese (not skilled as Mr. Leigh was in holding his breath
under water) was drawn, a perfectly helpless and appar

ently drowned man, up the bank, and the tangle of ropes
and boards by which the other insensible being swung came
but slowly up the high cliff, Monny, woman-like, forgetting herself and her own footing, as she reached down her
insufficient young arms in a wild impulse to help, lost her
balance, and, slipping on the crumbling sand, would have
gone headlong over the cliff into the breakers but for two
or three hands that caught her back.

Mr. Leigh's was among them, and as he set her on her
feet he fairly shook her.

"That ever a rational being should run such *senseless*
risks!" he said, transporting her, as if she had been a
kitten, several yards back from her dangerous position.

"I wanted to do something," gasped Monny, in the
grasp of Hercules, which was sufficiently vigorous to
suggest to the girl that he was good for a dozen ship-
wrecks more on the spot.

"Do what you *can* do, then!" he answered, in only a
lower note of that tone in which he had cried erewhile on
the shore, "Let go the rope!" "Go home this moment,
put on dry clothing, and see if you can get these poor
people something to eat."

The stringent vehemence with which he spoke was only
the involuntary vibration in the man of the tremendous
shock that the sight of Monny tumbling over the cliff had
caused him. He had not been really aware of her presence
at all until that instant; and the perceiving how drenched
and shivering was this delicate, girlish frame, all un-
cloaked as Monny was now in the storm, thrilled him
with some apprehension that all the mortal exposures of
this night had scarcely stirred before. Thus to send her
where her sympathies could be expended with safety to
herself, and some practical benefit to the sufferers, was
his only thought; but in this strongly-moved moment it

found expression in a style which certainly savored, as no word of his to Miss Monny had ever done before, of the "domineering."

But meeker than ever was Moses, — for Moses had not been a light-tongued girl making fun of a great man as a paltry one, — and brought to repentance by such a night as this, the maiden heard and obeyed : yea, as Mr. Leigh turned to examine the insensible men whom they were preparing to carry away, Monny paused only for a word of inquiry about them, then, softly calling her dog, she ran through the gale and the darkness for the Hines house. Panting enough, she arrived there, but stopped merely to call Susannah to the door, and tell her, for the poor wife's sake, that they were bringing the captain straight on to the house, and that they did not know but he might be still alive. Then, taking her cloak, she went straight on for home ; Mrs. Doane, who supposed that some of the villagers were along with her, being very glad to have her return at once to the shelter of her own roof.

All alone, however, with Duke George, Monny ran swiftly up the long, pitch-black lane, in the small hours of the night, in her desperate eagerness to reach what she had so longed to find in the last hour of looking helplessly on at masculine power and skill ; viz., woman's opportunity to be a little useful. That, it seemed, was still at home, — cooking victuals, to be sure. Instead of hanging over that wild sea, every throb of her heart straining with the strain of those struggling lives, where should she have been the last hour? Industriously putting the kettle on for tea.

Well, the convicted Monny ran for her sphere now with might and main : how she shone in it will be seen in another chapter.

CHAPTER VII.

IT must be confessed that Miss Monny Rivers was not prepared to shine in the kitchen department of woman's sphere by any previous practice. In the sewing department she was very excellently accomplished, having been in the habit of teaching poor girls how to cut and make their own dresses by patterns. But although she had learned that it was desirable for all women, of whatever station, to have skill with the needle, she had never made the same discovery with reference to the culinary art.

Her aunt Helen was a lady whom cooks never deserted in a huff. The apparently unforcible Mrs. Slabwell yet kept an American domestic establishment, with the usual Milesian retinue of servants, rolling on the softest and smoothest of wheels year in and year out: so it had never occurred to Miss Monny that break-downs in the kitchen, requiring the mistress personally to officiate there, were among the contingencies of life. In short, the present contingency was the first time in Monny's mortal existence that she had been summoned to produce " something to eat " on her sole responsibility.

True, she had once attended a lecture by Professor Blot, aunt Helen having bought a ticket to the course as one of her social duties. On that occasion of privilege, as Monny remembered now with remorse, after she had dutifully minded the composition of three varieties of syllabub, the procession of ladies solemnly filing up to the professor with their individual spoons for tasting, so

tickled her fancy, that she spent the rest of the houi drawing a caricature of the same. She could have wept now,
recalling this levity. But at least, she said to herself, as
she ran splashing through mud and water, she could ran-
sack the larder, and set forth its cold provisions in order.
And for hot provisions, certainly the first preliminary
would be a fire; and, consoled by remembrance of the old
proverb that it took a fool to make a fire, she arrived at
the dark house, and rushed for her chamber. There she
changed her wet garments with more care for herself than
she might have staid to take but for fear, that, if she
should even sneeze on the morrow, a certain man would
regard her as a troublesome imbecile, who ran *senseless*
risks (the risks of men were taken to some purpose); then
plunging down to the kitchen she attacked — that new
cooking-range of special memory. The new stove was
insanely rich in modern improvements; and, in spite of
the proverb, getting a locomotive in running order would
not have looked much more formidable to Monny than the
firing-up of this engine, stuffed, as the grate was at this
hour of the night, with dying coals, too dead to be re-
vived into burning again, yet decidedly too alive in their
deceitful grayness to be plucked out by the maiden's bare
fingers; which tender implements, in the impotence of
shovels, and the wild impossibility of discovering the
peculiar yank of the dumper, the neopyhte stoker at first
attempted to thrust into the heap. A considerably wise
fool, indeed, was required to make a fire in this machine;
for when by dint of iron spoons, pewter skimmers, egg-
beaters, all the tinware in the pantry that would scoop
(the bowls of the pewter implements pleasantly melting
off with the heat of the cinders, and leaving Monny dig-
ging away with the handle), — when by these sacrifices,
and the indispensable fingers wound in wet woollen rags

and making dexterous dives all the while, the mountain of
hot embers was at last triumphantly cast out independent
of dumpers, and the empty grate joyfully crammed with
kindlings, then began the snarl of dampers, seen and
unseen, which bewitched the thing before, behind, and on
all sides.

To know how to open and shut these attachments, what
was the effect of their opening or shutting, and when they
were open or shut, — this riddle might have been longer
in the solving, but that the hurricane of wind which was
blowing at present pronounced on these points with such
staccato of belching smoke or roaring flame, that Monny
only strangled a few times, and singed off some front
locks of her hair, before she had all the stops of her new
instrument drawn out, and kindling-wood, charcoal, and
the solid anthracite itself, going at full blast. In the
latter stages of this combustion she had flown about and
cleared the kitchen of ash-pans, and wrecks of tinware
(she proposed to pay for her damages), made clean her
fair begrimed hands with soap and water, filled high the
teakettle, and begun to set the table, and still Duke
George was her sole companion. No feet yet came on
the doorstone. Having an impression that the masculine
digestion would survive, even after shipwreck, in some of
its native contempt for cakes, Monny had examined wistfully the only supply of meats which the small family had
on hand in this warm season ; viz., a pound or so of beefsteak, and a pair of chickens. She was gazing into the
refrigerator at these provisions, especially at the chickens,
which seemed to be in some mysterious state, — not exactly
raw, yet not ready for the table : she was desperately
wishing that she knew how to get them ready, — when there
was a noise of men arriving at the house-door, and directly
the welcome Susannah bounced into the kitchen.

" Sakes alive, honey! Hev you got such a blessed fire as dis yer agoin' all by yerself? And all the nasty ashes — how ever did you know how to dump him? "

" Are they alive? " asked Monny, appearing from the pantry, thinking first of those two corpse-like figures that she had seen lifted out of the deep.

" Jess what we've been doin' so long, tryin' to see if they was clean done gone forever. De young one, de little furriner, he come to pretty soon: he was mostly stunned, an' he'd swallered some ob de sea; but dey roll him, an' rub him, an' he come to an' speak. But he's powerful weak, an' he's got to stay to de Hines's. And de cap'n — dey work over him all de time; an' missis she rub him, and give him hot tings, an' at las' he breve jess a little. He dunno nuthin', an' he's got bones broke; but he breve: so mebbe he'll pull troo, after all. An' de doctor's dere now: so missis is comin' home berry soon, an' his Honor, who is one mighty angel ob de Lord, sure, an' de winds an' de sea obey him! " . All which Susannah poured out in a breath, as she was getting off her wet outer garments and over-shoes, and lighting a lamp.

" An' his Honor told me to put de men right up into his room to change 'em. Dere's tree of 'em come along wid me, an' waitin' now in dere soppin' close in de entry; an' dere's more a-comin' wid his Honor: so, seein' you've got tings a-goin' so bright an' shinin' here, I'll jess fly right round up-stairs, an' get dere dry close de fus ting; Missis tole me where to find 'em." With which discharge of words the handmaid vanished; Monny, feeling that she must not detain her an instant now, reserving her questions about supper till she should re-appear. But Susannah was long gone: in fact, one of the sailors, another youth of about twenty, less robust than the older men who made most of

the crew, fell in a fainting-fit, soon after he was got up-
stairs, followed by violent chills and nausea; so that with
the care of getting this patient to bed, and hunting up
clothing for the others, Susannah was quite taken up for
the present.

Meanwhile there was a general arrival at the house of
Mrs. Doane, — Mr. Leigh and six more of the shipwrecked
men to stay there; this house being nearer the scene of
the disaster than any other, except that little cabin occupied by the Hines family, which was more than full
with the two men who could not be moved, and the poor
woman who was the wife of one of them. Also they
had brought the baby in this company, to relieve the exhausted mother of its care while she watched her husband
hovering between life and death; and when the bed-quilt
in which it had been wrapped to bring it again through
the storm was unwound by the kitchen-fire, disclosing a
plump little girl about a year and a half old, with black
eyes shining like buttons, and when Monny had brought
one of her little cashmere morning-jackets, and improvised
a tunic for the darling, in addition to such dry garments
as the Hines family had been able to reclothe it in, the
small shipwrecked was in much more comfortable case
than it had been any time before that night.

Nevertheless, when it had taken slow and solemn survey
of the new premises, with its black eyes growing bigger
and blacker every moment, it began to cry aloud with fear.
Its wondering baby-soul may have stood still through
either awe or attention during the various cracks of doom
through which it had passed: it had certainly endured
being dragged, head downward, through thunder and sea,
and all the other terrors of the night, with comparative
quiet; but, now that it was entirely safe and sound, the
poor little daughter of Eve considered that it was time
to have an attack of nerves.

Mrs. Doane perceiving, through whatever nice learning in infant shrieks, that the much-tried baby was in a fever of fright rather than in any physical distress, and being imperatively needed up-stairs as well as Susannah, left the screaming child entirely to Monny's devices. The tenderest of these were wholly unavailing to pacify it. The fair face of the new nurse was regarded, to be sure, with a moment's toleration by the wondering black eyes, then, happening to remember that it was not the order of beauty that it was accustomed to, the lost baby yelled in Spanish with madder outcry than ever.

Monny was distractedly tugging the kicking infant up and down the room, feeling quite ready to cry herself, when a pair of strong arms were reached suddenly over her head, and Mr. Leigh, who had just emerged from his room, dry clothed, strode off with the little howler. The miraculous thing was, that it ceased to howl immediately, — a miracle which the discarded nurse beheld, through all her relief on the baby's account, with some mysterious touch of disturbance on her own. Apparently the magician took no very laborious pains. With the baby on one arm, only saying to it now and then some merry, coaxing word, he was all over the house, in the darkness or the light, as he went from one room to another, looking after the men ; yet that restored infant purred confidingly away on his shoulder, plucked delightedly at his whiskers, drank peacefully out of the porringer which he held to its lips, — that identical porringer which it had madly dashed out of Monny's hand when she wooed it to imbibe just such another milk-and-sugared mixture as it drained the dish of now, — and then went to sleep, with its small Catholic nose buried in the heretic minister's coat-sleeve (the child was a girl, and probably accepted the heretic for the sake of the minister, — the child was a girl). The minister,

to be sure, after administering the porringer, did take two
or three quiet turns up and down the front sitting-room,
empty just then, stroking the bewildered little head that
had been through so much, till it sank off unconscious, tc
be pillowed, sound asleep for the rest of the night, in Mrs.
Doane's bedroom. But had not she, Monny, stroked its
head, and with much affection? and it had only bounced
the more.

The young woman who saw herself thus vanquished in
the supreme feminine office of baby-tending by a man
surveyed his doings only furtively and from afar, being
extremely busy the while in enlarging the table accommodations, etc. For being the most unsuitable person in
the house to be running about among men more or less
déshabillé, bringing them fresh changes of clothing,
Monny's labors were still confined below stairs, where
as yet she had no assistant. Susannah, indeed, supposing, after the young lady's exploit with the range,
that she was equal to any thing, called to her down the
back stairs, just as the minister was disposing of his
baby, to say, —

"Miss Monny, dere's some ob de men might begin to
hab dere supper now, if you'd jess clap dat ar beefsteak
right on de coals, and let it go fur as 'twill, an' I'll be
down in a minute an' knock up somethin' else for de rest.
De gridiron is in de pantry. You jess take de tops ob de
stove clean off, an' clap him right on de coals. Turn him
fus one side an' den todder, you know: dat's all."
According to which bulletin of instructions Monny flew
for the gridiron, cast down as to her failure with the
baby, but lifted up as to her triumphant success with
the fire. For the patent range, with all the stops out, was
by this time a red-hot furnace, — alas! too fiery a furnace;
for the steak, "clapped right on de coals," was burnt

to blackness before ever the amateur cook supposed t
time to make the first turn of the gridiron. "Oh, I
didn't know there was such a power in fire!" moaned
Monny, as, turning up the gridiron, she beheld her broiling. But there was no more steak in the house; and
heroically serving with the burnt side upward, that nobody might be snared by her cooking unawares, she
carried the platter to the table, where Mr. Leigh was
just seating three or four of the men. Rather more
hopefully she brought in her tea and coffee; for she had
made a cup of tea some moments before for the sick man
up-stairs, according to another bulletin of directions shot
down the back staircase by Susannah; and, as Monny
could follow directions accurately, her tea had been pronounced "fus-rate" by the critical Susannah. So she
had joyfully proceeded to make not only a large potful
of tea, but one of coffee; making the latter by exactly
the same rule which Susannah had imparted for the tea;
viz., "A small teaspoonful to a pusson," pouring on
boiling water, and setting the pot in a merely warm place,
to "draw."

If Monny had been a drinker of tea and coffee herself,
she might have had a grain more intuition about the making of these beverages; but she drank neither. She had,
however, a floating impression that coffee had some distinctive need of being settled, and that eggs were used
in the process, — yes, she remembered just now Kitty
Ellison picnicking with Mr. Arburton, in "A Chance
Acquaintance."

"Mr. Arburton saw her break the egg upon the edge
of the coffee-pot, and let it drop therein, and then, with
a charming frenzy, stir it round and round." Blessing
the instructive reminiscence, she repeated this passage
now to herself, as if it had been a recipe, and supposing,

of course, that the settling operation must be the last
business before carrying the coffee to the table, she broke
her egg, stirring it violently in with a long-handled spoon,
scalding her much-enduring hands with the hot splashes,
then rushing for the table to pour out the delicious slops
(every sailor of them had declared for coffee instead of
tea) before the virtue of the stirring should expire.

Alas, again! and alas! The clear amber stream that
was wont to pour from aunt Helen's and Mrs. Doane's
breakfast urns was sufficiently removed, even to the eye,
from the weakly muddy tide that Monny's coffee-pot dis-
charged, for the mortified cook to perceive her failure, as
did also the watchful Mr. Leigh, who took the vessel
from the girl's trembling hand, ostensibly to relieve her
of its weight, but really to set the whirling fluid down
to recover itself after its "settling," Monny, meanwhile,
hearing that "Do what you *can* do" thundering in her
ears with quite awful echo.

Certainly, however, there was no thunder, nothing in
the least awful, in Mr. Leigh's present manner. He was
carving that steak as if it were so delicious, that, smitten
himself with a sudden and vast appetite, he must needs
divide unto his own plate all the most beautifully charred
portions thereof; then, when Monny was looking the
other way, or when he supposed she was, he so adroitly
pared the rest as really to extract some quite tolerable
morsels for the sailors. Just now, moreover, Susannah
made a providential transit through the dining-room with
a mammoth coffee-pot in hand, whose contents she had
been distributing up stairs, having herself snatched some
unknown moment to brew the same when Monny was
absorbed with the screaming baby. Mr. Leigh, having
eyes everywhere at present, arrested the handmaid, suggesting, with an artful plausibility that was rather a new

growth in his character, that she fill the sailors' cups with the remains of her coffee, as perhaps the coffee-pot on the table was a little *cooled*, and had best go back to the fire. By these inventions the famished mariners did not go quite hungry, it will be seen. As for Mr. Leigh, pouring out unto himself enormous libations of Monny's successful tea (he had a marked preference for coffee), he washed down therewith his plate of bitter cinders without a grimace.

None of these specious proceedings deceived, however, the young waitress on the table, who rushed into the kitchen the second Susannah had set foot there, to seize from her hand that decoction of egg-water tinctured with coffee-grains which had " cooled," dash it out of doors, and return the empty coffee-pot to the black woman, who seemed to Monny at that moment the perfect ideal of her sex, with, " Make some more coffee ; and let me see you do it, every inch."

" Bless you, honey ! mos' likely you didn't make him strong enough," responded the expert, pouring in the Java by the teacupful, instead of poor Monny's little teaspoon measures. " Men always want a great deal more power in dere vittles an' drink dan women. Jess bring me a egg to clear him — dere — so — you break him in, shell and all, de fus ting ; " and Monny, beholding, saw at which end of the process of coffee-making Kitty Ellison stirred in the egg with that charming frenzy. " Now I pour on de hot water," continued the illustrator, " when de teakettle don't fairly bile, but only kiu .ei tich- l ers, an' den I set de pot jess where he'll bile deep an' steady, but still, as you may say, softly, 'bout ten, fifteen minnits, — ten minnits'll do for now, — an' by dat time de rest ob de men'll be down for dere supper, an' den, ef I ain't here, you take him off an' pour in jess a little

cold water to settle him fore you carry him to table mild
and lubly so as not to rile him a grain." And Susannah
was back in the dining-room before these words had well
left her lips, taking a comprehensive look at the table,
then saying in Mr. Leigh's ear, —

"Your Honor, dere's a pair of parbiled chickens in de
fridgrator dat I can make a hot stew of in no time ; but
I'se got to fly round fus up stairs along o' some trousers
an' tings dat's jess been sent from de village to help fix
out de men."

"Well, if you will give me the chickens, I think I can
manage the stew," said Mr. Leigh in the need there was
for hastening supper, and being informed by Susannah
that he could not officiate just then about "de trousers
an' tings."

Monny did not hear this dialogue, as she was bringing
a fresh plate of bread from the pantry ; but she noted how
Mr. Leigh rose up, and went into the kitchen with Susannah, then, presently hearing that heavy-footed handmaid
travelling up the back stairs again, she a little wondered
what Mr. Leigh was up to in the kitchen all by himself.
So, stepping in range of the open doors, she looked out
to see, and, by the stars above, if he wasn't making ready
that stew-pot with all the *savoir faire* of a first-class
hotel cook !

Dismembering in the twinkling of an eye those formidable animals that she had not dared to meddle with,
stowing them snug in the kettle, pouring in some mysterious jellied gravy out of a dish, sprinkling away with
dredging-boxes, — Monny's cheeks, which were vivid
enough before with all that she had been through, began
to burn like pomegranate-blossoms at the sight. Here
was a royal Alfred who would have minded the peasant-
woman's cakes, and *not* burnt them. Monny had an in-

tense respect for capacity, and some inward sense that she was herself apt and willing to learn, and did not rightly belong among the blunderers, and, through all the awe with which she had bowed before the hero who had conquered the death-raging flood, there began to stir in her now, some instinct of her own personality not to be utterly abased and abolished, — a passionate inquiry as to why this potent masculinity was equal to all things, small and great, and she to nothing. Was the secret in some quality of nature, or of training whereof she had been highly defrauded? asked the girl, as she watched his Serenity setting the pot over the fire. Then suddenly, as one who arraigned the universe to know why her attainments were knowledge of syllabub in three kinds, while he was solidly furnished to the occasion, whatever it was, she made an indignant dive at the man, demanding, "Where did *you* learn to do chicken-stews?"

The royal Alfred turned at this onset, to behold the pomegranate cheeks, the eyes blazing like two stars, and made leisurely answer, "Well, I think I came by this accomplishment (knowing poke of a drumstick under water) in rather disorderly ways, not to be recommended to young ladies (scientific shake of the dredger). Surreptitious suppers with my mates when I was a boy away at school, fowls roasted in the small hours of the nigh over fire-grates not especially designed for cookery (sagacious adding of a little more hot water to the stew), — these furnished my first practice, I believe, in this art, perfected afterwards by some camping-out experiences with my brothers in college vacations, when our servant fell ill," continued Mr. Leigh, rather lingering over these explanations, noting what a picture Monny made the while. It was not the mere scarlet of her cheeks, and the white of her forehead, and the tossed glory of her

hair, but the rueful, half-defiant, passionately in-earnest air
with which she spoke, and listened, only half appeased, to
his words of reply, then silently turned, and slowly with-
drew to the dining-room, her head flung back over her
curved shoulder, her eyes dwelling on that supper-kettle,
as if it contained some problem of destiny. Mr. Leigh
watched this receding vision with a musing smile, thinking what a beautiful, wilful, mysteriously charming child
it was. He thought this for a moment, perhaps it was a
long moment; but then, for charming children were as
yet not quite ascendent over his permanent mood, his face
grew abstract with graver musings as he waited at his
novel post: he was thinking of the men in the other
room, how the very sea had cast up to him the old
problems.

The shipwrecked crew, most of them of Anglo-Saxon
speech and blood, were all gathering there now, — in the
dining-room, which was the largest room in the house, it
having been the kitchen of the original square dwelling,
since built out in indefinite extension in the rear. This
now central room still retained its huge old-fashioned fireplace, on whose hearth Monny had bethought herself to
kindle a bright blaze, round which the sailors instinctively
drew as they came in.

Skipper Brickett had not named amiss these depraved
seamen, who half in drink, and wholly reckless, had
dared needlessly, and with a woman and child on board,
a gale off a highly dangerous coast. Monny, who had
seen merely rough sailors before, had never seen such
faces as came into view around this hearth-fire: the New-
York minister had seen — oh, how many of them!

As he came presently in among them now (Susannah
having finally appeared to serve up the stew, and wait on
the table), the girl, whose last impulsive ebullition had

subsided, to leave her again keenly watchful of Mr. Leigh,
grew aware of some mystery of power in him far rarer
than aught which the night had before revealed of his
character.

They are, to begin with, the very rarest of beings, for
all our democracies and philanthropies and soul-saving,
who can ever meet those below them by any deep social
chasm with an absolute simplicity. The straits of mere
physical danger, it is true, make all flesh one; but many
a gentleman who will go gallantly and nobly into fire or
flood to save a beggar's life at peril of his own is honestly
embarrassed, the moment he gets him out, to know how
to strike a sufficiently common chord of feeling with the
poor man to enable him even to express comfortably to
him his thanks. There was no such difficulty with Kenyon
Leigh, for all thanks to him were instinctively hushed by
the perception that he shrank from personal praise with
some self-withdrawal that was even bashful; so that one
could quite imagine, seeing him among men who owed
him their lives, the blushing, excessively diffident boy
that this hero had once been.

Probably, by the way, to the make-up of heroes of
the most genuine kind, there goes, much oftener than the
superficial observer would fancy, that intense sensibility
which is one of the roots of shyness. At all events, the
present remains of this temperamental trait in Kenyon
Leigh had some indescribably winning charm in a man
of a type that is wont to have a certain necessity to
dominate, — that touch of the aggressive, egotistic, which
we have almost come to expect as the inevitable alloy in
men of great abilities, and positive, passionate convictions. Some living force of these, only the more effective
for his peculiar personal modesty, yet went with him
everywhere; and it was a significant thing that a man

who made this supreme impression of character, should have been nowhere more magnetic than among the most utterly fallen and degraded of beings. What is often called the "magnetic" man is wont to have it as his prime characteristic, not to exalt, but to lower, all standards : such would-be leader, not merely of the degraded, but of what are only termed the "vulgar" masses of men. is apt to take their tone, — to hide whatever privileges he has had of learning better things in a vulgarity more essentially vulgar than that of the simple ever is or can be. Of this demagogue style, as of every and all species of acting, Kenyon Leigh was incapable : if he had some unconscious gift for hiding his privileges in the presence of the unprivileged, they were hid in his lowly sense of that eternal mystery which has made men so to differ. Too far into that mystery he looked, not to see the remorseless bequeathing of evil, how much of all human character and condition comes not by the personal doing or deserving ; how, in all that we call free choice, something was fatalized ere the man was born, — this old, old riddle, that every thoughtful mind must struggle with, this minister felt only more keenly than another.

With this insight he looked into faces like these of "The Rattler's" crew ; and there was a touch in the mingled expression of his eyes, which would have reminded those who had known that rare lady, of his dead mother. It was a look which one sees sometimes in women of sweet and noble natures, who, reared amid all opulent refinements, pass through life with a kind of angel's incredulity of evil. Too pitiful over the sorrows of humanity to chide its sin, all the crimes of the world seem to them born of suffering : they lean out from the porches of their own sheltered lives, dropping, indeed, a bounty which has no winter in it. In this heavenly ignorance the man had not been able to abide. If his mother's blood in him made him yearn over the fallen with some instinctive, "Lord, lay not this sin to their charge," he yet realized that the source of every thing which is respectable in the race has been in the power of the human will to struggle, not only against the difficulties without, but the defects within; and the mysterious gift which he had to quicken this power in others thrilled in some incorruptible recess, even hearts like these.

Yes, the shipwrecked men, rising up one after another from their irregular meal, gathered round this being, who, flush on the high meridian of younger manhood, had so perilled his life for theirs. They gazed at him as if they were under a spell; strange gleams beginning to grow in their dark faces, — signs of that struggling aspiration towards the greatness and goodness of another which is the creative germ of moral life.

A girl who, from a faculty of her artist nature for finding something interesting in every thing that lived, and the soft heart which did not ask too severely whether it lived well or ill, — the creature in hard conditions, — who from these qualities, and the universal attraction of her fair face, had been wont herself to have a peculiar ease of approach to the ignorant and lowly, silently contrasted the influence which pleased with an influence like this. The former, the feminine influence, thought the girl, accustomed to please, was instinctively shut away by every order of man from every really serious hour. So she interpreted to-night that distance which was in the sailors' manner towards herself, as compared with Mr. Leigh, — a distinction not wholly due to the mighty debt which they owed the latter. And restrained of all the gracious young service, which, pitying them for the dangers they had passed, she was eager to render to these poor men, Monny shrank timidly away, struck with a sharper sense of being useless and *de trop*, and lost in mournfuller ponderings on woman's sphere and its limitations than all the previous humiliations of the night had caused her.

"The Rattler's" crew, indeed, watched both Mrs. Doane's boarders with marked attention, — the girl who looked the crown of her sex, as the man did of his, — they watched them both with that pathos of homage which one sees sometimes in the lowly towards the elect of their race; and that homage, in truth, did make them draw apart from the woman, but nigh, with some strange outreaching, to the man.

There are two kinds of sympathy very precious in this world, — that of the being "who with all our faults loves us still," and of the one who best grasps our situation. The eternal sentiment of sex has so put some hint of the former sympathy even into the attack made by the praying women of the grog-shops on the dram-drinker, for instance, that he takes, half-pleased, his buffetings, and signs the pledge, partly in repentance of his vice, and partly flattered that the lady thinks him so much worth the saving. Still it is probable, after all, that, in its most genuine hour of self-abasement and struggle, the fallen life is most strongly helped by the other kind of sympathy, — that of its own sex, — a man's distinctive charity for another man being based on the fuller view which he can take of the force of his temptations.

Certainly, in such men as were these wild sailors, it was a sign of the absolute contrition which thrilled them at present, that they saw in the fair girl, whose refined loveliness shone like a star under the homespun roof, a being alien to them as the very stars, before whose face their disordered lives fled away. But they brought them back

before the man, making some strange, silent review of
their dark memories, dimly wondering if the passions
which in themselves leaped in blind brawling and carouse,
only less dreary at the last than the sluggish torpor, the
dead routine of toil out of which the madness broke, — if
these forces had indeed any kinship with the energies
which in him could flame so in peril, and breathe such
peace when it was past.

Peace did this man breathe? Oh, Great Hearts of
humanity, walking whatsoever haunted ways between the
lion and the pilgrims, calm do their lifted brows seem,
touched of no mortal weakness?   Nay, be sure that unto
them, and with only fiercer combat than others know, hath
somewhere been the lone fight with Apollyon, striding the
whole breadth of the way, fire-breathing, roaring hideous,
"Here will I spill thy soul!" Yea, life's temptation, its
tedium, albeit in far other forms, were known to Kenyon
Leigh as to these poor turbid souls : never else, indeed,
had they drawn to him with such yearning inquiry.

Kenyon Leigh was not given to perfunctory exhorta-
tions : he only looked at the sailors with his strange, penetrating eyes as he sat among them, filling out, with some
little talk of the sea, the waiting moments while the impromptu beds for all this company were being prepared.
So they did not suspect the clergyman until they came to
part for the night ; Mr. Leigh having said no grace at the
irregular meal, as he noted how two or three of the sailors
furtively made the sign of the cross when they sat down
to eat.   For the sake of these poor brethren the Protestant bread went unblessed : but now, when the mixed company, all gathered round the hearth-fire, were going to
their short sleep as the dawn was at hand, the minister
rose up ; and mindful of the death to which they had all
been so nigh, simple as a child saying its evening prayer,
he knelt down with, "Let us pray."

And the sailors who made the sign of the cross made it now, falling on their knees with the rest, or whatever sign might witness to the power which made this man, who out of his robes had not even what is known as the clerical look, a priest forever after an order higher than Melchisedec's. Out of the book could this churchman pray on occasion ; though the soul of its old prayers, with their simple, reverent phrase, was in his, as his fervent, impassioned voice arose. Haply the heavens into which he prayed were dim enough to these wild beings, most of whom were men who crossed themselves neither in faith nor fear ; but not dim was their belief in him who poured the petition. Now that he saw them not, their wide-open eyes, brimming with tears, never wandered from his face ; they swayed towards him as if to partake of his nature : yea, distinct at last, the divine longing dawned in these darkened souls, — not cupidity of heaven, nor terror of hell, but the passion for purity uncompounded.

It was a picture of thrilling contrast, — the shining face of the man on the height of humanity, the marred, marred lineaments of these in its depths ; but the wonder, the beauty of humility there : was it that he could so feel his brotherhood with them ? Nay, but that they could feel theirs with him.

Mystery of one mortal life drawing its tides through generations of honor and of worth, and of another whose currents flow poisoned from their spring ! — the hour when any soul of the latter first discerns all the vantage-ground of the former in how much more than external things, not so strange were its poor human impulse to curse God, and die. But the loyal delight which the most miserable of men will take in every gift that crowns some exemplar of their race, — herein is not only pathos, but a seed of promise which surely awaits only nurture for all fulfilment.

Monny, gliding in from the bedroom, where she had been for a look at the sleeping baby, paused in a dim corner of the many-angled old room, spell-bound at sight of those streaming, upturned faces ; then with an answering quiver in her own young heart, that rose up in her sobbing throat, and 'sent a gush of tears from her eyes, she stole away again, and left them alone with their d:liverer.

CHAPTER VIII.

" AUNT PERSIS, do you suppose men can do every thing better than women, — *every thing?*" repeated Monny, with an emphasis that swept all mortal doings from pole to pole.

It was the fifth day since the wreck of " The Rattler ; " and Mr. Leigh had gone up to Boston to put the captain, who was but just able to bear the journey, in the hospital, the man having escaped with his life, but still with injuries so severe as to require for a long time yet constant supervision of the best medical skill. With the captain had gone wife and baby, the replenishing of whose wardrobe had been Monny's grand care for days past; also, as the last of the crew to take service again on the sea, the young Portuguese sailor, who had been half-drowned on the night of the wreck. These all departing in care of Mr. Leigh, the old house had settled back to its normal quiet; and Monny, straying down to the porch, and falling into an afternoon revery there, had looked up out of it, and propounded the above question to Mrs. Doane as she appeared in the open doorway, indulging once more in the leisures of knitting-work.

" Did you see how Mr. Leigh hushed that baby the other night, when none of us could hush it?" pursued Monny; "and, whatever he pretends about the way he came by the rest of his all-knowingness, he hasn't lived out for a nursery-maid," declared the girl, reaching this one solid point of certainty in her speculations as to the right of Mr. Leigh to be so aggrandized with faculties.

"Now, Miss Monny," replied the widow, coming out to sit on the stoop as she waited for a fresh skein of yarn which Susannah was to bring her from a certain bureau-drawer up-stairs, " 'twas the most natural thing in the world for that baby to take to Mr. Leigh. In the first place, living on shipboard, 'twas a great deal more used to seeing men than women ; and, in the second place, Mr. Leigh brought it all the way that night to the house in his arms."

"Yes, missis," chimed in Susannah, appearing here to hand the skein of yarn over Mrs. Doane's head, and add her contribution to the philosophy of life, "and his Honor 'ud carry it so strong. A baby knows in a minuit whether you carry it strong or not."

"I carried it with all my might," protested Monny, recalling the strained arms with which she had lugged to and fro that writhing infant.

"Jess so, honey, and 'pears like a baby wants to feel dat dere's some might left over. Seein' dey are all flyin' to pieces in dere little tantrums along of dere own nerves and weakness, a woman's nerves and weakness kinder drives 'em wilder. Whereas, a man dat handles 'em strong and cool and easy sorter calms 'em down, unbe-known as 'twere. La! women are poor critters, and even a cryin'. baby knows it," declared Susannah. With which voice from Ethiopia going back on her sex, Monny was quite quenched ; but as the handmaid vanished, and Mrs. Doane bent over a knot in her skein of yarn, she mur-mured at length, as if thinking aloud, —

"That's just what some of the anti-woman's rights essayists say, — that men, whenever they have a mind to try, can do every earthly thing, even woman's work, bet-ter than women can do it."

"Now, my child," replied Mrs. Doane in her calm, elderly fashion, "I'm afraid you read too much all that heap of books and magazines you've got in your room this summer on woman's rights. If you girls that are growing up nowadays are going to lay seriously to heart all the stuff that you see printed for and against women, certain you'll blow to all points of the compass to once. There, she hasn't brought me just the right hank of yarn after all," abruptly declared the matron, and forthwith she went in doors in pursuit of the correct thing.

Monny, remaining still in the shady corner of the porch where the vines clustered thickly, was soon lost again in revery. The central figure of her meditations was certainly the Rev. Kenyon Leigh, but she was by no means weaving round him any dreams of sentiment. Monny was much too great a stickler for the "proper order" to be burning even hidden incense of tenderness to any man unasked. Then, although the fashionable preacher, spoilt of women, had dissolved to her so utterly and forever as the man called Kenyon Leigh, that she wondered at her own distempered fancy in creating such a chimera: and although the extraordinary figure which had now risen on her vision in its place occupied her thoughts wholly as a man, and not as a minister, still the fact of Mr. Leigh's profession remained in her consciousness ; and for Monny to imagine herself a minister's wife was the one impossible imagination to her.

Miss Rivers then presents at this time the phenomenon of a young maiden to whom an unmarried man has become a subject of intense speculation, although he figures in no outermost circle of her fancy as her conceivable lover. That this was a possible feminine condition, the sceptical may be aided to believe, if we admit that there might perhaps be traced in the coolly abstract examination which the Rev. Kenyon Leigh was undergoing in this young head some subtle, far-off connection with what could be called matters of the heart; that is, if the young lady thus occupied with the image of a gentleman was not asking what *he* thought about *her*, she was very profoundly asking what the order of men of whom Kenyon Leigh was a type thought about women, — the personal question, it will be seen, only in a general form.

Monny's saying that she wished to be approved of the serious minds, the men who wrote the solid essays and reviews, was her girlish way of stating the fact that she had come to have, with her growing years, an especial admiration for powerful thinkers dealing with what are called practical questions. This taste in so imaginative a girl arose partly perhaps from the instinct of a thoroughly healthful nature to seek that which was opposite to its own line of gifts, but still more because the old Puritan character, renewed with whatsoever strange blossoming in this fanciful maiden, was still there in great strength: over and above all dreams of beauty, she inquired earnestly into life.

She had, as we know, been especially led of late to study what this weighty order of masculine intelligences thought of the feminine; and she had suffered what might be called a pain of the heart from whatever slights these admired sons of wisdom put upon her sex. And now there had walked into her immediate knowledge and observation a very commanding specimen of "the serious mind;" and, lo! he came scorning women. This was the aspect under which the Rev. Kenyon Leigh became a subject of such profound reflection to the maid sitting on the vine-covered porch. She could not forget that he had once proposed to leave that house because a young lady was boarding there. Now that the coxcombry which she had formerly attributed to the New-York minister was removed as far from her idea of him as the east is from the west, this proceeding of his was simply an overwhelming argument to prove that such men habitually avoided the frittering atmosphere of women whenever it was possible.

Weighed down by these thoughts of gloom, Miss Monny was only roused by the step of Mrs. Doane again on the porch, as she called to Susannah in the yard with some remark which told that Mr. Leigh was expected by the evening train, and that "high tea" must be prepared for the traveller. Or rather, since that phrase was not current with the Cape-Cod woman, her direction was, that some addition of "hearty vittles" should be made to the evening meal for a minister who was not addicted to pie.

This suggestion of Mr. Leigh's return moved Monny instantly to forsake the porch, and go up to her own room, where arraying herself for a walk, she departed, intending that the minister's arrival should find her absent.

Monny's impulse in the present days to avoid Mr. Leigh was as much more active than her former one had been, as a very decided sense of embarrassment in another's presence is stronger than a *nonchalant* indifference to it. Being a well-bred young lady, and no pert hoiden by nature, Monny was quite appalled now to remember her past style of demeanor to Mr. Leigh; and yet some obstinate remnant of perplexity about him made it mysteriously difficult for her to find the fitting new behavior: so she simply slipped out of his way to avoid behaving to him at all.

Going down the lane, seaward, she still went on, however, with her silent commeasuring of man and woman. Down the long lane, past the little Hines house, where

she had been so often during the last few days, out upon
the sea-banks, and away to the point off which "The
Rattler" had gone to pieces, its human freight brought
in by the mighty daring of one man, — to this place came
Monny; and its reminiscences were well calculated to
confirm her present depressing idea of power, force, as
the only symbols of high human worth.

These same qualities in their purer spiritual manifesta-
tion, — had she not felt them to be the root of that mysterious influence so unconsciously exerted by Mr. Leigh
over the souls of those debased men whose bodies he had
plucked out of the deep ? Monny could see their wild
faces now uplifted to his around that hearth-fire; and
she was undoubtedly right in her feeling that not easy-
going toleration of the worst that is in him, but stimulus
of the best, is, finally and at the last, what the lowest
human being really longs for, as well as needs.

All the everlasting old saws that she had heard about
the supreme moral influence of women snapped in utter
brittleness to the girl in her present train of thought: the
world seemed to her all a man's world, in the stress and
strain of whose real issues women had no part. This
minister who could so bow himself to the refuse of New-
Orleans wharves was the same man who had been bored
at the idea of a young lady under the roof where he was
to pass a few summer weeks. Was it merely the "young
lady" division of the female sex that he had such a dis-
gust for? queried the girl; and she had an odd thought
that she would like to have seen how he would pray for
women of the same class as were those sailors. Then
this fancy was blotted by a peculiarly disturbing cloud, —
a thought of all the nonsense mixed up with the devotion
of women to ministers; and with a sense that this was
a most besnarled creation for her sex, Monny climbed

down one of the hollows of the bank to the beach below, where she roamed till the sun fell low over the sea, and she heard the railway whistle blown at the station of the little village, and anon the train rolling past her as it threaded its narrow way down to the end of the Cape.

The passenger expected by Mrs. Doane had duly alighted at the station, but had disappointed the stage-driver there by deciding to walk to his boarding-place, and even to carry his baggage; that is, a bulky brown paper parcel which he had with him, quite cumbersome enough to be called by that name. Swinging this load in his hand, he set out on his walk home, proceeding by the extremely roundabout way of striking first for the seashore. With his rapid step, he was soon beyond the little village, and traversing the thickets of bay and boxberry, and all the unfenced wild that he had come to know so well, and which apparently he was very glad to be returned to. Still it might not be safe to assume that any thing more than a merely general sense of satisfaction made the elasticity of his step, the light of the clear glances which swept the lonely barrens and the sea: he certainly did not look like a being dependent on any particular thing, still less on any one creature, for his joy. No, as he walked with his brisk, strong tread, and that indefinable port of the man unsubdued to the domestic yoke, it seemed a little singular that women should ever have wasted their hearts on one whose whole air so suggested, in defiance of Genesis, that man was created to be alone, and that he found it extremely good.

Still he had, as we know, very active ties of a certain sort to his fellow-creatures, and the complications which had arisen from his endeavor to do his duty by one of these was the occasion of his present little ramble. Yes, as he approached the shore, his way of glancing about him in mere pleasure at the prospect changed to the definite expression of a man surveying the landscape in search of some one. The minister's eyes were very keen and bright, and could pierce afar; moreover, this coast was so bare, one could look along it for miles and see any creature astir on it, unless it might be hidden by one of the hollows of the bank: so, having explored certain of these, he descended at once to the beach below. He had scarcely reached this level when he discerned at a distance a feminine form sitting motionless on a pile of driftwood, not far from the sea-line, with a dog taking short runs along the water's edge, as a dog might who was making an occasional jocular snap at a beach bird to relieve the dulness in which the grave mood of his mistress left him.

The minister, at sight of these figures, made the momentary pleased start of a man who has found what he is looking for; but the next moment he somewhat slackened his rapid pace, while, for the first time during his walk, a shade of embarrassment crossed his face. Monny and her dog in this place vividly recalled to him that morning of his first introduction to the pair frolicking by the waves; and he remembered just now all the fate which he had had to affront the young lady from the beginning. He concluded that she felt very severely affronted with him in his taking away of her Popish books. That incident had occurred, it will be remembered, on the same day as the wreck; and he had been well aware, that, in the time which had elapsed between that day and his going up to Boston, Miss Monny had behaved to him with an entirely new reserve, a grave distance and silence, which he found an extremely unsatisfying change from the enlivening doses of derision to which she had been wont to treat him. So, in a hope to dispel the memory of the

proceeding whose causes he could not explain to the
maiden, he had bought for her in Boston the budget of
literature which he had now on his arm.   A budget it
was: first, he had laid in a stock of such saints as
Francis de Sales, Thomas à Kempis, etc. ; then, because
all this type of spirituality lacked something to his own
robust mind, he added Marcus Aurelius, superadding
thereto a volume of Matthew Arnold's essays, in a dim
notion that this writer's study of the stoic philosopher
might a little break him to Monny's reading.   His faith
was probably very dim that she would really read any of
these books at all : still certain other moralists of attractive
literary style went into the pack.   Then, as a sweetener to
all this seriousness, a handful of comfits, which might
really be to the girl's taste, he added some of the latest
English and American novels (quite unread by himself),
and some volumes of poetry, gotten up with extreme richness of binding and illustrations.

It had seemed to him highly natural in Boston to make
up this parcel to propitiate the pretty creature at his
Cape-Cod boarding-place, whose last phase of wrath
towards him had left him so dull and forlorn.   Equally
natural he thought it, when he alighted at the station, to
go in search of her in her favorite haunts at this hour,
and to take the books along with him for presentation on
the spot ; but now, when he was fairly in sight of the
maiden, he suddenly woke up to the perception that he
had been a great bungler in all his management about
those ill books from the beginning.

He realized this still more forcibly when Monny, moved
by the watchful attitude of her dog, as he suddenly
descried the minister in the distance, to glance herself
along the shore, rose instantly upon that glance, and
moved swiftly away, vanishing with Duke George by the

first opening which allowed one to reach the bank from the beach below. The gentleman and the young lady were too far apart for the ceremony of exchanging bows ; but Mr. Leigh felt that he had been perfectly recognized, and that this sudden flight of his fellow-boarder was the cut direct. Naturally, on this reception, he lingered about the beach for a while, to allow the feminine rambler undisturbed freedom of the bank : so Mrs. Doane's high tea was decidedly waiting when the returned traveller at last sat down to it. Miss Rivers was in the house, — the presence of Duke George announced that fact, — but she was nowhere visible ; and not greatly ministering on this occasion to that secret satisfaction with which women, especially when they have themselves spread the board, behold a good masculine appetite, Mr. Leigh soon left his landlady alone at the table, and went to his own rooms.

There, however, with the usual male instinct to settle up *somehow* an affair that is hanging at loose ends, he opened the old-fashioned little dark cupboard in the wall, where Monny's Holy Fathers were in hiding, not with the slightest intent of returning them, — he was never further from that idea, — but merely to count out, saint for saint, from the lavish pile which he had bought for Miss Monny, the precise tale of books which he had taken from her. These were not many ; but judging, that, in the young lady's present mood towards him, gifts from his hand would not be acceptable, he despatched this exact equivalent of books, and no more, to her room by Susannah, with no explanations whatever. Then, having shoved into the darkest corner of the Puritan dark closet the saints in their indecency, he flung in after them Marcus Aurelius, Matthew Arnold, novels, and *editions de luxe* of poetry, pell-mell. But as the novels were extremely stupid, and the elegantly bound poetries decidedly too elegant not to have been an embarrassing gift for Monny to receive at this time from Mr. Leigh, and as she had not only read Marcus Aurelius, but had been first led to read him through that identical volume of "Essays in Criticism" by Matthew Arnold, which she had devoured every line of, — in view of these things, she was not in a way to suffer at present for want of any thing that the dark closet contained.

She was consciously suffering, however, when Susannah came in on the above-mentioned errand in behalf of Mr. Leigh, from the memory of her rudeness in running away from that gentleman down at the seashore. She had not the least idea that he came that way expressly to seek her, — the cars always gave her a headachy longing herself for a ramble in the fresh air, — but she felt the incivility of not having staid to greet him after his absence. She did not know what mysterious nervousness had put wings to her feet at the very sight of him. She could only hope that he had not perceived her, at least that he had not perceived that she perceived him; and she would not appear at the tea-table, lest her conscious face should betray the fact that she had seen him before.

Either because she was so pre-occupied with this matter, or because the vast depths of Mr. Leigh's domineering made an abyss that she had given up all attempt to fathom, Susannah's entrance presently with the substituted books made scarcely more than a passing ripple in her thoughts.

CHAPTER IX.

THE very old truth, that we only know the value of things by losing them, the Rev. Kenyon Leigh proved, with much astonishment to himself, in the days that now followed, when he found that the vanishing of that disrespectful nymph whom he had known as Miss Monny Rivers from his daily ways took therefrom some brightness, which he missed as if it had become a necessary ray to his life. The maiden was still under the roof, but she might almost as well have been at the antipodes. Her former reticence was of a kind that the minister could amuse himself by trespassing on. To pause when he saw that airy approaching figure, and waylay it with some of those "perfectly needless and uncommonly stupid" questions with which he evoked its frosty, keen morsels, its sudden impatient flashes of reply, —how often Mr. Leigh had indulged in this recreation, and how valuable a recreation it was to him, he was not in the least aware till all its opportunities were ended. The manner, by the way, in which the minister had taken this diversion, it was not wholly strange that Monny should have construed as "lordly." Extreme simplicity of character and the sovereign extreme of pride have this in common, that both are unperturbed by anxiety to please. Solicitude as to the sort of figure which he himself was making in the eyes of others was, in general, peculiarly absent from Kenyon Leigh; but of late, with reference to one young mortal, the personal question,

What *she* thought about *him?* had begun to deflect this hitherto single-minded character.

He did not wish to make too unpleasant a figure in Miss Monny's eyes : he had a mysterious longing for her to fly in his face again, and yet an unwillingness that she should take that obnoxious view of him which made her fly in his face. In this paradoxical state of mind the man was as newly scrupulous not to intrude on the maiden's reserve as she was newly vigilant in guarding it. Meanwhile, across this double gulf of distance her image came to haunt with extraordinary persistency his thoughts. Of course he had to think about his fellow-boarder somewhat, — to think how he should make up with her. He must watch a good deal her goings-out and comings-in to see if he could anywhere seize a favorable opportunity to say or do something amiable, merely to show himself in a kind of human light to a young creature whom any one would be sorry to have seriously vexed and offended. With these duteous cares, he slid into much thinking about Miss Monny, which could only be referred to a charm for his thoughts in the subject itself. A very idle charm he would have confessed. His judgment, which still kept its cool, parallel line beside the path of his imagination on this theme, smiled at the preposterousness of the fancy which invested, for instance, such questions as "Where did *you* learn to do chicken-stews?" with some character which made the vivid moment when the girl had flown at him with that mighty demand recur again and again to his memory. Her mingled air that night of a mutinous child and a solemnly earnest woman, — it was a part of the same glamour that was always about her, the suggestion, the hinted depths which made her mere silent figure, pacing in the sunset along the orchard line, a picture, which, to tell the truth, the minister had formed a habit of keeping his western window-blinds always closed, their slats turned cunningly downward, expressly to survey unseen.

It was the very newest ambuscading under the sun for the Rev. Kenyon Leigh. Pink beauties and pale ones, blondes and brunettes, and all the shades between, had this minister, whose ways had been so full of fair women, beheld, with eyes by no means blind to their beauty. He had seen them as the flowers of the field; nor more than the flowers of the field did they take tribute of his thoughts in hours of work and study. But this dreaming girl under the apple-trees, revolving, Heaven knew what follies in her half-drooped head, — that was the minister's sober idea of her, — all the same, it had been a mysterious refreshing to him to lift his eyes, as he sat writing in the languid close of the day, and see her there; and he missed her now that she came no more. For Monny took her little airings no longer in the western yard. Not that she had ever discovered her observer behind the guarding blind; but she had grown conscious of the very side of the house where abode the man whose existence she had formerly forgotten, save when he insisted upon thrusting on her the importunate fact. All her daily routine of life, indeed, in the old house, was broken up. The first thing she had done, when the Samaritan labors incident on the shipwreck were ended, was to march into Mrs. Doane's kitchen, there to make most thorough-going, experimental study of the whole science of cookery. We may remark here, that, as any full-grown girl of intelligence may do, Monny became mistress of this art in a very few days, in all its ordinary branches. And as to ascend from these to every flourish of the extraordinary requires only the ability to read cook-books, which instructive works are usually writ-

ten in quite elementary phrase, it appears that the future
households of this nation are not necessarily doomed to
starvation, because Miss Rivers's former night of domestic
ignorance may perhaps be paralleled in this school-going
generation among many American girls who will need
personally to mix the family bread in all their after-lives.
There is, doubtless, a kind of education which spoils the
housewife: nevertheless, this young lady turned out very
superior bread on her second baking, simply because, in
one way and another, she had attained to a culture which
gave force to her brains, and a sufficient respect for every
necessary task to do it with her brains. She was so
cultivated a being as to have learned that luck cannot be
counted on in this world to bring any thing right, and
that, as a rule, it can be counted on to bring every thing
wrong. Thus, while Mistress Doane, who would have
pronounced at first that her beloved Miss Monny was too
brilliant a genius ever to make a good cook, concluded
next that this same genius enabled her to do whatever she
chose, as by inspiration, all the genius there was in the
swift progress made by her young apprentice consisted
in the unerring accuracy and skill with which she seized
and followed her instructions. To do things by brilliant
guessing and fitful dashes was a kind of inspiration that
Monny had learned long ago to trample under foot in all
serious work; and the preparing of human food, she
rightly considered, since her memorable experiences on
the night of the shipwreck, to be very serious work, and
a knowledge that she would never more be ignorant of.
But, as she had been accustomed to do serious work
which required infinitely more severe concentration than
these arts of the kitchen, she mastered them, as we have
said, in brief space; and having gotten up on her sole responsibility several dinners of some elaborateness for the

family household, and bestowed broths, bread, and cakes
of her own making, on all the sick and poor that she
could find in the neighborhood, she rested on her laurels
as cook, and being already, as we know, a good dress-
maker, looked round for more worlds to conquer. Not
being a fool, she did not suppose that there was any
inherent virtue in cooking and sewing when the circumstances of her position did not require it, even as this
same fact of her not being a fool would have prevented
her from despising or slighting these tasks if they had
been necessary.

So Monny was again pondering the question of woman's
business in this world with some troubled inquiry, which
prevented her from returning, with any sustained power
of work, to her easel.

One afternoon of these perplexed days, she was straying on the shore, nearly two miles from Mrs. Doane's,
where, the high sea-bank sloping away, there was a long
line of salt-works, mostly abandoned, however, and not
far away somewhat of a pier, where boats ran in from
the mackerel-schooners belonging to the little village.
Two or three children of the latter, whom Monny had
had in her studio at various times, left their play among
the salt-works as the young lady came along, and ran to
join her. A pleasure-yacht, whose manœuvres Monny had
idly noted during her walk, was making now directly for
the shore; and, to please her juvenile escort, she went
down to the pier to see the gay craft a little nearer.

She was turning away, however, as its boat, containing
two or three young men, came with rapid strokes towards
the landing, when, one of its occupants rising up and
waving her a salute, she recognized Mr. Halstone Roosevelt, a young New-Yorker of her summer acquaintance,
and paused where she was.

The party were soon on the pier; Monny's admirer, for this was another beau in search of the exiled belle, presenting his two comrades, whom she met now for the first time. All these young men, very graceful specimens of the *jeunesse dorée* of America, bowing with *empressement* round this rose in the wilderness, gave the dejected rose at the moment, perhaps, a pleased sense as of her little court come back again ; or it may be the girl's natural gayety bubbled with re-actionary fulness just because of its melancholy suppression of late. At all events, Monny had a sudden accession of high spirits, sparkled with more than her wonted brilliancy : the amateur sailors had their adventures to relate, of course, and the maiden's laugh rang out with its old joyous sweetness.

Another man, approaching unseen behind the line of ruined saltworks, caught that merry echo with a start of glad surprise: it was the Rev. Kenyon Leigh. It was his first intimation of Monny's neighborhood : her usual walks were to less frequented places than this ; and, coming himself directly from the village, he had nowhere seen her on her ramble. Feeling deterred in these days from seeking to meet his fellow-boarder anywhere when she was really alone, here, where she was amusing herself, as he supposed, with the fishermen and their children, and in her old lightsome mood again, was a favorable place and moment to thaw reserves ; and, with highly sociable intentions, the minister stepped on to join himself to the company. A pace or two farther, however, as a gap in the projecting timbers gave him a glance at the company, he stood still with a rush of most extraordinary sensations.

Those handsome young yachtsmen, gotten up with the last refinement of amateur nautical costumes, certainly made a very effective and pleasing group in their pictur-

esque flannels round the delicately robed maiden. They
were thorough-bred youths, and were paying her their
devoirs with every respect. What insane impulse had
the Rev. Kenyon Leigh to take them up by their dandy
waistbands, and sling them into the sea! Especially
savage was this impulse, and particularly unjust, toward s
Mr. Halstone Roosevelt; for his demeanor to Miss Rivers
was of the most reverential: he spoke least of the three;
he was the lover among the admirers. Moreover, the
minister, instead of scowling at that young man from
behind some old vats of saltworks, was bound in common
courtesy to go forward and shake hands with him as one
of his own parish of St. Ancient's, whom he had not seen
for a twelvemonth: yea, the youth, whom Mr. Leigh had
doubtless heard in his catechism, was not so changed in a
year that his minister did not recognize him at a glance.

We hope it will be remembered that the latter was
on his vacation, when we confess, that, if he had spoken
out his sentiments towards that silent admirer, their very
mildest utterance would have been, " Confound his impudence!'' and that there rose before him as the most
intolerable of mortal visions Monny walking into his own
church in New York as Mrs. Halstone Roosevelt.

These emotions swept the minister's soul one astonished moment; then, looking on that gay young group, he
felt suddenly old, and stricken in years. Turning sharply
on his heel, he walked away through the soft sand as
unnoticed as he had come.

The hour when a strong spirit in its maturity, a nature
that has come almost to hate the conduct that is not
founded on reason, finds itself seized with an infatuation, an impulse which it acknowledges to itself to be
the starkest 'olly, is a strange one. Kenyon Leigh had
lived through no such moments in his existence as these

moments wherein he walked back by the wild sea to the solitude of his own room. Arrived there, he went straight to his writing-table. He took up a pen : the name which he was about to write was that of Mrs. Van Cortlandt. With his habits about corresponding with women, to begin a correspondence with that lady was to begin marriage-proposals to her : indeed, such was his intent. He dipped the pen in ink, poised it, threw it down with a great revulsion which ended for ever and ever all thought of that marriage. For the first time in his life he now distinctly said to himself that he should never marry ; for he knew that there was but one wife in the world that he wanted, but one of all Eve's daughters that he had ever wanted, — a girl who put her soul to the fashions, who had seldom said any thing to him but the giddiest impertinences, who had a manifest personal aversion to him which he had wasted an unconscionable amount of time lately in thinking how to dispel. All this madness — and the mere sense of wasted time, to men who have disciplined themselves to make the most of the hours, is wont to be a very sharp awakener — the awakened minister reviewed. When, where, and how had the lunacy come upon him?

If it had come through avenues of the heart's own wisdom ; if some kindred thrill of a spirit fearless, resistant as his own of shams and impositions, had made the girl's impertinence to him a fascinating impertinence ; if, through all the disguise wrought by the untoward circumstances of their first introduction, some hint of her real self had yet penetrated, — these intimations were subtle, intangible, and the man strove against them at present as the very crown of his delusion. He had seen with marvelling other men under such hallucination about some utterly commonplace pretty woman ; and he had seen the hallucination end — with a very few months of marriage.

Yes, he had lived long enough to see that over and over.

Kenyon Leigh was no cynic: he was only a man in whom a judicial habit of mind co-existed in an extraordinary degree with a hiddenly fervid and impetuous heart. Unswamped by whatever emotions swept the latter, it was the instinct of his brain to take calm note of facts, look at things in the light of the evidence, distrust all impressions which these did not sustain. There were certainly no facts, no external evidence, of any such qualities in this girl as would justify the extraordinary spell which she had laid upon his fancy; and he roused himself to break it. Under the impulse of this resolution he made a sudden move to the western window, and flung wide those masking blinds behind which he had so often watched for a fairer vision than the sunset. The sunset streamed goldenly into the chamber from which its rays had been so long debarred; and lo! not under the apple-trees, but approaching along the road, was seen at the moment that other vision, — Miss Rivers. Not escorted by the yachtsmen, — those gallants were nowhere in view, — the maiden was riding aloft in the chariot of that ancient mariner, Isry-Chris. Aunt Isry, along with a variety of other bundles, was likewise stowed in the cart. The pair had evidently been on one of their marketing trips to the village store, and Monny had somewhere forsaken her admirers to ride home with them. The equipage came on to Mrs. Doane's door, where uncle Chris began to clamber out; but Monny, setting her light foot on the wide tire of the Cape-Cod wheel, sprang to the ground before him, and ran into the house.

It seemed that she was going home at once with the Isry-Chrisses to make one of her visits at their cottage across the Cape.

There were a few moments of echoing bustle in Monny's
rooms, then the sound of the light feet flying down the
stairs, of Mrs. Doane's voice bestowing the usual motherly
injunctions on her young boarder about taking care of herself; there was the noise of Duke George howling his
grief and wrath as Susannah chained him up to prevent
him from following his beloved young mistress; then,
with its strangely assorted company, the cart rolled away.
And to the boarder left in the western chambers silence
as of the grave seemed to fall on the house.

CHAPTER X.

MONNY'S present visit to the other side of the Cape had been wholly unthought of until the arrival of " The Golden Fleece ; " for by this classic name was christened the yacht owned by Mr. Roosevelt, and which had touched at Lonewater solely because Miss Rivers was staying there. The party was bound for the coast of Maine, and farther north ; but Cape Cod was not so worn out a region to summer idlers from New York, that a young man of ingenious fancy could not find very plausible reasons for stopping a few days to explore it more nearly than from the deck of a vessel. In fact, as Monny walked slowly up from the pier, with her gallant convoy, towards the little village and Capt. Gawthrop's house, to which she could do no less than show the way, she could but perceive that she was likely to see much of the devoted young Halstone, if his yacht made the proposed stay at Lonewater.

Apparently the pleasure which it had been to her to see a little of him did not hold out to the requirements of seeing him too much ; for having consigned the young men to Capt. Gawthrop, who met the party on the way, scenting possible boarders from afar, and availed herself of the very opportune passing of uncle Isry's wagon to return to Mrs. Doane's, she had scarcely ridden away with the old pair when she resolved on taking flight forthwith to their cottage. She had left Capt. Gawthrop setting forth such inducements to the yachtsmen in the way

of excursions in the neighborhood, that she doubted not
" The Golden Fleece " was anchored for the ensuing days ;
but as, when she made her adieus to the party, their stay
was not absolutely decided, now was her chance to run
away without too glaring a discourtesy, and according'y
she determined to run.

So Monny crossed the Cape with the Isry-Chrisses, and
took her old place in their cottage, — the little best room,
or parlor, on the ground-floor, permanently adorned by
the spare bed.   Here she slept and woke ; and posing Isry-
Chris, — he had been her model for the picture of the old
fisherman drawing up his boat, — she painted some valiant
hours to the final completing of that picture.

But, having lost courage for any further efforts in art
just now, she spent the hours roaming out of doors, reading, or musing on the only book she had brought with her,
— a certain French book which she had never opened
before.   This was a volume of abusive sayings about
women, compiled from all literatures by the industry of
Monsieur Emile Deschanel, and entitled " Le Mal qu'on
a dit des Femmes."

Monny's reading was not usually pursued on the scrap-
book foundation ; but this little volume, which, struck
by the title, she had bought when laying in books for a
general study of the woman-question, was impressive to
her now from its very fragmentariness, making awful suggestion of the original unknown sources whereof these were
but the droppings.   Droppings they were from corrupt
ages and from the disenchanted minds that are in every
age, all rendered into a tongue whose very idioms seem
made for airy scoffing ; and however decorously weeded
was the little book by its editor of too gross utterance,
and tied with a posy of French compliment to the sex at
beginning and end, it was still very melancholy reading to

the maiden, — a quite appalling response to her present effort to penetrate the secret mind of man concerning womankind.

True, many of the writers of these things were essentially jaded spirits, looking cynically at all life, and finding, in the disappointments of love and the follies of woman, only a more pungent theme than another on which to exercise that kind of ghastly insight which comes of a culture that has refined the head, but somewhere missed the heart, — that has made critical and exacting every taste, but wrought no true delicacy of feeling. But though some perception of this fact reached Monny, still the insight of the book was too subtle after its manner, the analysis of her sex too keen, up to a certain point, not to oppress her with a vast and nameless oppression. One notion that was haunting her at present gathered dark confirmation from these leaves; viz., that the intellectual man in all his varieties had some mysterious feud with woman; if he was sensitive to her charm he yet rebelled against it: what meant the strangely mingled cry of adoration and of cursing that went up from so many of these bitter pages?

This young admirer of the intellectual man saddened so over them at last, that she closed the French scrap-book, and began to turn the scrap-book of memory, — of her own personal observation. There was her aunt Helen's married life, the domestic history which she knew best, and which would so well bear knowing. She had never thought about that lady's marriage before; for it is not natural to the young to think of the marriages of their elders, whom they have always seen in the same easy domesticity of relation, as affairs that were ever in the making. But she wondered now if her aunt had not chosen the husband she had, expressly because, being socially above him, he would respect her through life as no other husband would; the unequal scale between man and woman being righted, as it were, to a level balance by this makeweight of aristocracy on the feminine side. A man of a generous heart and a plain head, which no elegant culture had made subtle and mocking in all its thoughts, nor scholastic learning had made severe, — perhaps this was the only kind of husbands, the uncle Slabwell kind, thought Monny, who absolutely, in their secret hearts, respected wives to the end, however madly all sorts of men made love to women when they were young and had not come to philosophy.

Mr. Thomas Slabwell certainly had not come to much philosophy: he was a shining example of how much well doing there is in the world with no right thinking behind it, or no thinking at all. Of this order of virtue, indeed, the domestic man, idolizing wife and children, finding in devotion to their comfort all the chief enlargement and purifying of a life whose aims would otherwise be narrow and sordid, is probably as solidly worthy a specimen as can be shown. A solidly well-behaved man was Monny's uncle-in-law; yet he had really no fixed principles of right and wrong, save as he could see that family interests and affections were somewhere touched. Show him a battlefield where that sacred queen of the family, woman, was threatened in any of her sovereign claims on the race, and hot shot would have had hard work to finish him, or the last ditch to choke him up, till he had seen those claims established. But, beyond such convictions as these, the nothingarian was all at sea.

It was quite possible for Monny to have, as she certainly did have, a sincere affection for the uncle, who, a mere marriage-connection, had cared for her as for a child, and yet to miss in him all that strength of the

man " who lives by law, acting the law he lives by without fear," and to know in her young way that only in
such spirits reside the really creative forces of virtue.
And now, when by a perhaps not wholly fantastic cor-
relation of ideas the notion grew on her that her uncle's
fireside was so completely his altar, just because he had
no other altar, shrine neither of religion, learning, nor
art, to kneel at; and that high devotion to these latter
shrines men felt to be somehow hampered and hindered
by any ties to women, — these fancies were peculiarly
dejecting to the girl, all whose ideals in the other sex
were beings of thought and aspiration.

It will be perceived, that, wherever Monny's study of
the woman-question had begun, it was virtually ending
in the husband-question; albeit she was so little given
to talk of husbands, that her *chaperone* aunt had begun to
be terrified lest the girl had got some unnatural notion
of spending her existence in singleness, the more entirely to devote herself to art. But no: if aunt Helen
could have seen with how much deeper concern the maiden
pondered now woman's place as a wife than she had
ever done her place as an artist, she would have been
assured that Monny had formed to herself no plan of life
which excluded life's young dream of somewhere finding
and being united to the perfect mate.

We pass on here to say that she did not find that mate
in Mr. Halstone Roosevelt, which young gentleman made
his appearance one of these days at the Bay shore, armed
with a rifle for hunting — foxes. It was not quite the
season for hunting that animal, even if he had been more
numerous than he was on Cape Cod in these years. But
Capt. Gawthrop was certainly a *cicerone* who told remarkable stories, and the young man was in a way to
believe any story which gave him a pretext for exploring

that opposite side of the Cape where Miss Rivers was now sojourning: so the credit of the fox-hunting fable may be divided between them. The solitary sportsman found the young lady slowly rambling by the sea in the neighborhood of the fisherman's cottage; but his reception by her, although not discourteous, was yet so utterly hopeless, that, being a young gentleman, Mr. Halstone sailed away on his yacht next morning from the Atlantic shore of the Cape.

Monny had little to reproach herself with concerning this lover, with whom, indeed, her acquaintance had been brief and transient enough to promise a healthful recovery from his disappointment. Nevertheless, she returned to her abstract speculations after this incident, more dissatisfied with her life, past, present, and to come, than ever, — a decidedly increased sense that the earth was a painfully entangled sphere.

Life on the other side of the Cape, however, would not be any further entangled by yachtsmen at present: so, on the day after the sailing-away of "The Golden Fleece," Monny decided to return to Mrs. Doane's. Towards nightfall, therefore, when uncle Chris had finished the day's fishing, the old horse was put to the wagon, and Monny set forth over the roadless sands lying like a ribbon between the great widths of waters. So vast they seemed to-night, with the unbroken dome of the sky making another immensity above, and the wide sighing of the pine-trees as wandering winds from the two seas blew over them with the sinking sun, the mystery of nature grew too mighty at last for this young heart, overcharged with that other mystery of life; and with a glad re-action she saw the dear lights from Mrs. Doane's windows shine across the waste. Jumping down at the familiar gate, she ran up to the porch with such a rush of home-coming joy, she even forgot all 'Le Mal qu'on a dit des Femmes.''

Hope of Monny's return to-night had been quite given up by this hour ; and when her roguish bright eyes peeped slyly round the half-open dining-room door, where Mrs. Doane was just distributing a waiterful of dishes for the morrow's breakfast, what a glad start and outcry of the matron, threatening all the dishes ! what a bounding-in of Duke George, who, napping on the western door-stone, had not heard the sand-muffled wheels come up on the other side of the house, and had to make up for his lost chance at the gate by thrice-devouring transports of affection now ! and black Susannah, dropping the sponge she was setting for bread, and flying in from the kitchen, — altogether there was such a greeting as if Monny had been round the world.

There are beings whose briefest absence from a dwelling every breathing thing in it seems to feel. Sometimes it is a gentle, unobtrusive presence whose coming or going makes this change in the house-atmosphere, in some way so quiet as to be undefined. Or, again, these lights of the home, and such a one was Monny, burst in like a sunrise on the positive gloom their departure has made : there is a stir of anticipation, a sense of revival after collapse ; they seem always to bring news, though they bring only themselves ; and albeit the present home-circle comprised but a dog and two old women, one white and the other black, Monny's coming was with a little tumult of acclaim. This rejoicing echo floated out into the front entry, telling who must surely be arrived to a man, who, coming in from a solitary walk in the summer night, just now entered the house that way On his morning walk the day before, we may remark here, he had witnessed the sailing-away of " The Golden

Ficece,"—a departure seen by him with such a sudden
great rising of satisfaction as reason had had to put
mightily down. Which exercise did not in the least prevent him from standing still now, with a great throb of
the heart, as he heard that voice, as it detached itself
presently from the other voices, a light step coming
fleetly on towards the inner door leading into the entry
where he was; for Monny had taken a lamp to go up to
her rooms by the front stairs. Opening narrowly the
entry-door, she slipped swiftly through, and turned, so to
shut it as not to damage the nose of Duke George on the
other side, whose company just then she did not want
up-stairs. Then, facing about, she first discovered Mr.
Leigh, standing with some arrested action, as if about to
hang his hat on its usual peg behind the front door.
Monny also stood arrested for an imperceptible moment,
a strange medley of memories small and great rushing at
once over her mind,— memory of Mr. Leigh's last return
after absence, and how she had run away from speaking to
him down at the seashore; of that other time when he had
stopped to greet her on her own home-coming from a for-·
mer visit to the Isry-Chrisses, and how she had laughed-at
him then the instant his back was turned. With a curious
compunction, a desire to make amends, she recalled now
these trifles; while, mingled with them, rose a vision of a
black night and a terrible sea, and one swimming out into
them every inch of the way by death; and again she
thought of the very books she had been brooding over
these days past,— the over-subtle, morbid, mocking minds.
Heaven knows what blessed sense of contrast to these
men, in the open-browed Anglo-Saxon before her, half-
consciously thrilled the girl, as, after that instant's pause
of vivid and various reminiscence, she stepped impulsively
forward, and with some sweet young grace of spontaneous

trust, which cannot at all be described, put out her soft hand in greeting.

The man who took it looked down on the winsome, smiling face upturned to his, which to his consciousness had never smiled on him before, which now for days, that seemed like ages, he had not seen ; and, wheresoever reason went, all life for the moment seemed concentrate to him in but one longing, — to gather this restored darling into his arms, and kiss her. He by no means did this; he by no manner of means made any outward movement to do it: how was the inward motion yet half translated, though he only took the lamp from the maiden's hand, and set it down by his hat on the table, with little questions about her visit, any subterfuges that would detain her? Too many men had brightened at Monny's coming, and darkened at her going, for her not at last a little to perceive, what, if she had been a vainer or more self-conscious girl, she would have perceived some time before ; viz., the sort of interest which this "meddler" took in her. For the rest, while Kenyon Leigh had a world of self-control, he had but very little power of self-disguise ; and the wiles of a lover to keep the beloved face in sight a few moments longer were too utterly new for him to practise, for them not to have even a boyish transparency.

There was something else that grew transparent also. For what with the passionate personal sentiment which was on the one side, and on the other all those abstract speculations which had had so much of a personal starting-point of late in the individual man Kenyon Leigh, a sufficiently magnetic atmosphere vibrated between these two beings at the moment to communicate, to a nature so sensitive as Monny's, something of the secret mind of the man who thus stood delaying her because of the charm her presence was to him. And she saw, what was the truth, that he struggled against that charm as a weakness. Yes: in Kenyon Leigh's secret mind judgment approved not, nor reason sanctioned, his present action; and to all this lingering there at the foot of the old stairs, dallying with a spell whose strength these moments but too well taught him, his inclination, but not his *will*, consented.

Did the latter suddenly regain the mastery? Or did the maiden, who, while she answered gently and respectfully to whatever Mr. Leigh said to her, was yet mysteriously disturbed in all that confiding friendliness with which she had stepped to greet him, — did she make some movement so decided to end this interview that it could not be prolonged? Certain it was that the man finally went most abruptly, nor stood upon the order of his going, but first, and with a swift, instantaneous departing, flashed up the stairs, and shut himself in his own room.

This leave-taking was sufficiently remarkable to add decidedly to the dazed maiden's trouble; and in some rising inner commotion, whose chief sense as yet was bewilderment, she took up her lamp, and, mounting the staircase alone, likewise shut herself up in her room.

To that chamber entered, about ten minutes later, Mistress Doane, to find the young lady who had arrived home in such gay spirits cast desperate into a chair beside her bed, whence she launched at the astonished matron, the second she opened the door, this quotation: "In all time women have had a predilection for fools!" (It was a quotation surging up into her memory just then from Monsieur Déschanel's bitter book.) "Well they may have! well they may!" cried the girl passionately. "For the fools really care for the women they make love to with their whole nature." Monny felt sure now, for ever

and ever, why aunt Helen had married the husband she
had : Mr. Halstone Roosevelt, too, she saw in such new
worth as a husband, it was a thousand pities that young
gentleman could not have tried his fate at this moment.
(Mr. Halstone was by no means a fool, only too young
to have developed up to Monny's hitherto masculine idea
of wisdom.) "The fools," she repeated excitedly, "do
not take a fancy to you with one side of their minds, and
disbelieve in you with the other. That is the way the
wise men do. I see it in the books. They disbelieve in
the character of women. The solid qualities of character
which win respect and esteem, the qualities which men
honor and prize each other for, — they do not believe
women have those qualities ; and yet they admire them.
It is an admiration that hurts all round," said the girl in
a quivering tone that was indeed as of one wounded.
"It hurts the admirer too. I say it hurts him too ; for
all that Oxford professor writing, in a sentence that I
thought beautiful when I read it weeks ago, says, 'The
highest conception that humanity ever has formed is that
of power losing itself in affection.' *How* losing itself?
— how?" cried the girl, her voice thrilling with its passionate searching. "The way Mark Antony lost himself,
and all the men in the stories who have cared for women
against their right reason? You should not care for what
is against your right reason. To take pleasure in what
you do not respect — there will be a dissatisfaction in that
pleasure, there will be no peace. I see it in the books :
there *is* no peace."

All the love-stories, French and English, that she had
ever read, rose up in the girl's mind as she made this
passionate lament, seeming to her only to show through
some febrile atmosphere of half-simulated joys all the
fathomless tumult of the heart unstilled ; — these memories

really floated over her thought: still the widow's surmise, that something besides what was "in the books" had thrown Monny so suddenly into this strange excitement, was true enough also.

Very sure was Mrs. Doane that she had heard Mr. Leigh's voice speaking with the girl in the entry; and, much marvelling what a man who she felt certain was Monny's secret admirer could have said to put her into such a mood, the matron had yet the instinct to answer as if indeed the books had been the only disturbance.

"Now, my child, that ever you should go over to Isry-Chrisses' to keep on with all that reading that worries you so! I thought certain you'd drop that kind of books for these few days at least."

"No, I shall never drop them!" rejoined Monny with energy. "I shall read all I can find of those books! They show you great truths at last; and truths, however dreadful, are what you should wish to know in this world, and not delusions," said the maid with solemn fortitude.

"The man who made that sneer," she went on, "about the preference of women for fools, in one particular French book that I've been reading, full of the satires of men of all nations and ages about women, — that scoffer, in what he meant for scoffing, spoke the substance of a truth. I remember now it is often remarked that the most brilliant and superior women are apt to marry commonplace men, — the kind of men whom the wise men call *fools*, I suppose," said Monny, repeating the word defiantly, as one who indignantly championed the same fools.

"Of course they would; for such women, just because of their superiority, would see clearer than other women into men and things, and would know that finer than all the fine heads in the world is a good and a believing heart."

And ah! even as Monny made this en phatic declaration, there came a piercing sense that the man who had
met her at the stairway, and whom she had seen in situations which sift to the last atom the qualities of character,
— that the *heart* of this man was just where he could be
supremely trusted, save in this mysterious exception of
his attitude towards womankind.

Needless to say that neither in the Rev. Kenyon Leigh's
manner, nor in his inmost thought, towards this young
specimen of womankind whom he found so charming, had
there been any thing, that, in any current acceptation of
the word, is called disrespect. Nevertheless, in the passionate agitation which had shaken the maiden since she
came up the stairs was a feeling as if something like what is
expressed by that word had come nigh her. Poor Monny
did not pause to consider that all her ways since her
acquaintance with Mr. Leigh began had been eminently
calculated to convince him that she did *not* possess what
she had described in her own phrase as the solid qualities
of character. Nor, in fact, would his failure to credit
her with those qualities now have in itself alone wrought
her into such a state of mind. She had been thinking
very humbly of herself of late, and with much awe of
Kenyon Leigh; and if he had met her merely with the
greeting that awful personages give to humble ones, saluting her with removed benignity across the gulf, her feeling
at least would not have been of indignation. But it was
her perception, that, while believing her a frivolous girl,
he was still attracted by her, — it was this mixture of
things which had made her gathering wrath and woe.

Her little outburst of words to the matron had been
made the more unreservedly, because, as yet, in her conscious thought, Kenyon Leigh had no nearer place than as
a kind of typical being, — a representative of the general

sentiment of the superior man towards her sex. But types and representatives could apparently be subjects of very poignant reflection ; for Monny fell now into a silence which made the wise widow, only suggesting afresh the injuriousness of too much poring over books to young constitutions, and putting a few soothing touches to the furniture here and there, say to the perturbed girl very soon her motherly good-night, and leave her alone.

Monny's perturbation did not subside with solitude. She was very far from imagining, not being a vain girl, the real extent to which Mr. Leigh had lost his heart to her : there was only a perception of some of that sentiment in his manner towards her which she had been used to in her admirers, mingled with the new, strange element, which made him, as it were, an unwilling admirer. This was her whole impression, but in her present mood it was enough. She felt confronted in living reality with a truth which had been growing darkly on her through all her late readings and speculations ; viz., that the being who charms is not necessarily the one who is esteemed. This truth, which, as well as its converse, must be called a truth in the relations of men and women, however melancholy the issues it is capable of containing, came down on Monny as the final stroke of all her recent tribulations of thought ; and the sick wail of the period went up at last from this pair of red lips, " Oh, it's a dreadful thing to be a woman ! "

Meanwhile at this same hour, in the opposite chambers, beyond the thickness of two partition-walls, a man of heroic stature was preparing to do what heroes have had to do before, — to run away. Alas ! in this most undignified attitude I was obliged to show the Rev. Kenyon Leigh at the very outset of this history. Then, however, he was running only from the apprehended folly of an-

other : now he had to run from his own. And ah! that
strenuous flight which is the flight from one's self must
be farther than to a neighboring boarding-place, or up
a staircase. Yea, his apartments in New York were the
nearest limit at which he proposed now to stop : thither
·he intended to go on the morrow, and to come back no
more.

The somewhat marked tendency of the weightiest of
men to fall in love with the lightest of women is a form
of human fatuity which has received bountiful satire in
this world : likewise, that other fatuity in these affairs,
which makes some gentle, especially sensitive, piece of
femininity so apt to select as her life-owner a man whom
all his fellows recognize as the most overbearing despot
of his sex. From these undoubted phenomena male observers have generalized the statement that women love
best the men who treat them worst; the more feminine
the woman, the more clearly appearing her innate passion for being trampled on. And, even as the masculine
critic has made this deduction from the latter order of
cases, the feminine censor, to whom the former is naturally most impressive, has decided that intellectual men
prefer mindless women for wives, whether of the giddy or
the passively amiable variety. Notably, for example, in
those pages where the novelist spreads the panorama of
life, is the woman author wont to select for her most remorseless strokes of punishment the superior man who
thus passes by his proper mate to be become enamoured
of the slight creature. Nor does she ever fail to imply
also that he has *deserved* all his scourging by the Furies
for his deliberate preference of the lower to the higher,
— his base ideal, in short, of womankind. Thus George
Eliot's Dr. Lydgate, whose manly life-blood is murder-
ously drawn by his blonde vampire of a wife, — this man

of noble quality, we are carefully told at the outset by
the famous woman who depicts him, had " spots of com-
monness ; " to wit, " that distinction of mind which
belonged to his intellectual ardor did not penetrate his
feeling and judgment about women."

Evidently the trait thus described, the taste which
made him find the high-flown Dorothea, for instance,
" troublesome to talk to," and Rosamond's the delight-
fully relaxing society, in his unlessoned bachelor days.
— most evidently this was the accursed spot which would
not out in the author's view of him till he had drunk to its
lowest dregs the cup of torment mixed for him by that
same blue-eyed Rosamond.

But, in spite of these high examples, we are not quite
ready to admit that our hero was spotted with common-
ness, because of his extraordinary fancy for the kind of
girl that he yet soberly believed Monny Rivers to be.
No : it is our view that he was really no more in love with
folly than those soft little sisters who will marry the
tyrants are with tyranny. He was in love with a temperament which may often go with folly, but which was
as intrinsically attractive to his opposite temperament as
is the man of forceful nature to the especially delicate
and dependent type of woman ; and because poor Gri-
selda mistakes mere self-assertion and hardness of temper,
or, haply, some accident of brawn and muscle, for the far
finer qualities which make the really strong man, it is not
proved that she loves ignobly, only that she has that
frequentest of all earthly fates, — to dream that she has
found a substance where there is nought but a shell. No :
all these seemingly mad marriages, whatever madness of
misery they may and often do end in, end thus because
the qualities which so irresistibly attract are there only in
seeming, or are not supplemented by other qualities : the

attraction proceeds from a true instinct, and, like every
thing which is instinctive, expresses, subject to the due
checks and limitations, a sacred want.

The swift decision with which Kenyon Leigh had said
to himself, on that memorable afternoon of a few days
before, that he should never marry, had been no fitful
whim of a fevered moment, but a conclusion permanent,
with all his perception, not only of the depth of his feeling for one particular woman, but with the perception
also that hers was the only type of woman that he should
ever desire for a wife.   No being could possibly be more
astonished than he was himself at this discovery : in no
human brain could an opinion be more clearly registered
than was in his, then and still, the opinion that Mrs. Van
Cortlandt was the suitable wife for him, and not the girl
whose caprice to bestow a smile on him just now, instead
of a frown, had been capable of turning the world upside
down to him.   He did not argue with this amazing experience, — he was a man, in more respects than one, of the
simple old heroic temper, — he did not analyze primitive
emotions.   He said, that, if he staid where he was one
other day, he could no more be sure of his power to
depart; and, it being characteristic of him to take some
immediate outward steps in the direction of any difficult
inward resolve, he was this moment packing whatever
books he had in these lodgings to be ready to leave on the
morrow by the ten o'clock train.

There was no atom of a prig in Kenyon Leigh's composition.   Too broad and generous at all points had been
his life and training, that he should have the conventional
pattern of minister's wife set up in his mind as the only
proper wife for him.   He simply thought Monny Rivers
an impossible wife for any serious man whatever, engaged
in any arduous work in life   For he by no means asked

alone what the butterfly could at last be to such a husband, but what could such a husband be, what could he really do for the happiness of the butterfly? His infatuation for the girl was quite strong enough for him to have flung to the winds the question how he could live with her: he could not so dispose of the question how she could live with him.

It may be suggested that this was a man whose express business in life was to develop the serious side of people: why did he not set himself forthwith to create a soul in the Undine who had so bewitched him, — to mould this maiden, now in her plastic years, into whatever manner of mate he approved? — a favorite idea with many merely secular men in choosing a wife.

Well, such an idea as this never occurred to the Rev. Kenyon Leigh: he could have gone round the world, and preached regeneration to every creature in it save only this one; it was the one piece of imperfect human clay mysteriously removed in his mind from any thought of fashioning it anew. He had decided, as we know, what Monny did with her afternoons, and what she did with her mornings, and what she thought about when she walked under the apple-trees; and yet to see her walk under the apple-trees had been an indefeasible pleasure still. Just as she was, as he thought she was, he could not marry her; but, just as he thought she was, there is no denying that he had fallen in love with her, and that sentiment in the pure heart will have an element of reverence in it, will make to itself a kind of altar, whether the temple be there or no. Yet none the less beside his sentiment of worship for this maiden stood all the while his mental conception of her — a recognized disproportion of things, a non-correspondence between cause and effect, which in this man's nature made a kind of panic.

It was not a nature subject to panic : nothing had more impressed Monny on the night of the shipwreck than to see how, the instant he fairly drew breath out of water, he so recovered his habitual equilibrium, it seemed impossible to realize at all the terrific struggle out of which he had just come.   And indeed nowhere, perhaps, do great rulers of men and things more show their greatness than in this very case and entireness with which they pass from some tremendous commotion to calm ; and the secret probably is that the calm has never really been lost at all ; that, in their utmost hurricane of action, there has been an inner centre of quiet, never invaded, controlling all the passion with which every faculty must move, so that in its fiercest energy there is no frenzy.   Certain it was that this strong swimmer, not in the black whirling caldron of the midnight sea, nor even in those spiritual tempests of a year before, which had left unreached that sane, sound core of purpose in the man which had brought him home so soon as he found that what he voyaged for lay not beyond the seas, — not in these shocks had Kenyon Leigh known the sense of chaos, and the rout of reason, but in the contrary currents set in motion by a girl's smile. Contrary they were, giving no promise, if he yielded to them, but of unrest forever, — Monny herself could not have so testified as could the man who had met her in the dim old entry, to the absence of all peace from a passion wherein charm and esteem do not go together.

Assuredly he profoundly esteemed in Monny Rivers many excellent qualities.   He thought her guileless and open as the day : it had been her first supreme attraction to him.   Nor had all her exceptional behavior to himself prevented him from seeing that she was habitually both well-bred and sweet-tempered.   An innocent, lovely, bewitching plaything ; but he could not relegate her to any such place in his life as one gives to playthings : the paradox was true, that, if he had loved her less, he could have thought of marrying her more.

And so, while the long leaves of the Balm-of-Gilead tree swayed in the moonlight at the open window, the books were packed, a kerosene lamp flashing into the depths of the Puritan dark closet as the old Romish saints were rummaged out therefrom by the minister's unforgetting hand, headlong went those brethren into his departing boxes, then a very few moments more sufficed to toss all other properties which he had at Cape Cod into a state for transportation.

And, these things being accomplished, he sought the repose of the just.

.

CHAPTER XI.

THERE arose next morning in the eastern chambers of Mrs. Doane's house a much dejected young woman and an utterly discouraged artist.

To young Monny Rivers unquestionably belonged the title of true artist in this, that she only valued her vocation as it might enable her to shape in some outward form life's inner meanings. When, therefore, those grew dark and doubtful to her, as they did now, her brushes fell from her hand, and all her skill therewith seemed to her only some poor trick which she had insanely wasted years in acquiring. That sense which had finally settled on her, of a primary, ineradicable discordance between the two halves which make up the whole of humanity, reached, with its blight, to every sentiment, emotion, and aspiration of that humanity which she had ever essayed to express on canvas. So taking a sick-hearted look around her studio this morning, with a mere dreary wonder as to what had sustained her through all that drawing of lines and mixing of paints, she went down-stairs.

It was not quite breakfast-time; and Monny wandered out into the much elongated back regions of the house: it ended in two wings, in one of which was the summer-kitchen, while at the extremity of the other was a room known as the milk-room, although Mrs. Doane kept no cow at present. In this latter room she found the widow.

"Are there any errands that I can do for you to the village?" asked the young lady, after she had said her good-morning, one of the prompters of the question being her habitual impulse to avoid the family meal-times : which impulse was about the only sentiment that she had left actively alive this morning.

"Bless you, my dear! nothing in the world that I think of,' replied the matron. "I've just sent Susannah for the milk, as little Bobby Gates is lame yet, with a nail he run into his foot two or three days ago : so I told his mother I'd send till he was all right again.

"But Miss Monny," added the matron, as the girl was turning away, "there's something I was thinking of only a minute ago, that you used to do for me, if you're not too busy."

Monny paused at this intimation that there was any thing remaining in the offices of life to which her powers were adequate; and Mrs. Doane forthwith opened the refrigerator, taking thence a roll of very superior-looking butter. She imported, while she had these high-priced summer boarders, what she required of that article for table-use by way of Boston market, as the lower portion of Cape Cod is not a rich grazing country.

"I was thinking just now, as I took a look at this," began Mrs. Doane, — "it came last night with the fruit on the train, the real gilt-edged butter from Worcester County, and a nicer flavor never was," said the house-keeper with satisfaction, — "I was thinking how you used to ornament the butter-plates years ago, making pictures in the butter, natural as life. Don't you remember? Now, if I cut off a round of this, would you make one to put on the tea-table to-night?"

"Oh, cut it all up!" said Monny carelessly. "I will do the whole, if you wish. Is it soft enough to model now?"

"Well, I think just about as you used to like it. The

ice is all gone out of the refrigerator: so it's only about
half hard," said the widow, beginning to cut the butter;
while Monny was already gone to pull some straws from
the corn-broom, and then out of doors to select some
splinters from the wood-pile.

Returning presently with these implements, she rinsed
them in a bowl of water, and, sitting down by the old
deal-table, drew towards her the plate on which Mrs.
Doane had placed the first round from the golden butter-
ball, and began her work. The latter, meanwhile, had
taken the shortest cut to her kitchen; viz., across the bit
of grassy yard, enclosed on three sides, like a little court,
by the walls of the house, with its two queer extensions
long drawn out under their sloping roofs. The housekeeper, crossing this outdoor space, had bestowed a look
on the corn-cake in the oven, and manipulated the dampers of the range, to deaden the coals a little for broiling;
then, bringing a large plate or two, she came back, and
divided the rest of the gilt-edged butter into the proper
sections, laying them round on the plates in readiness for
the artist's hand. As the Centennial Exposition was not
yet quite arrived, with Western sculptresses making a
specialty of moulding heads in butter, Monny was not at
all aware that the material in which she wrought was
classic. She had never experimented in it herself, save
for the literal purpose of decorating Mrs. Doane's table;
but, in the very peculiarity of her mood this morning, she
presently bent over her work with a certain absorption.
It was two or three years since she remembered to have
made any butter heads; and, perceiving that her skill
had increased in that time, she went on elaborating her
grotesque material, with a half-melancholy, half-ironical
impulse to do well this ridiculous work which was her
long farewell to art, being quite sure this morning that
she had done with painting pictures forever.

"Susannah has come with the milk, and I'm just going to ring the bell," announced Mrs. Doane, appearing by and by at the inner door. "You'll come to breakfast, won't you, Miss Monny?" she added, pleased that this boarder, who was always avoiding the other boarder, was entrapped for at least one meal.

To the matron's disappointment, however, Monny replied, "No. I want to stay and finish these now, if you will please tell Susannah, when she has done waiting on the table, to bring me a little breakfast out here."

The widow, having keenly in mind last night's mysterious disturbance, did not venture to urge the maiden further, but, shutting the door at her request, went to preside at the breakfast-table.

Monny worked busily on, only interrupted by Susannah crossing the little grass-plot from the kitchen presently, to ask what she would have for breakfast, and coming again to bring the chosen viands on a waiter. These consisted of corn-cake, a boiled egg, and some sliced peaches; which breakfast Monny consumed at intervals, while she still shaped with her sticks and straws the plastic substance before her. A little child on tiptoe, tugging desperately to lift the handle of a churn, its baby mouth pursed up, and its fat cheeks puffed out with the effort; a man with a milk-pail, letting down a pair of bars, the head of an eager cow being thrust over them; the face of a dreaming girl looking out of a dairy-window, and forgetting to skim the cream, — these simplest little fancies Monny wrought out on one round of butter after another; but the born cunning of her hand and its long-practised skill were in them.

Meanwhile there were boiled eggs and corn-cake on the orderly breakfast-table in an inner room, and coffee and chops, and baked potatoes, and such other substantials of diet; but the minister listened, with some inner strain which decidedly interfered with appetite, for the light-coming echo of a certain footfall, hoping against hope to hear it through all the long-drawn-out melancholy meal. At last, however, having pared peaches with infinite slow nicety, and then forgotten to eat them, he rose with one of his abrupt movements, and vanished up-stairs.

With thoughtful, knitted brow Mrs. Doane went slowly out into her kitchen, meeting, at the foot of the back stairs, Susannah, who came down from making the beds to ask, with astonished glitter of eyes and teeth, " Is his Honor gwine away? His rooms has got an all-clared-out look, an' portmanter an' things standin' up on end ready to start."

" Sit down, and eat your breakfast right away, Susannah, and don't be talking!" said the mistress, in a tone of asperity quite unusual for her to employ to her long-familiar handmaid. " The minister is going up to Boston of errands, may be, or to dedicate a church, or something. We are not to be noticing things about boarders," pronounced Mrs. Doane. But the extinguisher which she had thought prudent thus to put on Susannah's curiosity by no means satisfied herself. She stepped directly across, therefore, into the milk-room; but Monny was not there. Having finished her breakfast and her artistic efforts, she had strayed listlessly out of doors, and was now wandering, bareheaded, down the lane in rear of the house. Thus the matron could not enlighten the alarmed per-plexity which Susannah's announcement had caused her by taking a fresh look of examination at the young lady, who, she was convinced, had to do at present with what-ever was unusual in Mr. Leigh's moods and movements The widow had by no means failed to observe his mood all breakfast-time, and to connect it with Monny's extraordinary mood the night before, however mystified she was as to the point of connection ; and, lost in conjecture, she was going rather absently about some little affairs she had to mind in the milk-room, when she heard approaching — not Monny, but Mr. Leigh.

This unaccustomed prowler through Mrs. Doane's back kitchens was, in fact, seeking his landlady to ask her for whatever bill might yet be unsettled against him, and to inform her of his intended departure at ten o'clock ; for he intended his going only the more firmly since his disappointed longing at breakfast to see once more the bright face which he was to bid farewell to forever, since every lapsing moment of that pain had but shown him anew his necessity for flight. But he suppressed strange emotions as he passed now from one to another of the queer old rooms : it was a cleaving pang to part with the very walls of the old house where he had found that pretty shell, — only a many-tinted, lovely shell ; yet he had heard in it the murmur of the infinite sea.

Well, the man who was thus grappling with fate came somehow to the milk-room, discerning the widow's honest back through its open door. She was standing, at the moment, before the big old table pushed against the opposite wall, where Monny's butter-plates were still displayed ; and, as she heard the step of her ministerial boarder, she had a sudden impulse to show him those works in butter. Now Monny, in her generally increased sensitiveness of late about Mr. Leigh, had more straitly charged her landlady than ever before to keep locked and hidden the secret of her studio. But showing butter-plates, thought the Puritan casuist, was not showing pictures ; and, as the minister paused on the threshold behind her, she turned about before he spoke, holding out to him one of the plates, with —

"Did you ever see any thing, sir, prettier than that which Miss Monny has just been doing?"

Arrested by the name, Mr. Leigh mechanically took the dish extended to him, beginning to say, —

"Where in the world do you get such a wonderful stamp?" But the words had not passed his lips when his eye recognized the fact which the matron hastened to assure him of.

"There's no stamp about it at all, sir: she does them all out of her own head, with little sticks and straws. She did all those while she was eating her breakfast here," said the widow, drawing forward the other plates to the front of the table.

Naturally Mrs. Doane could not know as did Mr. Leigh, who had much knowledge of art, how very extraordinary the butter-plates were; nor could all her surmises about his interest in Miss Monny measure the sensations with which he bent over that table.

He saw every thing on it at a glance, — the remains of Monny's breakfast: a fearfully suggestive sight that was to him. It suggested to him on the instant that utterly forgotten deed of his, viz., where and how he had taken his first breakfast under Mrs. Doane's roof; and, whether or no that famous meal was "hot" in the eating, it certainly "burnt him up" now to remember it. An awful sense of having driven out this dainty girl, in her white dresses, to take her meals in the uttermost back kitchen of the house, where, taking them with one hand, she executed with the other, in a fine sarcasm of the ogre who had thus exiled her, things whose first stroke he could not have made to save his intolerable life: this sensation transfixed him. Mysteriously must his guilty brain recall the very viands whereof that shameless meal was composed, — fried fish, for one thing: all their bones stuck in his throat this moment. Perhaps that was why he could not speak, but stood staring dumbly at the butter-plates, with a mingled feeling of himself as a ruffian fit for the hulks, of having been justly doomed, how many meals since, to find no nourishment in victuals, for want of that same exiled presence, and, under all these unquiet surges of the breast, some indefeasible rising wave of joy.

Did it rise because he heard Monny coming? for she was coming, very slowly, over the narrow loose boards laid for a walk to the well through the dewy, thick grass of the little court. Slow with melancholy trod the maid: there had been no strength for sarcasm in her this morning, only a little sad satirizing of herself as she wrought the butter-moulds so carefully. Nor did she lift her brooding, downcast eyes now, till, as her languid foot was set on the low sill of the open door, Mr. Leigh's voice suddenly startled her. His glance did not meet hers: only his side-face was towards her, as he stood still bending down over the table, while he said, without the preface even of good-morning, —

"Miss Rivers, to have done these things you must have done many other things in art. I beg — I beg that you will show them to me, — something, any thing, that you have done."

The widow, who was hovering with some alarm in the background, drew an inward breath of content as she saw Monny's startled look at this address pass into a questioning one, then her hand go slowly to her pocket, from which she took a key, laying it with no more ado on a corner of the table.

"That is the key of my front room," she said. "You can unlock it, and go in, if you like. A few of the pictures there I have painted this summer, and all of them at some time."

The softer maiden voice spoke in the same tone of
restrained quiet that the man had spoken in; but the effort
of restraint was a little more apparent in her accents.
And so soon as these words were said, still without having
met her interlocutor's eyes, she passed directly on across
the little room, and out its opposite open door, continuing
thus her indefinite rambles around the house. For Mr.
Leigh, he took up the key forthwith, and went for the
door that it unlocked.

The Puritan widow, who had tried a little casuistry with
what seemed to her thus far very promising results, after
thoughtfully allowing the minister a certain length of time
alone in Monny's studio, concluded next that she had
better go up, and wander conveniently round a little in
the young lady's apartments, in case there was any further
occasion for her to act as a providence. The matron
acted in all these proceedings of hers wholly by instinct,
being by no means of a sufficiently speculative turn of
mind to have framed to herself any theory that would
quite account for all the behaviors that she saw going on.
But instinct in women is truly a great matter: so, armed
with a dust-brush, — housekeepers can always dust, and
pictures need a great deal of dusting, — the good soul
ascended.

Very opportune was her coming to Mr. Leigh in the
studio, on whom, it is safe to say, none of all the world-
famous galleries of art that he had beheld had ever
wrought as did this little gallery that he found hidden in
the old Cape-Cod house. And he needed at last the substantial figure of his landlady, a woman who had known
about this amazing Monny from her babyhood up, to
assure him that what he saw was really not a dream.
One pretty keen sense he had had, to be sure, of being
awake; viz., when he took up the girl's sketch-book

where it lay on the table, — the familiar thing he had seen her carry about for weeks wrapped in a shawl. Opening it now, he was doomed to behold at once its dated inscription, and to feel Monny mocking at him in every letter of it; for he perfectly remembered the morning when that inscription was entered. Well, he was presently absorbed in hearing Mrs. Doane's communications; for, inspired by such a listener, the tongue which had been so long unwillingly silent concerning Monny's toils and talents waxed eloquent indeed.

Then, when this useful woman descended the stairs again, she went in search of Monny herself. That young lady, with all her frankness, was not one easy to approach with gossiping questions on such an affair as her acquaintance with Mr. Leigh had become; nor was the woman who had known her so long at all sure yet what the sentiment on Monny's side of the affair was. So the diplomatic widow confined herself strictly to business in what she said to her young boarder. She found her stooping among the flower-beds, gathering petunia-seeds. The petunias sowed themselves every year in the borders, growing like weeds there; but Monny was searching about now for the early ripened flower-heads, pouring their tiny little globules of seed into her hand as something very precious indeed, when Mrs. Doane woke her out of her absorption with, —

"Miss Monny, the minister says, if you please, when it is perfectly convenient he would like to see you upstairs. I think he wants to ask you something about the pictures: he is mightily taken up with them," was all the matron ventured to add; with which words she retreated at once within doors.

Monny had scattered all her petunia-seeds at the first words of this summons; but, after standing irresolute a few moments, she turned, and went slowly into the house by the front way.

The self-controlled Kenyon Leigh was at bottom an impetuous man ; and, when he heard Monny on the staircase, it seemed to him that no speech with her would be possible to him, without uttering some of the wild words of penitence and adoration that his heart was full of. But the first sight of the maiden as she timidly appeared settled all that tumult, leaving only one supreme solicitude, — to help, to sustain her where she wanted help. What she wanted above all things just then was to be perfectly calm and composed ; and she was secretly struggling against some mysterious tremulousness of the nerves which was bearing her desperately near to tears. To break down and cry at this moment would have been horrible to Monny, in whom was not only all the instinct of reserve and restraint which distinguishes the lady from the mere impulsive female, but her general feeling of being disheartened, hurt, and wounded, was by no means wholly attributable to the man in whose presence she stood. ·And what of it was connected with him was a very indefinite business that she was far from ready to put any such definite point to as would seem given by a display of emotion. No : she did not wish to make a scene herself, and any demonstration of sentiment on Mr. Leigh's side could scarce have failed to be highly distressing to her.

Young maidens right maidenly, even when they are pleased with the admiration of the other sex, are much less eager for downright love-making than seems commonly to be supposed ; and Monny's inner history, of late, had not been calculated to diminish her shyness. But, if she did not want a lover this morning, she was in a mood to value most keenly that somewhat uncertain article for women to deal with too extensively, — a man's friendship. So the friendly, easy, quiet words which made Mr. Leigh's first utterance to her were as well timed as possible.

"Mrs. Doane tells me that you have never exhibited any thing. But some of these pictures would surely bring you recognition now as an artist; and nothing will be easier than for me to get them advantageously placed for you in New York, if you will trust me. I should like to know what of your work you value most yourself — and these pictures that are turned to the wall, if I might see them also?" he concluded interrogatively.

The girl's fluttering pulses had calmed with every moment of this address; and she was presently walking around her studio with Mr. Leigh, only remembering her impressions of him the night before as some more of those absurdly false impressions that she had been having about this man from the beginning. Monny had, indeed, the readiness of all large, sweet natures, to reconsider her own adverse judgments, to believe herself mistaken: life was yet a new strange book to her, in which it was so easy to read amiss.

It seemed entirely natural to the girl that Mr. Leigh should have all knowledge. That was not true, of course; but it was true, as Monny at once perceived, that he was not only an enthusiastic lover of art, but a most rare *connoisseur*, especially for an American. He had never drawn a line himself; but certain circumstances had so highly developed in him the critical faculty in these things, his judgment of a work of art was a recognized authority. And, what is not invariably found in the critic, he had as fine a feeling for the sentiment of a picture as for its mastery of technique.

To all workers in any field that is called art come hours

when their pursuits seem fantastic and unreal to their very
selves: the truths that imagination shapes in her airy
forms become air indeed, and all that the picture, the
poem, the romance, were created for, dissolves, even to
their creator, in the insubstantiality of the medium through
which he works. This despair which the philosopher, the
thinker in the world of facts, can scarcely know, had been
very heavy of late in this lonely young girl, with her
much pondering on the more tangible forces of life; and
to find no subtlest meaning that she had tried to render in
her pictures lost on this critic, and that this order of man
gave the kind of recognition that he did to an artist's
work, — these things were verily to her now like bread to
the perishing. Some of the pictures turned to the wall
were of her latest work, that she had thus hidden, in very
misery to behold them, in the circuit that she had taken
around her studio before going down-stairs this morning.
And as she turned them out now, one after another, she
stood waiting for Mr. Leigh's verdict on each one, much
like a child that brings up its task, and stands beaming,
wistful, watching to see whether you will approve or no.

"I suppose it would be more superior not to be so glad
to be praised," she broke out suddenly, bethinking herself
that she was perhaps plainly showing the pleasure that
she felt, as indeed she was, in the gathering radiance of
her face. "But I *am* glad, I am," she repeated *naively*,
as confessing what was perhaps a fault, yet which must be
owned in truth. "It is so many, many long years that I
have been painting pictures, and afraid very often that
they were all good for nothing. I am a great deal older
than people think," she added, meeting some gleam in
Mr. Leigh's eyes as they turned from the pictures to the
young picture of her face. "I shall be twenty-one years
old next month."

"That is very old indeed," said the man of thirty-four, smiling down on this veteran, who announced her approaching birthday as if it was about her sixtieth. Monny's simplicity was as adorable to him as if he were not the simplest of beings himself. But a man's simplicity is never like a woman's, and Kenyon Leigh's was eminently unlike Monny's. The trait which sometimes gave to his manners an air of bluntness, and disregard of appearances and opinion, showed itself in the more gracious maiden in the artless openness with which she betrayed, as now, her sensitiveness to those matters.

"Men, I suppose, are not so?" she continued interrogatively, with her persistent solicitude about the masculine standards. "They do not like to be praised for their well-doing?"

What she was secretly thinking of was of Mr. Leigh's own exceeding shrinking from praise on the night of the wreck; and it was quite a satisfaction to her when the unconscious hero, not in the least suspecting what was in her head, yet answered in a way to suggest that there were some directions, after all, in which he was not wholly independent of all the meed of mortals.

"Surely, in every work that is an effort to interpret truth, men are very much sustained and stimulated by the recognition of others; and I have been marvelling how any man could have achieved such work as has the painter of these pictures, in such obscurity. Greater than your gifts, greater always than any gift, is the devotion that so cultivates the gift. It is so plain that you have the true artist's passion for perfection, one may dare tell you that the little pictures I have mentioned, — those where you attempt least, but where you have developed an admirably pure style, and one absolutely your own, — that those are your best work; although this Lenore here " (he paused before a large canvas, on which was portrayed the maiden riding away with her ghastly lover in Bürger's wild ballad), this, and two or three other such in the room, are the performances that would most astonish the public. And as performances, considering especially the years at which they were painted, they *are* wholly astonishing."

"Astonishingly bad," laughed Monny: she could laugh with real lightness now at her outgrown work. "I know the horse is out of drawing, and the lurid lights are impossible, and the man is neither dead nor alive, instead of both dead and alive, as he ought to be. I hoped, myself, the simple pictures you have chosen might not be so full of faults as the others, because I could make thorough studies for them from the life. But then, about those simple pictures — I have had times of being dreadfully afraid that they were not worth doing at all."

"It will be a re-assurance for those times to have the suffrages of others, and be sure you will have them, of a few, as to the rare worth of some of this unpretending work of yours. It is not often that there is any need to urge young talent to make a public venture. But in your case, I am sure it will help, and not harm, the artist. And for the rest of us," added Mr. Leigh, after an instant's hesitation, "if you had not hidden your gifts so deeply, you would not have left a stone-blind, stupid man to fall into what is always a severe mortification, — the finding that one has failed to show any honor where honor was very greatly due."

"You must not think I do not owe a great deal to lessons," said Monny, veiling the little trepidation which these last words caused her by keeping close to the professional question. "I had a very superior master at one time, — an artist from Paris, astray in New York for a while, — who gave me lessons two whole years, and took the greatest pains with me. Here are some of the very studies I used to do with him," she said, going to a square mahogany table pushed against the wall, — a large old-fashioned card-table, piled with sketch-books, a variety of boxes containing art-materials, and two or three great folios of drawings. "If you would like to see them?" she said, looking up, with her hand on the under-most one of the folios.

"Certainly. I should like to see any thing, every thing, that will account for you at all."

Mr. Leigh knew very well that only genius would account for Monny, but he was extremely glad to look over the drawings, as it was a business capable of much prolonging: so, as Monny sat down at one side of the table, he seated himself at another, and began to examine the old studies she had done at school with the master of whom Mrs. Doane had before told him.

It was a very long while since that particular folio had been opened, and Monny had no precise idea of its contents; but, giving it directly into Mr. Leigh's hand, she sat quietly by herself while he drew out in turn, and examined, the miscellaneous collection with which it was stuffed. Somewhere in the course of this survey he came upon a certain half-painted picture in oils of a youth about twenty, painted cabinet-size, on a piece of prepared board such as artists use. This picture, as it appeared, drew from Mr. Leigh the exclamation, "What a hand-some young *caballero!*"

Monny's eyes, from where she sat, had fallen on the sketch with the same merely ascertaining glance, to see what it was, that she bestowed on whatever Mr. Leigh took out of the long-forgotten folio; but she made no answer to his remark, and he observed that her glance just then wandered off into a very absent gaze.

A slighter-natured girl than Monny — she herself, probably, a week later — would have blushed to have this
picture, representing what it did in her history, fall so
unexpe.tedly into the hands of the man who sat by the
table.   But the constant, delicate color that made so
lovely her soft cheeks neither deepened nor paled now ;
the dreaming eyes showed no trace of disturbance ; her
attitude only took some peculiar stillness, as of one who
lis ens. '

Long was it before Mr. Leigh laid down that sketch,
not because of its artistic merit : it was plainly a piece
of Monny's early, immature work, and he had noted it at
first only because of the superb type of physical beauty
that the face represented.   Perhaps because that type
seemed to him so wholly un-American, or because of the
highly romantic pose and air that the very young hand
which had painted it had given to the figure, he did not
at all imagine the sketch to be a portrait, nor did it even
occur to him that his taking of it out now had any connection with the revery into which Monny had fallen.
But it was that revery which made him sit motionless
himself, his eyes apparently occupied with the piece of
painted board before him, although, after the first glance,
he was really not seeing at all the handsome youth portrayed thereon.

He was seeing, with those mysterious glances which
see while they appear directed to another object, the rapt
away face of the maiden as she sat in the morning light.
It streamed full upon her from the front windows of the
apartment, the table being against the side of the room,
her seat near the wall, while, Mr. Leigh's position being
rather diagonal to hers across the table, his back was
partly towards the light : he never forgot any detail of
this scene.   What was to burn these moments into his

memory forever was yet hid from him : in their passing
they filled consciousness to the brim, not with anguish,
but delight, — that large delight which lifts the soul in
knowing that the being beloved is worthy of all beloving.
Whether this joy would ever hold any personal hope for
himself or not, it was still a joy which made the lover
almost forbear to breathe, lest he should break the dream
which touched that young face with the same sweet musing seriousness that he had so often seen it wear before,
and marvelled how so light a creature could have so deep
a look. "Stone-blind and stupid" indeed, he seemed
to himself to have been : yet his old sense of mystery
about this maiden was but enhanced, transformed ; in her
every movement to him now was a kind of sacred wonder. What was she listening to? What was she seeing
with those dreaming eyes?

Well, Monny in these moments was really listening,
listening to a long-ago echo from her past, — certain remembered strains of dance-music in a high-bannered hall,
where martial emblems were of right, and morning faces.
A nation's nursery of heroes it was, and heroes that
should be, looked the gallant young figures, brave in uniform, graceful in their young slimness as the maidens who
went whirling with them in all that splendor of light and
flowers and music which makes such enchantment of a
girl's first ball.

Yes, it was Monny's first ball (it had come, by certain
chances, when she was a mere schoolgirl, not formally
out) which had risen on her vision when the minister took
out that picture ; and what she was chiefly striving to see
with those intent eyes was her own self of five years
before. Outwardly she had not greatly changed. The
young girl whom she saw waltzing on and on in that flying
throng, with one partner always coming to claim her

anew as the music beat wilder and sweeter measures with
every latening hour — between that girl's face and this
maiden's, who mused so fair in the morning light, time
had as yet marked no difference so wide that Monny
should find such difficulty in realizing that vision of the
ball-room as indeed herself. But it was not her outer self
of the past that she was thinking of: it was the inner
being, her notions of life at that period, her conception
of men and things, — that horizon of the mind may sweep
through vast changes between the ages of sixteen and
twenty-one ; and it was her sense of these altered measurements which made it so hard for her to identify her
present self with that girl of sixteen.

Now, the words which we shall have to put down as
Monny's first utterance when she woke out of the reminiscences that I have indicated will be considered, doubtless, as a shining example of feminine inconsequence :
nevertheless, her mind had travelled logically (being a
woman's) to just the subject which she introduced.

There had been something in that backward look into
the past to make her vividly contrast her ideas of then
and now as to what was admirable in masculine character ;
and Mr. Leigh at this moment made a nearer move into
what may be called her regard than he had ever done
before. Simultaneously with this feeling came a solicitude
that the man who had approved her work should approve
also herself. The deathless feminine wish to be thought
well of personally by the being whose opinion is valued
for one's talents moved her instinctively to put in a little
plea for herself in a direction where she thought she had
been at a disadvantage in Kenyon Leigh's eyes. So,
turning those dreaming orbs back upon him, she began
gravely, —

" I have learned lately," — he looked up, expecting to

hear of some new form of art that she had been studying,
— "I have learned lately, a little — *to cook.* I should not
burn the steak up now."

At this solemn announcement Mr. Leigh burst out
laughing. The tension of will with which he had been
holding emotion in check ever since Monny came up-
stairs was too suddenly relaxed for him to help it.

"Truly I should not," Monny repeated, taking this
merriment as a sign of some scepticism about her new
accomplishment. "I have practised all the common
kinds of cooking for all the meals with Mrs. Doane. And
she said I learned quicker than — than some girls," said
Monny; which was putting very mildly indeed Mrs.
Doane's commendation of her quickness. But the young
lady advanced even this bit of self-praise only in her
eagerness to stand well with her new mentor.

"Very extraordinary that you should," the mentor
replied, still laughing. Monny's want of culinary skill
had *not* been one of the items which had made him decide
her an impossible wife. "Very extraordinary that a brain
which has mastered the difficulties of such an art as
yours should be apter to learn than the thick skull of
some ignorant Irish girl," — a view of things which certainly implies that Mr. Leigh was a more advanced
philosopher than some of his contemporaries.

"Were the dinners last week," said Monny, brightening, — "were they worse than — usual?" she asked bashfully, intending no slur on the dinners of the house, only
desiring to present modestly her part in them.

"I have no fault to find with Mrs. Doane's dinners,
except being left to eat them so much alone," ventured
the gentleman boarder.

"I cooked two of them all by myself," announced the
young lady boarder, — "without any directions, I mean,

with Susannah only helping me : I was head cook. And all the other days I helped Susannah and Mrs. Doane.''

Between the one sensation of finding that he had ignorantly eaten dinners cooked by those sacred hands, and the other sensation of learning that there really were some causes beside total abhorrence of himself that had kept Monny away from the table of late, Mr. Leigh was speechless ; and, before he could recover himself, his interlocutor went on, —

" I could never be so sorry to spoil any picture as I was to spoil the steak for those poor hungry men when there was no more steak in the house. But it was not my fondness for art that made me so ignorant,'' she said, having in mind all the homilies she had been reading on woman's sphere. "I could have learned to cook too (it is very simple) ; and I would have learned long ago, if I had thought about it before. Truly,'' she pleaded, opening her earnest eyes on Mr. Leigh, as if she stood at the bar of the whole masculine world, entreating its fair mind on woman's case, — "truly, it was not because I despised the useful duties of life that I took to painting pictures. I began when I was much too little to know any thing about those distinctions. I cannot remember any time in my life when I did not try to make pictures ; only if I had not had some good lessons after a while, if Monsieur Durocher had not come, I think I should have gone on making the wildest waste of time and strength, trying to do all the impossible things for which I was not prepared by any knowledge. I think that is the kind of work that strains and wears you out ; not hard study under good masters, but to work blind, and untaught in all the necessary rules that you can hardly find out for yourself, except by such long ways as use up all your force in just discovering the bare methods of good work. And so, it seems to me, thorough training is profitable for women too," argued Monny, encouraged to deliver her burdened mind by the attention of the court.

"Not that I am a worthy example myself, in art or any thing else," she went on. "I have been full of all wrong ideas, which I did not get over, even after I had lessons of Monsieur Durocher: there were many false ideas that I seemed to have to grow beyond, all by myself. I mean, art used to be to me, above all things, a way of escaping from the every-day world to a more romantic one : I thought real life prosy and humdrum, and not worth painting, especially in America. But later I came to see how much beauty there is in every-day things everywhere, all the fine and noble moments there are in what seem very common lives ; and then I began to try to paint pictures that would bring these truths out a little. And since the real world is where we have to live, and where we ought to live, satisfied and believing, I thought, if I could paint any little picture that would help to show those things clearer, perhaps that might be called a kind of usefulness too." Having expressed which diffident hope that she might not fall wholly short of woman's prime duty to be useful, Monny suddenly paused, fearing, that, in her explanatory eagerness, she had grown quite incoherent and tiresome.

But the present listener would have found Monny's words perfectly intelligible and profoundly interesting, if they had been much more broken than they were : hearkening to them indeed, and watching the expressive young face of the speaker, he had a sense of making acquaintance with some entirely new form of heroism. A man able to know that a certain quality of attainment in art, no matter what the native genius, represents always such a long scorning of delights, and living of laborious

days, as may be called heroic at twenty-one years, —
Kenyon Leigh found something very touching in this fair
creature to whom delights so beckoned, making her artist's
battle ; while added to all its difficulty was this mysterious
feminine trouble lest her desert should be counted her
demerit.

In this sympathetic mood he probably found something
vastly consoling to say concerning life's various fields of
usefulness : certainly, as he answered Monny's last words,
her face went brightening on into some fulness of satisfaction which could only have arisen from laying hold at
last of a lively hope that to be a good artist did not necessarily imply a poor kind of a woman.   While this talk
went on, shrill blew the departing whistle of the ten o'clock
train from the railway-station of the village, and the Rev.
Kenyon Leigh was *not* on board.

And had this pair really done misunderstanding each
other?

CHAPTER XII.

CERTAINLY they seemed to understand each other marvellously well in the now ensuing days. Whatever deep correspondences were in these two beings by nature, — and there were very deep ones, — it might have been expected that education would still have separated them too widely for much that could strictly be called mental sympathy. Yet they talked together by the hour; and although any one who had known well the Kenyon Leigh of old would have perceived, perhaps, that this new man made love to Monny with every breath, still lover's words were as yet what he dared not venture on: so something besides variations of "My angel" must have made up at present this exhaustless conversation.

Certainly the girl did not know the things that the ripely educated man, thirteen years her senior, knew, in any such way as he knew them. But it is not nearly so much inequality of mere attainment as a difference in the entire mental habit, which is wont to put such a gulf intellectually between even very bright girls and men of thought and masculine culture. This bright girl, as to her nominal education, had had a very flimsy one. Private governesses had taught her in childhood (they are not, in America, the learned class of female teachers, as a rule; and the instructresses of Aunt Helen's choice did not make the exception): later, Monny had been placed at an ultra-fashionable, ultra-expensive, New-York boarding-school, where nothing was really well taught but the

French language and dancing. Mrs. Slabwell had the most sincerely good intentions in thus schooling her niece. In that lady's ears the very words " female college," not to mention any such wild innovation as a " mixed college," had a startling sound. Such institutions — all the newer schools, in fact, aiming at a more solid education for women than had been usual in Mrs. Slabwell's girlhood — the matron had utterly ignored in selecting schools for her own daughters, having a suspicion of something a little too miscellaneous in the class from which these ambitious students came, a little crude and rude, not to say revolutionary, in the very atmosphere where such strong knowledge was absorbed by women: still less was this radical atmosphere to be thought of for the book-loving, art-gifted, young Monny; since any especial endowment of brains in a girl, the lady considered, had a native tendency to the abnormal and dangerous. So the New-York boarding-school befell Monny, with the two well-taught branches. But as thoroughly to master the French tongue is really a work of no mean mental discipline, and as Monny did attain to that end by grace of this school, learning to speak and write the language there with rare purity and ease, and as she learned also to dance like a sylph, with but very small tax on her time, more utterly fruitless places, in the way of young ladies' schools, might easily have befallen her than this ornamental establishment, which actually attended to two ornaments with thoroughness. Moreover, there came to her in the New-York school the great educational good fortune of her life, — a real master in art.

This wandering Frenchman, who, in the declining years of an unsuccessful life, had drifted over to America a while, had in himself every requisite of a great artist, except that last combination of qualities which makes

origiṇal genius. He was a master of all mere technical
skill in painting, and he had a lofty ideal. The divine
spark which he found in such preposterous lodging as the
breast of an American boarding-school miss, he set himself to guard the more fiercely, because he considered it
doubly exposed to extinction both by reason of Monny's
nationality and of her sex. An American was to the
Frenchman a raw, hasty, superficial creature, the last
of beings to make an artist, and a girl something beyond
the last. Nevertheless, the spark was there; he recognized it: so, all the more because of the small chance he
saw for it to live, he fostered it with a kind of furious
fidelity, as Monny herself had said. Her guardian sup-
plying her liberally with money to gratify this as any
other harmless whim, not only was Monny enabled to
recompense her master, who would have bestowed his
time on this extraordinary pupil whether she could have
paid him or not, but her master was enabled to obtain for
her many valuable facilities for study, even in her boarding-school surroundings.

So this precariously taught girl had had, in one direction
at least, some true and systematic training; and the habit
of accuracy, of patient searching after truth, which she
had acquired in her study of art, doubtless went somewhere into all the other studies which she apparently pursued, after such a random and superficial manner, through
her miscellaneous reading of books. For her general
culture seemed, to a highly cultivated man, of astonishing
extent and solidity for her years: aside from a lover's
fancy, her mere attainments were probably not astonishing at all in the sense of their being beyond what any
bright girl should be equal to.

The art in which Monny had creative power was one
whose labors were necessarily ended with daylight: her

school-tasks had been, for the most part, so shallow, she had skimmed them lightly and in the briefest spaces of time, and at school, as elsewhere, gone on always reading; then, in times when it was impossible to command the more concentrated mood required for all inventive labors sufficiently to work at her easel, a book could still be taken up; so, even amid all the distractions of society incident to her career as a young lady, she had still done much reading. We pause over this matter; because, although the girl of whom we write was a young lady of leisure, on whose so-called schooling much money had been spent, it was still a fact that all which was most valuable in her general education had come through what could be called "studies at home," pursued in odd moments.

One sees, by the way, in the newspapers, some occasional notice of a certain Boston society by that name, to guide American girls in their reading. All the present writer knows of that society is such notices: but I think no woman who can look back from even a few years of maturity, to see in what beggary and blindness as to all the vital sources of knowledge her own school-course left her, — I think no such woman can hear of that society without recognizing in it one of the most needed and practicable of all the new efforts for helping her sex to wider knowledge; for, schooled or unschooled, the normal course of women's lives will still make, for the very large majority of them, studies at home, pursued at interrupted times, their main hope of real culture. Nor is this hope, when once rightly seized, at all a barren one.

Young Monny Rivers certainly had been fortunate above many another in having had from the beginning all the books she wanted, and in having escaped also, in very large measure, all that kind of mental tasking, which, doing little to strengthen the brains, does a great deal to exhaust them, "mocking and deluding with ragged notions and babblements of learning, instead of worthy and delightful knowledge," as John Milton describes the school-cramming of his day. As there is evidence that this cramming is monstrously on the increase since his time, and that there is a particularly barren form of it particularly rife in American schools for girls as well as boys, worse fates might well have befallen our heroine than an aunt Helen through whose beneficent folly this unworn young brain had had leisure to find out for itself, without a society, how to make some fruitful studies at home. No one will pretend that this unguided reading of a girl was the best possible education for her; only that she had absorbed from it much knowledge which was worthy and delightful knowledge, and not the utterly disjointed notions and babblements of school text-books with which so many a bright girl's education seems to end. She was not learned: but she had some cultured sense to discern between the good and the spurious in the literature of which she had read so much; she had an eager passion to know, to attain to clear ideas and just views, that she might base her young life on them; and she had some adequate notion of the conditions of search and study by which these are attained. She could be called, therefore, an educated being. The man who found her mind so interesting was certainly much more educated; but the very crudity which was necessarily in her thoughts on many subjects, the girlish speech in which she expressed them, was charming to him, since the crudity was of a sort that ripens, and which has an attractive freshness even in its immaturity.

There may be readers who will find prosings on education and the like quite intolerably out of place just here, since it is well understood that love is a madness, and the genuine lover in a state of total inability to discern whether the charmer talks sense or nonsense. We assure them that we are not at all impugning this general theory: our only point is, that this particular lover had such a prejudice in favor of reason, he was liable to lucid intervals. And in these intervals he was such a fearful bungler in all make-believe arts, he could hardly have been trusted to keep up successfully the pretence of finding folly and wisdom all the same thing, especially as the young woman in the case was visited by rather penetrative flashes of insight into the secret minds of men who made love to her. It seems to us fortunate, therefore, that there were some rational topics of conversation mutually possible to this *particular* pair. Moreover, a man does not usually appear to his best advantage when he is taken too violently out of all his natural modes of speech and lines of reflection; and, since Miss Monny had become so desperately charming to our hero, we suppose that all who wish him well will desire that he should now become equally charming to her. I do not know whether Kenyon Leigh was of the class of professed conversationalists or not; he was a man whose life was very largely lived in thought; he was accustomed to express his thoughts in words: what he had to say, therefore, on thoughtful subjects, could scarcely have failed to be interesting. It is certain that all which he said and did and was grew ever more and more interesting to young Monny Rivers. Indeed, this man and maiden were so utterly unlike, and yet so deeply akin, they had but to show themselves as they really were, to speak their own natural language, to find each in the other a supreme charm. And so, through all these wise conversations on impersonal subjects, they grew so well acquainted at last, that there came an afternoon when they had a little conversation somewhat personal and highly foolish. This dialogue it will be the need of our tale to report. All that wise and edifying discourse on themes ethical, æsthetical, and philosophical, which filled the long hours that the pair had spent together before the afternoon when this foolish little dialogue befell, will have to pass unrecorded. It will be understood that those talks were as deep as the small-talk which we are about to note is shallow. Yet, since the most momentous waves of human life often widen from some idlest little pebble of word or deed which the merest sportive chance has tossed into the current of things, in telling the tale even of a serious man, we must pass over his thoughtful words to give his trifling ones in some detail.

The place was the minister's study, and the time somewhere in the long summer afternoon following the early dinner-hour of half-past one. Miss Monny usually made whatever change she made from her morning toilet during the day, after, instead of before, that meal, adopting the rural fashion. The minister had a notion that she was about this pleasing duty now, and he was listening to hear her chamber-door open, planning to beguile her into bestowing her society on him a while, before resuming work in her studio. His own domain the young lady was still sufficiently shy of entering to make some strategy necessary to bring her there. So he had spread out on his study-table at this hour certain matters which we will assume to be objects of interest. But whether they were old engravings, curious books, or remarkable specimens of seaweed that he had picked up in his morning ramble, we need not pause to inquire; for, whatever the exhibition was, it was the merest pretext to insnare the visitor.

Well, the deep trap was got ready: there was a little echo from the maiden's door-latch, a soft rustle of skirts in the entry, the minister appeared on his threshold, and — "'Will you walk into my parlor?' said the spider to the fly."

The fly came walking in. Whether or no it was the prettiest of little parlors, it certainly was one of the prettiest of little flies, quite especially so this afternoon. It had got its hair up since dinner with some bewildering new grace: there was a gleam of gold chain about its neck. Its gown seemed to the man of the study, with its shimmering white and faint azure, to be made out of a piece of the summer-afternoon sky; but more prosaic observers would have perceived that it was only a demi-toilet of pale-blue underdress, hair-striped summer silk, with a white overdress of very fine embroidered Swiss muslin moderately frilled with lace. On one of the rolling folds in which the front of this snowy overdress was caught back had lodged some little gossamer waif, of a golden-brown color; which alien substance the admiring observer of Monny's afternoon toilet bent respectfully forward to remove. He found it rather a mysterious substance, something that might have been tiny locks of Monny's curling hair, which had thus shed themselves down on her gown : only hair did not usually fall out in exactly that way, at least, not from a man's scalp; viz., in a little strip of *woven* fringe about an inch and a half wide and twice that number of inches long.

" Oh, my rainy-day friz ! It must have dropped out of the box when I put away my morning switch. I had forgotten I had that friz," said Monny, looking down, and blushing a little that Mr. Leigh should have found any speck of disorder about her toilet. As for blushing at being detected in the use of artificial aids to hair-dressing, women were quite past blushing for this cause at the period of our tale, the year 187–, when the somewhat Fijian immensity of chignon which has so prevailed during the last decade had reached its most swollen proportions preparatory to a re-action in favor of the present simpler styles of arranging hair.

Rainy-day friz! *morning* switches! To the dazed masculine being who still held that atom of commercial hair between his thumb and forefinger, these words suggested a whole assortment of such lendings. Monny's morning hair, then, was a kind of second-best variety, that she had just taken off to put on — the contents of another box.

I confess at this moment the heart of his biographer does a little ache for Kenyon Leigh ; for, although he was not of those lovers who count up with a kind of appraiser's eye the " points " of the fair one whom they favor, he *had* observed the beauty of Monny's hair, and it chanced to be so arranged this afternoon, that, if any of it was put on, really the whole of it must be. So as his unpractised eyes now turned the first investigating glance of his life on a lady's head to see where nature ended, and art began, and could find no possible joining-place, what could he conclude, having understood that these things were managed to deceive the very elect, but that his beloved wore a solid wig?

Well, even under this startling hypothesis he stood firm: he still preferred Monny, hairless (but for the shops), to any other woman whose hair should sweep the ground. Virtue was presently rewarded in this man, as surely such virtue ought to be. Monny's tresses certainly never made a more luxuriant display than they did this afternoon, and there was not a hair on her head at this moment that was not growing quick out of the live cuticle that covered her ridiculous young skull. Ridiculous, I suppose, philosophy must pronounce the head, which, being provided by Nature with so bountiful and beautiful a covering as was Monny's, yet buys unto itself a switch, and at certain times and seasons actually wears it. But this absurd young daughter of the nineteenth century and its Fijian decade stood smiling tranquilly away there in the speechless face of the man as she said, —

"Oh! you do not like switches — I remember."

What Monny mistily remembered at the moment was sitting on the doorsteps once, with Clara Macey's switch, and being very pert to Mr. Leigh, in some old days which seemed so far off and impossible now. She wondered exactly how odious she had been at that time. The recollection somehow prompted her to go on now with a little winsome tone of arguing, —

"But truly, switches are a great convenience in the morning, when you are in a hurry to get to work right away, and do not want to spend the time to stuff yourself up with combs."

"To stuff — with combs," repeated Mr. Leigh so helplessly, Monny clapped her fair hand on her crown with an expository gesture as she said, "This way, you see."

The beholder so evidently did *not* see, the maid, laughing and blushing, pulled up to view a high back comb, over which she had heaped the soft masses of her hair to the fashionable altitude of the day. Monny had, in fact, curled all her hair in the morning in its own natural curls, and then loosely gathered them, while still damp from the brush, into a long invisible net. This informal little *coiffure* of the morning she had changed by simply pulling off the net, and arranging her curls, which had dried in all manner of graceful shapes in the confining net, high on the top of her head, leaving a few of them to fall free, while the others were looped over and around the comb

Also she had enhanced the slight natural waves of her hair by winding its front locks on two crimping-pins. Being less dependent on these implements than girls with naturally straight hair, she had not put them in over night at all, but only for a few hours in the morning, laying her switch round in a braid to hide them.

Any woman on reading the above description, which we trust we have made explicit enough to satisfy the most earnest inquirer, will at once perceive that the heroine's hair in the afternoon, when she wore only her own, would make twice the display that it did in the morning, when she wore also a switch. The hero, however had not quite mastered yet this new mathematics, in which to take away was to add, and *vice versa*. We return, therefore, to his case by stating that the foundation of this airy architecture of crimps and curls which Monny had built up on her head for the afternoon, being the comb, she had not moved it with impunity: some hair-pins fell out, and, after an ineffectual attempt to refasten the comb, down fell the whole shining cloud of tresses, and, lo ! not a hair of them fell off.

Fortunately this lover had held so fast to the woman through all the fluctuations of her hair, there had been no violent transitions in his face as one moment he mentally saw every fibre of Monny's hair vanish into a box, and the next moment its restoration in this indubitably genuine magnificence which now tumbled down over the maiden's shoulders. Still some atom of a gleam did come into his face as that spectre of the wig was so utterly abolished, — a look which made the wondering girl say, —

" Oh ! did you suppose *this* hair came off too? Oh, no ! This will pull," she laughed, winding her hand in her fleecy mane, and giving a vigorously demonstrative jerk to the head on which it grew.

"The proof is not satisfactory," said Mr. Leigh with
affected solemnity of tone, as he gravely advanced, perceiving how a lover's opportunity could be stolen to lay a
hand on that sacred head. "In all serious tests it is cus-
tomary to allow the audience to pull."

Like a frolicsome kid, Monny butted out her pretty head
for a consenting second, but she shied bashfully away
again when the coveted privilege was scarce tasted; and,
partly because she was a little fluttered by these new
familiarities, she ran out of the room, saying, "I will
show you my switch."

Back she presently walked with that thing of folly in her
hand, and held it out to Tertullian, — a nice little straight
switch, matching her own locks in color. He took it with
a delicious sense of becoming very intimate with Monny.
Intimacy with Monny was by no means easy to establish,
for all her frankness, and often childlike absence of punc-
tilio. She was emphatically a maiden who was at once
near, and very far. And, really, conversations ethical,
æsthetical, and philosophical, had never brought quite
that nearness, that enchanting sense of domesticity, which
the man felt in being honored with these confidences
about the switch. So he examined that object in his
hand with most respectful attention, even discovering the
three tails whereof it was composed, the tiny loop whereby
the humbug was pinned on.

"You see it is neat and *clean* as can be," argued the
young lady, composed now with all that calm abstraction
which naturally belongs to the logical frame of mind.
"It is not 'nasty heaps,' nor 'graveyard hair,' at all, as
the satirical writers say. You would suppose, from the
way those writers talk, that we went shearing the heads
of poor dead women all in their sepulchres to get our
switches, — that we were a kind of ghouls and body-
snatchers."

She looked so unlike a ghoul, with her bright, bright face blooming out of the lace neck-ruffle of that sweet gown, the listener could but smile. But the maid went on with all the seriousness of one who has the correct information to diffuse on a much misunderstood subject, —

"The real fact is, that the false hair is all cut from the heads of live women ; and the women like to sell it so as to have the money, — in Germany, and the other countries where their hair grows so fast, and they do not have the American climate to make it fall out and grow thin so early — do you truly think switches are a great weakness and folly?" the debater suddenly broke off, her mind including just now under the word "switches" the whole subject of woman's personal adornment, all the feminine fondness for pleasing array.

"Have I not just been taught that any one who should so slander this commodity," returned the gentleman, tenderly stroking the switch, "would only prove his crass ignorance of the great laws which have created commerce? — excess of product in one zone, and deficiency in another. But as I see one American head which the climate appears to have spared" —

"Oh!" laughed Monny, winding one hand in the flowing ringlets which Mr. Leigh's teasing glance surveyed alternately with that superfluity of a switch which he still held, "my hair is not so very thick. It is a kind of hair that puffs out when it is loose, but all goes to nothing when it is done up in solid braids." And she illustrated the notningness by giving a tight twist to the tresses in her hand, which, indeed, having the silken fineness of fibre belonging to some varieties of curling hair, made much less show in braids than hair of a coarser quality.

"Except for causing suffering Germany to languish in her commerce, I should say, then, it was a kind of hair that ought never to be done up in solid braids," returned the man, secretly reluctant to see that sweet shaken hair wound up again.

"Oh, everlasting curls are so monotonous!" replied the maid.

"Monotonous!" murmured Monny's admirer, wondering what about Monny could ever deserve that name. Then, merely to stir her up anew on the subject which kept her sitting so near, making those fascinating expositions as to how she did up her hair, he held up that almost invisible morsel of a rainy-day friz, looking from it to the head of the girl, whose own sunny locks hung on her temples like a golden fleece, as he asked, "And where, where, *where*, do you bestow this miserable string?"

"Oh, I never wear that at all!" said Monny, dimpling. "That is how I forgot it was in the box. I bought it, thinking I might want it some time. All the girls have them, for a convenience, when they are going to parties in the evening." The secret fact was, that Monny had a little personal dislike of false frisettes, as she made a distinction herself between stuffing out one's back hair, and wearing foreign locks dropping over the very forehead : still, since "the girls" wore them, she was bound to defend frisettes also. So she went on, "You see, you can crimp your own hair to look much prettier than any of those false crimps."

"Yes. I see that perfectly," replied the man, surveying the golden crinkling cloud which Monny's own hair made at this moment over her brow.

"So, of course," the maid went on, much too absorbed in the general argument to note any complimentary personal allusions, "if you are going to a party in the evening. you wish to save your own crimps fresh for that occasion. And it would be *truly* silly to shut yourself

up till evening, and still worse to show yourself, even
about your own house, not fit to be seen, in crimping-
pins."

"Certainly," responded the auditor, with the gravity
which he felt to be expected of him.

"So you have a false frisette, and you put that on in
the morning, right over your crimping-pins, with a little
ribbon or a braid; and there you are, all nice for the
whole day, and your own hair snug underneath in crimps,
ready to be taken down for the evening. I mean all this,
of course, when the weather is moist, which takes out
most crimps, except the false ones. Then, some of the
girls," added this expositor, wishing to make an exhaustive review of her subject, "have a rainy-day hat, with
false frizzes sewed round inside the brim. But I think
that *is* a little *too* barefaced; because, if your hat *should*
happen to blow off, it would give men a chance to
laugh."

"I think so," replied the present representative of that
sex, exploding with laughter, as Monny's revelations at
this point, and especially the air of serious reasoning with
which they were made, became too much for him.

"Do you dislike these things *very* much?" asked the
girl, still solicitously, of the amused man.

"On the contrary. Their utility has been so ably
argued to me, that I think of buying one of *these* things,
to begin small, for myself," declared Mr. Leigh, holding
up the imponderable bit of frisette. "I think the kind
that is sewed inside the hat will be the most convenient
arrangement for me. Since you do not wear this, can
you not lend it to me, to show in the shops as a sample
of the goods I want?"

All lovers will talk some nonsense which sounds not
very brilliant in the repeating; and these nonsensical

words of the Rev. Kenyon Leigh were merely uttered as a
cover to his serious intent of retaining the article which he
had vilified as a "miserable string," the same suddenly
striking him as a precious keepsake, since it belonged to
Monny.   " You really have no use for it?" he repeated.

"No," replied Monny, the smile which had gleamed
across her face at the fancy of a row of frisette curls
bobbing round Mr. Leigh's manly brows, becoming a
little bashful, as she said, "But I had some crimping-
pins in this morning my own self, and the switch worn
forward, in a coronet braid, to hide them. That is one
use for switches; and then I wear mine in other ways.
I really wear it very often when I braid up my hair."

Here, certainly, was an excellent opportunity for the
minister to exhort the young lady, over whom he had so
much influence at present, to set an example to her insane
sex by wearing her hair *au naturel* thenceforth. But
probably he was in that state of mind about Monny, that
her veriest follies were charming to him ; or it may be
that he had secretly found a very sweet young dignity in
the air of Monny's head with all that puffing-up of its
beautiful hair, made by the crimping-pins and the skilful
placing of the high-topped comb (the Fijian style in its
worst enormity was really capable of being made a grace
by some women, and that was what kept it going).

Certain it was that he still smiled so tolerantly at all
these confessions, that the maiden added, with her abid-
ing desire to show her sex in a fair light, "And many of
the girls have switches of their real own hair. I mean
hair cut from their very own heads."

"But this is not such?" returned the man, who was
attaining to such critical judgment in switches as to perceive that the hair in his hand was scarcely of so fine a
fibre as Monny's own soft locks.

"No: that was bought in a store," replied the girl. "I have never had my hair cut off at its full length but once ; and then — it was lost," she added hastily.

"Lost! And can it not be found?" involuntarily asked the lover, feeling as if priceless treasure had been cast away.

"Oh, no, no! it was lost — in a trunk. I was travel ling," replied Monny still more hastily. And with these words a sudden and most extraordinary blush flamed over her face.

Slight little blushes had touched this sensitive face before during the present interview, as some bashful feeling would come to the girl that she was pursuing a very ridiculous subject of conversation with an intellectual man ; but those soft fluctuations of color were not like this mysterious rushing red that so suddenly lit her cheeks to fire.

The very color was scarce to be forgotten. Any eye that saw for the first time Monny's translucent complexion kindle with one of her infrequent, intense blushes would be struck by the mere hue : it was the rose of the auroral lights, of sunset clouds. One involuntarily thought of those skyey tints. No color of any flower that blooms out of earthly soil seemed vivid enough to compare to that bright, rushing blood.

It paled in a moment, but then came pulsing back again ; and the embarrassed girl, rising up abruptly, retook her switch from Mr. Leigh, and, saying "I must go do up my hair again," fled confusedly out of the room.

What had startled her so? Maidenly shyness at sitting there any longer in her tumbled hair, a sudden access of personal consciousness in the midst of that *naïve* abstraction with which she was arguing the case of "the girls"? Kenyon Leigh's musings on that bright, burning blush, that hasty flight, probably did not go back of some such thought as this — not now. But a severer analyst than a lover would have recognized that Monny's embarrassment was scarce to be accounted for by any cause of the moment: it was an agitation too unlike herself. For beneath all her sensitiveness, her swift-changing moods, there was some quality of repose in the girl very unwont to be shaken into such a loss of self-possession as had marked her last fluttering exit from the room.

The desolated man left alone in the study could only realize, as he instinctively did, that this time Monny would not return. She did not. He had to gather up his bait of curiosities for another day. Nevertheless he felt that much remained to him from this intercourse — for one thing, the rainy-day friz. Consider the condition of a lover when he cherishes tenderly the charmer's *false* hair; when he hunts through all his possessions disconsolate at finding nothing quite choice and delicate enough to wrap the treasure in.

In the midst of this affecting spectacle of devotion which the Rev. Kenyon Leigh now presents we must pause to affirm that the present chapter is not intended to stimulate the trade in false hair, — Heaven forbid! Undoubtedly the Fijian style of hair-dressing conduced neither to the general health of woman, nor to the natural growth of her scalp; nevertheless, in its worst rage, total baldness at twenty-one was not a common condition, even among fashionable young ladies, although this might well be inferred from the Jeremiades of our day on woman's folly, some echoes of which had, doubtless, blindly lodged in the brain of the inexperienced minister. All the folly he found, however, in Monny's account of the girlish artifices of her mates, probably struck him as folly which had an extremely innocent side, — a discovery which ve

think some women of the day who are so severe on their
sex would do well to make.

It is a great pleasure to be pretty and to be eighteen:
and, when that short-lived pleasure is over, it would seem
that some memory of it should remain to the woman to
soften her judgment of the girls, even in their little vani-
ties, — their wish to be prettier every minute of their lives
than it is at all necessary to be. There *is* a very innocent
side to this folly; and how briefly lasts, as a rule, all of it
that can really be called folly!

That young defender of the girls, who was still one of
them, had evidently quite forgotten her hair now, in some
mysterious memories which her talk on that unique subject with Mr. Leigh had strangely evoked. Dropping her
switch absently on the toilet-table of her chamber, whither
she had so swiftly gone from the minister's study, she
stood, with her unbound curls falling round her, lost to
every thing but those silent reminiscences which still, in
the solitude of her own room, sent the blushes to her
cheeks. Presently she moved towards the door connecting
her two apartments, and went into her studio, walking
slowly, and still with that brooding, abstracted gaze as of
one who recalls, detail by detail, something long forgotten.
By that table against the wall, piled with folios, she paused,
and took from among them that same collection of her
old school-studies which Mr. Leigh had looked over the
first time he had ever been in that room. What she
sought was the picture in oils which he had called "the
handsome young *caballero*." It was soon found, and a
curiously troubled glance the girl now bestowed on it.
All that unruffled calm with which she had seen the picture
in Mr. Leigh's hand on the gone-by morning was broken
up. Yet this trouble in her face seemed scarce of regret,
no pain of loss; only the same confused, bashful, blushing

distress which had so overcome her when she hastened
out just now from Mr. Leigh's presence.

She laid down the picture, and began a search through
all the drawings dating back to her school-days : she was
examining if any other sketch of that same face was
among them. None was found ; and, laying the folios
back in their place, she took up again the picture of the
superbly handsome youth. Not stealthily, but very quietly, — her agitation had calmed in these moments, — she
carried it towards the old-fashioned fireplace in the room.
On its hearth some new impulse seemed to arrest her for
a moment, drawing her across the room, the painted
board still in her hand, to an easel which stood by a
window in the most favorable lights for working. A new
canvas was on the easel, the colors still wet upon it.
The picture portrayed a single powerful figure in the
garb of a Knight-Templar : it was painted life-size, and
about half-length. A certain card-photograph, which the
artist had possessed herself of unknown to its owner, was
pinned up on the easel : the knightly painting on the canvas had the face of the photograph. The mediæval armor
of the figure was evidently being copied from some old
engravings that were lying about.

With a shy, mysterious movement that seemed stirred
by the picture on the easel rather than by the one in her
hand, the girl slowly lifted the latter, holding it at arm's-
length, approaching it to the other picture, not too near,
but still with a survey that evidently compared the two
faces. And ever such a strange, triumphing tenderness
grew in those alternate glances as they sought the face on
the easel, as they lingered on it last and long.

Was it the artist that rejoiced so with that mysterious,
wondrous joy which seemed trembling at itself? Cer
tainly the progress marked by the two pieces of work was

immense. Modelled from the beginning was the unfinished face on the easel with some power of handling that
nothing else of all Monny's work approached. The likeness was already a living one ; but, for that matter, so was
the likeness of the face she held in her hand, — a face
she had painted before she was seventeen. Even in those
years Monny could seize a likeness. This latter likeness
she carried back now to the fireplace, and laid it between
the old-fashioned andirons. There was a box on the
hearth filled with the dried pine-needles which the little
Cape-Cod boys bring round in bags, and sell at the door
for kindlings.

Monny was a vast patron of pine-needles, as well as of
various other staples of small-boy traders, for which she
had no very urgent use. The pine-needles had a use
now ? heaping them high on the hearth, she applied a
lighted match to the pile, and in this aromatic blaze the
picture of the handsome youth went up.

CHAPTER XIII.

THAT new picture on the easel absorbed Monny as no work had ever done before. Her studio became an absolutely interdicted place to all mortals but herself. It was, in fact, the recent passing of this decree, banishing Mr. Leigh from her room, which had added stimulus to his ingenious efforts to draw the maiden into his own room, as exemplified in the last chapter. She grew so miserly, however, of her time now, few and short were the visits that he could secure from her there or elsewhere: in fact, meal-times were about the only times at present that he had for seeing the young lady.

"Can we not even know the *subject* of this extraordinary picture?" he asked one day, going with Monny up the front stairs after dinner, and managing to delay her a moment in the upper entry before she unlocked her studio-door, to disappear for the rest of the afternoon.

"It is a — battle-piece. I have not painted a battle-piece before since the lunacies of my first works. There were some marvellous battle-pieces among those. The carnage was dreadful."

"This time, the life-blood spilt will be that of the artist," said the lover. "I have seen her growing pale every day since this murderous work began."

"It is such a strain," replied Monny, with a deep sigh of affected exhaustion, "to imagine heroes in this poor, degenerate era! So far, far back, I have to look for them — way back into the middle ages! One must needs grow pale with such an effort," said the girl, her secret heart thrilling with a thought how opposite from the words her mischievous lips spoke.

"But you must be obliged to borrow, even out of this miserable age, models for the corporeal outlines of those heroes. I do not hear them coming up stairs to the studio, — neither the soldiers nor the steeds. How do you study the grouping of your figures?"

"There is no group, not a steed. It is a battle-piece of — one."

"Oh! Is the warrior falling on his own sword?"

"Never! never! He is not the warrior to do that."

"Will he do the deed and repent it? — he had better never been born.
Will he do the deed, and exalt it? — then his fame shall be outworn:
He shall do the deed, and *abide* it, and sit on his throne on high,
And look on to-day and to-morrow as those that never die."

As the lover stood in admiring amaze at the sudden burst of dramatic fire with which these lines were recited, the girlish voice thrilling rich and resonant with such a depth and compass of tones as one would scarce have imagined it to possess, Monny turned in its lock the key on which her hand rested, and in a second she had passed through the door, having opened it narrowly as possible. From within showed only the half of her tantalizing face as she peeped back through the crack to say wickedly, —

"It is time now for that afternoon slumber of mine The feeble-minded must have naps, — naps five hours long, by daylight."

Wherewith swiftly clashed the door, and clicked the little bolt in its lock; and the man was left speechless without, wondering what other of his base misconceptions

of Monny in the past the witch had found out, and stored
up in remembrance against him.

Bitterness was no longer in these remembrances. In
fact, from the very brokenness of the moments in which
any speech could now be seized with Monny, the *naïveté*
with which her admirer openly laid in wait for these scraps
of intercourse, the pretexts with which the engrossed
artist put him off, — from all this there grew an infor-
mality of talk between the pair in which their acquaintance certainly went not backward, although the long talks
were suspended. All the sportive side of the girl's character began to come out, unafraid, during these days, in a
thousand *espiègleries*, caprices, as native to her as the
foam is to the wave ; and in this dancing temperament, as
in the serious young soul beneath it, Monny Rivers was
created to be a perpetual charm and benison to Kenyon
Leigh.

In many ways his life had been lived at an intense, too
intense, a strain. It is not the radical, hurling his axe
unquestioningly at the root of every tree of abuse, who
really wears himself out, but the man who has at once
the radical hatred of what is wrong in society, and the
conservative vision of all the long and slow gathered good
liable to be uptorn in exterminating the evil. Men of
this balance of mind, especially when they are men of
such poetic sensibility as was Kenyon Leigh, are probably
wont, as a rule, to spend their lives rather in eloquent
exposition of the world's disorders than in any active,
practical attempts to right them. Especially are they
unlikely to choose a pulpit as the standing-place from
which to right them, at least in the present age. This
minister, perhaps, never preached in his great city church,
when, in the varied crowd that filled it, there were not
men who came there, drawn by very wonder to see this

man, so simple, calm, and strong, stand up, and with his
most luminous, instructed mind, rest all that he had to
say of life and death on those old hallucinations of a
crucified Jew. He was sincere, as we have said, in this
simple faith of his : nevertheless, to him, as to another,
existence was full of burning, unsolved questions. He
was a man who could not live without some theoretic largeness of belief in life, could not be satisfied with dabbling,
however diligently, in any mere surface of the stream of
human evils ; and he saw too well how elusive were all the
real sources of that stream to have the self-complacency in
his toils which comforts more shallow men. His mental
traits would never be altered, and it was not in his character to slacken any of his manifold labors. Such spirits
cannot ease themselves by throwing down any of those
burdens of humanity which they are framed to bear with
so vicarious a pain : a great counterpoise of happiness is
the only balance which will save even the strongest of
them from some morbidness at last.

This most unimagined deliverance had come of late to
Kenyon Leigh : he had not laid down any thing of the old,
but he had taken up something strangely new. Yes : while
it would be a very inadequate stating of the case to say
that he had had a long fit of the blues, which, falling in
love, he had forgotten, it was still true, that, in this great
experience of the man, the minister had got his new start.
Certainly sermons did not progress much just now ; but
the influence which was at present a distraction from all
work prophesied of a future when it would be a stimulus
to work wonderful and new with all the wonder and newness with which life was opening to Kenyon Leigh in
these days, which had now begun to thrill with a hope
that Monny might be his.

So, since the minister had got at last his vacation just

as he had given it up, a respite from all the jarring grind
of life in a burst of the music of the spheres, we trust
the severest censor of ministerial vacations will forgive
him for wanting a little more of it. For about this time
he went to New York to arrange for just a small piece
more of holiday. He was really only proposing to extend
his vacation to its original limit, an early date in October,
which had been fixed for his return when he went on his
late foreign tour. But, when he had landed at New York
in the summer, he had informed his church-wardens, or
whomever he had to inform, that he should take his pulpit
again a month earlier than he had been expected to,
intending then to spend only a few weeks at Cape Cod.
But, since Cape Cod had become the centre of the world
to him, he now wished to claim again his original grant of
vacation. And since this was the first time in his mortal
career that he had ever taken one day's vacation on a
lady's account, and as choosing a wife is usually allowed
to be an affair of moment, especially to a clergyman,
we repeat our entreaty that the hero be not denounced
as a hireling shepherd for being just this once a laggard
at his post. It was really almost impossible for him to
ask Monny formally to marry him just yet, for want of
a chance to see her long enough in the privacy which
such questions demand, because of that terrible battle-
piece of one which kept her so invisible. But, as she
had begun to throw out hints that it was growing towards
completion, there were hopes of days beyond more propi-
tious for declarations, if the suitor could be on the spot.
He could not think of leaving the spot. So he went to
New York to arrange about the supplies for his pulpit.
When this business was despatched, he would not leave
the city, of course, without attending to one of those little
rites with which courtships, by civilized man and by sav-

age, have, in all ages of the world, been carried on. He
wished to make Monny a present. *What* should it be?

The solicitude with which the present suitor pondered
this question language cannot describe. Was it treasures
in the way of literature or art that he thought of for this
oblation? Not at all. Something of fresh or rare in these
lines he would take back to Monny from the metropolis as
a matter of course. But if he had had the markets of the
world to choose from in books, or objects of art, or *vertu*,
not in these would have been *the* gift to the maiden that
his soul was set on. *The* gift must be something to —
wear. Monny could not help knowing how he admired
her genius and her sense, but *did* she know how he doted
on her clothes? She read largely the same books that he
read : nothing would be easier now (however it was a few
weeks ago) than to select books for Monny. But to give
her something most exquisitely difficult to select, most
absolutely feminine, to suit her taste where it was so
subtly delicate a matter to suit it, that only a lover of the
last devotion, the most appreciative worship of every
refinement of her being, could possibly succeed in the
feat, — this was the man's dear ambition.

Jewelry he set aside at once. In the first place, he did
recall so much of the conventional etiquette in these
things as to have a notion that very costly presents from
a gentleman to a lady who was not formally betrothed to
him would be a little premature, have some air of antici-
patory reliance on her favor, an audacity of presump-
tion that he would shudder to be guilty of. Then jewels
he would have to depend on a shopman to tell him the
intrinsic worth of ; they could not be his own sole selection : there would be an utter spoiling of his idea. No,
the something to wear must not only be something of his
very personal choice, but it must be most personally fitted

to Monny; not a necklace or a brooch that any woman could wear.

Well, at last, as the very acme of all that was most baffling in the feminine toilet, he bethought himself of those objects which women wear on their heads, called hats and bonnets; those things which now they tilted over their noses, and anon perched precarious afar on the farthest reaches of their back hair; which this season were all buttoned up askew over one ear, and *presto!* the next season, all peeled up on the other — the lovely method that he began to discern in this· madness! A hat, a new hat, was what he would buy for Monny. He trembled at his own daring; but still, when, after their long circling round, his thoughts had once alighted on that form of present, they clung to it as to no other.

Behold our hero, then, in a milliner's shop. By what process of inquiry he arrived at that precise depot of elegance, the millinery parlors of Madame ——, most *recherché* of all New-York milliners, he got there. Also he got in, although the establishment was as good as closed at present; all its hands being secluded in some invisible work-rooms, preparing for the fall openings, which would not occur until Madame's polite class of patrons should be returned to the city. Madame —— herself would doubtless have recognized at once the very widely known person of the rector of St. Ancient's, where so many of her bonnets went to church; but that milliner was much too elegant a being to be yet permanently returned to town herself. However, Mrs. ——, her chief deputy milliner, who reigned in her absence, although she did not know who the stranger was, having come to New York herself only within the year, could not resist this imposing figure of a gentleman so devotedly bent on buying a bonnet for a lady out of town. So the Re-

Kenyon Leigh was honored with a distinction to which no patron of Madame —— had ever before attained, — a grand opening was made solely for himself.

Behold him, then, in the centre of the chief millinery parlor, — a long *salon* curiously mixed of shop and drawing-room, but now in so dismantled a state that not much was to be seen in it beyond a forest of empty little stands of wire. This forest, however, was soon made to blossom utterly beyond the rose, as the milliner took from great cavernous drawers which were let into walls and tables in all directions, the choicest of Madame ——'s new trimmed hats and bonnets, hiding their richness there until the fall openings.

These head-pieces were so infinitely more incomprehensible as they nodded at him from the bodiless wire stands than they had ever been coming into church as the apex of a fine lady, the minister began to realize all the magnitude of his undertaking: the sweat stood on his brow.

"Was it to be a hat for driving, opera, church?" asked the milliner.

He should like a hat that *could* be worn to church. "But still a handsome hat," quickly added this back-slidden Tertullian, forgetful of the rigid plainness with which women should be attired at church.

"Was the hat wanted for immediate wear?" asked Mrs. ——.

"He should like it to be worn right away," the customer said, thinking of next Sunday, and the little Orthodox meeting-house of Lonewater.

The milliner made a rapid shifting of the wire stands, massing directly in front of the gentleman all the head-coverings most suited to this precise turning-time of the seasons, opening new drawers, and adding more hats to the collection.

The gaze with which the man surveyed this collection was curiously unlike the masculine blankness of gaze to be expected. It was a look, which, while touchingly helpless, was withal so critical, such an unhappy shadow in the eyes that went wandering over the *chefs-d'œuvres* of Madame —— as of a being haunted by an ideal dream of beauty in the shape of a hat utterly unfound there, — this was really a variety of the *nil admirari* air to stir both the pride of the milliner and the sympathy of the woman. She stood silently conjecturing what was the probable personal style of the destined wearer of that hat. Her first notion, of some stately queen of society, who could carry off a great deal of bonnet, began to be displaced by the wiser second thought, that if the case was of a veritable *grande passion*, as clearly it was, then, of course, it was a case of the attraction of opposites. The lady whom this tallest of men had fallen in love with would not be tall: no, if she was not absolutely *petite*, it would be a mercy.

Well, that mercy had been vouchsafed. Monny was not *petite*, still she would not have been called a tall young woman : so the milliner was really approximating to some correct notion of the figure of the unknown. Whether along with this new notion came an idea of girl-ishness, she ventured to inquire, —

" Is the lady *very* young and ? " —

" *Very* young and beautiful," replied the admirer, with the promptest decision.

"Ah ! Then she can wear the most trying things. The simplest hats are really much the most trying," said the milliner, who understood her business. " Nothing so sets off the face that can bear it as a hat of a certain striking and elegant simplicity. But only an absolutely fresh face can venture on those things," declared Mrs. ——, turning to some drawers where were stored against the coming winter opera hats for the young beauties in their first season.

"Elegant simplicity; that is precisely the lady's style of dress," said the customer, eagerly catching at the word, and beginning to follow the milliner all round the room, opening the drawers for her.

If any one fancies that the transaction in which the Rev. Kenyon Leigh was now engaged was one in which that vein of shyness which still somewhat inhered in him would at all appear, nothing could be a greater misconception. To see nothing at all but his object, when that object was a great one, was a marked characteristic of this man; and the wholly unembarrassed and absorbingly earnest quest with which his own eyes searched the drawers (he could look into them right over the milliner's head), and the perfectly pellucid candor with which he gave any information about his lady-love that could facilitate the finding of her affinity of a bonnet, — these things made the milliner more and more ready to ravage the shop for him.

"Blue, I think you mentioned as a favorite color with the lady, and that her complexion was fair?" interrogated Mrs. ——.

"Most exceedingly fair," declared the admirer.

They were looking into a drawer now whose hats certainly only the exceedingly fair could afford to put on. Hats like a snowdrift of white velvet, with white plumes, and some little knot or wreath of blue; then pale-blue velvets, white-plumed and white-wreathed : among these lovely head-pieces was one charming *chapeau*, somewhat plainer than the rest, which the milliner drew forth. It was a white-chip hat of the finest quality, its only trimming a very rich ostrich-plume of the loveliest light blue, sweeping back over the half-high crown, and a wreath of convolvulus, dyed in the solid color to match the plume, running along the brim of the hat, which was rolled smoothly up, and faced with black velvet, in a style destined to become very popular, but which just then was entirely novel on this side the water. The anxious eyes which were looking over the milliner's shoulder saw at once in this hat something which really looked like Monny. Here were no flaps and streamers of silk and lace dragging on one side, and variegated bouquets bunching on the other, with birds roosting around promiscuously, as in the compositions which the milliner had shown him in her first idea of the lady who could carry off so much bonnet. Mrs. —— perceiving, with but a glance at her customer, that she had found the right thing at last, began to explain to the neophyte, that, this hat being of chip, it was entirely suitable to be worn to church; that the delicate blue of the plume and wreath was the most choice of all created shades of blue; and that the darkening touch imparted by the black velvet brim was just the touch appropriate to September.

This having in the hat the very touch belonging to September struck the awed man as so fine a felicity, it offset the little anxiety he had felt lest the black-velvet brim added too many colors to the hat; for one fundamental principle that he had grasped in the bewitching mystery of Monny's toilets was that she wore the very fewest colors at a time. But the milliner, on a hint of this trouble, gently assuring him that a lady of elegant taste would be certain to wear always a black suit with this particular hat, so the black-velvet brim, instead of introducing a new color, would be only another point of harmony in her toilet, — with this suggestion his eased mind was enabled fully to accept the black-velvet brim.

So there remained only a single point of doubt, — an ornament where the plume was fastened on, that flashed with some metallic sharpness of glitter not quite suggestive of Monny's style to her admirer.

"You do not like the aigrette?" said Mrs. ——, as he indicated this too-lustrous object. "It can be changed for another in a moment. Still this is a very elegant one. I am not sure that we **have** another quite so choice."

The gentleman's reply revealed that his thought was, whether the hat could exist without any spangle or bangle at all.

"Something would have to replace the aigrette, if it were taken off," mildly pronounced the milliner. A plain velvet bow, either of black or blue, would answer," she said, and disappeared for a moment. Returning presently, she brought with her bias strips of blue velvet and of black, and, deftly twisting a knot of each, she laid them on the hat, each in turn, that the gentleman might choose which he preferred.

"Put your soul to it." He recalled Monny's old dictum in matters of the toilet, and was ready to put his soul, every immortal spark of it, to deciding whether that bow should be of black or blue. As he stood thus concentrating all the brains of the Leighs — and there was a great deal of brains in the family — on those two rags of velvet, I trust it will be acknowledged, in excuse of the feminine world who had so adored this man, that he had some adorable qualities. After a silent travail of mind over the blue bow, which ended with the fear that it would introduce an alien element, as he could not find any blue velvet anywhere else about the hat, he begged the milliner, Would she please hold the black bow on once more? And the milliner held it on. But the black bow seemed too black to him; until, lo! he actually originated an idea. "Could that kind," he asked, pointing to the wreath, "be stretched out, or could some more of it be pieced on, so as to wind over the bow, and thus soften the blackness a little?"

"Certainly," replied Mrs. ——, astonished at the millinery genius of the man. The spray was a very rare one : but they had just one duplicate of it, on another hat of a different style ; she would take it off at once, and cut it for this hat. So she stripped the other hat, and twined some more convolvulus over the black-velvet bow as if it grew there ; and, behold, the thing was achieved at last, — a hat which was just that marvel of quiet beauty and elegance which Monny's hat should be.

Elated with his success, the man even dared a second purchase. There were some simple little garden-hats, very fashionable this summer, made all of white lawn, shaped by slender little reeds on which the lawn was puffed. Seeing a half-dozen of these hats stacked on a table, he remembered that Monny had worn such a one during his first weeks at the Cape, and that one morning, when he had seen her go out with this snowy head-covering, which he thought marvellously becoming to her, she came home bareheaded, the light thing having blown off her head into the sea. He had missed it ever since, and now he had a chance to replace it. Taking up one of the hats from the table, he perceived, with his present critical eye in millinery, that the lawn was not of the finest, and he asked the milliner if she had other such hats, in a better quality of cloth. She replied that the ready-made lawn hats did not come in any finer material, but that she could have one made to his order in an hour or two, in the finest of lawn. And he gave the order immediately.

"They sometimes trimmed those garden-hats very tastefully," said Mrs. ——, "with flutings and bows of the lawn, edged with imitation Valenciennes lace. Should the hat be made in that way?"

"Certainly, if that was prettier. But he should not wish any thing of imitation about it." And the milliner wrote down " real Valenciennes " on the order.

"Would he have a little colored ribbon fluted round under the brim, with strings of the same? It was an addition; and the lady could easily take it off if she did not like it. Should the color of the ribbon be blue also for this hat?"

The gentleman said that there was a very remarkable kind of purple sometimes worn by the lady.

"Mauve?" suggested the milliner. The man looked helpless at that word, but said he should know the particular purple if he could see it. So he was shown boxes of ribbons in all imaginable shades of violet and lilac; and, picking out his particular purple with the slow but sure sagacity that he had all along displayed, the milliner approved it as a very choice shade of mauve, and the second hat was settled. If we were to mention the figure paid for his two purchases, it would be seen that this was one of those lover's attentions which it were really well should cease after marriage, as Monny certainly could buy her own bonnets with far less expenditure of money as well as of vital force. But the milliner, discerning, of course, that the more money the lover could pay for his bonnets, the happier he would be, had the benevolence to fix prices accordingly; and, paying her unconscionable bill, the purchaser joyfully departed, carrying with him the blue-plumed chip in a bandbox, and ordering the other hat to be sent to his hotel.

After this performance in ladies' shopping, it was, of course, the easiest of tasks for the hero now to buy a dress-pattern of the best black silk for good Mistress

Doane, a gay striped shawl of the newest fall styles for
Susannah, and, that he might carry every inmate of that
beloved old Cape-Cod house something to wear, he wound
up with a new collar for Duke George.

The morning having been consumed by these pursuits,
he next went to lunch at his old club-house, having
ordered all parcels sent to his hotel, save the bandbox
containing the hat arrived at with so much toil and pains :
that precious possession never left his hand. It chanced
that almost the first man whom he met at his club was that
eminent light of the New-York medical profession, Dr.
Herophilus. The two not having seen each other before
for a year, they sat down to table together ; and, as the
serious reader will be glad to know, Mr. Leigh forthwith
toned up his mind, after the enervating occupations of the
morning, by plunging into a vigorous discussion of European politics, and such other weighty matters of men's
discourse.

Now, Dr. Herophilus was a creature of learning and
skill, — a highly knowing member, in fact, of the knowing sex. Why, then, should the thoughts of so masculine
a being stray ever and anon, as they did, from those large
themes which he was discussing with his companion, into
certain curious little surmises about him of the merest
personal sort? The truth was, that Mr. Leigh, in various
ways, touched him with a little sense of surprise. For
instance, he had supposed that his early return from
abroad had been moved by a characteristic eagerness to
be at his work again. But here he was, in superb health,
as the professional eye could see, yet coming up to town
to put supplies in his pulpit that he might stay summering
at Cape Cod through all the September breezes, which,
one would say, would soon sweep somewhat chill over
those lonely sands. Then, Dr. Herophilus *did* observe

the bandbox. As a family-man he knew it infallibly for
what it was, — a lady's bonnet-box.

To be sure, the Rev. Kenyon Leigh had been seen
before in his life laden with rather odd parcels. Not that
he was what is properly called an eccentric man : he had
been reared as a gentleman, and ordinarily he made no
startling deviations from what are conventionally styled
the habits of gentlemen. But, while he did not parade
himself in the vocation of express or market man, he was
capable of carrying a provision-basket as unconsciously
as another man carries a cane, if in his walks he chanced
on a place where a full provision-basket was directly
needed, and no one else directly at hand to fetch it. So,
at one time and another, the rector of St. Ancient's had
been seen with such matters in his hand, that perhaps
there was no variety of luggage which it would have been
entirely astonishing to see him carrying about town, except
that precise variety which he had with him to-day. Of
course Dr. Herophilus, having also the habits of a gentleman, asked no open questions, since his companion volunteered no explanation of this most suggestively feminine
appurtenance which the latter handled so delicately, bestowing it, as he sat down to table, first in one spot, and
then in another, before he could be satisfied that it was
absolutely well placed. Still the bandbox wrought on his
secret mind.

The fact was, that there was already lodged in the
physician's mind a little circumstance with which these
wandering impressions of something unusual and very
newly domestic about the Rev. Kenyon Leigh made a
kind of conjunction. Mrs. Van Cortlandt had landed in
New York from a European steamer a few days before.
Her first stopping-place had been her town residence ; but
it was early yet formally to open that, and she had signi-

fied to Dr. Herophilus, whom she had called in professionally, her wish to find a *very* quiet seaside place, *utterly* removed from society, in which to restore herself for a few weeks. She had, in fact, mentioned Cape Cod as the place she had thought of for this recuperative retreat.

There was nothing the matter with the lady's constitution beyond a little temporary fatigue consequent on her Atlantic voyage ; and her attempt to get sent by a physician's prescription to that precise spot where the Rev. Kenyon Leigh was sojourning had quietly tickled the medical mind. For it is perhaps needless to state that every one who personally knew Mrs. Van Cortlandt knew her long designs on the rector of St. Ancient's, save that gentleman himself. And as there was a Mrs. Herophilus, this Benedict was naturally well posted in all the fine points of the widow's strategy. That strategy, it seemed, was growing bolder. For Mrs. Van Cortlandt to be following the minister quite so openly as to take board beside him in the extremely isolated region where he had now hidden himself, — this was a remarkably new advance on the widow's old feline policy. And still more remarkably new in the Rev. Kenyon Leigh was the policy of putting supplies in his pulpit when he could be there himself. What did it all mean? queried the doctor.. Had the huntress really brought down the game at last in some of the opportunities of her late European tour? Was there to be a little quiet fixing-up of things down there in the Cape-Cod desert, afar from town gossip, and would the minister retake his pulpit in October a married man? All these speculations to come out of a bandbox in which was hiding — another woman's bonnet.

Still the speculations did not hang very well together, even in the originator's mind. In the first place, his professional interview with the widow had not exactly given him the impression that there was as yet an actual understanding between the pursuer and the pursued. What *did* it all mean?

There are certain men, and the invulnerable rector of St. Ancient's was eminently one of them, concerning whom even their own sex ask, with some curiosity, whether they will ever really marry, and who the woman will be. Will they be conquered at last by a supreme charm, or entrapped by a supreme artifice?

Perhaps Dr. Herophilus, merely in the interests of pure philosophy, wished to see whether Mrs. Van Cortlandt and the Rev. Kenyon Leigh furnished one more proof of that saying of Mr. Thackeray, quoted in the early part of this history, as to the sure reward of female determination in such pursuit of a man. Or it may be that he was moved by a simple marital desire to carry Mrs. Herophilus, still summering out of town, a striking bit of news at this particularly dull season. But whatever his motive, certainly with as smug a countenance as was ever worn by any feminine gossip throwing out an apparently careless remark as a bait to catch personal information, this man of science said, somewhere in the midst of views on Bismarck and the Ultramontanes, —

" By the way, this hamlet at Cape Cod that you find so charming — is there a habitation there where a lady could board? Mrs. Van Cortlandt has just arrived home, as you may know, and was speaking to me yesterday of her wish to find just such a place as yours seems to be."

With these tentative words, the doctor, who was making a very hearty luncheon, — having breakfasted unusually early, and expecting to dine extremely late, — helped himself to another slice of the fowl he had ordered. It was a superior kind of bird, served with some French sauce which he ladled out just now in a very absorbed

way, whether because he was ashamed of himself, or
because, while looking very intently at a dish, one is well
placed to flash an apparently careless glance into a face
opposite

He might have looked at the face opposite half an
hour, it would still have remained a complete enigma to
him.   Nothing is so absolutely fathomless sometimes to a
sophisticated world as pure simplicity.   The only effect
on Kenyon Leigh of the woman's name which had been
thus fired at him was to make him wish most cordially to
do her a service.   He wished it more cordially than if she
had been any other member of his parish.   Not quite as
he would have heard any other name had he heard the
name of Mrs. Van Cortlandt; not that he thought of
the woman, so suddenly recalled out of the total oblivion
into which she had fallen to him, with any shadow of
compunction.   Clear as noonday was his sense that he
had never paid her any significant attentions; no less
clear was his unconsciousness that she had ever paid him
any.   But in his great experience of a real passion, and
in that deepened reverence for all women which had come
with his adoration for one woman, he had some sense as
if he had done Mrs. Van Cortlandt an irreverence in his
thought by having ever entertained even a fugitive idea
of her as a possible wife when he did not love her.   His
feeling was but an undefined one; for it was like an inconceivable chimera to him now that he had ever had any
marrying thoughts of the widow at all.   Still some
memory of such thoughts, vaguely stirring in his consciousness, were probably at the bottom of his especial
eagerness to serve her now, — the eagerness as of one who
has some little reparation to make.

Then another feeling, still more unformulated, may
have entered into the abounding welcome with which he

was ready to invite marriageable ladies into boarding-places of the most suggestive neighborhood to himself: he had drawn his last breath as a bachelor, so far as there being any woman in the universe, save one, who could ever more be the object to him of sentimental attentions. So married he felt himself already to be, for time and for eternity, he could plant the handsomest of widows and maidens round him right and left, in that large liberty towards all womankind wherewith his bond to one woman had set him free forever. Sweet is emancipation to a naturally liberty-loving soul; and joyful to a naturally benevolent spirit the finding itself suddenly enabled to extend to a whole sex just benevolence, and no more, in a world where it has been a little difficult to show them just that attribute, and no more.

Thus altogether the minister responded with the most exuberant heartiness to the remarks which the artful Herophilus had thrown out as a trap.

"Certainly. There is one house in the town" (he was thinking of Capt. Gawthrop's) "where I am almost sure Mrs. Van Cortlandt could have board. She will understand, of course, what accommodations are to be expected in these remote places; but nothing could be more obliging than the people. And I am certain she could be made quite comfortable there," he said, aware that Mrs. Van Cortlandt could pay for whatever "comforts" she wished added to the Gawthrop arrangements. "Tell her from me that I can thoroughly recommend the little town as a perfect retreat; and I believe, also, the house will be satisfactory enough. Stay, I will write her a note myself, and tell her where to telegraph if she wishes to go at once." And, calling a waiter to bring pen and paper, the Rev. Kenyon Leigh was presently writing his note to Mrs. Van Cortlandt.

The man of science sat as nonplussed as ever a man of science was who had indulged a moment's fancy to play the gossiping fool. Some such names as this he began liberally to bestow on himself in his mind; for, with all his nonplussed state, he saw the writing of that note go on with a kind of remorse. The fact was, the physician happened to know the beautiful widow too well to think her at all the wife for Kenyon Leigh. And was it possible that that gigantic piece of innocence, as he sat there writing to her, did not know that he was writing to a woman who wished to marry him? *Was* he extending to her a merely humane invitation to take a neighboring lodge in his wilderness? and was he, Dr. Herophilus, the means of it, — the means which was to bring this blind victim into such deadly near range of the sharp-shootress? It is verily to be suspected that the doctor was somewhat a believer in Mr. Thackeray's philosophy; for he saw the most fatal liabilities in the isolation of the minister and the determined widow, through the weeks to come, on these Cape-Cod sands.

So he sat discomforted, as meddlers should, while the minister wrote his note, directed it, and, calling the waiter again, sent it by a private messenger to the lady's house, that she might receive it at once.

The Ultramontanes did not come up again after this little interruption; for the minister informed his friend that he had to take a run to Philadelphia before returning to the Cape, and had still some more business in the city: in short, he presently shook hands and departed, taking with him that Pandora bandbox out of which had verily flown certain winged mischiefs, wheeling their dark flight, to bring the widow, the maiden, the minister, to most fateful meetings.

CHAPTER XIV.

I] was Saturday evening when Mr. Leigh came again
to the Cape. Mrs. Van Cortlandt he had nowhere
seen; but that lady, on receiving his note in New York,
had lost no time. Engaging her boarding-place by telegraph, and making her journey thither by steam, the
minister, moreover, using up a day by his trip to Philadelphia, she arrived at Capt. Gawthrop's house just one
train in advance of the train which brought Mr. Leigh
again to Mrs. Doane's. At the latter house that evening,
there was, after tea, a little scene in the front sitting-
room. The returned traveller had deposited on a table
there sundry packages of the sort which make returned
travellers in general so interesting; viz., the presents
which he had brought for the household.

So, while Mrs. Doane unrolled and beheld her dress-
pattern with that profound thrill of satisfaction which
black silk of the best quality conveys to the heart of
woman, and while Susannah performed a true Ethiopian
dance of delight over the brave glory of her new shawl,
and ran to find "his Honor," who had become invisible
at this moment, Monny dipped into her two bandboxes,
and drew forth with blushing amaze their contents.

She tried on both the hats by the ancient gilt-framed
looking-glass. She took them off, and looked their dainti-
ness all over by the kerosene globe-lamp. To the last
shadow of a shade each of them suited her taste and her
style. She had the blue-plumed hat on her head, and the

half-transparent white one poised like a snow-wreath on her hand, when Mr. Leigh came into the room.

"Real Valenciennes on a garden-hat! Oh, what awful extravagance!" cried Monny, as the first manner of salute which she could trust her voice to make to that gentleman. For, knowing very well that a lawn hat with such trimmings had never been made but to a special order, she was thinking of all it implied for Mr. Leigh to have discovered any language in which to communicate detailed directions to a milliner.

For himself — the novice in buying ladies' bonnets stood looking at the adored one's head to see how the chip hat became her. "Her hair is pretty, but she isn't pretty in her hair," was a remembered speech of Miss Monny, which had terribly haunted him in the milliner's shop, warning him that not only the hat must be pretty, but Monny must be pretty in the hat. Well, surely nothing could be prettier than Monny in the chip hat, except Monny in the lawn one, and *vice versa*. She tried them on now by turns; she whirled slowly round to be looked at; then she stood still, with the garden-hat on her head and the dress-hat in her hand, to admire again the points of the latter.

"It was — made a little different at first," said the anxious man, drawing near, and looking down also on the hat, which Monny was turning about under the lamplight. "There was a glittering substance there," pointing as he spoke, "which I thought might not quite suit you; and so I had it cut off. But I have brought it, in case you wished to fix it on again;" and he solemnly drew from his vest-pocket the aigrette wrapped up in tissue-paper. Then he proceeded, in words very crude indeed, but which were strangely significant to Monny, to explain about that experimenting with the blue-velvet

bow and the black one. Did she suppose she would have
liked the blue one better? he asked, in such a tone as if
he might be going up to weep on his pillow because he
did not get the blue bow after all.

Monny looked slowly up at these quaint explainings
(Mrs. Doane, having offered her thanks, had vanished
discreetly out of the room), and the maiden's eyes met
her lover's with a long, silent gaze.

Considering all that had been in the early acquaintance
of these two, pretty things to wear would have been a
very dangerous line of presents for the man to make to
this keen-eyed girl, if there had been one grain of false
quality in the impulse which had moved him to just these
gifts. But she saw to the bottom of his thought, and
knew that not as one pets a beloved doll, humoring its
doll-like fancies, had her lover brought her tokens like
these. A longing to make the *amende honorable* to Monny
for all his early mistaken judgment of her, to tell her
how charming to him was the very lightest foliage of her
character, as well as its enduring roots of worth, — in this
lover's longing, —

" Once, and only once, and for one only," could Kenyon
Leigh master the high science of ribbons and flowers and
feathers ; and for once in the world a New-York milliner's
bonnet became poetic as over it the understanding eyes of
these two met in a look wherein all was spoken.

Words were not spoken here, however; for just now
Duke George must push the unlatched door with his nose,
and walk in, Susannah in his wake, ostensibly to take out
the dog, but really because she could no longer restrain her
curiosity to see what " his Honor " had brought for Miss
Monny. So the bonnets were displayed to this fresh
audience ; and then Monny bent down, and clasped his new
collar round Duke George's neck, and Mrs. Doane was

called in to see bonnets and dog-collars, and altogether it became a family scene again.

So we will glance at that other house, half a mile away, where, also, was a newly-arrived traveller. Mrs. Van Cortlandt was standing at a window of that house, looking out, while her maid unpacked her trunks, into the misty night which wrapped all the strange, low-lying Cape shores. She was triumphing in the thought that this was her last journey after Kenyon Leigh. She did not pretend, even to herself, that he had ever yet paid her any lover's attentions. But the briefest term of courtship, whose first step would be absolute assurance for the last, was just what she had expected of the man; and a most prodigious first step for him, she counted it, that he had invited her here. Moreover, she knew that all the latter days in which she had seen Kenyon Leigh, at home and in Europe, had been peculiarily favorable days for her. This was true. Who shall say how all that mysteriously fatal pressure which the years exert to reduce every ideal aim to the commonplace standard had wrought on Kenyon Leigh to bring him to a mere *mariage de raison* at last? It is time to adjust one's self to life as it is, to follow no longer the young dream of what it is, had been an underlying thought with him about all things during this thirty-fourth of his, — the storm-tossed year, — and there was the old appointed anchor of marriage and a home. It had been, indeed, the hour for the woman who had always pleased his taste, and skilfully had she improved it. She had gone abroad when he did, by no means, however, on the same steamer: when he returned home, she also set sail, but, very decorously, by a later ship. Her art had always been perfect.

The whole secret of power over others, she believed, lay in dexterity of scheming: by this she had won the invulnerable Kenyon Leigh, and by this she meant to be that power with him after marriage which she had not been with her first husband. For, although men were by nature absorbed only in themselves, she believed women of sufficient art and subtlety could overcome that nature. History made abundant record of such women. Ninon de l'Enclos, with her lovers at sixty; Diana de Poictiers, adored by a young prince who could neglect a fair young wife for a woman always old enough to be his mother, and growing on into old age even, without abating one jot of her charm to him; Cleopatra, who attained her greatest fascination only with ripe years; Helen of Troy, who was forty years old, and Heaven knew how much more, when her lovers kept the world in arms, — these were women who had really swayed men with lasting ascendency, — the most powerful of men, — and who could thus work their will in the world with even more than a man's autocracy, — with the autocracy of the woman who rules the man.

And these sovereign charmers, the beautiful widow said to herself, had always had two conditions in their lives; viz., they were old enough to have made exhaustive study of all the weaknesses and caprices of men, by adroit managing of which they swayed them; and the way of their improper lives had enlarged that study by knowledge of many different men. She herself was now thirty-five, just coming into that accomplished prime of years; and she had had one husband, who being decorously under ground, she could apply in a second marriage all that she had learned through the failure of her first.

What this perfectly correct American lady emulated in those shining names among the improper sisterhood was their *power:* she thirsted for power. For thus far in her life, with all her beauty, elegance, wealth, and un-questioned entrance to society at home and abroad, Mrs

Van Cortlandt had been a consciously unsuccessful woman. She could not build up any thing, — not a permanent place in a husband's heart, nor the supreme social leadership which she had aspired to: for to win even the latter influence, external advantages alone do not suffice ; there must be talent, energy, sympathy, some qualities more vital than Mrs. Van Cortlandt had ever cultivated in herself.

She had some fantastic notion now of building up the church. The mysterious attraction which that institution seems so often to have for jaded women of the world, their notion of it as an institution especially dependent on feminine patronage, wrought on her mind, inducing her to weave some very curious visions of pageantry round her position as the wife of Kenyon Leigh. The hereditary palaces and other honors naturally appertaining to the highest dignitaries of a State Church, as to the lord-bishops of Mr. Leigh's own church in England, the splendor maintained by Romish cardinals, the brilliant social figure that some of them made, — all this, which her long residence abroad had familiarized her with, floated before her fancy as something which she would reproduce in America.

She well anticipated that she might have a little trouble in ingrafting her plans for making the church imposing in this world on the mind of Kenyon Leigh, who had long ago marked down to an extremely low figure all the time that he could spare for what is called " society." She would find her second husband, of course, like the first, wedded to some of those invisible rivals which every woman had to fight in a husband's heart. If, in this case, the man was not wedded to his club, his cigar, some excitement of masculine sports, or to still more doubtful pleasures, he was wedded to his whims. The fashiona-ble woman really called by no more serious name than "whims" the intense absorption of Kenyon Leigh in his work. De Tocqueville speaks of a certain fine lady who invariably ran out of any apartment that Napoleon entered, because "he was always talking his '*silly*' politics." The man whose topics of conversation did not interest *her*, though he were Europe's conqueror, was simply "silly," and no more.

The woman who proposed, so soon as she should be his wife, admirably to reform the devoted minister of all his "whims" and "silliness," happened to be a very selfish woman. But it is unfortunately true that there has so often been nothing in a woman's own mental training to give her any just notion of the requirements which an intellectual man's tasks make upon his life, that many a wife who by no means deserves to be called markedly selfish, honestly regards as mere whims (which she pardons more or less as affection rules her) the absolutely indispensable conditions under which her husband does his best work. These things being so, the dutiful, domestic, uncritical woman, asking nothing for herself, the genuine satellite wife, has probably deserved all the praises with which her meek brows have so often been crowned by men of talent and ambition hard driven in the ways where those endowments lead.

Kenyon Leigh had never wanted a satellite wife : satellites were not only uninteresting to him, but peculiarly oppressive. But he was a hard-driven worker ; and Mrs. Van Cortlandt had so regulated her existence before him for the last four years as to suggest that her own natural tastes would choose just that way of life which would blend most undisturbingly with his.

She was a wife to have been perfectly fatal to the great preacher. High in the hills of God this eagle had his rest ; but he soared on only mortal pinions — their flight could be broken. This most alien spirit, this poor restless woman, had strings to have bound and chafed to death precisely a man like this.

Did she cherish of intent ruinous designs on the happiness of the man she proposed to marry? Oh, no! her designs were merely for her own happiness. Youth, in its maddest chase after pleasure, never runs quite so desperately as does the elder worldling after some toy which seems to promise deliverance from *ennui*, — that tormentor whose scourge finds out the soul which has successfully lapped itself from every other earthly ill. Indolence which will not rouse itself to any useful activity has been seen to take on the fiercest energy here; and this disappointed woman of fashion, with her chaotic dreams of the four years past, stood to-night at a point in her life to dare all things for their fulfilling.

CHAPTER XV.

THE next day was Sunday; and Monny must go to church some time before the hour for service, as she had been playing the church-organ for weeks to allow young Clara Macey to go away and take music-lessons of a master, who, summering in a certain country-place, would take vacation scholars at less than his city prices. This particular morning Mrs. Doane accompanied Monny in her early walk, not to disturb the decorum of the regular meeting-hour by so secular a sight as a tin pail, which she was going to carry filled with broth to a sick man in the village, Skipper Benway.

Mr. Leigh, to spare Monny the annoyance of local gossip, was not accustomed to walk with her to church, or, indeed, anywhere about the village; but this morning, seeing how his beloved became with her matronly escort a mere family party to which any general acquaintance might join himself, he snatched his hat and ran downstairs to go early to church likewise. The widow turned, and sanctioned his company by gravely bestowing on him some stalks of the caraway-plant, which she called dill, — that herb sacred from immemorial Puritan usage to break the fasts of long sermons. Monny blushed radiant beneath her blue-plumed hat, his gift, — she was arrayed, for the rest, in a black silk walking-suit, according to the prophetic milliner, — and the three set forth together.

The road they trod was unfenced, stretching away on either side into such a waste as is this narrowed portion of Cape Cod, —only a dryer sandbar that the Atlantic has thrown up, and the beach-grass roped together, to keep the waters from claiming their own again.

But hints of the coming autumn, which would soon make beautiful with color all the shrubby sand-hills, touched already here and there the wilding bushes which overran them ; land-birds that were half sea-birds rose out of their nests in these thickets, flying over them from bay to ocean, and from ocean back to bay ; out on the great sea-roads white sails were growing and fading in the horizon's blue, or those long smoky banners that an ocean steamer trails, — altogether the walk was so delightful to Kenyon Leigh, that he quite forgot its proper place of termination : this, for him, was certainly the foot of the church-gallery stairs. But arrived at that spot, although he really had not premeditated it, some spirit in his feet, some " Whither thou goest I will go," took him straight up the gallery-stairs after Monny. She was a little in advance of him, talking with the male leader of the choir, Capt. Puffer, who had been politely waiting for the young organist at the meeting-house door to give her the hymns, which he had just obtained from the minister. So Mr. Leigh went up into the singers' gallery quite on his own invitation ; but, once arrived there, he could not tear himself away.

It was in itself a most enchanting loft to the New-York churchman. Two hundred years there had been an Ortho-dox meeting-house on this site. The first one had a thatched roof, through which the early settlers fired their muskets at the Indians. Of course, though the founda-tion-stones were thus ancient, the frame-building had been more than once rebuilt since that primeval thatched structure which had blazed out its gospel to the heathen through the roof.

Still the present edifice dated so far back as to be a

pure specimen of the old Puritan meeting-house in all its
barn-like glory. The only thing about it suggesting the
present age was the organ, a very good one, but looking
quite astray in the old-fashioned high gallery, stretching
straight from wall to wall, opposite the pulpit-end of the
church, and garnished with obsole c frills of faded red
curtain, pushed aside in little huddled flaps here and there
along a brass rod; nobody being moved to so radical a
step as taking down these long-d.sused modesties. In
all small boys of the congregation, we may remark, existed a deathless and never-quenched desire to sit in the
gallery. There were tempting tiers of vacant seats on
either side of those occupied by the singers, but Capt.
Puffer kept the entire gallery rigorously closed to all but
the choir. The Cape-Cod small boy, however, imitating
the strategy of "stowaways" on board ship, would sometimes hide himself in the hold of one of the remoter
gallery-pews until the choir was well out to sea, singing
the first hymn in full face of the risen congregation.
Then the young church stowaway would steal slowly up
to view from his hiding under the pew-seat, seeming "to
snatch a fearful joy" from the very sight of Capt. Puffer,
who with his mouth stretched wide in the delivery of the
tenor notes, one hand holding his book, and the other
beating time for his band, was certainly powerless to deal
with intruders, except by a flash of his wrathful eye, till
the hymn was ended. In some of his moods, however,
the musical captain would pounce on such a trespasser so
instantly after the conclusion of the hymn, that Mr
Leigh, from his seat in the congregation below had seen
such skirmishings round those gallery-pews as made him
aware of the jealousy with which they were guarded
against all outsiders. What was he himself, but an out-
sider, who, in deference to Capt. Puffer's prejudices, ought

certainly to go below at sermon-time — unless he should
join the choir? This sudden idea came to the famous
preacher of St. Ancient's with a perfect fascination. Such
a delicious sense of being —

> "Out of the ages of worldly weather,
> Forgotten of all men altogether,"

would there be in sitting in the singing-seats with his
sweetheart, carrying a bunch of dill! He stuck those
greens in his buttonhole, and, gravely taking up a sing-
ing-book, obediently found the page as Capt. Puffer gave
out the tune for the first hymn.

At this movement the distinguished new addition to the
choir was naturally invited to take a head seat; but he
discreetly declined this honor, choosing his place quite at
the foot of the bass force of the choir.

The rehearsal was not an extended one, only a long
metre, a common metre, and a short metre tune for the
three hymns of the Orthodox service; and then the bell
began to boom in the belfry overhead, the choir laid down
their books, and, while Monny's fingers wandered over the
organ-keys into an *andante* movement from Beethoven,
the congregation came into the pews below with an inquiring glance towards the pulpit to see who was to occupy it
to-day; for the installed pastor of the church had gone
this summer to make a long-desired visit to a son married
and settled in San Francisco. So the pulpit had been
"supplied" ever since Mr. Leigh's sojourn in Lonewater;
the supplies generally representing the two uttermost ex-
tremes of ministerial experience; viz., the superannuated
old fathers who had retired from the active ministry, and
the very young sons who had scarcely entered on it, to
wit, theological students who came down by the cars on
Saturday night, from Andover and elsewhere, to make their

maiden efforts before this little congregation by the sea.
To-day it seemed to be the fathers' day; for, with the
last strokes of the bell, a white-haired old man walked
slowly up the aisle, and took his place in the pulpit. Just
in the wake of the minister came Capt. Gawthrop, ad-
vancing to his well-placed pew in the centre of the house,
whose door he held wide while Mrs. Van Cortlandt swept
in, her landlord closing the door after her, and turning to
seat himself, and such of his family as were with him,
elsewhere, discreetly leaving a lady with so grand an air
to occupy the pew alone. Mrs. Van Cortlandt certainly
had the grand air; for in regions where that air is held
to be quite unmistakable — at European courts, for instance — the beautiful American was never taken for any
thing less than a duchess, till her nationality was known.

The proud woman had entered the little meeting-house
with but one object, — to see Kenyon Leigh, and he was
not there — unless on the chance that he had come in
later than herself, and was seated somewhere behind her.
In this hope, glad was the widow when the antique congregation rose up at the first hymn, and faced round
towards the choir to see them sing it. But, thus enabled
to sweep the house at a glance, she still believed that he
was absent, until, lifting her disappointed eyes in pure
ennui towards the high gallery, lo, there she beheld him,
the rector of St. Ancient's, perched up in a Cape-Cod
conventicle, singing bass at the foot of the choir!

Now, Mrs. Van Cortlandt knew Kenyon Leigh quite
well enough to know that a freak like this was not characteristic of him normally. This was true. It was entirely
characteristic of him to fill up any scanty Sunday-school
library, of whatever sect, that fell in his way, to preach
in any sort of meeting-house that asked him, to go walking, in short, over his church-lines, in all directions where

his business really led him to walk over them. But he
never walked over them for mere display. "Go to now,
I propose to be a Liberal," was never the style of any of
his departures from the conservative ways of his church.
His parishioner from St. Ancient's knew, therefore, that,
while it might perfectly be expected of Mr. Leigh to
officiate at the pulpit-end of this little Cape-Cod church,
yet for him to officiate at the singing-end of it was a
stretch of broad-churchmanship *not* to have been expected
of him. And she asked, as did Dr. Herophilus over the
bandbox, " What did this newness mean? "

The man, to her knowledge, made no pretensions whatever to tuneful powers. It appeared now, as he warbled
away there, that he might have by nature a very good
bass voice ; but it is doubtful if he had scarce exercised
it before in singing since his college-days. How had he
broken out so suddenly as a Presbyterian vocalist? How
came the Rev. Kenyon Leigh to be so surprisingly of-
ficious in that which was not his business?

The astonished lady in the congregation pondered these
questions with much exercise of mind. To behold the
man so familiar to her in the chancel of St. Ancient's,
with the great congregation crowding every standing-spot
of the edifice, while the grand strains of the Te Deum
Laudamus rolled round his head ; to see him aloft under
that white-washed roof, singing so painstakingly, in the
chopped metres of the Orthodox hymn-book, —

> "Let us awake our joys,
>   Strike up with cheerful voice,
>   Each creature sing;
>   Angels, begin the song,
>   Mortals, the strains prolong,
>   In accents sweet and strong," etc. —

to Mrs. Van Cortlandt this was something of a sight

So dutifully he inclined his famed head to follow the lead
of that minstrel, the chief bass (a squat sailor, who sang
in a voice like the growl of the surges over the bar) ;
so softly he brummed away on the more ambitious slurs,
and let fly on the notes he was sure of, with a laudable
intention to sustain the organist when he could, and not
do any harm when he couldn't — this *was* a little of a
spectacle.

Not that it was absurd; no, the immortal charm
which there is in simplicity and right good will, and the
inalienable dignity with which these qualities crown any
action, made the Rev. Kenyon Leigh never absurd, even
when he was in love forty thousand fathoms deep. But
if this musical performance of a man whose gifts were
not in music escaped the ridiculous (the tradition remained ever after in this parish, that Mr. Leigh was a
magnificent singer, only that he would not let his voice
out to throw the rest of the choir in the shade), an all-
pervading air of unusualness about Kenyon Leigh did not
escape Mrs. Van Cortlandt.

Is there some positive coruscation about a lover? Certainly the enamoured man in the choir did not once turn
his head towards the organist, and most certainly she
did not turn hers towards him : nevertheless, the pair of
feminine eyes that watched so narrowly from the pew
below soon travelled from the man to that young lady
who was officiating at the organ. Naturally she could
see only her back, the outline of a girlish waist, a rich
curl or two of fair hair falling from the simple coil in
which most of Monny's tresses were wound up to-day;
poised on this hair a pale-blue plumed hat, whose turn
and style suggested the very inside heart of Paris. Of
the face, nothing like a full profile-view even could be
caught ; only a glimpse now and then of a line of soft

cheek and throat as the player bent a little this way or
that to manipulate her organ-stops.

The hymn ended, and Mrs. Van Cortlandt must face
away from the choir again, and sit down with the rest,
which she did, feeling vaguely startled out of the secure
mood in which she had entered the church. Still her
apprehensions were but dim; her opinion of Mr. Leigh's
make-up leading her to be peculiarly unafraid of rivals,
especially in young girls. Nevertheless, she began to
recall — for she had immediately decided that the amateur
organ-player was that other summer-boarder at the house
where Mr. Leigh was staying — every item that she had
heard concerning the young lady.

She had first heard of her that morning, in the talk
of her maid Tonson while she was dressing her hair.
Tonson was a British woman, who had been for years in
Mrs. Van Cortlandt's service, — first as child's nurse, and
afterwards promoted, for some marked talents that she
possessed, to be the lady's dressing-maid. These talents
were not so much in the line of toilet services proper as
in another line of gifts sometimes highly valuable in a
lady's maid, viz., the gift for gathering gossip to regale
ears too polite to gather it for themselves. Tonson's
gossip of this morning had seemed to Mrs. Van Cortlandt
of but very little value. The maid, who knew perfectly
all the matrimonial designs of her mistress, had duly
crammed herself the night before in the Gawthrop
kitchen, from the lips of the cook, with all details about
Mr. Leigh and his boarding-place; and in the course of
this babble the name of Miss Monny Rivers had been
often repeated, with all that dressing-up which so popular
a star naturally received at the hands of a native boasting
to a new-comer of the distinctions of the town in its
transient as well as permanent inhabitants. Thus, trans-

mitted from the kitchen through Tonson, Mrs. Van Cortlandt had heard a long chronicle of the toilets and talents
and beauty and beaux of Miss Rivers ; but, so far as she
had given a thought to this tiresome heroine at all, she
had conceived her to be some very average city girl,
glorified in the ideas of this primitive region into a beauty
and a belle.   She gave so much more thought to Miss
Rivers now, that she was impatient for the congregation
to be dismissed in order to secure a good look at her face.
But only the short prayer had yet been, of the Orthodox
service ; and long prayer, and Bible-reading, and more
hymns must be ; and, when these were got through with,
there was the affliction of the sermon to be endured.

No affliction, no sense of endurance, meanwhile, did
the sermon bring in that charmed gallery where sat the
famous preacher, and heard, heard how devoutly ! — as
the dear old soul in the pulpit preached on the everlasting
decrees, and proved to a hair, — that every good and perfect gift (such as Monny) cometh down from the Father
of lights, for no merit or deserving in the receiver, but
fore-ordained to him, of Heaven's own divineness, before
the world was.   And so in the gallery and the pews the
sermon went on to its end.   The benediction was said,
and from the gallery and the pews came the people.

Mr. Leigh shook hands with Mrs. Van Cortlandt in
the church-entry, not far from the foot of the gallery-
stairs.   The lady, stepping aside a little out of the passing
current of the people, as she stood to talk with her rector,
it chanced that her back was directly towards the gallery-
stairs when Monny presently descended them, chatting
with some of the female singers of the choir alongside
and behind her on the rather narrow stairs.   Monny's
attention being thus diverted, she did not observe whom
Mr Leigh was speaking with, until she reached the foot

of the stairs, where he was waiting expressly to present her to Mrs. Van Cortlandt. Mr. Leigh had mentioned the evening before that a parishioner of his would probably come to take rooms for a few weeks at Capt. Gawthrop's; but he did not know then that she had already arrived, and, although he himself had seen her from the gallery when she came into the church, Monny had not seen her: so this introduction was a little sudden to her.

Now, Monny was a lady, and being presented to a stranger was not ordinarily an ordeal to make her blush with diffidence. But, as she was introduced to Mrs. Van Cortlandt, a blush — so intense that Mr. Leigh had never seen her blush so before, save once — must needs sweep her face, suffusing even her white brow with a faint pink, and fanning her cheeks into that marvellous bright bloom which Monny's color was at its highest. It was, perhaps, the sudden surprise of the lady's great beauty, so impressive to her artist's eye, and partly the fact of her being Mr. Leigh's parishioner, and probably, still more, the peculiar scrutiny with which the long-lashed gray eyes of the New-York stranger explored her young face. Then she blushed, of course, to find herself blushing; and, as a part of her little nervous flutter, her left hand (both hands were bare, as she had just come from playing the organ) went up with some unconscious movement to the curl of hair falling on her shoulder.

Beautiful women instinctively observe each other's points. They are apt, especially, to observe both the points in which they themselves excel and those in which they are deficient. Now, each of these women had in a different way a very rare beauty of complexion. Monny's order of complexion was one common enough among the soft-skinned American girls: the rarity in her case was only in the perfection of the kind: it was the absolute perfection of a transparent rose-and-white skin. But Mrs. Van Cortlandt's complexion was not only a perfect one of its style, but the style itself was extremely rare. The fairest Circassian beauties, perhaps, have something such a skin, — of texture and tint so firm and pure as really to suggest breathing marble, the whiteness having only so much of a creamy glow as belongs to the hues of living flesh, and not of stone. Mrs. Van Cortlandt, well accustomed to know that her paleness was more beautiful than all the color of most fresh-colored faces, would probably anywhere in the world have noticed a complexion like Monny's, beautiful enough to make her silently debate whether her own was really to be preferred or no. And the beauty of Monny's little hand she would certainly have observed anywhere, for an opposite reason: her own hands were extremely ugly. They were very well in gloves; kid gloves being apparently shaped to fit lean and ugly hands. A really beautiful hand can seldom be perfectly gloved. But one cannot wear gloves always; and, divested of these coverings, Mrs. Van Cortlandt showed a hand so bony and large-jointed as to be hard to the touch even, for all the luxurious softness of her life. And, because of the current notion that hands are peculiarly a sign of lineage, this defect was more vexatious than would be believed to Mrs. Van Cortlandt's pride.

Now, these two personal points about Monny, which the widow would have noted anywhere, she *had* noted somewhere in her life before. Yes, she grew certain that she had seen just that strikingly vivid blush, that peerless hand, yes, that very movement of that hand, before. This impression of reminiscence came to her with her very first look into Monny's flushing face; and although, as that face regained its more normal hues, and the young lady's manner its usual composure, the sense of likeness to some one seen elsewhere was lost a little, still her first impression had been too strong to be shaken : somewhere on the earth Mrs. Van Cortlandt was sure she had beheld this girl before ; where, she could not as yet recall. But, as she stood uttering her graceful common· places to the maiden, she was inwardly following that baffling clew of suggestion, feeling that she should yet seize it when she was alone.

Meanwhile, as the two ladies exchanged the conventional remarks of a first introduction, Mr. Leigh turned to greet one and another who had waited, out of the little congregation, to pay their Sunday respects to him. There were such a number of these, and they had such manner of communications to make, as almost to suggest that the rector of St. Ancient's had "taken duty" at this Orthodox church. And indeed, although he had never yet preached in its pulpit, he had attended so cordially to some contingencies of more private ministerial service which had befallen in the absence of the regular pastor, that the latter had been enabled to prolong his California visit for an extra period, through the kindness of this distinguished sojourner in his parish.

Mrs. Van Cortlandt had not lost a movement of Mr. Leigh's since Monny came down-stairs ; and, guarded as was his manner in public towards the maiden, the widow had yet discerned some hints in that manner which did not add to her tranquillity. Possibly something of a lover's pride would pierce even through the mere little ceremonial of introducing the young lady to his New-York parishioner. And then again, while he was engaged with those villagers who had staid to speak to him, he stooped once, and picked up the girl's pocket-handkerchief for her as it was accidentally dropped. This was certainly the slightest and most ordinary of all conventional courtesies due from gentlemen to ladies; but for Kenyon Leigh to render that courtesy just then was *not* an ordinary thing, as Mrs. Van Cortlandt knew. Certainly, as a well-bred man, Mr. Leigh dutifully picked up the pocket-handkerchiefs of contiguous ladies, when he saw them fall; but he was extremely apt not to see them. And the angle of vision to him at which that pocket-handkerchief had fallen, as he stood turned away from the ladies, giving audience to his villagers, was an angle at which he never would have perceived the fall of a feminine pocket-handkerchief — in the past.

There are two classes of men who can see a lady's movements perfectly well with the back of their heads. One is the lover, who has this remarkable vision with respect to one particular woman only; and the other is what may be called the born lover of the whole sex. This latter man, in the atmosphere of charming women, is genuinely pre-occupied with them, finds every thing else less charming: he cannot miss any chance of serving them, because he never for an instant forgets them. The assiduities of this knight — when he is a man, and not a mere beauish monkey — make the *petits soins* dear to the hearts of women (or just as dear to their vanity, when they have no hearts); for the evident fact that he pleases himself in the pleasing courtesies he renders is the most delicate of all possible tributes.

Mr. Leigh had never belonged to this class of men. No: it must be confessed concerning him, that Eve was not more distinctly a new creation to Adam, when he first beheld her in the garden, than had been woman to Kenyon Leigh in the person of Monny Rivers, when he woke from his deep sleep of thirty-four years to watch

that maiden walking under Mrs. Doane's apple-trees, and
see in her the incarnation of a sex whom it was man's
one want and joy to wait on. A being whom he was
possessed by a desire to communicate with, to make her
look ₁ t him, if only in anger — the impossibility of losing
her out of his own consciousness made it somehow un-
tearable to be himself lost out of hers. He would have
liked her to spill her pocket-handkerchiefs from morning
till night, that he might recall himself to her by picking
them up. Such having been his state of mind in those
early days, naturally, in the present riper ones, he had
so blossomed in *petits soins* towards Monny, that he forgot himself even in the church-entry, far enough to use
his lover's faculty of following her every motion whether
she was within his apparent optical range. or not. And
this new grace of gallantry in Kenyon Leigh was noted
by the widow as something which had certainly descended
on him since she saw him last. What was its quality and
extent? she mused. Had the back of his head become
transmittant of vision as to all fair women, or only one?

Silently she pondered this question, but finally decided
not to drop her own pocket-handkerchief to see.

The trio all went home by separate ways after leaving
the church-entry. That is, Mr. Leigh lifted his hat in
farewell to Mrs. Van Cortlandt only a short distance beyond the meeting-house grounds, leaving her then to go
along the main street to Capt. Gawthrop's, while he
turned up the lane leading to Skipper Benway's cottage.
For Mrs. Doane had spoken a word to him after church,
reporting the sick man, who was dying of a rapid con-
sumption, as enjoying one of his more comfortable days,
and desirous to see Mr. Leigh, whom he had conceived a
great adoration for, if he could conveniently call after

morning church. Accordingly, the minister was going round that way before returning home; while, as for Monny, her way was along the main street, in the opposite direction.

The lady she had just parted with had stirred no memory whatever in the girl's mind of having been seen before: nevertheless, on Monny's side too, the interview had left very peculiar impressions. So she was not sorry to-day to part soon from the village acquaintances whose way joined hers for a little along the main street, and to go on alone with her absorbing thoughts over the quiet road which took her home.

CHAPTER XVI.

MRS. DOANE had reached home somewhat earlier than Monny did; and having seen that the luncheon-table, which Susannah had spread, was all right, — on Sunday dinner was served between four and five o'clock, — she had gone up-stairs to water some house-plants which filled a window in the little upper hall of the house, and which the extra duties of Sunday morning had left untended till now. She was moving the plants out of the direct sunshine, that watering at this meridian hour might not injure them, when Monny arrived, and came musingly up the stairs, breaking impulsively out of her revery, when she saw the widow, with, —

"O aunt Persy! *did* you see how perfectly beautiful is that friend of Mr. Leigh's, — the lady who has come to board at Capt. Gawthrop's?"

"Yes, I saw her," said Mrs. Doane, plucking a with-ered leaf or two from a luxuriant begonia. "She has a face to be seen."

"The most wonderful perfect face of a woman I ever saw in this whole world!" cried enthusiastic Monny as she dropped into a chair.

"Do you really think that she is handsomer than you are?" involuntarily asked the matron, looking down on the girl, who sat radiant in the reflected lights of the sunny window, making to Mrs. Doane's partial fancy a picture much more attractive than the lofty lady who had sat so coldly alone in Capt. Gawthrop's pew.

"Me! me!" cried Monny, seeming to find more ex-clamatory power in somewhat doubtful grammar. "My face hasn't the very first foundation of handsome, which is a nose."

" Now, Miss Monny, whatever is the matter with your nose?" asked the widow, pausing, watering-pot in hand, to examine this hitherto unsuspected deficiency in the fair face before her. "I'm sure it isn't a crooked nose; and it's neither too big, nor yet too small."

" Look at Mrs. Van Cortlandt's nose, — and oh the line it makes with her forehead and her upper lip!" cried the artist adoringly, — "and then you will see what's the matter with my nose and all my face. See what it would go to in marble — *my* face!" pronounced the girl, with the most impersonal air of settling that physiognomy forever. "Let any sculptor make an exact portrait head of me, and then you would see that I haven't a feature, — not a feature."

" Oh!" was all that the Cape-Cod woman could reply; since, in her idea of the meaning of words, Monny's ex-pressive face was the very last face in the world that could be called featureless. Then she silently concluded it a wise provision of Heaven, to save from the snare of vanity a girl whose looks had been praised ever since she was born, that she should rate herself at this nothingness.

" But if you were to cut Mrs. Van Cortlandt's face out in wood or paper," Monny went on, "draw the barest out-line of it — any thing that would show its beautiful forms would show all the wonderful perfect face it is. Real beauty is bred in the bone," declared the artist. "It is not true at all, that it is merely skin deep. Mrs. Van Cortlandt's complexion is beautiful as the moonlight on the snow: but, if the flesh of her face was all faded and furrowed and shrunken, you would still see the perfect structure beneath ; some of its beauty can never, never die. That is a face to have !'' concluded the maid, with such a lowly sigh Mrs. Doane sufficiently forgot the profitableness of small self-esteem in young ladies as to their looks, to say, —

"Now, Miss Monny, *do* you not know what a pretty girl you are yourself?"

"Oh, anybody can be a pretty girl!" replied Monny slightingly, — "any girl who has not a particularly bad complexion, or awkward figure, or some such severe drawback. Prettiness is cheap as can be. You have only to consider your own personal points a little, so as to wear what is most becoming. But a beautiful woman, beautiful as Mrs. Van Cortlandt is beautiful, need not dress at all ; that is, she can wear the very costume of the noblest art, which is always mere plain drapery. And she can put her hair away all smooth and close, without a wave or a crinkle, into a simple low knot behind, and look like a queen as well as a Madonna, — every thing that is elegant, as well as every thing that is most spiritually lovely. Indeed, to wear your hair as opposite as possible to the prevailing fashion — especially when you wear it in the direction of simplicity, and the fashion is elaborate — will always make a woman look either perfectly distinguished, or perfectly dowdy ; only, in ninety-nine women out of a hundred, it will have merely the dowdy effect. You see, all the elaborations of *coiffure*, all adornments of dress of every kind, have been invented, not in the interest of the truly beautiful woman, but to make the best of all the flimsy order of looks — such as mine," concluded Monny, with another of those abased sighs that she had been heaving during this colloquy.

So dejected was it, Mrs. Doane again so forgot her prudence as to say, "Now, my dear, do you really con-

sider yourself one of those girls whose good looks are all
in their furbelows? Many's the time that I've thought
you look prettier when you come running home from the
beach through the rain, in your oldest black waterproof
cloak, than in most any thing you wear. And although
that New-York hat you've got on to-day is mighty becoming (and I never saw you in a regular dressed-up hat that
was more so), still the white gypsy Mr. Leigh brought you
is a grain prettier on you still; for I've always noticed
you everyday hats are a little more becoming to you than
any dressed-up hat, howsoever pretty."

"That's because I've got no features, and wide hat-
brims harmonize me a little."

Harmonizing hat-brims were to Mrs. Doane a flight
beyond even Monny's recurring monomania about destitu-
tion of features, so she found no answer to make ; and the
girl murmured, in an under-current of thought, —

"But I can't wear wide hat-brims to church, nor old
black waterproof cloaks. And the style which does *not*
become me, aunt Persy," she added with conviction, "is
the dressed-up style of grave dignity; such a style as
Mrs. Van Cortlandt's, which is dressed up, I mean, in
the sense of its being a proper attire to appear at church
in, or in a city street. All those full Watteau folds and
wide-hanging sleeves of her plain mantle had the simplest
majestic grace on her, but they would mop me up into
the dowdiest bundle. I haven't the figure for it."

"Now, Miss Monny, there never could be a mortal
woman with a better shape than yours, down to the ends
of your fingers."

"You have to dress to your face," insisted the young
Hebe, "your whole general appearance ; and you would
see that my figure is *not* equal to that style of dress. I
am not tall enough for very long lines in my costume,

except when I wear a train. But Mrs. Van Cortlandt, without adding an inch of train to her native height, in just a street walking-dress, is tall enough for all the lines made by long hanging veils and Watteau mantles. It is a great gift," sighed Monny again so deeply, Mrs. Doane laughed out, —

"Child, I think you have gone out of your head, a'most, about that lady. She is a very imposing-looking person, I grant. But the Lord has made us all: and she has no greater Maker than the humblest," declared the widow, secretly wondering if the strange lady could have dared to look at Monny with any such haughty stare as she had turned on herself in the church-entry; for Mrs. Doane had been obliged to deliver her sick man's message to Mr. Leigh while he stood there talking with his New-York parishioner.

"Indeed, aunt Persy," solemnly insisted Monny, "it *is* a very great gift to have such a face and figure as that; for it enables you to follow in your very dress the law of the grand simplicities. You do not have to modify it to your own imperfections and small style. You see, with most women, dress must always be a compromise between their taste in the abstract and the necessity of considering their own personal peculiarities. That fact does not seem to be always recognized," said Monny, with the gravity which she put into all this arguing. "I remember, for instance, to have read in a social essay by some man, that you could judge of a woman's character more by the way she wore her hair than by any thing else. Now, that is not true, except with very important modifications," declared Monny weightily. "It is true, for example, that plain hair on the brow looks serious and simple; while crimps, by comparison, look frivolous and artificial. But it is also true that fluffed hair softens

the line of the forehead, and can be arranged over it so
as to bring many an imperfect face into a little truer
measurements," urged the artist. " So, although nobody
would ever think of painting the Virgin Mary with little
curls dropping over her forehead, or such a face as Mrs.
Van Cortlandt's, all whose divisions are true to the absolute ideal of art—crimps are yet favorable to *my* forehead, for instance, which is too high " —

Patiently, even on the Lord's Day, had the pious
Orthodox dame listened to these themes thus far; but
Monny's last point of self-criticism seemed to her com-
pletely crazy.

" Really, now! if a good broad forehead isn't a fine
point in a woman, as showing that there's room in her
head for sense, what is?" broke in the astonished New-
England woman, who could never have been brought to
appreciate the Greek ideal of feminine beauty. " La,
child! if you will put an extra touch, sometimes, on your
natural curly locks with crimping-pins, and shake them
down in a way that does no justice at all to your forehead, I can stand it; because, as soon as ever you get
absorbed in any thing, you push your hair right up, and
show what a nice full forehead you've got under the
crimps," said Mrs. Doane, comfortably informing Monny
what a dead failure was her simulation of a Greek brow.
" What I was going to say was, crinkly hair, one way or
another, is as natural to you as straight hair to that tall
lady, who certain is *too* tall to have curls and crimps
flying. I thought myself, when I first saw her standing
up in the church, with her head clear up to the heads of
the men, and quite above so many of 'em, that she was
too tall a woman ever to look well *anyway*," declared the
widow, unable to forbear this small dig of criticism at
the lady who had so managed to upset Monny's usually

well-balanced sense. "She looked all right, to be sure,
when she stood by Mr. Leigh in the entry. I grant that,
put her beside him, they make a pair most striking and
grand to look at," repeated good Mrs. Doane, being
already conscientiously moved to soften the invidious
remark she had let slip about a stranger, and Mr. Leigh's
parishioner.

"Missis, missis!" here sounded in startling outcry
from the foot of the stairs. "De ole yaller hen dat's
been missin' dese tree weeks, jess come cluckin' up to de
back door, grand as can be, wid ten new chickens! · De
pore ole fool! — when de winter storms'll be blowin' afore
ebber dey grow dere fedders!" At this summons from
Susannah, the matron quitted her plants and the maiden;
for the latter did not follow her down-stairs, even so exciting an event as a brood of late chickens not having power to
draw Monny out of the present current of her thoughts.

Mrs. Doane's last words had inadvertently struck the
very keynote of all those thoughts. Monny had seen
nothing all the way home from church but just those two
figures beside each other, — Mr. Leigh and Mrs. Van
Cortlandt. They were emphatically, as to looks, a man
and woman of whom all beholders sensitive to harmoni-
ous looks involuntarily think, "What a pair they would
make!" Both of them were so above, respectively, the
average stature of man and woman, yet so perfectly pro-
portioned to each other in height, — to see them as they
stood, the man glorious in his strength, the woman in her
great beauty, one might say indeed that the gods had
come down to dwell among men. And there were even
finer correspondences to the eye in the pair than these:
for, if Mr. Leigh had an air of nobleness which is never
found independent of character, Mrs. Van Cortlandt had an
air of fine distinction ; and, although that air can perfectly

exist without any character at all, the difference between it and the former mien is not always discernible at first glance, even by more experienced observers than an ardent girl.

Monny could not doubt in these days that Mr. Leigh had chosen herself to be his wife, without doubting the honor of the man. Nor in these days could this young heart conceive of the remarriage of a widow but as a profanation. Monny had not got far enough yet in this world of mistakes to know how often a second marriage is a much truer one than the first. But if the maiden's fancy could not whisper of her own lover and of this woman shrined in her widowhood, "She might be a wife for Mr. Leigh," it *did* whisper, "Mr. Leigh's wife ought to *look* like that."

Monny had forgotten that there was any human opinion for her outside of the approval of one man : the world of persons, since she had fallen in love, had been all simplified to her into one person, whom alone she cared to please, until now, when her very absorption in this sole being suddenly caused her such a solicitude about the opinion of others as she had never felt before in all her life. The sense of a world fastidious and critical, to whose judgment she was exposed in a new, strange way, and with some new, strange need to be honored in it that another might not lose honor through her, — this feeling had begun in her with that first searching glance of Mrs. Van Cortlandt, which had so troubled her young cheek with blushes ; and its trouble wrought obscurely in her still. She went now to her own room ; and, in our aim to confess unto all the truth as it is in woman, it must be confessed that she marched straight to the looking-glass there, and took a long survey of herself, first in the hat she had worn to church, then in the other hat which Mr.

Leigh had brought her. Still worse, she even proceeded
to the trying-on of some of her old hats, — Gainsboroughs
and gypsies, — pretty caprices of head-rigging for out-of-
town summer-wear. As Monny tried on these girlish
hats, seeing all the while above her head in the glass that
Madonna face of the lady from St. Ancient's, she seemed
to herself a very cheap person, that she should have the
kind of face which this coquettish manner of hats especially became, — things that you could no more imagine on
Mrs. Van Cortlandt's head, she inwardly reflected, than
on the Mater Dolorosa's. There was, indeed, some substance of truth, probably, in the girl's artist-remark about
the harmonizing effect of wide hat-brims on irregular
features; for it was noticeable that any hat broad enough
to isolate, as it were, her radiant face, made a picture of
Monny at once; while the close-brimmed, conventional
little piece of millinery, half hat, half bonnet, which was
the most correct shape of the time for street-wear, was
only truly becoming to her in a hat as exquisitely chosen
as was that blue trimmed chip, in buying which Mr. Leigh
had shown such powers of divination. There began to
be a little poignancy, even in the tender thoughts which
had made these remarkable lover's gifts so deeply sacred
to Monny. Mr. Leigh, perhaps, wished her to know, she
mused, that he was content for her to wear such hats as
would make the best of her; but doubtless he would
have been more content if she had had a face which could
afford to be as indifferent about its bonnet as Mrs. Van
Cortlandt.

In making these disclosures of the mental exercises of
a young lady on coming home from church, we have
nowhere attempted to disguise the fact that they had to
do with very sadly superficial matters. Nor can it be
disguised, as we go onward with her history, that here the

girl's fate struck her, in her sensitive desire — overweening, if it must be called so — to be just what she should be in the mere external appearance. The woman who was to meddle so darkly with her fate began her power over her at this point, and began it from the very first moment.

No conscious reserve or discount was in Monny's admiration for Mr. Leigh's beautiful parishioner, who seemed to her at all points the perfect ideal of womanhood. But the perfect beings who send their admirers home with a particularly severe consciousness that their noses are out of joint, and an impulse to try on all their head-gear to see if there is any thing in which their insignificance may dare stand before them, must be classed among those beings who impress their own perfections as a standard from which it is a sign of defect to vary. Whether one woman who feels herself criticised by another is always moved to consider first if something in her dress may not be amiss, we need not decide. Certain it was, that all Monny's babble on that subject to-day had been moved by Mrs. Van Cortlandt; and apparently her soul was not fully eased yet, for she went down-stairs now from the looking-glass to babble a little more.

"Aunt Persy," she resumed, finding the old lady just returned to the sitting-room, after reviewing the autumn chickens, — "you see, aunt Persy, besides all the rest, Mrs. Van Cortlandt's style of dress is that of a very select upper few in society : it is the shabby aristocratic style, which is the most exclusive of any thing."

"Oh!" rejoined the widow, to whom the conjunction of those two adjectives conveyed no very definite meaning.

"I did not suppose it prevailed so much in New York as in some other places," thoughtfully added the young lady. "In Moralmount, for instance, some of the finest,

the truly finest, ladies always dress with that distinguished shabbiness on the street; and it is a style very
characteristic of the great ladies in Europe, in England
especially, if ever they go out on foot at all in the city."

"You are talking about the people who have seen
better days?" hazarded the Cape-Cod woman, groping
after a little clearer idea as to what the shabby aristocrat
was.

"Oh, no, no! not the shabby *genteel* style. It is just
the opposite. It is a despising of the genteel, a horror of
smartness as something too common, too much within
the reach of everybody. So the greatest ladies, who can
afford any thing, and who dress magnificently, of course,
on all dress occasions, show such an utter indifference to
looks and fashion in their walking-attire as no merely well-
off merchant's wife would ever do. I suppose," Monny
went on musingly, "this refined dowdiness originated at
first in a truly good and sensible idea, — that of shun-
ning the real vulgarity there is in very elegant dressing
on the street, as if you had nowhere else to show your
fine clothes. But what the refined dowdy style has developed into is an affected style of plainness, — not affected
by Mrs. Van Cortlandt, but by most ladies, — a kind of
carelessness in dress, which is very carefully studied indeed, and one of the most laborious of all styles to follow.
It would be for me, at least. I should make mistakes in
it: I should never remember to observe what was the last
new wrinkle it had adopted to show itself above the
fashion. Certainly, as a shabby aristocrat, I should be a
most dead failure," declared Monny dejectedly. "But,"
slowly added the girl after an anxious pause, "it is a
style of dress that to the general eye looks most plain and
unpretending, while to the select few it looks select: so I
suppose it would recommend one all round. It would

seem to set a good example. I have never thought
about setting examples, I have not been of consequence
enough," murmured Monny, still with a troubled look in
her hazel eyes, as she stood leaning meditatively over the
back of a chair.

The old woman, guessing well the future into which
those young eyes were looking to-day, divining what
made these very new phrases on Monny's lips about
recommending herself to all people, had patience still, as
she had had patience up-stairs, with what would otherwise
have seemed to her absurdly undue earnestness on the
most trivial of themes. And she was glad to hear just
now that quick, impetuous clash of the gate which generally announced Mr. Leigh's coming, trusting that the
presence of the minister would dispel the disquiet which
his parishioner had unmistakably brought.

"Miss Monny has been wondering, sir, whether all the
ladies in your church have such faces as the lady who has
come to board at Capt. Gawthrop's," said Mrs. Doane,
speaking first, as Mr. Leigh came in.

"Probably not," he returned, smiling. "I believe
Mrs. Van Cortlandt is everywhere acknowledged to be
very exceptionally handsome."

"Beautiful, perfectly beautiful," murmured Monny, a
little wondering that a man who usually chose his words
so well did not choose the higher and more appropriate
adjective.

But there was only one woman in the world who was
beautiful at present to Kenyon Leigh; and he had used
the highest word he could afford, even for Mrs. Van
Cortlandt.

The New-York widow went from the church-entry to
her lodgings in quite as absorbed a mood as Monny had

walked home to hers : she was wrapped in an intense effort
to make memory restore intact that broken chain of impressions which so haunted her. She caught the links at
last. Time, place, all the extraordinary circumstances in
which she had once seen a young girl like this Monny
Rivers, rushed clear and distinct on her mind. She had
seen her five years before, afar in a Southern city ; and she
had seen her on her journey to that city, — so strange a
journey, so strangely accompanied, — it was an immense
discovery to Mrs. Van Cortlandt, the discovery that this
fellow-boarder of Mr. Leigh's was identical with the
heroine of those remarkable travels. *Was* she the same
girl? could she be mistaken in a likeness which had
struck her, however confusedly, with the very first sight
of that face in the church-entry?

Ere nightfall this question, which grew a burning one
to the widow, was positively answered. It happened thus.
Tonson went out in the long Sunday afternoon to take a
small airing on her own account, and returned to say, —

" I reckon, my lady, that Miss Rivers comes over afternoons to lead the Sunday-school singing at the church.
For I 'card the closing 'ims of the children through the
windows, and see 'em all streamin' out pretty soon, an'
among 'em a young lady, from whose looks I said to
myself, ' That must be the belle to Mr. Leigh's boarding-
place they talk so much about.' So asking one of the
children, and findin' 'twas her indeed, I made bold to ask
the young lady herself, wen she came along, what was the
nearest way to the water-side."

The useful servitor, having well discovered that her
mistress came in from church in the morning vastly more
interested in Miss Rivers than when she went out. had
waylai l the latter on purpose thus to establish some speaking acquaintance with the young lady whom she might have
occasion to watch.

"And the moment she spoke," Tonson went on, "Lord, if it didn't come to me as if I'd seen that young lady before! Yes, when she turned round, and went back with me a little piece to show where the road went off, all her ways kep' giving me that blind kind of feeling as if I'd seen 'em before. But I couldn't nowise remember where, till sudden a little mite of a boy came runnin' out of a 'ouse, and called out to her, 'Ow oo do, Mith Monny Wiverth? Oo want to make my picter again?' An' wen I 'eard that lispin' child, I knew in a minnit just where I'd seen her. 'Twas in New Orleans, to the St. Charles 'Otel, five years ago, wen little Alfie (Mrs. Van Cortlandt's one child) was alive, an' I was his nurse, an' you 'ad Celeste for a maid, an' we went to New Orleans, an' this Miss Rivers was there to the St. Charles, where we staid. But of course you didn't notice her yourself."

The pulses of the languid lady, who was sitting at the moment on the edge of the bed, had quickened with great throbs at these words; but she said, with all outward indifference, "I have been asleep. And my hair has fallen down. Brush it out well, and put it up again. You think you saw this Miss Rivers in New Orleans five years ago? What did you ever see in the girl, Tonson, to make you remember her such a length of time?"

"Well, my lady," volubly replied the maid, as she wielded the brushes, "I 'appened across her pretty often to that 'otel wen I was leading little Alfie round the veranday to take the air, an' he asked her, the way little children do, wot her name was. An' though I 'eard that name last night, over and over, from 'Annah in the kitchen, I 'eard it with no sense nor knowledge that I'd ever 'eard it before, till that lispin' child, runnin' out just now, was like little Alfie callin' out of his grave again a'most them same words. For you see, one mornin' to that New Orleans 'otel, wen she stepped out on the verandny where I was walkin', little Alfie broke away from me, an' run up to her, an' says he, ' Ow oo do, Mith Monny Wiverth?' An I remember as she stooped down an' kissed him, an' stood a-pettin' him, she said, ' What a picture he would make ! ' They do say she's a regular hartist ; and pictures always runnin' in her 'ead perhaps made her speak that way to New Orleans, an' that little pipin' child to-day, I s'pose she's took the picture of some time."

Even when the rattling lips in her ear touched on those reminiscences of her dead child, the absorbed listener heard only what related to the schemes which she would hide close even from this minion of hers. So, nonchalantly as ever, she rejoined to the latter, —

"I will have some lavender-water, Tonson. So you really fancy the girl you have been talking of was this same Miss Rivers?"

" Certain of it, my lady, — no fancy at all, I remembered it all up comin' 'ome just now, — how 'twas with Mrs. Bingham of New York that she was stayin' there to that St. Charles 'Otel. An' there was with 'em, off and on, another young lady and young gentleman. Twin brother and sister they were, an' about one and twenty, I should say, for age, an' as 'andsome as pictures, both of 'em. An' they was orphans, an' belonged to Baltimore, but 'ad come down to New Orleans about their property, which a rich uncle, just dying there, 'ad left 'em ; an' their names was De Lancey. The young gentleman's name, I remember, was Mr. Carroll De Lancey."

The circumstantial memory is likely to be nowhere found in such perfection as in the lady's-maid and *valet-de-chambre* class ; for the ignorant mind being vacant of all subjects of thought, and the hands untaxed by any

arduous labors, the whole mental activity expends itself
in watching persons, — the world of fine persons, which
feeds curiosity the more, because it is at once in such
juxtaposition to, and so utterly removed from, the servant's life. Thus no human testimony could have been
more absolutely conclusive than the babble of this gar-
rulous maid, overflowing with details, and giving, at last,
the very names which proved, beyond all possibility of
doubt, the identity of Miss Rivers with that girl whom
Mrs. Van Cortlandt had so suspected and hoped that she
was.

It required a silent moment for even this cool woman so
to master her sensations as to say, still carelessly, —

"Of course, Tonson, you said nothing to Miss Rivers
about your notion of having seen her before?"

"Laws, no, my lady! I 'ope I know my place better,"
promptly replied Tonson, who had the true British lower-
class instinct for abasing one's self before "betters." "I
just turned round and come home, quite struck up with
thinking how curious it was to 'ave met 'his same young
lady way down to New Orleans, an' way 'ere to Cape Cod
a-boardin' with Mr. Leigh." ·

"I was introduced to Miss Rivers at that meeting-house
this morning," slowly pronounced Mrs. Van Cortlandt.
"She is supposed, therefore, to be of my personal acquaintance at present. There is no reason why I should
appear to take any especial interest in her."

"Laws, no, my lady! by no means," briskly replied the
maid, perfectly understanding this as a direction to herself to do all possible watching of Miss Rivers that could
be done, without appearing to watch her, and without in-
volving her principal.

"I remember," Tonson gossiped on, "'aving a notion
down there to New Orleans that the 'andsome young

gentleman, Mr. Carroll De Lancey, was the lover of that young girl whom it seems was Miss Rivers. But I suppose it wasn't so, or nothin' came of it, seeing that she's unmarried yet. 'Twas in the care of Mrs. Bingham, I s'pose, that she went on that long journey to New Orleans ; for I remember well that she came away with her : so, of course, she went there with her."

Mrs. Van Cortlandt knew that Monny Rivers did *not* travel to New Orleans with Mrs. Bingham, but in far other company ; but she made no reply, except to indicate that she had had a sufficiency of lavender-water.

Tonson put away the lavender-water, guessing no more than that bottle in her hand the deep plot which was slowly taking shape inside the proud head whose outside she had been laving. The young girl whom this poor tool had so artfully contrived to meet and accost, she had no malice against : her only aim was to serve her own mistress (who rewarded lavishly certain services) ; and all the dark extent to which she had served that lady mistress to-day, it was quite beyond Tonson's humble wits, cunning though they were, to imagine.

CHAPTER XVII.

MR. LEIGH politely called on his parishioner sojourning in a strange place, the very next day ; and never
had she seen him in brighter spirits or more cordial humor.
But his manner profoundly alarmed the lady who had
come to Cape Cod to marry him. In truth, nothing is
more hopeless for the bark of sentiment to put to sea on
than a certain particularly unchecked flood of good will in
the behavior of a being of the opposite sex: love is not
the shore to which that loud ocean of kindness rolls.

Possibly, too, the heart rang hollow from beneath all
those genial phrases of the caller, with some of that hol-
lowness which is wont to lurk in the best conversational
efforts of lovers with other than the beloved object.
Touches of a pre-occupation, which was not quite the old
pre-occupation of the man of books and study ; slight
lapses of forgetfulness, too hastily and brilliantly covered
not to be a little conscious, — signs like these may have
betrayed the man guilty of that abominable affront of
talking fluently with one woman while all his thoughts are
with another. At all events, when her friendly caller
departed, black was the mood of Mrs. Van Cortlandt.
Miss Rivers had not been mentioned during the interview,
since Mr. Leigh certainly would not bring Monny's name
casually into the conversation, and as yet he had no acknowledged right to speak of her otherwise than casually ;
while the widow, silently debating whether to make some
allusion to the young fellow-boarder, to see how Mr. Leigh

would be affected by it, or to ignore the girl as a being too unimportant to be inquired after, finally decided on the latter course, for she was a woman strong enough to let policy control her curiosity, even in a matter that she had a consuming desire to know more about. But her jealous thoughts fastened more and more persistently on that girl, and on the weapon which fate had strangely put into her own hand to strike the rival down, if this astounding thing could be true, that she had a rival, and in a mere girl. It may be that all the deadly uses of that weapon only gradually revealed themselves to her: still even to-day her creeping thoughts felt its edge.

Meanwhile, to-day, and during all the days of the present week, in the other Cape-Cod house the artist-girl toiled early and late at her picture of the Knight-Templar. She was not minutely learned in the history of any of those semi-military, semi-religious orders among the chivalry of the middle ages; but the picture was no anachronism. The simple, brave, believing spirit — it is the hero's type in every age; and this face of a man of the nineteenth century, marked though it was with the problems of his time, still looked out from those vanished trappings of the Red-Cross Knight with the same eternal qualities of character which make even mental modes like mere accidents of costume. The figure stood in the simplest pose; it portrayed no crisis of action; all the potentialities of action were in the traits of the face. The artist wrought at this head as she had never wrought before. She hid herself from her lover to perfect his image. It was something that she had secretly set herself to do before she would accept his love, as a proof that she was not all unworthy.

"That he may know I do not love him like a fool and blind; that I have counted up the jewels of his soul every one!"; she murmured to herself, and "Oh to make them shine in his face!" she cried in her throbbing young heart, as day by day the perfect face of Kenyon Leigh grew on the canvas.

> "As when a painter, poring on a face,
> Divinely through all hindrance finds the man
> Behind it; and so paints him that his face,
> *The shape and color of a mind and life,*
> Lives — ever at its best and fullest" —

Thus was it that the artist painted Kenyon Leigh's *perfect* face. His features were not faultless according to any classical standard. But sometimes a face rich in the latter kind of perfection floated before her in its adolescent beauty, as she traced the strong lineaments of the Knight-Templar: it was the pictured face she had burned to ashes in the old fireplace. It came, however, but as a faint passing memory, merely with its old suggestion of contrast to the face before her: the latter, and the man linked to it, absorbed all her being.

She had purloined a card-photograph of Mr. Leigh; then, too, as her picture advanced, she stole a kind of sittings after the following manner; that is, coming up the front stairs from dinner with her invariable escort, she would say to him, as she did one afternoon, "I am going to unlock my studio by and by, and let Mrs. Doane come in a while when she has got her knitting well in hand."

"And myself too?" very eagerly from the escort.

"If you will promise to walk straight from the door to the same corner I put you in the other day."

"And without even one look yet at the mysterious new picture?"

"Not a look. I have told you that you can be a little useful to me in the matter of — shoulders. Anybody can sit as a study for shoulders. The men of the middle ages were large creatures, I suppose. I wish my warrior to have the right proportions."

"Show him to me, and I can point out all his faults at once. There must be a great many of them, painting as you do in this solitary exaltation and self-sufficiency. It will make a failure of your warrior. He will not belong to this world."

"It is indeed a poor world for him," averred the maiden.

"Quite good enough," testily replied Mr. Leigh — he was getting mortally jealous of that man of the middle ages. "I wish to see him, that I may judge of his pretensions."

"You mock at them in advance. You cannot see him."

By this time the studio-door is reached, unlocked, and the maid, watching her chance, slips swiftly through it, holding the door narrowly open from within while she peeps back at the suppliant in a fashion that has grown tormentingly familiar to him.

"I shall soon know you, Miss Rivers, only by sections of your face. The effect is extremely broken — far from good."

" 'Quite good enough' — for the beholder. Half an eye ought to wither any man who so persists in begging invitations to the workshop of an extremely busy person. If he were not of the severely occupied sex, and it were proper manners, one might suggest that he take up some useful industry himself, to keep him from loitering at doors after he has received the broadest hints to go."

During these gibes the man is intent only on the sternly narrowing door, through whose straitening space he hastens to cry, —

"But you said I might come in and sit in the corner."

" Not till Mrs. Doane is ready. Wait till you hear her coming up the stairs."

" Why need Mrs. Doane come at all?" is the daring demand.

" To keep you in order, — keep you from giving those sudden great jerks of your shoulders which you did very troublesomely the last time."

" I was not practised then as a model. To-day I will stir no more than the brazen Brahma on my mantel-piece."

" No, no : you cannot be trusted. You will be travelling out of your corner, without Mrs. Doane to fence you in. Besides, I want to finish that group of you two which I began the other day, or to sketch a new one — an idea seizes me at this moment." And with these words the last crack in the door is closed, that inexorable bolt flies to, and there is no hope of admittance till Mrs. Doane comes up-stairs ; and the subjugated man walks meekly into the studio in the matron's train.

But if an American lover must be punished for falling in love with a young woman " seized of ideas " by being forced to do his wooing, after the fashions of Continental Europe, with third persons in the room, there could not have been a less offensive *duenna* than good Mrs. Doane. She had strictly kept her word of honor never to steal a look at the secret picture : still she had her surmises about it, and that not the lines of Mr. Leigh's mere shoulders were what Monny traced at these sittings, nor yet the " groups ; " which were merely various ludicrous carica-tures of her two visitors, which she often executed at a few strokes, behind her easel, to cover her real work there.

Thus to-day, when the minister and the matron were seated in their appointed corner, the artist set up inside

her large canvas a bit of sketching-board with this announcement : —

" This afternoon, Mr. Leigh, I will make a small sketch
of you as a domineering Churchman persecuting my ancestors in the days of the bad Stuarts. Mrs. Doane will
represent *my* people. She will be the faithful Puritan
matron, whose meeting-house you shut up, and call it by
such reviling names as ' conventicle ; ' whose cows and
things you take away to pay your unjust tithes ; whom
you impose on without end, till she is driven far over the
wide, cold ocean, to take refuge on Cape Cod."

" Or you might make a small sketch of me," suggests
Mr. Leigh, " as a faithful Churchman in the days of that
good Long Parliament. Driven out of my pulpit and my
little country parish for no crime but using the Prayer-
Book, hunted over the moors by the Roundheads, till
Mrs. Doane, the gentle Puritan matron, shelters me in
her house, lest an honest, if misguided, fellow-creature
perish of cold and hunger."

" I should certainly have taken you in, sir," said the
Orthodox widow, looking reverently up at the Episcopal
clergyman.

" H—m, h—m ! don't give up to him so, aunt Persy ! "
cried the younger champion. " Now, *do* you not acknowledge, Mr. Leigh, that your side behaved much, *much*
the worse? *Were* not the Puritans a great deal nearer
the right, on the whole?"

" It is, it mayhap," replied Mr. Leigh in the quietly
imposing recitative of a man quoting out of a book, " it
is not altogether to the discredit of the kindly race of·—
young ladies, that they are apt to take an interest warm,
yea, partial, in the deeds and sentiments of their forefathers. But truly the calm historian cannot gratify such
predilections. He must needs declare, that, although

the Puritans were honorably tenacious of their opinions
under persecution, still their own tempers were sullen,
fierce, and rude, their opinions absurd and extravagant,
and their whole course of conduct that of persons whom
hellebore would better have suited than prosecutions unto
death for high treason."

"You skip, you skip, *calm historian!*" challenges
Monny, popping out her bright face into full view at one
side of her easel, and dropping a brush in her gleeful
excitement at making a point against St. Ancient's rector.
"You are *not* 'cautelous' in quoting your authorities.
The first, the very first paragraph in your extract reads
so: 'The prelatist, the perjured *prelatist*, desires that *his*
predecessors should be considered moderate in their power,
and just in their execution of its privileges; when truly
the unimpassioned peruser of the annals of those times
shall deem them *sanguinary, violent*, and *tyrannical*.'"

"Breathes there a young lady with soul so dead,"
rejoined Mr. Leigh, endeavoring to save himself by assuming his most imperturbable air, "so devoid of all the
pleasing enthusiasms of her sex, that she stops to read the
prefaces of novels, of the 'Heart of Mid Lothian,' and
remembers every line on the cold page, like an attorney?"

"To confound the special pleaders who do not quote
fair, who garble Sir Walter Scott to their own uses, —
and he a Tory to begin with!"

"Well, well, too sharp young Mayflower! On the
whole, we will let his last words stand ungarbled. I
believe the conclusion of that whole matter is in these
words: 'Nathless, while such, and so preposterous, were
the opinions on either side, there were, it cannot be doubted, men of virtue and worth on both to entitle either
party to claim merit for its martyrs.'"

"That is the best sentiment of all, that has the right

sound," said Mrs. Doane, picking up her ball of yarn,
and straying out to the hall-window to cosset her plants
there a little. Then the blessed woman strayed softly on
down stairs, leaving the American lover to snatch for a
moment his national privilege of being alone with the
adored one. He had to be very wary, however, about
changing his tone too markedly, lest this incalculable
maid would sound an alarm for the *duenna*. So, with
some continuation of the teasing tone in which the late
conversation had gone on, he said, taking up a book
from a stand near by, inscribed with the name "Monny
Rivers," —

"Why does a being with such a beautiful name as
Anemone, not write out her name properly as it is?"

"To enrage Lord Dufferin when he sees me in my
boarding-school catalogue. Only I never have spelled
'Monny' with an 'ie,' which, of course, will make the
governor-general of Canada feel badly. He is the last
man, I believe, who has spent all his scorn on the names
of American ladies. Is it not a most presumptuous piece
of British interference — firing at us way over the bor-
der? Girls," she went on, "are obliged to make mince-
meat of their names, because they have such dreadful
names given them in their helpless infancy: so, when
they grow up, they have to trim them down as best they
can. The merriest and most unpretending girl I knew
at school was christened by such a name as Melpomene.
What could she do but write herself 'Mellie,' or 'Pom-
mie'?" demanded the maiden, who, as for her own name
of Anemone, really thought it so romantically affected
a name. it had required all her sentiment for her dead
mother ever to reconcile her to it.

"But Anemone, the wind-flower — to call that a dreadful name!" exclaimed the lover, who, for his part, sin-

cerely thought that no other name on earth could have
so exquisitely suited this ever-varying maiden.

But the perverse wind-blossom replied, "How would
a man like to be named after all the flowers of the field,
without waiting to see what kind of a flower he would
grow up into?"

"That grace has not been given him. He is not of
the sex that grows up into flowers."

"Certainly. He could be named Chamomile," laughed
Monny, "Juniper, Quince, Calycanthus, Pitch-Pine,—
all these names in the language of flowers mean masculine attributes (what are supposed to be masculine),—
fortitude, benevolence, time, and philosophy, 'I will protect thee.' Those are the meanings."

"Which of them means, 'I will protect thee'?" quickly interposed the lover.

"Juniper! As absurd a one as any," cried Monny.
"The Reverend Juniper Leigh! Wouldn't he be thankful
to write himself 'Junie,' or 'Nip'? Nip would be the
most mannish, I suppose, and extremely dignified for a
minister."

A girl who is bent only on warding off all possibility
of serious talk, and a man who is reconciled to any talk
by the one blissful fact that the darling is there, and the
duenna is not,—a pair so circumstanced will strikingly
illustrate what puerilities conversation can be reduced to
between two not wholly soft-brained mortals, and still go
on very interestingly to the twain.

Thus the next remark which the famous Kenyon Leigh
offered was to inquire most solicitously, "What does
'Anemone' mean in the language of flowers?"

"What *do* men study in all their colleges, that they
come out of them so ignorant of the barest rudiments of
knowledge? In my school botany there was a catalogue,

pages long, giving all the meanings of flowers in the most alphabetical order."

"No such delightful text-books are studied in men's colleges, — nothing half so interesting. This language of flowers is a quite unknown tongue to me. Tell me, what does 'Anemone' mean in it?"

"Do you dislike 'Monny' very much?" asked the maid, by way of answer; for she would have been content now to have been christened "Buttercup," or "Hollyhock," if those names had pleased Mr. Leigh's fancy.

"How *could* I dislike 'Monny'?" he replied, with such an emphasis the artist's head instantly disappeared behind her canvas, and she was severely absorbed in her work again.

"Have you ever been called 'Ana,' for a little name?" ventured the man; for, although the maiden's little name of 'Monny' was dear to him, he had a lover's fancy that a little name all to himself would be still dearer.

"Never," replied the busy artist. "I have always been called 'Monny,' for short."

"See how rich your name is in adaptations! Then the anemone is certainly one of the most poetic of all flowers. The old Greeks named it when they saw it swaying in the soft Thessalian airs. It keeps its lovely name under the waters, — the sea-anemone, you know, most beautiful of all the ocean forms, a plant just breaking into breathing life" —

"Oh! what they call a polyp!" interrupted Monny with a musical shriek. "A thing all a horrid mouth, and claws set round to feed it. I've seen him in the aquarium. Polyp Rivers! The worst, worst name that was ever done to me yet. O—h!" This prolonged outcry in which Monny's nonsense suddenly broke off was caused by a glimpse of Mr. Leigh's tall head as he slyly rose

up to make a raid out of his corner. But the swift girl
was too quick for him. Snatching her canvas from her
easel, and successfully keeping its painted side from
sight, she flashed, with her big but not very heavy
burden, through a door behind her, which opened into
her bedroom, whither the pursuer could not follow

There was a ringing laugh of victory on one side the
closed door, and on the other a man to whom nothing
was left but to go back to his own rooms, and — search
there for some book which would tell him what " anemone " meant in the language of flowers. He actually found
such a work there, among the possessions of Mrs. Doane,
lover of flowers, — a certain volume called " Flora's
Casket," which stood, with other faded little gilt-edged
volumes of the ornamental sort, on a small hanging piece
of furniture, made of pasteboard and varnished pine-
cones, which graced his study-walls. This work verily
expounded, with appropriate tags of poetical quotation,
" the language of flowers ; " and with a little search in
this new dictionary, " anemone " was found. " Anemone " signified *anticipation*. Her lover certainly had not
much else to sustain himself on at present.

But whatever capers the evasive maiden practised all
this week, her friskiness sobered into the most absorbing
earnestness as soon as she was alone in her locked-up
studio. She painted by the early morning light, and sometimes far into the night, even ; mixing her colors before
dark, and finding something that she could do on her
canvas, even by the yellow light of kerosene lamps.

And, by Saturday night of this week, the picture of the
Knight-Templar stood completed, — a great picture, whoever had painted it, and which, as the work of an artist
(man or woman) but twenty-one years old, was a creation
which would be called miraculous. It is a miraculously

rare thing, indeed, to happen to any woman's work, that
the supreme personal passion of her heart can absolutely
rush in one current with the creative effort of her mind.
This boon, with all its hidings of power, was Monny's.
She knew that her lover prized her gifts as she prized his;
and to show him those gifts at their best, and in a work
which should portray his very image as it stood glorified
in her young vision — this was a work into which she
could verily throw her whole undivided self. Young as
she was, she had attained already — through years of that
long travail of effort wherewith these gifts have birth,
and through the priceless discipline of some true training
— to a high degree of the artist's mere skill and knowledge; and now, strong and sure as the Atlantic tides
sweeping up the shore, came the inspiration.

Oh! — wayworn and weary as most gifted women must
come to their achievement, though its purpose thrilled
their earliest opening life — blessed indeed above women
was this maiden, toiling over her masterpiece far into the
night, since she was yet in those first young years when
the bright eyes could outwatch the stars, and the morrow
show only some sweet languor of their lids, some soft
paleness, making only tenderer the fair cheek: hers was
the *palma sine pulvere.*

CHAPTER XVIII.

THE next Sunday also was an eventful day to Monny; for she was to hear Mr. Leigh preach for the first time. He was to be the "supply" that day in the little Orthodox church of Lonewater.

Clara Macey had returned home during the week: so Monny was released from her organ duties; and at the usual hour, arrayed in a white walking-costume, — it was one of those intensely hot days which often come back in the first weeks of September, like a lavish good-by visit of the parting summer, — she set out for the village church with Mrs. Doane. A carryall had been sent to the house to convey the preacher of the day: but he left this vehicle to the sole use of the ladies, who could thus carry a third feminine passenger; and as the vehicle went somewhat out of its way to take up this neighbor, an infirm old lady, the church, when the carryall finally arrived there, was already crammed to overflowing with the people who had come from miles around to hear the man preach who could swim the Lonewater breakers in a midnight gale.

Now, seeing how crowded the church was, and that Mrs. Van Cortlandt was just coming towards it, quite alone, Monny bade the sexton take only the old ladies into those "best seats" which he had carefully reserved for Mr. Leigh's present household, while she waited for the New-York stranger, in order to transfer to the latter any advantage of her own about seats.

This little impulse of courtesy was the only feeling

stirred in Monny this morning at sight of the lady who
had so exercised her mind the Sunday before. She had
actually made her toilet to-day (she wore Mr. Leigh's gift
of the white-lawn gypsy) with the single aim of pleasing
one pair of masculine eyes, uncrossed by a thought of
Mrs. Van Cortlandt, or of what claims the dowdy aristocratic style might have on her future adopting, looked at
in the stern light of duty. Actually, as she stood waiting
now in the church-door, she had completely forgotten
what her own looks were, or Mrs. Van Cortlandt's, seeing
nothing, with that far-off light in her young eyes, but the
minister whose public speech she was to hear to-day for
the first time in her life. Yes, with the ever-gathering
exaltation of feeling in which she had painted her lover's
picture during the past week, the expectant mood that
thrilled her now, it was as if she had gone away with him
into some world apart, — just they two had entered in to
that place of separateness, and the door was shut. Shut
even to the related solicitudes that had moved her the
last Sunday before the lady parishioner of St. Ancient's;
and, modestly saluting that lady now, the two passed into
the church together, attracting every eye.

Very rarely, in truth, into one little meeting-house, or
into the largest one, come a pair of such striking feminine
figures as were these two beautiful women. Each of them
singularly set off the other; and both of them, in different
ways, looked immortal. The black-robed divinity looked
neither old nor young; yet no man would ever have described her as of uncertain age, or, in that rather dubious
phrase of compliment, as a well-preserved woman. No:
dateless of days, her beauty shone in its pale, starry
splendor, seeming by its own nature changeless; so perfect
it must have been created just as it was, subject neither to
growth nor to decay. The white-robed girl, on the other

hand, suggested such plenitude of life, it seemed as if nothing could ever drain the bounteous tides which fed those young pulses, so rounding every contour, making the mere gradation of tints, where her fair veined temples melted into the rose of her cheek, and that again into the whiteness of her round throat, like a symphony of light: for the moment, one forgot to ask what of all this would be left when the sallowing years should smite her; for the moment hers, too, seemed a beauty that could not be touched of time.

The minister, as he sat in the pulpit waiting for the last strokes of the bell to die away, turned a silent glance on the pair who drew so many glances from the congregation as they came up the aisle. Psychologists might say that some occult warning, in this moment, touched the soul of the lover, of danger to the maiden in the neighborhood of that widow; for he experienced some slight sensation like relief in seeing them finally seated, not together, but apart. But this passing feeling could probably be accounted for in a less fanciful way. Thus: the vivid picture which the beautiful twain had made as they moved together, led the eye almost automatically to compare them; and there were subtle refinements of feeling in Kenyon Leigh which shrank from any comparing of those two women. He had no more sense of having chosen one of them than of having left the other; for he did not assume that Mrs. Van Cortlandt had ever been his to leave, and his sentiment for Monny was too utterly supreme for him to think of her as a *choice.* Save for one intense moment of his life, he had never compared her with anybody; but that moment's comparison had been made with this very woman: and that precisely she, who so recently was on the opposite side of the globe, should be walking now into this little church of the wilderness, in such striking juxtaposition to Monny, was a coincidence which impressed him for an instant in some dimly unwelcome way.

It was all a very dim, feeling, however, — so dim that he may have recognized the pleasurable alternation that he experienced on seeing Monny parted from that suggestive companion merely as pleasure at seeing the darling of his heart, as he had always seen her, surrounded by untutored people, so distinct among them, yet so beloved. For Monny, giving her own reserved pew-seat, of course, to Mrs. Van Cortlandt, refused all other places, to blot herself, as the French say, in a little corner of one of the crowded aisle-settees, beside her ancient mariner, Isry-Chris, who proudly created this room for her.

Mrs. Van Cortlandt, as well as Mr. Leigh, was gratified to have Monny sit just where she did, because, in her sideways position in the aisle, the girl was particularly well placed for the widow to study her face at leisure. All that impression of surpassing beauty that she makes at first sight, mentally pronounced the latter, as she made this survey, is in the extreme variableness of her face, and the brilliancy of her eyes and complexion, set off by her curls, and that *ingénue* toilet which she understands so well. The very briefest kind of beauty: these mobile, vivacious faces are always the soonest lined: nobody will turn round to look at her ten years hence, thought the woman, whose face of imperial beauty people had turned round to look at during far more than one decade.

Mrs. Van Cortlandt fancied that those storied heroines whose long and late power over men she was so emulous of, had something like her own imperishable type of face. But probably gifts far rarer and more enduring than any mere physical charm belonged to those sirens who so miraculously triumphed over the years. There was, undoubtedly, far fresher beauty at Egypt's court than in the face of Cleopatra, "wrinkled deep in time." The quality that "age could not wither" was something deeper than her skin. No: even the perverted lives of Circean women would probably show another secret for their vitality than that deathly wisdom which prescribes as the best life-preserving recipe "a hard heart and a good digestion" (to the sex supposed to depend most on its digestion), and which warns women, as in the words of Landor, that "expression in the feminine face," viz., the outward sign of an inward sensibility, "is a beauty for which women must pay dearly and pay soon."

To be sure, there is a sense in which all energy of spirit makes its mark on the flesh, and that early. Thus, even to-day, when the light and bloom which this artist-girl seemed to radiate as she entered the church, a little died from her face, a close observer would have noted in it signs of thought and endeavor which contradicted all that impression of extreme juvenility, as of a girl scarcely more than half through her teens, which her dimpled fairness gave at first sight.

Well, Monny might smile at all the threatenings of time; since, from the first, she had drawn her lover by one of those attractions to which the charms of a face are but the merest lending. But the far deadlier destroyer than time, which the jealous woman who watched her was setting this moment on her track — what could the unconscious victim do against that foe? Yes, the plotter watched the victim while the opening services now began, led by an Orthodox minister who had come in among the hearers, and been invited into the pulpit, while the congregation rose up and sat down in the Orthodox places: all the while she studied that young creature in the aisle. Every outward sign that might aid her in guessing the

girl's most personal traits and temperament, the precise
shade of her social position in the city, — all these things
it concerned the widow's wily purposes to know. She
noted that preposterous old fisherman beside her, evidently her acquaintance, from the grand delight with
which he waited on her.   Isry-Chris, having a very tidy
old wife, got himself up for church with scrupulous neatness; but it must be confessed that he was transformed
by his Sunday clothes, from the hoary picturesqueness
which he had in his week-day ones, into a striking re-
semblance to the symbolic Uncle Sam in one of Nast's
caricatures.   The marvellous hitch about his trousers,
the indescribable fling of coat-tails and cravat, was,
doubtless, partly due to the fact that the chief pieces
of his Sunday suit had usually belonged to some other
man before himself, and partly to that indefeasible jaunti-
ness which a sailor, of whatever years, will impart to his
attire.   But Mrs. Van Cortlandt was precisely the sort of
fine lady to find the old man, in his grotesque simplicity,
an object to shudder at, and to make silent criticisms on
Monny, as she first distributed her own little hymn-book
to the unprovided ones near, and then looked over with
Isry-Chris in that hymn-book, big as a ledger, which he
had brought for his old eyes; her white hand holding
one side of it, and his horny brown paw grasping the
other, while she stood up beside him in all unconsciousness, singing, with something of the sweet voice of her
musical mother, in such melodies as the congregation
joined in.

Monny had always the good old Roman-Catholic virtue
of being able to say her prayers beside a beggar: but she
would really not have known to-day whether prince or
beggar were beside her; all her soul had migrated into
the pulpit with the man who was presently to stand up
there in an office in which he was yet unknown to her.

Now, to confess all the truth, ever since Monny's first
dawn of sentiment for Mr. Leigh, she had a little dreaded
to hear him preach. At first this had been because the
thought of him as a minister a little disturbed his perfect
ideal as a lover: she was so far from the type of young
woman who finds a clergyman as such a romantic character. And when the power of this disturbance was past,
when the man became so supreme to her that his vocation
no longer mattered to herself, then a new and far deeper
solicitude touched her, as to how it might matter to him.

That power of sympathetic insight which distinguishes
all fine feminine natures, and which so often enables a
woman to outrun her knowledge in true appreciation of
whatever concerns the man she loves, — this insight in
such a girl as Monny was like a divination. Thus discerning, as she did, what a masculine grasp of realities
characterized Kenyon Leigh, she could not imagine him
as dogmatizing on the things that nobody knows; and to
reiterate the things that everybody knows — he was too
original for that. But again: least, least of all, could
she imagine him as standing up in a pulpit to turn over
" all the riddle of the painful earth " as a mere problem
to exercise and entertain the mind with, however brilliantly.

Yet what could any preacher do, save some of these
things? was the query that haunted even this young
daughter of the Puritans, till Kenyon Leigh rose up, and
" his full flowing river of speech came down upon the
heart." That it should overcome this young heart like
a current setting from some new immortal seas was not
very strange, of course. But there was no class of minds
on which this preacher did not make somewhat the same
impression. This, by the way, was a never-ending marvel to some critics, who would have said that he would

only be appreciated by the very cultured, superior few, never by the many; and all sorts of extraneous reasons were sought, to account for his mysterious popularity with the multitude. The secret probably needed no such ingenious searching-out. It might not follow that all the crude ears that were always found in good proportion in that varied throng at St. Ancient's had been suddenly opened to perceive the superior force and beauty of this preacher's noble simplicity of speech, where the vividness was all in the ideas, — to perceive the superiority of this style, as a mere style, over that of the orators whose eloquence was rather in their sounding flights of words, and the liveliness of their arms and legs. Quite possibly, some of this class of eager listeners to Kenyon Leigh still thought, that, as to orators, those other speakers were the geniuses; while this was only a plain, blunt man, who spoke right on, in a fashion that mysteriously restored some lost purpose and enthusiasm and assurance to life, —a re-assurance which a great many different kinds of people were in want of; and this was what brought the crowd.

Seriously this might be so. The man did most singularly and peculiarly meet an especial and widely-diffused despair of our time; and whoever speaks to a general want will draw the general humanity to hear him, whatever his mere phrases be. The gift of Kenyon Leigh was, that he laid hold of the spiritual forces of life as other great leaders of thought to-day lay hold of its physical forces. They were just as actual to him. It was precisely that masculine grasp of realities brought to bear on things which are slipping out of men's belief as realities — just this quality in him, which had so troubled young Monny as to how it would find its exercise in the pulpit — which made his peculiar might there

He was like an incarnate deliverer from the spirit of fatalism, — the very St. Michael to that dragon whose constricting folds so tend to press the life to-day from out the moral will, in the rudest as in the most refined breast. Luther throwing his inkstand at the Devil could as easily have been persuaded that evil and good are twin-brethren, and both irresponsible puppets worked by the wires of circumstance, as Kenyon Leigh, albeit he did not live in an age to make precisely that kind of projectile of his inkstand. Of course, behind the unique mental organization that was at once so broad and so positive, there was the great illuminating light of a personal character which had its own way of shining.

"He don't do the scare, nor a bit of the soft sawder; he's got no delivery and no doctrines (nothing newer than the old Bible ones, that is); ain't so very deadly handsome; grand kind of a figure — but no more science of showing it off than a sheep. No, boys: I tell you what positively makes the rush after that new rector at St. Ancient's is, that he's a man himself of a kind of forty-thousand power to keep the strait road in a crooked wale; and by the Lord! if, in about five minutes of him, you don't begin to wish you was making more tracks that way yourself! Yes, sir: when I set out from the fair city of Destruction, there's a man I shall tie up to for the journey."

Thus the Rev. Kenyon Leigh was described, when he first made his advent in New York, by one of those youthful professors of gospel criticism who report the sermons for the Monday-morning dailies, as he sharpened his pencil in rendezvous with his *confrères*. And it may be that the more elegant critics who had puzzled over the riddle of Kenyon Leigh's popularity did not so nearly solve it.

Well, it is not necessary to make any extracts from

the sermon, or even to mention the text that was preached from this morning in the little seaside church, crowded with sailors, down to the lowest deck-hands from vessels lying in Sunday harbor at the next port, whose crews had walked over to Lonewater, getting news that the hero of the shipwreck was to preach there. Kenyon Leigh never preached down to any audience, and he did not preach down to this one; but perhaps that strangely sensitive young hearer whom he had in his congregation to-day could have nowhere heard him where his commission would have been made so clear to her.

Certainly there were men in the world who considered Kenyon Leigh as a great wasted power, as a man lavishing in an outworn profession a genius which in any other field than the pulpit would have made him a deathless name. But to-day, the girl, who, only a girl, was such a critic as in all his audiences the famed preacher had never had before, for none could so measure his greatness as did she, — this young hearer, listening through the deepening hush which always fell on Kenyon Leigh's audiences, and which held as if spell-bound this motley throng, was assured, with eternal assurance at last, that the man *was* in his true work, and that he did it with the rejoicing strength in which the true work is done. But then, he had got his new start.

And the woman who for years had heard this preacher, and yet could sit there to-day weaving her treacherous designs? Yea; and the most famous traitor in all history had sat under the preaching of the Master, plotting his treason while the divine sermon fell.

Oh, solemn exordium which must limit all exhortation that ever was or shall be! — "He that hath ears to hear, let him hear."

CHAPTER XIX.

MONNY went directly out when the congregation was dismissed: her seat in the aisle enabling her to slip quietly away from exchanging any of those greetings with the villagers which were usually a pleasure to her. But to-day her young heart swelled with emotions which made her long to escape from every-day speech. In the entry, however, she was met by the widow Macey, Clara's moth er, who had hastened to speak to the young lady, that she might invite her to go to dinner at her little cottage, not far from the church.

Monny knew that Mr. Leigh was to preach at the next town in the afternoon; that there would be an early dinner at home, after which he would immediately set off: so, on the whole, she went along with the pleased widow Macey. The widow's musical daughter, Clara (not at all a genius, but with talent and industry above the average), was now to go to the city for the winter, to continue her musical studies there, through Monny's influence; the latter having found a family where the girl could have board in return for giving piano-lessons to two children: so Miss Macey had only returned home for a brief period, to get her wardrobe in order.

Monny, who was not more generous than she was con siderate of the feelings of sensitive poverty, was quite adored at widow Macey's cottage; and after dinner the two young girls went out again together, — Clara to go back to the church to play for the afternoon Sunday school, while Monny turned aside to call at Skipper Ben-way's little house. There she staid to fan the sufferer, who lay breathing his life slowly away, or take the restless small children of the family out of doors, under the low apple-trees, and softly tell them stories there, to the res-pite of their overtasked mother.

Then, when the sun began to decline somewhat, she walked dreamfully home, hearing, as she had heard all the afternoon, that preacher of the morning, — home to the old house, so still in the sabbath stillness, and up to her studio, to shut herself in there alone, and kneel long before her picture of the Knight-Templar, which she had called completed the night before, · but which now it seemed to her that she must paint all over again. The warm, wide shining of the sea, the mighty sweep of the Cape-Cod skies beneath which she had walked home, — she longed to bring those breadths into her little room to paint that picture by; such largeness, it seemed to her, should be in the life that looked from it. Well, the sun went down in the great horizon without, and the little room grew too dark to see the picture in, and tea was over, before the minister came, who also had had calls to make, and did not arrive home until quite in the even-ing.

The low sea-breeze, that was stirring after the hot day, grew soft with a rich waft of perfume as he opened Mrs. Doane's little gate; for all over the porch, and high up on the walls of the old house, the sweet Madeira-vine was beginning to blow, whose long-waiting blossoms come with all the white tenderness of spring, all the depth of the ripened summer's fragrance — the man in whose heart love had bloomed even so, came swiftly up the walk and over the threshold, thrilled with but one thought. Flash-ing in his impetuous search from room to room, he caught at last the gleam of a white dress flitting up the stairs, in time to call softly to it, through the darkness, "Good-night, *Ana*."

So faint and shy that only a lover's ear could have heard it, was the returning "Good-night" that was dropped over the balusters : still its accent told that the lover's name was *not* forbidden.

Next day, Monny got out her palette anew, and mixed colors with great care, and thought she must surely re-touch the face of the Knight-Templar. But she did nothing, and finally concluded that she could do nothing until chance should procure her another sitting from her subject.

Well, the subject walked into the studio, all uninvited, soon after dinner; Monny, who had remained in a very subdued state since yesterday's sermon, having forgotten all her tantalizing tricks to-day of holding parley at the door, and then suddenly locking it in the suitor's face. In fact, slipping away from that teasing promenade which she had been wont to make with her lover from the dinner-table to the doors of her rooms up-stairs, she had actually passed from the entry into her studio, forgetting to lock the door behind her. The warped old door did not remain closed very securely, unless the bolt were slipped ; and, finding it thus a little ajar, the visitor, with the merest ceremony of a knock, marched in upon the artist.

"Where is Mrs. Doane?" the latter summoned voice to ask.

"She has gone away. I saw her starting for the village," replied the man, endeavoring to hide the intense triumph with which he made this announcement in the tone of one stating an entirely indifferent fact. Then he planted himself in the corner where he usually posed for his "shoulders," and assumed the immobility of a first-class professional model.

The artist now certainly had her opportunity, but she experienced a singular difficulty in improving it: she could not take a steady look into the face of the sitter. No: great artists among men have painted the women of their love, openly studying their faces, drawing the lines the truer, doubtless, for the inspiration of the beloved presence; but probably no woman could ever so paint her lover's picture, save as she adopted some such strategy as Monny's, who had followed a wise instinct in keeping a third person in the room, thus enabling her to maintain all her talk with Mr. Leigh in a vein of freakish nonsense, while she watched his lineaments unaware.

To-day she could not take up that old tone again; and, after fussing a little with her palette and brushes, she said, to break the too conscious silence which began to fall, —

" This is a hero of the middle ages, you know."

" Yes : up to date, that is all I have been able to learn about him," replied Mr. Leigh, to whom that absorbing hero had come to have such an actually objective existence as a rival to himself, he was divided between a constant longing to punch his canvas head and a sentiment of regard for Monny's work: so he only added the weakly carping fling, " Saracen, Jew, or Crusader, — which ruffian of the period is he? "

" Oh, he is no ruffian! He is the very ideal knight, — a Knight-Templar, one of the undegenerate days, I mean, before they grew bad and ambitious," said Monny, remembering Ivanhoe. " I suppose, of course, the first Templars, those who embodied the pure idea, were great heroes and true men. I had no books here to study up their history: what were the conditions, the vows, of the original order? "

" Well," mechanically began Mr. Leigh, " the first Templars were required to be of noble birth, celi bates " —

" Oh ! " interrupted the dismayed girl, as this before unknown bit of historical information was let fall, " oh ! — they were — *celibates !* O—h ! "

Among all the intonations of which that small word is capable, one of the most pining was Monny's *naive,* dolorous note, as she discovered that she had painted the man, beloved and adored, as a hopeless anchorite. Her arms dropped helplessly by her side as she stood looking blankly from the pictured face on her canvas to the living face of the man who was so identified with it. The latter did not know what was the matter, only that all those maiden defences with which his capricious idol had so bristled of late were down for a moment; and, lest another such moment should not come again in all the rolling suns, he rose up swiftly, and crossed the room to her side.

The girl, taken by surprise, could only make a startled movement towards her picture ; but she was too late to do any thing but hold her palette across the face of the knight, as a last concealment.

" It looks — a little bit — like — *you,*" she pleaded faintly, still striving to hide the telltale features on the canvas.

Mr. Leigh put his hand on the little hand that grasped the palette : he had never given *his* word of honor not to look at that mysterious picture, always meaning to seize the first expedient moment to look at it ; and now he put his powerful hand on the maiden's, and gently drew the little oval board from her hand. But it fell (he knew not where, as he saw the face it had covered) as he turned to the face of the girl who had painted it.

"O my darling, will you be my wife?"

"O Mr. Leigh, can I *ever* be good enough?"

So beautiful, so sacred, she stood there, with her dropped eyelids, and her fair flushing cheeks, he dared not kiss her — only to put an arm around her, and draw her to the high stool where she had been sitting before her easel. Taking a lower seat himself beside her, he turned thus to survey again the picture which he had seen as yet in but one swimming glance.

He took it in now, with its marvellous revelations of power, with all its infinitely tender suggestions of the love that had wrought such very indifferent material as he considered his own personal lineaments to be into this wondrous picture — he turned to the young creature who had done all this, and tried to speak, but could find no utterance, save to take up Monny's own little words, and say them for himself with his deep voice hushed and broken, —

"Can *I* ever be good enough?" The sweet face that was so near to his turned on him for answer such a look of adoring trust, he drew it softly nearer, —

"My darling, my darling!" In the rapture of first kisses no other speech could be.

CHAPTER XX.

"ARE you busy to-night, aunt Persy, or very tired?" asked Monny, looking into the familiar sitting-room soon after the evening lamp was lighted there. It was Tuesday evening; and Mr. Leigh had left the Cape in the morning, to fulfil some engagements which would compel his absence for two or three days.

"No, thank you, Miss Monny," replied the widow; "only some extra steps to-day, that's all, — what with getting Susannah packed off this morning, and teaching Jenny Hines how to wait on the table, and do such things round the house as a young thing like that is equal to."

"And you have not heard any worse news from your daughter Emily about the children?" Monny continued interrogatively.

"No, dear. I'm hoping the children won't be really dangerous. Only a mother, with little ones ailing at all, needs a help in the house that she's used to : so I thought I must send Susannah to Em'ly in this strait, and try to get along myself with Jenny, since neither of my boarders is of the fussy, exacting kind. Is there any thing you want me to do for you, Miss Monny?" the matron suddenly broke off, perceiving something peculiar in the girl's face and her lingering manner.

"No, no; but something I want to *tell* you," said Monny in a very troubled voice. "Something that's been on my mind all day; and it keeps growing bigger and bigger, — something *dreadful!*" she gasped.

Now, the widow had already been told of Monny's engagement to Mr. Leigh the day before; an announcement that she had naturally been expecting for some time. . So this intimation of desperate woes just now sounded rather strange to her; but, seeing the girl's evident distress, she said at once, —

"Come, sit right down here in the rocking-chair, my dear, and tell me what is the matter."

"Oh, the matter is that I have been engaged *before!*" cried Monny with a wailing burst of confession, as she dropped into the chair.

There was a little pause of surprise before the widow said, "*Have* you? Well, now, I had always supposed that you didn't really care for any of 'em. It seemed to me that there was none of all your beaux that you took a truly serious fancy to."

"No more there wasn't," declared Monny vehemently. "But there was one that I had a kind of fancy for when I was sixteen; but not serious. Oh! it never could have been serious, or it would not all have gone out of my life so, like a dream, — like something that never was. But, while the dream lasted, I was engaged to him; and so it has come over me to-day that perhaps I ought to tell Mr. Leigh. And how *can* I tell him?" cried the girl in an anguish of reluctance.

"Certain, dear, Mr. Leigh is not the man to be hard with you about such a thing, — only a passing fancy, as you say."

"But it will *seem* as if I have had something such a sentiment for another man as I have now for Mr. Leigh; and I never, never have. It will be as if I said to Mr. Leigh, 'I cared for that other man once; and now I care for you a little more.' Oh, how cheap it will sound!" lamented the girl, her spirit breathing the cry of love's

own passionate exclusiveness : " Set me as a seal upon
thy heart, as a seal upon thine arm ; for love is strong as
death."

" And there's something else all mixed up with it,"
Monny broke out afresh ; "things that will look most
wild and improper ; the strangest journey that I took once
to New Orleans, — I shall have to tell Mr. Leigh all about
that too, if I tell him any thing. It's been going over
and over in my head all day. You see, I have not had
time before to-day really to think of these things. Of
course, until Mr. Leigh asked me in plain words to marry
him, it wasn't for me to be offering him information about
my old beaux. And then I have been all swallowed up
in the picture — to make it truly like him. I felt born
into the world for just only that, — to paint his perfect
likeness : I could not remember any thing else. But
now the picture is done ; and I promised Mr. Leigh, when
he went away this morning, that I would not work at all
in my studio, but rest all the time till he came back. So
I have had nothing to do all day but think," said Monny,
who, like many another woman, had got more morbid
and unstrung by a few hours' solitary brooding over a
personal matter than by weeks of intense application to
a piece of work requiring all her powers, albeit the
anxious lover was right in thinking that the marvellous
work she had wrought in those weeks had been at a strain
which required rest.

The other guardian of this excitable girl here rejoined,
with her view of things, " Yes, my dear : you've been
swallowed up in doing the picture. And a wonderful
thing you've made of it, — more like Mr. Leigh than he
is himself. And how you make him look more natural
and alive, painted in all that queer old armor that he
never wore, than in his own actual coat and hat, which

he does wear, Heaven that made you with such gifts may know. But all I know is, that you do it by a swallowing up, which needs must be at some wearing cost to the nerves. And yet, instead of calming down after that excitement, and resting, as Mr. Leigh wished, you go swallowing yourself up again in something that worries you about an old beau, till it grows bigger and bigger, as you say yourself, — no doubt out of all its just and natural size."

"O aunt Persy! it is not a trouble I have imagined up. I only wish it was. You would be astonished yourself at my ever having done such things. You see, even aunt Helen does not know. She knows all about my being engaged that time, of course, but not what was mixed up with it, — not about my going to New Orleans. Mrs. Bingham advised me not to tell that to aunt Helen, nor uncle John, nor anybody."

"Mrs. Bingham? Who was she to give such advice as that?" asked the widow, astonished.

"She was a New-York lady, who knew all about the affair from beginning to end. And when she said to me, 'I would not tell your friends about this,' I did not. But I did not *promise* her not to tell (she never asked that) ; and now I *wish* to tell you, aunt Persy. Oh! I long to see how it will look to somebody else."

"And I wish to hear," said Mrs. Doane, thinking it high time that New-York ladies who instructed girls to keep secrets from their guardians should be disregarded. "Tell me all of it."

"I will, I will!" eagerly replied Monny. "It was a Southerner I was engaged to; that is, he was born in Baltimore, but he had lived mostly in Europe. His name was Carroll De Lancey."

"It was in Europe, then, that you became engaged?"

"Oh, no! It was before I went to Europe. It was all over then. It happened when I was at boarding-school in New York; and it all began by my having his sister for a chum."

"She was one of your schoolmates, you mean?"

"No, not exactly. She was never under rules, like a pupil. She was just a young lady boarder in our school. She had finished all her schooling in France, in a very aristocratic convent school, where some of the pupils were even royal princesses. She was very proud of her own lineage, which could be traced back to a De Lancey who was a Norman knight and crusader; but she was born an American. Her father was a rebel officer, killed in the war; and after his death her mother had lived abroad with her two children, till she died. And now Miss De Lancey had come back; and her friends had put her in my school, merely as a convenient place for her to stay in a few months, till her twin-brother Carroll, who was a cadet in West Point, should be twenty-one (because they had property affairs which could not be settled up till he came to that age), and then she was going back to Europe again, for she hated America dreadfully. That was all I knew about her at first; for she never spoke to any of the girls, but sat looking round her so sulky and splendid, just like a princess whose crown had been stolen, nobody could help watching her. And one day I saw her in *such* an attitude, I went up and asked her if I might make a sketch of her, she was so beautiful. And she turned, — she couldn't stir without making a new picture of herself, — she turned into such another attitude as would have scared me to death if it hadn't been perfectly glorious too, just like Judith cutting off the head of Holofernes. She looked at me that way a minute, without speaking, and then she rose up, with a

kind of slow sign to me to lead the way; and I took her
to my room, which was full of my drawings, for I was
studying art very hard then with my master.   And she
went from one picture to another, making a kind of stage
stops and starts, but not saying a word, till suddenly she
turned round and broke out, like any girl, 'O you divine
little genius!'   She was very extravagant in her speech,
you see; and then she was truly fond of pictures, having
lived so long in Italy.   And she sat right down, and
struck up a great friendship for me on the spot, and decided that she would be my chum.   And I grew very
fond of her indeed.   I liked all the girls, but I had never
had any truly dear intimate among them till Kate De
Lancey came."

"Well, now, I shouldn't have supposed she was one
to be very fond of," remarked aunt Persy, to whom
Judith cutting off the head of Holofernes, although doubtless a useful agent for exterminating the enemies of the
Lord, did not suggest the most endearing style of woman
for the intimacy of private life.

"Oh, yes, she was!" replied Monny, in behalf of her
Baltimore Judith.   "Those fiercely scornful ways she
had were a little bit put on, you see, — not vulgarly: it
was a behavior not at all like what artificial airs usually
are.   She was truly high bred, the most elegant and perfect young lady, whenever she chose to be.   But she did
a little like to astonish people.   And then she looked
down on every thing in America; and yet being too really
warm in her feelings, and like a girl, to be proud in the
icy style, she took on that tragedy-queen style.   Then
she was in such a fury against the North!   When we
were chums, she used to just rave round our room when
she was in trouble, apostrophizing her father's ghost, and
crying that Massachusetts had murdered him."

" Well, I should say that was scarce the behavior of
a young lady," observed Mrs. Doane, " when you were a
Massachusetts girl."

" Oh! somehow you couldn't get much provoked with
her," replied Monny. " You see, having lived in Europe
ever since she was a little girl, she was so really ignorant
of America, and about the North especially she made
such monstrous mistakes, you couldn't take it quite seriously enough to get angry. No : mostly when she stormed
so, I used to sit perfectly fascinated to see her attitudes.
She had the most wonderfully graceful figure, taller than
mine, and slim, slim and straight as an arrow, yet perfectly willowy and bending : why, you would have said
that I looked *heavy* beside her," declared Monny, with
such an accent as might have designated Barnum's fat
woman.

" To be sure," added the girl, " when she would go on
very bitterly about the wickedness of the war, I would
say, ' I'm glad the slaves are free ! ' I put that in every
time, — ' I'm glad the slaves are free ! ' And she would
say, ' Of course you are, crazy little abolitionist, stark
mad under your curls, just like all the rest. Aboriginal
Puritan you are : don't I know it? Haven't I seen your
very ancestress? — Rose Carver — Meat-axe — Standish —
whatever her name was. Hope I scorn to know their
names ! hope I scorn to know American history ! That
girl, I mean, standing up in their old boat, in the psalm·
singing picture " Landing of the Pilgrims," — the one
pretty woman they had in their horrid crowd to save
them ; and so they always put her to the fore, in a way
to show her off, in their " Landing of the Pilgrims."
Wouldn't I have landed them at the bottom of the sea !
only I would have fished the poor Rose out by the golden
locks, to be your ancestress, you dear.'

"Rose Standish was not really my ancestress at all," said Monny; "but that was the way Kate would run on, mixing every thing up, till she was all out of breath, and often taking a sudden turn to hug me, after her worst abusing of the North. You see, although she never left off abusing Massachusetts, we were truly fond of each other. She was an orphan, just as I was; and then she had other severe troubles which I had never had, such as money troubles. For all the great wealth she had been born to had been so swept away since the war, that, when I knew Kate, the property left to her and her brother in their own right was but a mere little remnant. But they had a distant relation, very rich, in Louisiana, Gen. Warwick, a kind of great-uncle on their mother's side, who had an idea of making them his heirs, for his sons had been killed in the war, and he had no near heirs alive. Well, Kate was always in a worry lest this old man, who was in very broken health (he had been a great fighter in the war), would die without making a will, in which case his money would all go to a certain Louisiana family named Regdon, whom he perfectly hated; for he called these Regdons traitors to their country, because, just before the war, seeing it coming on, they had sold out their Southern property to advantage, and gone to live in Europe, and so had nothing to do with the war; and all their behavior in this he considered most basely cunning and unpatriotic. Well, these Regdons, who were rich already, and whom Gen. Warwick wouldn't leave his money to for any thing, would yet be able to take it all in law, if he should die without a will, because they were one degree nearer of kin to him than the De Lancey orphans. And yet Gen. Warwick, being full of wild whims, Kate said, kept delaying to make his will. It seemed his views were what even

SoutLerners would call wild. He expected the wur could some time be fougnt over again, and the Southern Confederacy be restored ; and he wanted to leave his property in some way to help on that end. He wanted Kate's brother, I know, as the condition of being made his heir, to promise certain things that he was not willing to promise, because he had no idea of carrying them out. And so, being dissatisfied with Carroll De Lancey, he would often get into his head a plan of leaving his wealth to the State in some way (his own State of Louisiana), so as to forward future revolutionary schemes. I never clearly understood it all," said Monny ; " only that Kate's great anxiety always was this Gen. Warwick, and that he would make some kind of strange will, which would be set aside in a court of law, and so she and her brother get nothing at all. And Kate had told me of all these affairs before ever I saw her brother Carroll. I saw him for the first time at a cadets' ball at West Point. Kate and I went there chaperoned by Mrs. Bingham. Mrs. Bingham lived in New York, and hers was the only Northern family that Kate ever visited at all. She was the wife of Gen. Bingham, who had been bred to the regular army, before the war, you know ; and he had been minister to France, and in many other high positions, as he was a great public man.

"Well, way back in his boyhood, when he was being educated at West Point, Kate De Lancey's father was a cadet there too ; and the two were intimate friends. So when the war came, and they fought on opposite sides, and Kate's father was killed, Gen. Bingham mourned for his early friend, though he was a rebel, and ever after did any thing he could for his widow and orphans, though he was not their legal guardian. His legal guardians, I knew afterwards, could do nothing at all with Carroll ; and Gen.

Bingham had found him living a very wild life in Paris, when he was scarcely more than a boy, and had persuaded him to come home, and enter West Point, thinking, I suppose, that he would steady down there, and come out a fine man at last. Well, Mrs. Bingham's carriage used to be always coming to our school to take Kate to her house; and two or three times Kate had got holidays for me to go with her to Mrs. Bingham's, before we went under her care to West Point. Gen. Bingham was one of the official visitors to West Point, though he did not go with us to the ball. He was out of the country just then, and I never knew him at all; but his wife was a great lady, and I admired her very much."

"I suppose it wasn't a regular thing for you to be going to balls when you were away at school, was it?" asked Mrs. Doane.

"Oh, no!" said Monny. "I never had been at a regular grown-up ball in my life before. But a West-Point ball is not just like other balls; and Kate said her brother wanted her to come so much, she would go, if I would like it. You see, Kate herself did not care for going about in America; for, besides other reasons, she was engaged to a nobleman in Italy, though her friends did not greatly favor the match, which was another of her troubles.

"Well, I was wild for dancing in those days: it was the one amusement that I was truly fond of. And I had a new dress made, and I thought it would be splendid to go.

"And it *was* splendid," murmured Monny after a dreamy pause. "I can look back and remember, — just remember, you know, as you think of something that once was, but which moves you no more, no more: in that way, aunt Persy, I can think how the night of that

ball was all a wonderful joy to me. It was my very first
ball, and every thing was so beautiful and strange with
newness; and he, Carroll De Lancey, was most beautiful
and strange of all. The first sight of him was the greatest
surprise to me when he came to meet us at the boat. I
might have known. of course, as he was Kate's twin-
brother, that he must be in his twenty-first year. But
she, being a girl, had come of age, you know, when she
was eighteen; and, besides being legally free from her
guardians three years sooner than her brother was, she
had such a way of taking all the responsibility about
their joint affairs, I had a notion, somehow, of her brother
as still a boy, much younger than she; and there he was
a man, and like a young prince. He seemed older than
she, instead of younger, not having her fitful, impulsive
ways. He had her splendid beauty; and he was proud like
her, but in a more careless, unconscious style. He was
like her in every thing, and yet not like her at all: I
mean there was all the difference there is between a young
man and a girl.

"Well, he danced with me at the opening of the ball:
then I had a few other partners, because their names were
already down on my card; but after that he asked me to
dance with only him. He was one of the managers of
the ball: so, of course, he ought to have danced with all
the belles, to have taken out all the important young
ladies, in turn; but he was like his sister in his way of
doing just as he chose, and he said he wished to dance
with nobody but me. And as I was only a school-girl out
for a holiday, and not a young lady in society yet, I did
not mind myself about the proper etiquette of balls; and
so, after the first few sets, I danced with only him. He
was a perfectly splendid dancer; and we were trained very
carefully in dancing at Madame Melville's, so I could

dance all night and never be tired : and they played all
the sweet Strauss waltzes, and it was as if we went
through the air. And it seemed to me as if all life was
going to be like that," said the girl, with a look on her
face as if she gazed back into some incredible past, —
" only that, to whirl away in the Strauss waltzes, with
little sittings-down between waiting for the music to strike
up again, while your partner put on your wraps so delicately you could not stop to think whether it was more
affectionate behavior than should be on so short an acquaintance. I suppose he did — did begin to make love
to me that very night," confessed Monny, blushing at the
confession ; " and the next day he went everywhere I did,
although, of course, there were others in the company.
And we went on the river next eve· .ng in the moonlight ;
and he sang most wonderfully an old love-song, — sang it
all to me, though we were not alone. And, when I went
back to school, he came right on to New York, and staid
at a hotel, and came to see me at Mrs. Bingham's ; and it
was very soon indeed that we were engaged. You see,
you see, aunt Persy," pleaded the girl, " Carroll De
Lancey was not at all like a Massachusetts young gentleman. I mean, inexperienced as I was then in lovers, I
am sure I would never have allowed any other kind of
young man to go on so fast : I should have thought him
bold, and myself a forward girl to allow it. But it seemed
just as proper for Carroll De Lancey to make love at first
sight as for Romeo, or the lovers in the old pictures of
the golden age. He looked like those pictures : a wreath
would have been as natural in his hair as in Apollo's. I
made sketches of him as Apollo : I drew him in many
romantic characters — oh, how *could* it all have been? "
said the girl, again with that same look of wondering at
herself which her musing face had worn that morning
when she sat by her studio-table with Mr. Leigh.

What order of masculine personages wore wreaths in their hair aunt Persis did not clearly know, nor was Romeo the most familiar of characters to her; but she began to perceive that the girl whom she had always considered such a marvel of discretion amid her crowd of lovers had had her time of young rashness too. And she asked, with some renewal of critical feeling towards that New-York lady of the first society, " Did that Mrs. Bingham know about all this? Was it at her house that the young man sat to you for his picture?"

" O aunt Persy! he never *sat* to me anywhere: it was not so bad as that. All the pictures I ever made of him were from memory: it was easy enough to do that with his photograph (which I had, of course, after we were engaged), and with Kate always to look at, who had his very features. *Did* you suppose I ever was *intimate* with him the way I have been with—with Mr. Leigh? Never, never, did I have such an acquaintance with Carroll De Lancey — or any other man," declared the girl impetuously.

" Yes," Monny went on more quietly, " Mrs. Bingham knew about it very soon ; because Carroll De Lancey told her that he was going to marry me, and never anybody else. She told him that I was only a school-girl, away from my friends, and that he must write to them. I knew afterwards that she was sorry it had happened: she thought it was too sudden. She was not to blame at all. She had a great many social and other duties, and had not observed, you see; for, in all our acquaintance, it was only a very, very few times that I ever saw him."

" And did the young man write to your friends?" asked Mrs. Doane.

" Certainly; and I wrote o them too. They were in Europe. It was the year that my cousin Annie Slabwell was married, and her father and mother went abroad with her on the bridal tour that she made with her husband. So they wrote me back from Europe; and I remember uncle John's writing me that he should not object to Carroll De Lancey because he was a Southerner. He said all the honest men in the United States, North and South, would have to pull together yet to save this country from its rascals; and, since the old quarrel of slavery was fought out and ended, the next thing to be done was to forget it, and the best way to forget was for Southerners and Northerners to intermarry. I remember that uncle John wrote me out all those sentiments. And aunt Helen, she liked the family because it was an aristocratic one. And although they both wrote, of course, that I was too young, and things must not go any farther till they came home, still they did not really oppose, you see. And so I gave my promise to Carroll that I would some time marry him. And it all happened," said Monny, "in one short school-term. Kate's coming to Madame Melville's, and her asking me to be her chum, and the going to West Point, and my engagement to her brother, — it all came about in that single term; and it was at the end of the term that the New-Orleans journey was. At that time I was expecting aunt Helen and all of them home very soon; but they had not arrived yet: so I was going with Kate to spend the vacation in Maryland, at the estate of some relatives of hers, named Carroll, who had invited us.

" So I was packing my trunks. Kate had been gone to West Point two or three days, staying with her brother there, who had been taken suddenly ill; but I had left off severe anxiety about him, because Kate had written me back that he would be well and out again right away, and would be sure to come and see us a few days in Maryland. Well, I was doing my last packing, and I remen.bx: I had just laid in a trunk that very ball-dress I had worn at West Point, when Kate burst into the room, just come from the depot. She carried the most extraordinary big bundle, and locked the door behind her the second she was in the room. Then she tore open the bundle, and there fell out of it trousers and hats; and she began to strip off her own dress, and put on the trousers, as if she had gone mad. Yes, she had in that bundle a full suit of her brother's clothes; and she dressed herself in them from top to toe before I fairly understood any thing, though she talked as fast as she could speak. It seemed that Gen. Warwick had had a stroke, and was on his very death-bed, and had telegraphed to Carroll De Lancey to come straight on and see him. And the telegram had come to West Point while Kate was there; and, because her brother was too sick to go, she had determined to go herself, dressed up in her brother's clothes, and pretend to be him."

"Goodness alive!" cried the matron. "Pretend to be a young man?"

"Yes," said Monny. "I had seen her fix herself up to represent her brother before. It was for some private theatricals we had at our school. And the very wig and false mustache she had worn then were in our closet now; and Kate had them out and fixed on in a flash; and then she imitated her brother's voice and air so, it was his very self. Well, she said I must go with her, dressed up like a West-Point cadet too. She had brought a boy's suit of clothes with her on purpose for me."

"And what on earth did she want to drag you into her wild doings for?" cried Mrs. Doane.

"Why, for company on the journey. She said how could she go travelling a thousand miles all alone, dressed up in men's clothes, and nobody with her to know that she was a girl, if she should be sick, or any accident happen. Of course, I could not help seeing that would be frightful," said Monny. "Then I begged her to go in her own dress. I told her, if she would only go as herself, I would go with her in a moment, and she could explain to her uncle why her brother could not come, and take all his dying messages. And Kate said that was perfectly absurd : if Gen. Warwick saw her come into his room, only a girl, of no political consequence, instead of her brother, he would be in such a rage of disappointment he would die of rage on the spot, and then there would be no will made. And besides, she said, for two girls no older than we to go travelling without a *duenna* — 'twould be most vulgar and indecent.''

"Indecent!" cried the confounded matron. "And was it less indecent to go travelling in men's clothes?''

"I really think it seemed so to Kate," answered Monny, "she was so used to the European ideas. Anyway she wouldn't listen a word to my proposal. And she began to get very angry with me for refusing to fall in with her plan, for there wasn't a minute to lose. And I remember, in the midst of her distraction and storming, I put in the question, whether her brother approved of this, — of her going to Louisiana, pretending to be him. And she said that her brother did not even know Gen. Warwick's telegram had come ; that he was out of his head, and could not be told any thing. And that frightened me : I thought he was sicker than they had let me know, and I began to cry. And Kate dropped down on the bed, and cried desperately too, and said I could never go to see her brother, however sick he was : it wouldn't be proper. And the one only thing I could do to help him was to go on this journey with her ; and much he would think I cared for him, when he got better and found out that I

had refused to do such a little thing for his sake. And
It broke me all down, Kate's talking that way. Really,
you know, to stand making little moral objections when
people are going wild with distress, and begging you to
do something to help them, it does seem as if you were
just a hard-hearted, unsympathizing prig; and I began
to give way a little. And, the minute Kate saw it, she
began putting me into the cadet's clothes; and, before I
fairly realized any thing, we were in the carriage, both of
us in cadet's uniform, and on our way to the depot."

"How in the world did you get away from the school
in that rig? Where were your teachers?" asked Mrs.
Doane, feeling that somebody should have been present
to stay that scandalous flight.

"Oh, I don't know!" said Monny. "Kate managed
every thing. Servants always did just as she told them,
no more asking her questions than if she had been a
queen. I only knew there was a carriage standing ready
for us, and we got into it and off, with nobody to stop
us. It was about dark, and it had begun to rain, I remember: so the waterproof cloaks that we threw on to
hide our clothes looked all right; and I believe Kate carried her wig and mustache in her pocket, and put them
on at the depot, after she dismissed the carriage. But it
was in the carriage, before we got to the depot, that she
cut off my hair."

"Cut off your hair!" repeated Mrs. Doane, aghast at
every new disclosure of the actions of that possessed
young woman of the Southern Confederacy.

"Yes, I wanted her to. I couldn't do any thing with
my hair at all. Kate managed hers perfectly. To begin
with, her head was unusually small and round: it was one
of her beauties. And, although her hair was long, it was
very straight and smooth, so she pinned it in braids tight

round her head, and then put the wig right on over them, and that just enlarged her head to the size of her brother's : so, with the false mustache, she was his perfect image. But I had no wig ; and my hair, being curly and very long then, wouldn't stay at all tucked up under the cadet's cap, and of course, having once put on the disguise, I was all in a tremble for fear of being found out in it. And I had some scissors in my hand-bag, and I made Kate shear my hair all off before we got to the depot. We gathered up the hair as it dropped under the scissors ; and I can remember now Kate poking all round over the bottom of the carriage, in the dark, to feel if there were any stray locks : she said 'twould look like such a suspicious slaughter of innocents if newly-chopped off hair was left lying in carriages. And then we got to the depot, and she pulled me into some dark corner, where we changed our hats for the cadets' caps ; and she opened one of my trunks, and threw in it the hats and my cut-off hair, and, before I knew, we were on the night-train, and rushing out of New York southward."

CHAPTER XXI.

"WELL," resumed Monny to the auditor, who had come to listen very anxiously to the unfolding of this strange tale, "when we had got off sure and safe, Kate began to be in great spirits. I did not quite understand then how she could be so perfectly easy about her brother; for she had a devoted affection for him. But I knew afterwards that his sickness was all caused by his having taken too much wine in a student's frolic; that he had got so — *drunk* really — it brought on such fever and delirium, his mates got frightened about him, and tele graphed for his sister. But the doctor she had for him knew all about such cases, and just how long they would last, and that was how she could calculate so confidently on his being out again at a set time, while yet he was so sick that he couldn't be told any thing about the telegram, which was what seemed a little mysterious to me then. Kate's only explanation to me was, that the doctor said he had a strong young constitution, which would bring him out all right in a few days. And then she repeated what she had said before, that a little Puritan like me would be just the wife for Cal : when he was married, he would take better care of himself, and not be sick."

" Well, of all the deceitful hussies ! " exclaimed Mrs. Doane, who considered that her well-behaved Monny had been the victim of as precious a pair of young scamps as a slaveholding aristocracy ever produced.

" No," insisted Monny, " she was not deceitful, as she

saw things. Naturally she would not tell me, when I was
engaged to her brother, exactly what had made his strange
illness ; but I don't think she considered those habits any
thing really against him as a fine match. Her notions
were, that it was quite in the order of things for elegant
young men to be very wild before they were married;
that wives were expressly made to steady husbands down.
She had always a very funny style of talking about men,
as if they were somehow in the care of women, — I mean,
as if women were much the most competent to all affairs
where managing and contriving was to be done. That
was one thing which made her so gay on our journey.
She said she had got just the chance she had wanted all
her life, — a chance to be in a man's place, with a woman's
gumption. 'There'll be a will made that will stand in law
when *I* get to Gen. Warwick's bedside,' says she, 'which
it's more than likely there wouldn't be if Cal was there
himself, men have such pragmatical notions about giving
their word. Gen. Warwick will want me to swear eternal
enmity to Rome, of course ; that is to say, Boston : there's
nothing I'll swear quicker. What's the use of being born
in this atrocious country, if you can't take a little practical
Yankee view of things? Whom does Gen. Warwick really
want his estates to go to? Carroll and I, impoverished
orphans of a sire who gave his life and his fortunes for the
sacred cause,' said Kate, in that orating style of hers:
'Whom would he most hate and abhor to have them go to?'
she went on. 'Those renegade Regdons, snug and smug
already in all the unspoiled goods that they had the mean
long-headedness to run away with? Or Northern carpet-
baggers? — wouldn't they plunder it all, even if Gen.
Warwick *could* leave his money to the State by any will
which would stand in law ; which of course it wouldn't,
with all the fantastic conditions he would put in.'

"Well," said Monny, "I had always been used to hear Kate run on that way, and I had no doubt what she said was all true about Gen. Warwick's 'own wishes. Kate would never have tried to get possession of a fortune that others had a more *real* right to than herself," said Monny, correctly discriminating that the Southern girl's unscrupulousness was of the sort which extends only to means, not to ends. "But I felt more and more doubtful and troubled," Monny went on, "about the *way* she was going to get it, — the false clothes we were dressed up in, and every thing. Kate, she kept up all the time as brave and merry as could be : she said we were like Rosamond and Celia in the Forest of Arden. But it wasn't the Forest of Arden : it was the American railroad-cars, full of strange men — there were hardly any women travelling in the night-train. And when the daylight came next morning it was much more dreadful : I did not dare stir out of my seat in that cadet's coat without any tails ; and oh, my *feet* in trousers! So," continued New-England Monny, "Kate got out all alone at the places where our train, which was a through one, stopped for refreshments. I could not eat, anyway, as I began to have a sick headache with riding all night in the cars, and no sleep. But Kate took all her meals regularly ; for she said to take all your meals regularly, and let nothing interfere with them, was the very strongest mark which distinguished a man from a woman. And if you *could* have seen her buy herself a cigar after the meals, and pretend to take two or three puffs at it on the depot platforms while she looked after the baggage! No, Kate was really not a coarse girl," insisted Monny, as the face of Mrs. Doane took a freshly horrified expression. "It only seemed to be her way of keeping cool and unconcerned to amuse herself by putting all those extra touches into her part. And nobody found her out in it :

nobody, from beginning to end, ever imagined that she was no^t really a young man. But *I* got found out.''

"O).!" gasped aunt Persis.

"Yes, I did. It was when Kate got out at one of the stations. My headache was growing very bad then; and I put up my hand, not thinking, and leaned my head back on it a little, while the cars stopped. And a man in the seat behind me suddenly snatched the hand I had put up so, and whispered insultingly over my shoulder, ' Look here, pretty miss, a girl who wants to pass herself off for a boy while she goes travelling with her young man had better not have such hands as yours. Give me a kiss while your other spark is out of sight, and I won't tell your little game.' And all the while the terrible coarse man said those words, he held my hand so tight I could not pull it away, and I was going to cry out to the conductor, or somebody, for help, when it struck all over me that there was no help I could call for; that I had put myself, by that dress, out of the ranks of respectable girls; that I was a character who could be taken up by the police. It was the most dreadful sensation, to know that I was in my own country of America, where men, North and South, can be counted on to be respectful to all women who behave properly, but that I was in an appearance of such improper behavior, the worst man in any crowd was at liberty to speak to me just as he liked, and the best man could only think that I deserved it, and ought to be arrested by a constable. And while I stood dumb and faint, with this dreadful realizing that it was not the Forest of Arden, Kate came sauntering back into the car, twirling her false mustache. You see, the man behind me had seized the moment for all his insulting ways when the passengers were hurrying in and out of the car, and nobody paying attention; but, the minute he saw Kate coming back, he let go my hand. For, you see, he never imagined that she, too, was a girl in disguise: he believed that she was really my young man, and my spark, as he said in that slang of his. Well, the train started on ; and the man staid just where he was, in the seat behind us, from a curiosity to watch us, I suppose. And as Kate sat down beside me I told her right away, in French, just what the man had said to me, and all his behavior. But instead of starting up quick, as I supposed she woul l, to change our seats into another car, she just turned slowly and awfully round on the man, looking him straight in the eyes, while she said, in a low undertone that yet sounded more fierce than you can imagine through the rattle of the cars, ' You touch her again, or breathe one syllable of what you know, and I'll have your life !' And the man — he was a flashy-looking man, about thirty-five — actually shrank all away in his seat, as if death was going to spring on him right out of Kate's eyes. She wore, all through the journey, a seven-barrelled revolver in her breast-pocket, with the handle stuck up to show ; but you would have said her eyes were the deadly thing, rather than the pistol. And the man, looking at them, just whispered out, scared and abject, ' I promise to keep dark, sir ; but, if I might drop a friendly warning to ye, make her put her gloves on, put her gloves on !'

"At that, I tried (for all my gloves were in my trunks) to stuff my hands under the edge of my jacket ; and Kate she corrected me with, ' Crazy child ! put them into your trousers pockets, as a boy does.' You see, nothing could be more stupid than I was, or cleverer than Kate, from beginning to end.

"Well, while all this went on, the seats nearest us had happened to be quite empty, so many passengers had left the car at the last station, and Kate kept half turned

round in her seat, holding that man steadily in her eye:
and although I was terribly afraid that he would break
from under the spell which Kate seemed to have laid on
him, when the conductor came along, and give information
that I was a girl, and not a boy, he did not; he let the
conductor go by without a word.   And he never stirred,
or spoke again, till the train began to slack up to stop at
the next station; then he bent forward a little, and said
to Kate, as if he was a prisoner and she his guard, 'I
beg your pardon, sir; but the next depot is where I was
going to get off.'

"' I will see you landed, sirrah,' says Kate in her most
tremendous tragedy style; and, when the train stopped,
she just marched out with the man, and kept her eye on
him, from the very platform of the cars, till the train rolled
out of sight of the depot, where I could see him standing
still, as if he hardly dared to breathe.

"Well, Kate came back to her seat by me; and the first
word she said was, 'I am disappointed in you, Monny
Rivers, — completely disappointed.   In the theatricals at
Madame Melville's you did Juliet's soliloquy before taking
the poison so like a born stage-genius, I supposed nothing would be easier to you than a little bit of acting
like this.'   I answered that I could act Juliet because I
thought I *was* Juliet, I forgot myself entirely; but that I
could not forget myself now: I remembered every minute
that I was Monny Rivers, not in my proper clothes."

Of the two. Monny had the real dramatic genius; Kate
De Lancey was only theatrical: still it was the latter who
could bring all her clever mimetic talent admirably to bear
in a piece of artifice like this masculine masquerade, while
the girl who had made quite an inspired personation of
Juliet wholly lost her power.

"And then," said Monny, continuing her narration to

Mrs. Donne, "I gathered up my courage to tell Kate that I was not going any farther in those clothes. She asked me if I was mad. I told her no, but that I should be if I tried any longer to play a part that she must see I was a miserable failure in. I said, 'I cannot put people down as you do, Kate: I have not the majesty, nor the self-control. I am of worse weakness in this than you think. I came near laughing right out when you turned round on that man in such a blood-thirsty manner. I shook inside, both with laughter at the idea of his being so afraid of you, only a dressed-up girl, and with terror lest he would find you out. I shall laugh and cry pretty soon all in the same breath: I shall have the hysterics, like Lilly Lambert at school.'

"Kate said, 'Would I pretend that I was such a silly, sentimental idiot as Lilly Lambert?' then, when she found out that I was actually in earnest, we had a tremendous battle. What I proposed was to stop at the city of Jackson in Mississippi, where the train was to arrive very soon, go up to a hotel (taking one of my trunks), dress myself out of it in my own clothes, and then go on the rest of the journey with Kate, in my proper character. Of course I did not mean to desert her utterly. For I *had* started and come thus far with her; and, if there ever had been a possible moment when she would have given up the journey if I had stood out firm in my refusal to take it with her, that chance was lost now; and I felt I was so far involved in her action as to have no right to forsake her in that dangerous disguise that she had always been afraid to travel in quite alone. But I told her, for myself, I must go back into my own dress. I said, 'You have decided, that, when we get to New Orleans, it will be best for me to be left at a hotel there while you go on alone to your uncle's place, which you say is six miles out of the city. Perhaps he will live several days yet; and what shall I do all that time at the hotel? I shall be sure to get found out there, unless I tell lies that I cannot tell, and which would all be useless if I were willing to tell them: for the blushes will go over and over my face, if any man looks hard at me in these clothes; that is something beyond my power to prevent. And, when I am found out, it is not merely that I shall be put in the lock-up, but men who hunt out every thing as constables and detectives do will hunt out all about me just the same if I do not speak one word. They will find out who I came to New Orleans with; they will find out about you, Kate, and that you are another girl dressed up in man's clothes — and *then* what will be?'

" Well, Kate quieted down a little as I said all this; for, of course, she had been wofully disappointed in me, as she said, and she could not help being afraid that I should be found out again, and with far worse consequences, when she was not with me to crush people. So she sat silent, and thinking a moment, then she broke out, —

" ' Now, Plymouth Rock, now, Miss Bunker Hill, will you hear reason? If I give in to you on the main point, will you absolutely obey me in the details? If I consent to your changing back into a girl, you cannot go back into your own name: for I shall stay a man, and you cannot travel with me without taking my name; you must pass as my wife.' I asked her if I could not as well be her sister.

" ' Good heavens!' she said. 'If we leave the train for this business, haven't we got to stay overnight at Jackson; and what a frightful thing to be shut up alone in separate rooms all night at a strange hotel!' "

" Lord save her!" ejaculated aunt Persis, "if she wasn't just a girl, after all! Smoking cigars, and threaten-

ing men's lives with seven-barrelled guns, and yet too
timersome to sleep alone in a strange place."

"Of course," answered Monny, "we wouldn't either
of us have liked that. And I was expecting then that my
name would some time really be Mrs. Carroll De Lancey;
and so, as Kate said, it would only be anticipating the
future a little to take that name now, and I agreed to it.
So we left the cars at Jackson, and went up to a hotel
and staid all night; and Kate managed every thing so
cleverly,. just as when we left our school in New York,
that I went into the hotel a boy, and came out of it a
young lady, without anybody's detecting it. And our
names were registered at the hotel as Mr. and Mrs.
Carroll De Lancey; and we took the earliest morning-
train, and went on to New Orleans, and had no mishaps,
except that we forgot to have the trunk that we had
taken up to the hotel checked at the depot; and it was
left behind on the platform there. But we never sent
back for it: I told Kate there was nothing in it that was
worth the trouble. You see, it was that same trunk which
held the West-Point ball-dress; for my travelling-suit,
that I was all dressed in to go to Maryland, had been flung
into that trunk, hat and all, in New York, when Kate
dressed me in such a hurry in the cadet's uniform. The
uniform that I took off at the Jackson Hotel was in the
trunk now, of course; and there was not much else in it
but the smashed old ball-dress and my cut-off hair; and
so we let the trunk go, and never saw it again. And I
felt so comfortable to be in my own dress again, that,
just before we got to New Orleans, I went sound asleep
in the cars. I remember it, because it was the only time
in my life that I ever could fall asleep in the cars. But
all the night before, at the hotel, I had not been able to
shut my eyes for thinking what if we should be found out

in the morning: so at last I was fagged out enough to
drop asleep even on the train.   Well, I woke up out of
my nap with a great start.   Our train had stopped; my
head was on Kate's shoulder; and her eyes were flashing
lightnings (the way they did when she was angry) after
somebody who seemed to have just left the car.   I asked
her what was the matter.   'That sham duchess!' said
she, 'that humbug Madonna!   She presumes on her
beauty to be insolent.   I looked her down in her low-born
curiosity, — low-born she is, I say, for all her Queen of
Heaven airs, and style of beauty.   The one thing a real
gentlewoman does not do is to pry and peer.   I looked
her down.   She'll know a De Lancey the next time she
sees one: she'll know her betters, and try her stares on
somebody else.'

"'Why, what ever did she do?' I said.

"'Do?' says Kate.   'Wasn't I so pleased to see you
asleep at last, you poor little wakeful owl, I just hugged
you up a little, that you might sleep sounder; and with
your pathetic short locks, that I'd cropped off all uneven
in that dark old carriage, twirling in such babyish rings
over your bigoted Boston head, didn't I kiss you one small
kiss, forgetting that I was a man; and along must come
My Lady, and turn round with her slurring stare.   Eye-
lashes half a yard long ought to be sweeping round in
search of good sights, and not evil.   She's a swindle, with
her divine gray eyes — and a fool, a fool!   She might
have seen, through a forest of false mustaches, that I
kissed you like your mamma, and not like your lover of
an improper sort.'

"'O Kate!' I said, 'how *could* she help staring?
Don't, *don't* forget that you are a man again!'

"Kate said she wouldn't, and that she had forgotten
once in a worse way than I: so now she was more than

even with me, she said. You see, Kate was truly good-natured and generous. And that was the last of our mis-haps. Very soon we were in the main depot of New Orleans. And an odd chance happened to us there. I had barely stepped from the cars when I heard somebody saying, in such an astonished voice, 'Why, how come you here, Miss Rivers, and with Mr. Carroll De Lancey? Is Miss Kate along too?'

"I turned round, and there was Mrs. Bingham's maid Jane. Then I remembered Kate had told me on the journey that she was afraid of crossing the Binghams somewhere; for they had gone South a week before. Well, Kate seized Jane's arm now, and said quickly, 'Where is your mistress?' — 'She's gone up to St. Louis with Gen. Bingham,' says Jane.

"'When are they coming back?' Kate asked.

"'Gen. Bingham is not coming back at all,' said Jane. 'He's going on up the river. And Mrs. Bingham we some expected to-night, and that's why me and Halifax came to the cars to wait on her: but she hain't come; so she won't be here now for another twenty-four hours certain.'

"'Go and tell Halifax,' says Kate, 'to get two swift saddle-horses — one for me, and the other for himself — to go out to Ashcroft, Gen. Warwick's place. The general is dying. Tell Halifax to be here with the horses the quickest possible.'

"'This turns out good luck, instead of bad,' said Kate to me as Jane hurried off. 'The Binghams have rooms at the St. Charles Hotel: so you can be bestowed right there; while, as for me, I shall have no loss of time get-ting to Gen. Warwick. Halifax was born a slave in New Orleans, and knows the whole country round here.'

"'Shall you tell him who you really are?' I whispered to Kate. 'Halifax? no; Jane? yes,' said she. 'She's a shifty creature, and nobody knows what I may want of her yet.' So Kate took Jane aside, when she came back, and told her the secret. And Halifax came very soon with the two saddle-horses; and Jane hushed up her surprise, though she did give a little bit of a cry when she saw Kate spring on her horse just like a man.'"

"Mercy!" echoed the Puritan matron, with another cry.

"Oh, she carried it off wonderfully!" rejoined Monny. "Nobody ever mistrusted that she was not really Carroll, — no, not Gen. Warwick himself. She got there before he died, and the will was made as she wanted it, and he lived only a few hours after; and I had word of all this the next afternoon, when Halifax came riding into the city again, with a note from Kate to me, saying that it was all over, and I could tell Mrs. Bingham now, if she had got back.

"Well, Mrs. Bingham arrived about dark at the hotel, and I had just done telling her how I came to be there, when Kate came herself. Halifax happened to be in the room just then, taking some orders from his mistress, so Mrs. Bingham was forced to speak to Kate as if she was Carroll, till Halifax went out. Then she said very sternly, ' Kate De Lancey, take off those mad riggings, and go to bed!'

"'I shall obey you, madam,' says Kate, bowing very low and humbly. She had been trained in that French convent school in a beautiful respect to superiors; and she really liked Mrs. Bingham, who was a very queenly lady herself. So, with only those few words, and a lovely meek courtesy, she came right away to her room, our room, which we had together in the hotel, close to Mrs. Bingham's. But when she got there, with only me, you know, she tore off her wig and mustaches, and danced

round with her long hair tumbling over her man's coat,
and hugged me round the neck, and just went wild with
triumph. ' I defy them to do any thing about it now ! '
said she, — ' Mrs. Bingham, or anybody else. Will they
go embarrassing the hapless orphan of a murdered sire by
betraying what shifts she was reduced to to get her own:
They'll never do it. Gen. Bingham went to see Gen.
Warwick once, himself, to persuade him to provide for
Carroll and me in his will. And what have I done, but
pacify a poor dying old hero by promising what he asked?
And, if Cal doesn't fulfil, how can I help it? ' And Kate
whirled me round the room in her joy, crying that we
should all be rich now forever, and could be married
right away, the whole of us, and go to live in Europe.
And all I knew was that she carried every thing through
successfully; and, although Mrs. Bingham disapproved
dreadfully, she didn't see any way to interfere, I suppose,
at that late stage of affairs.''

"Well, no," admitted Mrs. Doane, "I don't know as
anybody could have seen it a clear duty to tell what that
harum-scarum girl had done, bad as it was, playing tricks
at death-beds. Since it seems the rich man had had
nobody in his mind for real personal heirs but them
two orphans, so, very likely, at the last he would have
left them his money pretty much the same, if the girl
hadn't done that wild piece of daring, to make sure.
Most likely the New-York lady, Mrs. Bingham, thought
so, and felt no right to do any thing that might stir up
strife about the will, seeing there was them who would
have been eager to set it aside so as to come into the
property themselves. But, anyway, 'twas a terrible
mixed-up business; and I hope — Did you go out to
that place at all yourself, — that country-place where you
say this Gen. Warwick died?" suddenly asked the

matron, feeling that it would be some relief to know that
Monny had been kept from the immediate locality where
a will was made under such conditions.

"Oh, no!" said Monny. "And Kate herself never
went out there again in man's clothes. She had brought
a trunk with her from New York; and she changed back
into her own dress that very night — Mrs. Bingham sent
Jane in to help her dress, I remember. Then Kate staid
hid in our room, and never stirred out of it till her
brother came: he came only two or three days after
us."

"Brother — came?" repeated Mrs. Doane in bewilderment.

"Certainly," said Monny. "Kate had left directions
for him to follow us just as soon as he was able to travel;
and, when he arrived in New Orleans, Kate slipped out
of the hotel by a back door, unobserved, met him at the
depot, came back to the hotel leaning on her brother's
arm as a young lady (coming in by the front entrance
of the hotel this time), making all the parade she could,
on purpose to attract attention. Her plan was, you see,
to represent that *Miss* De Lancey, the sister, was the
one of them who had just arrived."

"Mercy on us! If that girl wasn't the beat-all!"
ejaculated Mrs. Doane, as she gradually took in this last
transformation of Miss Kate.

"He got there, the real Carroll did," resumed Monny, "just in time for the funeral. So the brother and
sister went together, each in their own proper character,
to the funeral, and then together again the next day to
hear the will read; and from first to last nobody ever
guessed but that Carroll De Lancey himself was with
Gen. Warwick when he died, and that it was his sister
who came a few days later. You see, Kate never over

looked any least little circumstance that might help to mix her identity more completely with her brother's. For instance, all the time that we two were on the cars, travelling South, Carroll was absent from his school-quarters. His mates had him in hiding somewhere, away from the military academy: Kate had charged them to keep him so. I suppose the reason she gave them was that she did not wish the school authorities to know about his drinking so much; but she had the deeper reason of the disguise she was going to put on: she had to pro-vide, of course, against the appearance of a Carroll De Lancey in two places at once. And I know the cadets who had her brother in charge managed just as she told them. She was so beautiful, you see, young men would do any thing for her."

" Whom did you come back from New Orleans with? " suddenly asked Mrs. Doane, with some passing alarm at finding that Monny's girl-companion had so completely imposed on all beholders the idea that she was a young man.

" Oh! I came back alone with Mrs. Bingham," replied Monny, looking up unconsciously. " And I never saw Carroll De Lancey again. You see, I fell all out of love with him one miserable evening, right there at the St. Charles Hotel, so that in my heart I really wanted to break off my engagement then; but I did not feel it right to when I could give no positive reason. But, when uncle John came home, he broke the engagement right off. He knew positive reasons why I should not marry him. O aunt Persy! uncle John had found out bad things about him in Paris; that, besides drinking too much wine, he was very wild in other ways — in — in ways not to be talked about. Uncle John was more angry than I ever saw him before in all my life; for he found that he had

gone right on in all those unmentionable dissipations just
the same while he was engaged to me.   When I knew
that (aunt Helen told me), I understood then all my blind
feeling about him that unhappy night at the hotel when I
repented so that I was engaged to him.   It was the night
after the will was made.   Kate staid out at Ashcroft, but
Carroll rode into the city to spend the evening with me in
Mrs. Bingham's parlor.   She was in the bed-room of her
maid Jane, who was taken very sick, most of the time that
evening: so I was much alone with Carroll.   He wanted
me to marry him right away ; and perhaps his head was a
little turned by having come into his fortune, or he had
been taking too much wine again — oh ! I cannot explain
it, aunt Persy ; only I did not like his manners that night
at all.   I wished he would go ; I wished Mrs. Bingham
would come back into the room — and oh, I wished my
mother was alive !   I was so young — it was only a blind,
blind repulsion I had for him ; but I understood it all
afterwards," said the Puritan girl, whose Parisian-South-
ern lover had been by no means a villain, no betrayer of
innocence in high circles or low : he had merely plunged
so deeply into the world's old, old ways of evil, that, even
in these young years, the returnless delicacy of the heart
had passed away.

"And you say you never saw him again?" said Mrs.
Doane.

"No ; because we left New Orleans (Mrs. Bingham,
and poor Jane, and I) the very next morning, at daybreak.
It was the New-Orleans climate that had caused Jane's
sickness ; and the only hope of saving her life, the doctors
said, was to get her right off on the water : so Mrs. Bingham, who was very fond of Jane (she had lived with
her many years), started with her at once.   And she
took me with her merely because it was more proper, of

course, than for me to be left to go home with the others. But poor Jane died on the passage, and was carried home to Mrs. Bingham's only to be buried."

"Did not the young man come after you?" asked Mrs. Doane.

"Oh, yes! He came right on to New York. But, by the time he got there, uncle John had come home; and he saw Carroll De Lancey, and forbade him ever to come near me again. And I never have seen him since."

"And never have told your uncle and aunt, you say, about that journey South?"

"No," replied Monny. "You see, I was staying at Mrs. Bingham's when uncle John came. She had become like an old friend to me; for one day, in asking me about my parents, it came out that a younger brother of hers had been poor papa's most intimate friend in college — she remembered to have heard all about how he was killed. So, in all this trouble of breaking off my engagement, she was like a mother to me; and when she said, ' I would not mention this journey to New Orleans, even to your friends,' I did not."

"Well, doubtless she had good reasons. She seems to have meant the right thing."

"Indeed she did. And it happened, that, right after all this, I went to Europe in the bridal party of my cousin Harry Slabwell, who was married now; and his wife's father and mother and myself, all went in the party abroad. And before I came home from Europe I heard of poor Kate's death."

"Her death too?" repeated Mrs. Doane, startled for a moment (but the thought soon faded away) at finding how few were the original witnesses left alive to Monny's strangely entangled adventure.

"Yes: she died in Italy, in a year after her marriage

there to that nobleman she was engaged to.   I was truly
fonder of Kate than of any girl I ever knew : and, after
her death, her memory and that of her brother all mingled,
and grew in my mind to something sad and tearful : it
was as if he was dead too, and his faults no more to be
spoken of.   I do not mean that I had any tenderness for
Carroll De Lancey as for a lost lover, for I had not.   You
see, I could never have loved him truly ; for all the memory
of him faded out swiftly and utterly as a dream — except
the lesson of it : that lasted, and went deep.   I never
forgot that once in my life I had found a young man so
charming as to fancy that I wished to be with him always,
and yet that I grew sick to death of him all in a minute.
O aunt Persy, that was an experience I never, never could
forget !   Why, the very reason I have had so many beaux
has been because I did not dare, remembering my wild
delusion of being engaged to Carroll De Lancey, to receive
the exclusive attentions of one.   It is going with one alone
which really draws you into sentimentalities before you
know ; whereas, when you have many beaux, you just talk
nonsense to them all round, which does not lead to any
thing serious at all.

" No, aunt Persy, I have never had serious relations with
beaux except that once, nor ever allowed any young man
to behave to me as a favored lover does, except just Carroll De Lancey.   But if I tell Mr. Leigh about him now,
and he happens to remember all those young men who
were here to see me when he first came to this house, will
it not *seem* to him as if I have been giving my heart away
piecemeal all along, as if I have been truly a great flirt,
and began very improperly young indeed ? — engaged when
I was a school-girl.   How can I *bear* for him to have such
an idea of me ? " wailed Monny afresh.

" O aunt Persy ! " she broke out anew, " of course a

would never, never be right for me to marry a minister, if I were not in true sympathy with his life and work. But I *am* in *true* sympathy with the kind of minister Mr. Leigh is. If he were like some ministers, strict about trifles. or laying great stress on doctrines, and the necessity of belonging to his own particular church, why then I could not honestly profess to be a very strong believer of that kind. But I *am* a strong believer in him and in the everlasting righteousness, which is all .you can think of when you hear him preach. Truly it is the very spirit of that righteousness in himself which makes me adore Mr. Leigh so, and not his great talents. I could not love any man merely because he was talented. I'm talented myself," cried the artist-girl. "I mean, I know just what a poor little accidental trifle it is to be talented. To be born with some knack at expressing things on canvas or in books, — it is nothing. One may be very rich in those gifts, and yet live a low and ignoble life. Oh! I saw that when I was in Europe, in the great picture-galleries there; that there were evil pictures, as well as divine ones; pictures that it took a world of talent to paint, and yet which had better never have been painted. It was as if my eyes were opened to see all this by my acquaintance with Carroll De Lancey, which had first brought to me the great dreadful discovery, that this was a world where people could be perfectly beautiful, and yet have no morals. It was such a shock that I could never be dazzled by that kind of beauty any more, or think mere talents and brilliancy any thing to glory in, except as one would be glad to have any gift to make pictures live, or put words powerful, so as to bear witness to the truth.

"I never, never imagined," the impassioned girl went on, "that just the kind of seer of the truth whom I should fall in love with would be a minister. But it is so ; and I do want Mr. Leigh to know that the things he spends his life for, the things which have to do with character and conduct, are what I, too, set higher than any thing else in this world. And how can he believe that, if he thinks I have been of light conduct myself? Why, I suppose that even the least strict people, if they knew of that Southern journey of mine, would cry out, ' What a shocking thing ! That great preacher is going to marry a wild girl who played bold pranks when she went to school ! ' I never did," protested Monny, and most truly. "It is not a true piece out of my life : I mean it is not like any of the rest of it, — my running away to New Orleans in boy's clothes."

" No, dear," replied the matron soothingly, as the girl drew breath for a moment in her impulsive outpourings ; " and nobody but perfect strangers to you, who never even saw your face in their lives, would call you a bold girl."

" But I don't like even perfect strangers to be able to think any thing amiss of Mr. Leigh's wife. You know the least ill report about a minister, or anybody that belongs to him, — how it stains, how it stains ! " cried the girl. " And I cannot bear to tell even Mr. Leigh himself just this one kind of story. I mean, I should not be afraid to tell him, he is so generous to me, any most foolish, foolish little thing I had ever done that troubled me, if only it was not just in the line of *those* things, — the things which have to do with modesty. You know, aunt Persy, in those things it seems unpardonable for a woman to make even a mistake : the bare shadow of wrong-doing offends like the substance."

" Yes," rejoined the Puritan matron, " the world reckons, and rightly, that, between the women who do bad things and the women who are given to dancing on the edges of badness, there's no great difference : modesty is alike gone from both of 'em. So I don't blame you for disliking to stand, even for a moment, in the eyes of the man you are to marry, as among the careless-behaved girls.''

"It will *look* as if I must have been such a girl to have travelled a thousand miles dressed up first as a boy. and then pretending to be a wife, when I was not married. O aunt Persy! how will such behaviors *look?*" And with this word so often and distressfully repeated, the girl ended her long tale, and, leaning her round arms on the table before her, looked into the elder eyes with anxious longing to have her policy of concealment seconded.

It should be remembered, we think, when women are accused of being the concealing sex, that frankness about their mistakes is generally far more costly to them than to men, not only because of woman's greater sensitiveness to blame from those she loves, but because, while it is sufficient, as a rule, for a man to *be* right, a woman's ways must not only be right, they must *look* right.

The Cape-Cod widow, being a woman, shared Monny's own sense of the feminine relation to mere appearances; and she answered slowly, "I don't know that there's any clear call of duty for you to tell Mr. Leigh just now all this strange-sounding story. When you're a married wife, my dear, if it still burdens your mind as something you ought to tell him, 'twould come a great deal easier to you to speak to him about it then; but till then I'd let it all drop, seeing you are sure that your heart is no less whole towards the man you are going to marry, because of that old affair.''

"Indeed I am. I love Mr. Leigh not less, but always more, because of my memory of Carroll De Lancey, and the shocking disappointment he was to me.''

"I've no doubt of it," said aunt Persy; "and so there

seems to be no reason of the inward state why you've any thing to confess to Mr. Leigh, — mere outside actions, that you were led into, not of your own will, and which happened so long ago, I see no reason of conscience for you to speak of while it is so trying to your feelings; and I'd just go to bed and to sleep, my dear, and forget all about it," concluded aunt Persy.

It will be seen that both Monny and her elderly adviser had all the feminine reverence for truths, but not the masculine respect for facts. Women, in general, incline to attach a prime importance to intentions, — "the inward state," — as aunt Persy had it; while men do to the outward act. That is, something in the whole course of men's lives, in their larger dealing with the world of affairs, seems to teach them far more forcibly than it does women, that deeds are always more serious than intentions, for this momentous reason, that any thing which has once taken shape in action is always likely to trail some consequences after it, which, sooner or later, will turn up and have to be met. Notably was this proved true in poor Monny's girlish engagement, and all the tangled adventures which had grown out of it: five years had that affair lain dead, and no living soul had stirred the embers thereof; yet it was all there, ready to be blown up into a most burning scandal by an enemy.

This tendency of women, by the way, to exalt the spirit above the letter, is a great spiritualizing force, we think, in life and society, — a help to that perpetual re-asserting of the vital quality of things which the world always needs. But, applied to the conduct of affairs, would not this feminine virtue tend to become a peculiar vice of disorder? Would it be wholly fanciful, for instance, to cite Miss Kate De Lancey, with her reasoning that all means were right to secure Gen. Warwick's property to her brother and herself, because in his heart he *wanted* them for his heirs, — to cite this young woman as having merely carried out to some daring extreme the feminine doctrine of the " inwardness of things " ? This girl and her brother were two of those uprooted and unguided young lives which are among the heaviest damages of every civil war ; but, of the two, the girl had grown up by far the least damaged, by far the superior moral being. Yet she did, without a qualm of conscience, what nothing would have induced her wild young brother to do. He would not swear a promise, even to a half-crazed old man, which he had no intention of performing. Drunk or sober, he would not trifle with his word. He considered it the characteristic of low-born knaves to lie ; and, whether his scruples had their root in pride or principle, the practical result was the same, since his integrity was quite unshakable.

His sister well knew this, and had contrived her plot accordingly, making it impossible for him to undo any thing she had done, save by exposing a lady, and she his own sister ; that is, the one earthly device by which to tie up his " pragmatic " sense of honor, her ingenious wits had hit on, — she had tied it up with her own. Now, the girl was not false-natured ; but she had none of her brother's instinctive sense that to tamper even with the formulas of bonds and contracts strikes at law and order. Indeed, that law and order have been hardly won, and won by fighting, and that, if lost, they must be fought for again and by one sex, — this feeling seems sufficiently to penetrate the whole fighting sex to make a man, when he has any conscience at all, apt to show some conscience in the direction of those principles which underlie law and order. The feminine conscientiousness is prone to be keener in some other directions ; and hence, we fancy, arises that charge so often brought by men against women, of being lawless in any thing like business dealings ; the charge, also, that, whenever women have had political influence, they have shown a political immorality and unscrupulousness quite beyond that of men. Now, that women are the less scrupulous sex in questions of pure right — what they apprehend as pure right — certainly cannot be true : they made the most heroic of martyrs in the days of religious martyrdom : they have always been ready to die for love or religion ; that is, for a person or a principle, — any principle which really commanded the allegiance of their souls. But the principles on which governments are carried on probably very seldom do so command their allegiance ; for in the practical world pure right never obtains, only a very mixed right indeed. And women being most keenly alive to all this alloy of im- perfection in the best systems for establishing human justice, and not realizing, as men do, that these imperfect systems are yet the sole barriers against chaos and mis- rule, probably somewhat naturally incline to the dangerous liberty of making private interpretations, — of setting aside codes and formulas in the interest of some higher truth which they seek to establish ; to, in short, what scoffers would call the politics of priests and women.

It is not necessary to be a scoffer — to be either in the ignoble attitude of beings who undervalue their own sex, or the ungenerous attitude of those who undervalue the other — to see that there may be some grounds for the con- servative apprehension, that in politics the better woman might often be a more mischievous agent than the worse man.

CHAPTER XXII.

BEFORE Mr. Leigh's return to the Cape at this time, he took occasion to present himself to the Slabwells to ask his wife in due form of her guardians. They were finishing the out-of-town season with a few quiet weeks among the Berkshire hills, and there the suitor called on them. When Mr. Slabwell had somewhat recovered from his amaze at the idea of Monny's choosing a clergyman, he found points in the proposed alliance that were profoundly satisfying. Morals and money he regarded as the two indispensable pins of a human exist-ence: which of the two he considered the most essen-tial, it might be difficult to say, so absolutely fatal a lack he found in the life that wanted either. And certainly a man who was at once a minister, and the possessor of an independent fortune, presented such a conjunction of these two prime human values as might be called miracu-lous. Also, the devoted husband reflected that this gen-tleman of old family would be a nephew-in-law sure to please his lady-wife. Mr. Slabwell's own respect for old families, as we have before implied, was strictly limited to the female sex. No aristocrat on earth could surpass him in reverence for a born lady; but the only born gen-tleman that he had ever stood in the slightest awe of was the paternal Mr. Rivers, when he went to ask him for the treasure of his daughter. And as for Mr. Leigh, uncle John considered it decidedly that gentleman's place at present to stand in awe of him. And so he did. Scriously, the suitor's claims to ask for such a rare girl as his wife's niece were so thoroughly examined by Mr. Slabwell as to assure Mr. Leigh that his darling had grown up under the stoutest of masculine protection; and altogether the famous clergyman, and the undevout but very upright Mr. Slabwell, acquired, in the course of their transactions, quite a strong mutual respect. Aunt Helen, who was really of Monny's blood, naturally pleased Mr. Leigh still more, — a liking which was fully reciprocated by the lady. Thus Mr. Leigh was indorsed by the Slabwells; and appreciating on his own side all that Monny's guardians were, and finding, in all that they were not, only a new cause of tenderness towards the young orphan who in her deepest life had grown so alone and apart, he returned to the Cape — having fulfilled the other engagements which had taken him away at this time — at the end of a three-days' absence.

He came by that same early evening-train which had brought him so often; and a high tea awaited him, which, this time, was probably a truly exalted meal, as Monny graced the board, with no hints of running away; and, after the repast, the two went out for a pleasure in which they had never indulged before, — a walk together down to the beach.

It was a singularly soft, still evening for this region. The wild gales which blow about the equinox yet waited; and even by the ocean, whose opposite bank was the shore of another continent, — even over this mighty thoroughfare of winds, no breeze to-night seemed arriving. Calm sea and sky were all alight with the ineffable glory of a September moon shining at its full; and the long waves, falling farther and farther away with the outgoing tide, made only a tranquil cadence to the varying voices of the man and maiden as they came down the high bank to the beach.

"Here seems a good place to rest," said Mr. Leigh, leading the way to a certain spot on the beach which lured him to-night with an especial fancy. It was a great rock, half buried in the sand; and Monny, whose memory at the moment was less alert than his, sat down, unaware of any thing peculiar in the place, until Mr. Leigh added, —

"From this rock a certain young lady, inspirited by an extremely early breakfast and an exciting dog-race, first gave me a piece of her remarkable mind."

"Oh!" cried Monny in sudden horrified remembrance of the place and that matutinal dialogue which had opened her acquaintance with Mr. Leigh. "What *did* you think of me that morning?"

"I thought," said the minister conscientiously, "that you were very pretty and amusing."

"And after?" softly asked the girl, as her lover sat down on the rock beside her.

"That you were always more and more pretty and amusing."

"And after?" still repeated the wistful voice.

"And after, ever after, O my darling! what have I had to do but to be ashamed and ashamed that I once thought you *only* pretty and amusing?"

"Truly, I mean to be more than that," whispered the eager girl. "I wish to be all, all, that I should be. I have thought about this a great deal since you have been away. I have been reading the Prayer-Book, — over in the last part, the Appendix, I mean, where there are rules for the ordering of priests and things. I found something domestic there, an order about 'the manners of them that specially pertain to ministers,' — their households. I am charged to be ' a wholesome example and pattern,'" quoted Monny, from her researches in the Prayer-Book Appendix.

"No, little dissenter," laughed the minister softly, as the rueful, solemn accent with which Monny made her personal application of the Church orders was bewitching in his ear: "you are not quite up in the Prayer-Book yet. The charge is to *me*. I am to *make* you a wholesome example and pattern, 'as much as in me lieth.' The Church is very reasonable, you see, does not ask any impossibilities, only some decent endeavor on the part of the clergyman to make his wife behave."

He spoke playfully, anxious to dispel any unduly formidable notion of the responsibilities of a minister's wife which might be oppressing the young girl beside him; but his lightsome answer had a word in it which started into such painful memory her New-Orleans escapade, Monny took it up quickly,—

"To behave has always been my wish and my habit— I hope; that is — usually. Truly, as a general rule, I do not think I have been given to wild and strange conduct. But sometimes, in the press of very peculiar circumstances, one may do things not like one's real self, — things which should not be taken as true samples of one's character. Do you not think so? That morning when I talked to you so here (I have forgotten what words I said; but I am sure they were dreadful impudence), you do not believe it had been my usual style to lecture strange gentlemen with that awful boldness, do you?"

"Blessed child! it was the most unmistakable style in all the world, never, never, the style of a bold girl," the lover hastened to reply to the tremulous pleading that was in Monny's voice. "Why, darling, I had a fancy to come here to-night just because I loved you then, and always, always from that morning. And what man could ever love a bold girl?" said the simple wooer.

Again a word which struck sharply on that trembling

inner consciousness of the girl. She did not speak; but her lover discerned by the moonlight some expression in her face which made him say quickly, "Dearest, what is the matter? Let us go away from this place, if it is painful to you."

"No, I like this place," said Monny, controlling herself. "It is larger out of doors, it is very large to-night, — the sea and the sky." She was feeling as if the shining immensities that she looked on might widen her vision of what her duty was as to telling her lover that secret; for the calm decision not to tell him, which she had been able to come to in his absence, was singularly shaken by his return, his very presence so moved her to confidence. Still she trembled to speak.

Meanwhile the lover rejoined, to the maiden's last words, "Not larger than my confidence, my delight, in you, darling, just as you are : yonder ocean is not more boundless than that trust and joy. This doom of 'specially pertaining to a minister,' he went on, improving the phrase which Monny had fished out of the Prayer-Book to put the arm of a proprietor (an extremely covetous one) around the maid as he spoke, — consider it not so deeply. You must not fancy that the change in your name is going to necessitate any mighty change otherwise."

"Oh! there are many changes I shall expect, I shall wish, to make," said Monny, readily lured away from the disturbing subject she was secretly struggling with, to talk of easier things connected with her future relations. "Balls and such gayeties I shall be so glad to give up : for I was getting very tired of them even before — before I knew you, Mr. Leigh. Not that I thought it wicked to dance ; for I have not been brought up to think that way, and I took immense pleasure in dancing when I first came out. But that kind of pleasure lasts such a little while :

when once you have been through the whole round of
fashionable amusements, it is much the same thing over
again, and leaves such a sense of emptiness as work does
not, because that is never quite the same thing over again.
And my work, too: I shall be willing to change all that
now — to give up art.''

"You give up art? What an inconceivable idea!"
ejaculated the astonished man, as Monny reached this
point in her offerings.

"Surely," said the girl earnestly, "all the daily hours
I spend now in painting pictures will make a great deal of
time to help you. Can I not do something about your
sermons? — copy them, I mean."

"Precious martyr," laughed Mr. Leigh: "there are
two difficulties in the way of the immolation you propose.
First, I have never yet kept a private secretary; second,
when I do come to that need, I think I can find some
proficient in the art of penmanship whom I can sacrifice
to my sermons at a less monstrous waste and misuse than
there would be in making a mere scribe of a being whom
Heaven made an artist, and who has done her heroic best
to improve the gift of Heaven. Ana," he continued
seriously, "it has seemed possible to me, it has been my
hope, that, in the life which you have promised to live with
me, there might, in the long-run, be fewer obstructions to
your study of art — at least, not more — than those which
have been in your past life, and which you have so marvellously overcome. I certainly know women of society
whose homes are in nowise neglected, and who yet keep
up such a constant round of what may be called outside
duties and pleasures as must consume a very large part of
every day. And since Ana cares so little for the pleasures of these ladies, for ' the sugar-plums, and cat's-
cradles, compliments, cards, and custard which rack the

wit of all society;' and since she is certainly excused from
their duties, having been born to this especial duty of her
own of art, — I cannot see why this great *desideratum* of
time for her pursuits may not, one year with another, be
secured to her.   It surely cannot be a wild calculation to
hope for this, since I reckon, you see, quite from the
standard of the average woman, even the fashionable
variety of her who is not usually considered the most
energetic of her sex.   And have I not seen how infinitely
more than the average energy has one young girl in gathering up the hours?''

"Oh! I have always had to gather them up in order to
do any thing at all in art; especially since I have been a
young lady, — after I left school and came out, I mean.
I had supposed that my time was going to be wholly my
own then; and I was very much disappointed and troubled
to find that it was less my own than ever before in my
life: all the day seemed to be so frittered away, and
utterly spoilt for work, by mere social demands.   And
although, at last, I succeeded in reserving to myself some
regular morning hours to paint in, I had to do it by
dropping the whole business of making and receiving
formal calls, and ignoring so many other observances of
society as made me, I knew, an anxiety to aunt Helen.
And then the thought that I was discomforting her would
be such a weight on my feelings, that often, when I shut
myself up to paint, I could hardly do any thing at all; for
you know you need to have your heart at ease before you
can put your mind well to your work," said soft-hearted
Monny.   "And I tell you all this, not to complain of the
home which has been my only home for so long," continued the orphan; "for aunt Helen has always been kind to
me, and most careful for my good (according to her own
ideas), and uncle John as generous as possible, and always

interceding for me to have my own way. But what I wanted to say was, that no hinderances which I *could* have in — in a new home, would be any hinderance to me at all, where I had the strange new help of somebody who did not merely tolerate my pursuits, as my guardians have done, but who really believed in and strongly approved of them. Oh, if you *truly* wish for me to keep on in art, I cannot think what kind of heaven it would be to work with such a help as that always!" ('Tender demonstrations from the lover here somewhat interrupt the outflow of girlish confidences. It is resumed, however, with another anxious inquiry from the maiden), —

"And will not the people — your parish, dislike my being an artist?"

. "*Dislike* your genius! — I should think not," replied the lover proudly. "Why, when once you have exhibited your pictures, I expect to be known thereafter only as the husband of Mrs. Leigh. As the dearest earthly ambition I have ever had has been to wear that title, I shall naturally like to hear it repeated as often as possible."

"Seriously," returned the girl to these flatteries of the famous man, to whose face her own was so wistfully upturned, "there will be an idea, you know, that an artist will be both undomestic, and inefficient in parish duties."

"Seriously, my dear child, who on earth will the domestic business concern save our two selves? And even the most inexperienced mortal can discern one thing about this great domestic question; viz., that it is very largely indeed a question of finance. I mean that it is perfectly idle to say that the mistress of a house cannot safely and rightly delegate an immense proportion of all her cares, if she has no necessity to count the money-cost of thus relieving herself. Thanks to my fathers, money-necessities, which hamper all their days so many better men, have not

touched my life : I trust they may never come near yours.
Fortune does permit us, my dear, to arrange our establishment in the way most favorable to the ends we both
value most, and still to have something to spare for
others. We can the more readily provide for all this,
because neither of us care for great show and magnificence."

"Indeed I do not: indeed I would like to be poor with
you, Mr. Leigh, to live on very, very small means indeed.
You would see what a manager I would develop into
then," said Monny, not without some warrant for this
little boast. "I could dress — why, I could dress entirely
out of your old surplices," exclaimed the girl merrily.
"The white robes and the black ones, they would keep
me in toilets all the year round, and such riches of yards
as would be in them for trains! With those mighty
remnants to fall back on for clothes, I would so fix myself
out as to be a perfect credit to you on the smallest
of incomes. How big *do* you look in your preaching
gowns?" asked Monny, who had never yet seen her
gigantic lover magnified by those flowing habiliments, her
light way of referring to which must be pardoned to
her Puritan blood : she was not to the manner born.

This churchman's sense of the seriousness of his calling did not reside in his gown ; and he met the girl's little
sally with the laughing reply, " Big enough, I hope, to
suggest to the young person who was referring just now,
in rather an alarming tone, to her parish duties, that I may
not stand too ambitious encroachments on what I had
fancied to be my own peculiar sphere.

" Seriously again, Ana, this is a reasonable world, much
more reasonable, on the whole, than it has the credit of
being. When it sees man or woman truly devoted and
effective in any one work, it does not ask that such a

worker shall equally attend to all other works. My parish has, I hope, the average rationality : be altogether sure, my darling, that you can trust it never to ask a girl whose patient, wonderful young years have wrought what yours have to be any more 'efficient' than she is."

"Of course, I shall be most glad to help in the church charities, — looking after the poor, — I have always tried to do that a little."

"Have I not seen it?" said the minister.

"And any thing in this world that I can do to be useful to you, if they are things that I have *not* cared about before, I shall care for now. I have read," Monny went on with *naïve* earnestness, "that the wives of great men — those of them who were fortunate in their wives — enabled the men to be much greater by supplementing all their labors, sparing them the drudgery of their tasks ; that even the wives of scientific men have learned to be thus helpful. It seems there have been many of these women. I was reading this summer about Dr. Priestley, who discovered dephlogisticated air, I believe it was, — made a great many investigations in airs, the reviewer said, which were of immense importance to science. And he said that Dr. Priestley was able to accomplish such great things because he had a remarkably capable wife, who relieved him from all earthly cares. And I read, too, that it was through another devoted wife that animal magnetism was discovered ; that some scientific man, experimenting one day with a live frog, happened to put him down near something that was electrized, and the watchful wife observed how its leg twitched — poor little frog ! " Monny exclaimed with involuntary lament, in the midst of her gravely-delivered scraps of biography.

"I think so ! " — Mr. Leigh laughed aloud at the abrupt termination of Monny's solemn quotations, — " a pair of

them to torment him, decidedly a family of cruelists for
Bergh to look after !

"It is conclusively settled now," declared the lover,
"that I am *not* a great man ; for I am everlastingly certain that I do not want a supplementary wife. Mrs.
Priestley especially, I am bound as a churchman to object
to. Some of her husband's mischievous activity might
have been curtailed, perhaps, if she had been a less capable woman. The frogman's wife I will not pronounce
on ; but surely I cannot indorse a woman who contributed
to the enlargement of such a schismatic as the Rev. Dr.
Priestley."

"Reverend?—I did not know that he was a minister,"
murmured Monny.

"Certainly, he diffused rather more dephlogisticated
air in the domain of theology than anywhere else," said
Mr. Leigh.

"I remember now," rejoined the girl, "that he was
some kind of religious come-outer, to begin with. But I
read about him in ' The Popular Science Monthly ; ' and
all that remained in my mind was his scientific discoveries,
and how the reviewer extolled Mrs. Priestley as a model
wife. He said that all efforts of her own would undoubtedly have been miserably weak and worthless, if she had
aspired to any original research, like the vainly ambitious
women of to-day ; whereas, by making herself an adjunct
to her husband's labors, she was instrumental in the ac-
complishing of truly great things. And I remember the
reviewer wound up by saying, ' Honor to the wives of that
type,' in a way which so seemed to say, ' Dishonor to those
who attempt to do any thing of themselves,' it discouraged me dreadfully about painting pictures."

"Dear child," replied the lover, who had listened, fascinated by the mere music of the pensive tone in which

Monny bewailed herself over "The Popular Science
Monthly," "old Dr. Johnson ought to be forever alive to
say to every mortal man of us, your afflicting reviewer
with the rest, ' My dear sir, endeavor to clear your mind
of cant.' We must all live by cant sometimes, the
shallow generality, the idle hearsay, — we must follow
these in many perplexed things until the true light dawn.
But when that comes, when a man has had the illumination which I have had in you, my wonderful Ana, he must
be an extraordinary bigot and blockhead to have any ear
for the old cant afterwards. As to the general subject
of woman's rights, I suspect there is plenty of cant on
both sides of it : my tastes, I suppose, have been conservative on the general question. But it is a question that I
do not pretend to have studied, and I see no need to study
it now — to settle any general questions in order to decide
that it is your particular right to be an artist."

"I know, I know that you will be most generous to me
if I go on in art ; and it has been very good of you to jest
about the useful wives, and say that you will be content if
I am not one of them. But I *want* to be one of them, —
to be the very, very average woman indeed, in the sense
of living all my life for your sake," said the girl, voicing
a passion which was so infinitely deeper in her than the
artist's, no reviewers were needed to stimulate it. "If I
could be the greatest artist that ever was, it would never
console me, if I thought that I missed thereby the chance
of lightening your special burdens a little : it is something
I cannot *bear* to miss, — the hope of being some near and
personal help to you which nobody else is."

"My own beloved," said the man solemnly, for the
girl's words had touched deep chords, "really to bear
another's burden is not in our mortal power. But to keep
another happy and in good heart while he bears his burden

himself, that is love's gift, and it is the divinest gift on
earth. That gift, that help, you are to me in a degree
beyond all words to utter, — a help indeed which none
other is, or ever was, or I had imagined ever could be.

"And see now," he went on more lightly, "what cant
beyond all other cants it is to talk of the model wife as
if she were some stereotype pattern, warranted to suit the
universal man ; when I, for instance, should find your
reviewer's model wife, whose husband must provide all
her work or her play, the most formidable lady that I
could possibly take on my hands. For there are no frogs
to watch in my study ; and how could I supply her with
my 'drudgeries,' when I have always been mysteriously
unable to do any work well, if I tried to cut out and
shirk the drudgeries thereof? And, perhaps because I
have lived too long alone, I must confess that I should
not want the most admirable supplementary lady in the
world to be talking to me, even about the Sunday schools
and the charities, at all times and seasons. Behold what a
miserably unfit husband I should be for the perfect wife !
But the imperfect one, the abnormal woman, the genius,"
he said teasingly, "I have the singularity to think that I
might possibly manage with her. When she was revealed
to me one marvellous morning, I began to whisper to
myself, 'I could forage for this mate. Some of its natural wants are known to me. It were good for it to have
its bread and water sure, and with no turmoil of their
getting ; and for that Heaven has enabled me to provide.
It would choose regular habits : so do I. It will wish to
spend much solitary time at its work ; ergo, when I shut
myself up alone to study, it will not feel itself wronged
and neglected. Ah, this bird of the empyrean,' thought
I, 'rare and strange as it is, if I could win it to be my
home-bird, there would be this enormous basis of hope

for future happiness, that so many of its wants and ways are in my line of wants and ways. This unnatural girl, with a pursuit of her own,' I said, 'is the one feminine being who would not be wholly an enigma to me.' "

Thus spoke the man to whom a being who should fill all life's large spaces of thought and endeavor with only the fondnesses of the heart, however fond, with the mere ebb and flow of emotion, however pure, — to whom such a being, let it be confessed of Kenyon Leigh, would have been, however fascinating for a little time, at last utterly wearisome and exhausting.

"O my darling, my darling!" protested the lover anew, "I always loved you, always wanted you for my wife: not to long for you was impossible. But when I thought you were what these *doctrinaires* of yours would call the normal young maiden, in the sense of your having no special occupation but — to be charming (although Heaven knows you were too charming to me for me to pass any severe criticisms on your office in the world), was I not forced to think that such powers of charming must needs pine for a gayer atmosphere than was permitted to a work-bound life like mine? And now, my own Ana, that I know you as you really are, all the deep sources from which your young brightness was fed, do you ask if I am content with you, glad in your great gifts, in the expectation that you will cultivate them through life? Dearest, believe me, you are all in all so absolutely what I would have you, that if I had ever dared to dream of such a possible wife. of a joy so perfect in this world of ours where perfect joys are so seldom found, — great satisfactions for great desires, — I should have thought myself as wild as Greek Endymion, maddening for the moon."

Solemnly, as all deep feeling speaks, these words were spoken; and it would seem that they might quiet even the fluttering young heart that heard them with an eternal re-assurance.

Apparently it was so for a little. When the thrilling silence which held the lovers for a moment was again broken, it was by the voice of the girl, saying in a tone low and gravely sweet, —

"I *do* believe you, Mr. Leigh, that you wish me to go on with my work. And be very sure indeed," continued the earnest maiden, "that mine is not a kind of work that will ever in the least have to be considered beside yours, — with reference to interruptions, I mean. Interruptions will be comparatively of no importance to me, because, if I lose one day, I can paint another; whereas I understand very well that a man's work can never be put off in that way. Because almost all the work that men are engaged in — men who are in what is called active life — has this necessity, that it must absolutely be done within a fixed time : when the hour strikes, the minister must be ready with his sermon, the lawyer with his brief, and so on. That is one reason why the women's-rights people seem to me very wild indeed when they urge that women can practise professions just as men do. For of course it would be a very strange kind of home, it would be no home at all, where both the master and the mistress were driven by avocations that could not be interrupted. It is certain, that, if one had this necessity to have his working-time kept sacred, there must be the other to guard it."

The man who was to be "guarded" listened in charmed silence to all this grave discoursing of Miss Monny. The way in which this very emotional and imaginative girl yet betrayed her descent from the much-arguing Puritans by her earnestness to be logically right on the most every-day matters, this little debating fashion of Monny's speech, perpetually fascinated Mr. Leigh, albeit there was often a touch of amusement in the mood with which he listened. Just now he smiled only an inward smile as he looked down on his young protector to ask when and where she had made such an exhaustive study of the whole duty of woman.

"This summer," she answered with all seriousness, "I have read a good deal about woman's sphere. Dr. Priestley seemed to be in the magazines *apropos* of some celebration. The centennial of his birth has come round lately, has it not?"

"That came round, my dear, between forty and fifty years ago," replied Mr. Leigh. "But there has been a statue erected to him in England lately: that is what you have seen notices of."

"I suppose so," said Monny, who had taken no profound interest in Dr. Priestley or his birthdays, save as his domestic life had furnished a text for preachments on the model woman. "So many centennials are being celebrated just now," she added, half in excuse of her inattentive memory, — "America's next year, and this year Michael Angelo's fourth centennial."

It was the merest chance which had brought the great sculptor's name to Monny's lips; but it was a chance fated to give a particular turn to her thoughts. Michael Angelo had been an especial god with this artist-girl. She adored his character as well as his genius. And now, as his name dropped accidentally from her lips, it crossed her young fancy that there was some likeness between the great master who had so long dominated her ideal world and the man beside her, although the latter had never handled any implements of the former's art. Men are allied quite as much through the greatness of their qualities as through any similarity of their mere talents; and the spirit, at once fiery and austere, of the great sculptor, writing on his immortal statue, "Sweet is sleep, and sweeter yet is it to be of stone while misery and wrong endure," — this spirit, in its strong hatred of the evil, and passion for the good, might well seem reproduced in Kenyon Leigh to the girl who loved him. Certain it was that at this moment her fond imagination spanned the centuries to compare her lover to the immortal artist, so many of whose words are as memorable as his statues. And Monny's thoughts could not make this comparison to-night without remembering Michael Angelo's love for Vittoria Colonna. Nor could she recall just now the Marchioness of Pescara, the mature, gifted woman, the widow, lovely in her ripe years, without thinking of — Mrs. Van Cortlandt. Yes, there flew back to her now on the wings of all these wandering fancies her first impression of that beautiful woman as she stood beside Mr. Leigh in the church-entry, her sense of the wondrous way in which the pair graced each other. Now, as then, any jealous thought was impossible to her of the widow. But her original feeling about Mrs. .Van Cortlandt as the resplendent type of all the fair women Mr. Leigh had known before herself, came back to her now with such a renewal of the thrilling wonder that she could be preferred to such, she lifted her face to her lover's, with the bashful, slow-dropping-words, "Have you never — cared for — loved — any woman before me?"

"Never!" The answer came so full and strong, the girl forgot every thing else to respond, "Nor I. I have never truly cared for any man in this world before. Little fancies — I have had those; but they are not love — are not worthy to be called so. Are they?" pleaded the girl with a passionate eagerness which overbore all timidity; for Mrs. Van Cortlandt had suddenly dropped into the sea, and the image which rose on 'Monny now was Carroil De Lancey.

"Never, never!" reiterated the man with a fervor of emphasis, which, on his side too, gathered force from a hidden thought; for he remembered at this moment his own "little fancy" for Mrs. Van Cortlandt. Here, then, were two most truthful beings, looking into each other's eyes, speaking, one would verily say, heart to heart, who were yet keeping back a secret each from the other, — a secret of the same nature. There was this difference between them, however, that the man had not the slightest feeling that his secret was any thing that he ought to speak of. He would have considered himself no gentleman if he had mentioned to any being on earth, even the nearest and the dearest, any such inchoate, never-fulfilled views towards a lady as had been his regarding Mrs. Van Cortlandt. The girl, on the other hand, suffered from the fluctuating conviction that she ought to confess. The words she had said, however, had been as pure of all conscious intent to falsify, or even evade the truth, as the man's had. She scarcely knew what she *said;* for she had spoken from an impulse to quiet within, not to disguise without, that resurgent trouble, which, whether her wandering thoughts strayed to woman's sphere or to Michael Angelo, lay in wait to seize her.

It is possible that this trouble might yet have found some outlet in speech to her lover, as she sat beside him on the moonlit shore, had not a familiar sound just here broke in upon all conversation. It was the bark of Duke George coming rapidly nearer, and soon echoing along the edge of the cliff above their heads.

"Somebody must be with him. There must be something wanted at the house," said Monny, starting up;

and as the dog presently came plunging down the bank, ecstatic at finding the truants, Mr. Leigh's "Halloo!" soon brought a responsive "Hi!" from Susannah; and in a moment or two more her dusky figure showed, outlined against the sky, at the top of the bank.

"Please, your Honor," she cried, as Mr. Leigh took a few strides upward to hear her message, "de missis hab sent me to say dat word hab jess come to de house dat poor Skipper Benway is gwine fast. An' his wife, hearin' dat your Honor hab come home, she send word to know if it be too much trouble for your Honor to come over and speak wid de dyin' man once more, at de last."

The minister could make but one answer to this, and forthwith he led Monny up the bank. When they had reached its top, the girl said, "You will get there much quicker, you know, by walking straight to the village, across the sand-hills; and I will go home with Susannah and Duke George."

Thus, therefore, they parted, Monny going home with the black woman, and Mr. Leigh striking directly across the waste for the cottage to which he had been summoned.

CHAPTER XXIII.

MRS. VAN CORTLANDT was at the cottage before
him, making a charitable call, in prophetic anticipation of seeing Mr. Leigh, having learned his habit of
visiting there. She had brought some flowers with her,
ordered express from a Boston greenhouse. The door
of the sick-room stood open into the little kitchen, in
which latter room Mrs. Van Cortlandt now sat, making a
figure which an artist might have painted for a picture of
high-born beauty ministering to the lowly. But in fact
the lady was a great embarrassment to the lowly. The
very flowers she had brought, with their exotic richness
and professionally elaborate arrangement, suggested funeral decorations to poor Mrs. Benway ; and she dreaded
to have the eyes of her dying husband turn on them, lest
they should seem to him an unkind anticipation of his
burial. Moreover, one of those painful contrasts which
cannot be softened in the narrow quarters of the poor was
present in a frolicsome two-years-old baby, which, having
had its long nap indiscreetly late in the day, was running
about now with an ecstatic sense of being out of bed at
candlelight, and of having much sleep laid up for many
hours. The exhilarated baby, in fact, had been so bor-
rowed and petted by the neighbors during the long sickness in the house, as to have become a rather demoralized
baby in other ways beside its sleeping habits. Thus it
would keep informing Mrs. Van Cortlandt that she was
making too long a call, by striking at her with hostile

little hands, and ordering her to " dow away, dow away !" with all its infant might. That the grand lady should see her child misbehave thus while the parent life was ebbing added some touch of maternal mortification to the poor wife's sharp sorrow; and altogether Mrs. Van Cortlandt was not a consoler.

All the difference which there is between the truly great personality and the merely imposing one was felt when Mr. Leigh came in. Not humiliation, but help, was in his very presence: he even relieved, as it chanced, poor Mrs. Benway's soul of those deathly flowers; for, noting practically that their heavy fragrance thickened the air for that laboring breath, he swept them all up with both hands, and carried them out into the kitchen. As it chanced, he set them down there on a low table, where baby, slyly straining on its little tiptoes, reached after them with that grip of the baby-fist which makes up in tenacity what it lacks in comprehensiveness, and, dragging the whole pile of costly blossoms down on the floor, revelled in the delicious mischief of tearing them all to bits. There would certainly have been loud outcries from the small destroyer, if Mrs. Van Cortlandt had interfered with this pastime, and she did not. No: in the little kitchen whence all others had withdrawn now, she sat silently shredding her bitter thoughts while the babe on the floor shredded the flowers; nor was the infant's mind further than hers from the soul that was passing.

Life, almost to the last, wrestled hard with death in the strong-knit frame of the poor sailor; and the minister, so powerful to lift the gasping sufferer into more easy attitudes, and yet more powerful to sustain the parting spirit, did not leave until all was over. It was midnight ere this release came; and Mr. Leigh then started for home in an abstraction in which he forgot Mrs. Van Cort-

landt. He went a few paces, then suddenly remembered
his manners, and came back to offer his arm to his lady
parishioner, who must walk at this late hour to her lodgings. The proud woman whom he had forgotten, sharply
affronted as she felt, had risen to her feet even to go after
him; for she had lingered through all this long waiting-
time at the cottage for an opportunity that she would not
let slip to-night, at whatever cost of pride. So, taking
the arm of her tardy escort, she went out from the little
house. The great moon of the night was riding high in
the zenith now; and no foot was abroad so late, save that
of a neighbor who came up the lane to straighten the dead
man for his burial. It was so short a walk around the
corner, and along the main street, to Capt. Gawthrop's,
that, very soon after leaving the cottage, Mrs. Van Cortlandt began, —

"There is a trouble on my mind, Mr. Leigh, that I
have been wishing to speak to you about."

"Shall I call on you to-morrow?" replied the clergyman, as the lady was slackening her steps rather suggestively.

"I think there will be time to speak of it *now*," said
Mrs. Van Cortlandt, suppressing another angry sense of
slight.

The man who had been much preyed upon by ladies
with troubles on their mind which they must open at somewhat untimely seasons had never found this lady one of
that indiscreet company before. But he could but fall
obedient into the lingering pace which the widow set, and
prepare to give ear.

"The trouble is one which wholly concerns others, not
myself," said Mrs. Van Cortlandt with her usual slow,
refined utterance. "A very great calamity is likely to
befall our friends the Roosevelts unless they are warned

of certain facts which are in my possession. It is so
painful an interference for me to undertake personally, I
naturally conclude to ask you, as their pastor and mine, to
discharge this duty in whatever way you may think best."

The pastor listened to learn his duty. "There is a
young girl in this place whose" — the lady hesitated with
the proper diffidence of a lady forced to speak of delicate
matters to a gentleman — "whose past has a perfectly
ruinous stain. The young person was never of my acquaintance, but accident informed me of all the facts of
her misbehavior at the time. It was several years ago
that her scandalous affair occurred. It was very skilfully
covered up, I fancy; so that she has been received ever
since as an honest girl. Her face is a striking one, and I
recognized her the moment I met her here. But of course
I did not feel called upon to betray what I knew about
her, until I learned that she was likely to marry a man
whose family would naturally sooner see him dead than so
married. And he himself is utterly ignorant, of course,
of these antecedents of hers. She has, as I have said, a
striking sort of face, one that at first sight gives a certain
impression of beauty. And being a lively, extremely talkative young person, she has a great attraction for *very*
young men," said the widow, thinking it wise to admin-
ister even these small thrusts in her stabbing of Monny's
image in the breast of the *not* very young man who was
listening to her. "Several such," Mrs. Van Cortlandt
went on, "young men of society and fashion have been
here this summer, I find, as her admirers, — Halstone
Roosevelt among them. He was here in his yacht a few
weeks since, it seems; and I have no doubt, from what I
have heard, that he is so deeply interested in the girl as to
be seeking her in marriage."

Infinity is not wider than was Kenyon Leigh's thought

from any imagination that his betrothed was the being whom Mrs. Van Cortlandt was speaking of. Not even the small innuendoes which she mingled with her deadly aspersions against the unknown girl in the least suggested Monny to him.

"Talkative!" to describe by that cheap word the charm of Monny's rippling speech would have seemed to her lover a kind of slandering of her. No: he had a strong sense of bewilderment at learning that not the maiden whom with never-to-be forgotten sensations he had seen Halstone Roosevelt salute on the pier, that not Monny, was the magnet who had drawn the young yachtsman to Lonewater, but some unknown frail deceiver sojourning there. He felt quite overwhelmed with surprise, but with no other emotion, as he replied to the widow's mysterious tale with the question, "What is the name of the girl you speak of?"

"She is at your own lodgings : she is that Miss Rivers whom " —

The man dropped the woman's arm as if he had been struck. "Miss Rivers is to be my wife!" shot from his lips like the bolt from a thunder-cloud.

Mrs. Van Cortlandt had not quite expected to hear this. She believed that very damaging inroads had been made on Mr. Leigh's fancy by his young fellow-boarder; but she could never have believed that the fortress which had cost her a four-years' siege had surrendered in a few short weeks to a mere curly-haired girl. Still her self-possession did not forsake her at this crisis. She answered firmly, —

"There is only the more reason, then, for me to repeat that she is a ruined " —

"Madam!" imperiously interrupted the man, "have you not understood me, that, when you speak to me of

Miss Rivers, you speak to me of my wife?" And without lifting his hat from his head, or making any sign of adieu, he turned on his heel, and with the speed of wrath went on his homeward way.

The lady thus left had but a step or two more to reach her gate; but she did not take them until she had listened with straining ear to the last echo of that rapidly receding footfall. It might return: she had a fear that it might. When it did not, she turned and entered the house, with one sense of satisfaction piercing through all the emotions which raged in her breast. In the blind game she was playing she had just grasped one new item of knowledge which would serve her well.

Meanwhile Mr. Leigh went at a flying pace over the road between the village and the house that held Monny.

Entering the familiar little entry, he heard the soft rustle of skirts at the head of the stairs, as a young figure leaned half out of a door there, and then was stealing noiselessly away again.

"Darling, my own darling, *do* come here a moment!" he called to her, with some low, yearning cry, to which Monny came down over the stairs like a bird to its mate.

What did he want of her? Nothing. Only to fold her quick and close in his arms as he had never quite done before, to press her soft cheeks to his: he had no word to say beyond, "Dear child, it is quite midnight. You should not sit up so late."

" I wanted to see you come home," whispered the girl.

"I wanted to come," vehemently replied the lover, thinking, not of the lingering death-bed where he had been a willing watcher, but of the insult which had come after it to this young creature, which had made his feet devour the road in an instinctive impulse to be protectingly near her.

"I wish it was our own home indeed," he went on. "I wish Ana's name was Ana Leigh this moment, and my right arm around her forever. Tell me, dear," he added, drawing the girl to sit down beside him on the stair, "why need we part for very long when we go away from this blessed old house, which I must leave very soon now, you know?"

He had not precisely intended before to urge his young betrothed to an immediate marriage; but now, if this was a world where innocence like hers could be struck at by calumny, he wanted at once to stand visibly where blows at her must be struck through him.

"What can there really be to delay for?" he argued. "Wedding-clothes?" he inquired, with his new considerateness for the feminine point of view. "Certainly dressmakers would be willing to hurry. They seem to me the most obliging of women," he declared. arguing from his experience with the New-York milliner. "And, besides, I am sure you never wear any thing now that is not beautiful enough for any bride in the world. *What* can there be to wait for?"

Profound silence had fallen on Monny during these words. The coy demurrings, which, under other circumstances, she might have opposed to her lover's entreaty, came not to her lips now: one absorbing pre-occupation held her mute. Yes, in the hush of the deepening night, when every companionship grows more dear and tender, with a sense of all the solemn mysteries which compass our lives about, — in this hour, with her lover's breath on her cheek, Monny was again mightily impelled to tell him all that secret. Or could she not wait, as aunt Persy had suggested, till she was his wife? And he wished her to be his wife so soon! A very brief waiting-time, then, it would be. Surely she might delay this little while.

All this silent tumult within resulted at last in these sudden words, with which she abruptly broke silence, —

"Mr. Leigh, I want to join your church."

"Darling, you are in it now. I have no church but that of the true believers. The church of my fathers is only that outward form of it which I love best, because I am at home in it. I hope very much, of course, that you will like to join that too, in due time."

"But I mean I want to join it now, — here on the stairs. Lay your hand on my head, — the ministerial hand, — and say over me, not the congregation blessing, but a little private and particular and individual 'God bless.'"

The girl was not trifling, her voice was any thing in the world but trifling ; and the ministerial hand, and oh ! the lover's hand, was laid on the fair head, and " God bless my own wife ! " was said, — " God bless her ! "

" And forgive her all her sins, negligences, and ignorances," Monny subjoined, making her own rubrics. " If she have any sin that she know not if it be a sin, wash it away, and make her meet to be a minister's wife, — such a minister as Kenyon Leigh ! " The sweet voice broke up with a sob ; and with a sudden impulse the girl reached up, and for the first, first time, threw her arms around her lover's neck. He drew her on his knee with that long, clinging clasp, living one of love's immortal moments as this tender heart throbbed so fast and fluttering against his, but never, never once imagining that heart was quivering with a secret which it longed, yet dreaded to tell him.

It was in the strain of this man's own nature to consider that people ought to ask pardon for their ignorances, and realize that it would be very hard for them to find it too (if they were people who had had opportunity to know), when ignorances wrought such endless mischief in the world. And that Monny should make just that peculiar rejoinder to his plea for their early marriage seemed to him only characteristic of the intense purity of her nature and aspirations. That benedictory little ceremonial she had asked of him was quite one of her darling ways. And he found it too altogether like the maiden to control very soon, as she now did, the impulsive outburst of feeling in which she had flung herself on her lover's breast — there was never too much of Monny.

"No, no! I wish to talk calm and steady," she said, withdrawing insistently from the arms that would detain her, to sit in her former place on the stairs. She was nerving herself again for the great confession; for that little absolution which she had craved of her lover had not brought peace, after all. She had not felt quite confirmed, not quite in the church of the true believers — no, not with the hand of that bishop of her soul on her head. The true believers must tell.

She was going to tell now. But the unconscious man beside her, swaying to her apparent mood, rejoined to her last words with, "Calm and steady then, let us talk over things, and consider how, when I go back to New York, that dreary period can be shortened during which I must take a journey even to look at my darling."

"Shall you truly come often?" asked Monny, still temporizing, still taking up any little remark that might postpone the subject she so dreaded to begin.

"Every other day at least," declared Mr. Leigh. "And the other day to come and go all the long miles. There will be a useful minister of a parish! But see how every thing would be simplified if we were married. How can I even buy a house for us to live in without consulting its mistress? And how can I consult her, if she is not there? Evidently she must be there. Evidently, therefore, we must be married, perch a while in hotel-apartments, whence we can go forth and look us up the perfect dwelling at our leisure. That will be the convenient, the delightful way to begin our new days; and what do we care for the parading way? I see this very moment how my apartments in New York can be broadened out by taking in the next suite of apartments, — rooms that can be made over into studios and boudoirs and every thing."

"Is there nobody in the rooms now?" murmured Monny.

"None but miserable bachelors, who have no rights that a married man is bound to respect. Oh, I can get rooms, — if not at my present hotel, then at another, — oceans of rooms; and then, with two of us to find it, how soon we shall find a house! And, when that is found, I have a famous British housekeeper all ready, — a woman competent to move us into it with our eyes shut. I brought her over from Europe this summer for the very purpose. Seriously, there came on my steamer one Mrs. Bunleigh, who was housekeeper at a gentleman's country-seat where I used to make holiday visits when I was a lad at an English school. She is that paragon of all housekeepers, the English trained housekeeper, and wishes to sojourn now in this unworthy land, because of her two grown-up sons, whom she is just starting in certain lines of trade in New York. This excellent woman dropped me a true British courtesy on the streets the very last time I went to the city; and, as I stopped for a word with her, it appeared that her present situation so humiliates her she desired to change it. She is housekeeper in the family of a wealthy merchant of the city. Her grievance there is a social one. Being a perfectly grammatical woman, and of dignified, not to say commanding, presence, her American mistress has given Mrs. Bunleigh a seat at the family table. It was plain that Mrs. Bunleigh had no respect whatever for a civilization which admitted its housekeeper to such intimacy. Dearest, authorize me to notify to-morrow this priceless woman to hold herself ready to respect the privacies in our house."

The wooer had turned his talk on all these little trifles of domestic detail in a thought to carry his main point by easy, unalarming stages, with the girl who sat so pensive, yet whose little remarks now and then encouraged him to hope that she might be gradually accepting his idea. Thus now, as he paused in his eloquence over the English housekeeper, Monny said, —

"Am I not going to be a great expense to you, and no profit, if you hire British housekeepers? Do you know that my fortune is only a very little one, that I am not worth much myself?"

"No, I did not know that: it is a great disappointment to me to learn it. How many golden dollars would these make, melted down, I wonder?" said the doting lover, lifting one of the shining curls, which at this hour were all tumbling down in very picturesque disarray. "By the way," he added, "I remember your telling me one day that all this wonderful hair was cut off once, and lost, or thrown away. How came you to do such a sin?"

A sudden shiver ran over the girl at these words. The secret that she was just going to confess unasked, it yet shook her to have her lover stumble on so unaware.

"Dear little wind-flower, you are cold!" was the man's exclamation at the sensible thrill which quivered through the young frame beside him. "I ought never to have called you down into this chilly entry, knowing well how slow I should be to let you go again. I hear Susannah coming up the back stairs to bed. We shall see the whites of her eyes if she sees us sitting here, the selfish man keeping his darling up when she ought to be asleep."

And he kissed her, and they parted — and she had not told.

Mrs. Van Cortlandt knew perfectly well all the main facts of that journey to New Orleans, which she meant to use for the ruin of Monny's good name: we mean she knew those facts, not in their false appearance, but just as they really were. She was, as the reader will have surmised, that lady-passenger on the cars near New Orleans, styled by Kate De Lancey "the humbug Madonna," whose curious scrutiny of the two young travellers had so incensed the Southern girl. That had been the widow's first sight of Monny Rivers as she lay asleep on the shoulder of the apparent young man. Her attention even then had been first drawn to the girl by the beauty of her hand, as, in the unconsciousness of slumber, it drooped conspicuously over the back of the car-seat. Mrs. Van Cortlandt, with her extreme sensitiveness to that point of personal beauty, had studied the perfection of this hand for some moments from her seat a little in rear of the two ; and, when she presently had occasion to leave the car with other passengers, she turned round to look at the sleeping girl, just as Kate, " forgetting that she was a man," was moved to kiss her. This salute, under the circumstances, had certainly a highly indiscreet appearance ; and Mrs. Van Cortlandt, with her European ideas of things, immediately assumed that this was some young scion of aristocracy travelling with his inamorata of an irregular character. And, as she came to this conclusion, it was not the face of the supposed young man, but of the *girl*, whom her downward-glancing eyelids swept with scorn. It was this look which had so roused the fury of the easily roused Miss Kate.

Now, it had also chanced, that, two or three days after this encounter, Mrs. Van Cortlandt, bowing to her New-York friend Mrs. Bingham, in the breakfast-room of the St. Charles Hotel, saw under that lady's distinguished care a young girl, whom she presently identified as that sleeping damsel on the train. The chaperonage which the girl at present enjoyed proving at once to the widow how utterly she herself had misconceived the young traveller's character and position, she naturally took a fresh survey of the latter in her present wide-awake condition. And, as the young figure settled itself at the breakfast-table, Mrs. Van Cortlandt observed that beautiful hand go up to the head with its childish short hair, that there came then a rather odd expression of bewilderment, succeeded by a singularly brilliant blush, which made the girl's face fairly dazzling for a moment with its radiant illumination. Every one knows how a gesture will cling to the memory : the merest little way of turning the head, or lifting the eyes, — such slight peculiarities of movement, — although they may be not in the least strange or eccentric, seem to have some gift for fastening themselves on the attention beyond any outline of features in repose. Monny had some little characteristic way of throwing back her hair ; and at that hotel breakfast-table she put up her hand with this involuntary movement, when, finding her hair missing (for the instant she had forgotten that it was cut off), all the consciousness that was connected with those recently sheared locks made her blush. The striking blush, the beauty of the hand, the peculiar movement of the hand, — all these were seen in conjunction five years after in the entry of the little Lonewater church, and seen by Mrs. Van Cortlandt, to the infallible identification of Monny Rivers with that young girl at New Orleans.

There had been yet another bit of sequel to the affair ere Mrs. Van Cortlandt left the St. Charles; to wit, after the veritable Carroll De Lancey had arrived at New Orleans, and his sister had resumed her own name and attire, the young lady chanced one day to meet face to face, in a corridor of the hotel, Mrs. Van Cortlandt. A cat might look upon a king, but no mortal on Kate De Lancey or her friends as she did not choose to be looked at. Accordingly, when Miss Kate now recognized the "sham duchess" of the railway-train she stopped short, gathered up her sweeping feminine array, and taking one of her "Judith" attitudes, with an access of antagonism towards this woman which overbore all prudence, the reckless girl broke out thus, —

"When you sneer again at an innocent baby of sixteen, look out that it isn't my sister-in-law to be!"

Having launched this oracular utterance, the haughty beauty swept on her way, leaving Mrs. Van Cortlandt, of course, sufficiently confounded. Kate's marvellous black eyes had flashed so absolutely the same blazing glance at Mrs. Van Cortlandt now, which the latter remembered from that fiery young cavalier in the cars, the widow, notwithstanding all the affront she felt, stood gazing after the young lady in a sense of some extraordinary mystery. Then, seeing her stop far down the corridor to speak to a servant, Mrs. Van Cortlandt waited to waylay the latter, who, when she came up, proved to be Mrs. Bingham's maid Jane.

"Who is that handsome young lady who spoke to you just now?" asked Mrs. Van Cortlandt of the maid.

"Miss Kate De Lancey of Maryland, ma'am."

"One of the Baltimore De Lanceys?"

" Those same, ma'am."

" Are any more of the family here?"

" Miss Kate's twin-brother, Mr. Carroll De Lancey, came last night" —

" Ah! you mean he came several days ago with a very young girl."

Not to quote this colloquy further, the end of it was, that Mrs. Van Cortlandt extracted from Jane, who had dressed Miss Kate when she changed her masculine for her feminine attire, the whole secret of that young lady's extraordinary personation of her brother. Jane was a most trusty servant, and no tattler: but she looked upon Mrs. Van Cortlandt as a friend of her mistress; and the widow's questions were so directed, that the maid was led on to tell the real truth in order to clear the character of Mr. Carroll's young betrothed from any such disreputable supposition as that they had made the journey together.

Now, poor Jane, who was even then ailing, took her bed that very day, of the malady of which she died. Mrs. Bingham was out of the city, and did not return until the next day, when her favorite servant was already in a danger ous condition, and, as it proved, very near her death. Mrs. Van Cortlandt, who had carefully recalled all these facts, said now that there was no human probability that it ever occurred to the dying maid to inform her mistress that she had confided to her the affair of the two girls. Certainly Mrs. Bingham had never mentioned the subject to her, Mrs. Van Cortlandt; and the latter, after Jane's explanation had furnished a complete solution to the enigma which puzzled her, had been glad to let the whole matter drop in silence.

It will be seen, from the foregoing sketch of the circumstances, that they presented to the woman whose interest it

now was to destroy Monny Rivers, this great conjunction
of opportunities; viz., that she could deal a deadly blow at
the girl with entire security to herself, whatever the result
of that blow; for she could declare, as an eye-witness,
that this Monny Rivers once took a long journey as the
pretended wife of a very fast young man. And, even if
the falsity of her tale was found out, no one was alive to
whisper that she, the accuser, knew its falsity, — knew
that the girl's companion on that journey had been no
young man at all, but a girl dressed up in her brother's
clothes. Clad in this proof-armor for herself, Mrs. Van
Cortlandt had begun to-night her attack on Monny to Mr.
Leigh, seizing upon what she had heard of young Halstone
Roosevelt's flame for Miss Rivers as the most plausible
and telling way of introducing her slanders. She had
imagined that Mr. Leigh's fancy for Monny was still
sufficiently in the bud for it to be nipped utterly in so
fastidious a man by merely dark hints from herself, — a
simple indication that disgraceful charges existed against
the girl.

"But what was to be done now?" the enraged woman
asked herself as she went up to her rooms after that
explosion with Mr. Leigh, in which she had learned that
Miss Rivers was already his betrothed wife. Sending
Tonson at once to bed, who came sleepily forward to
wait on her mistress, the latter sat down alone in the still
house for a long hour of intense thought. She had discovered one new thing in the very quality of Mr. Leigh's
indignation when he left her at the gate; viz., that he
knew nothing as yet, in any shape, of that New-Orleans
journey of Miss Rivers. For if he had known it, the
widow reasoned, he would have remembered it to-night,
so soon as the first passion of his wrath had passed; he
would have bethought himself of that strange adventure,

and of all the damaging construction to which it was
liable; and conceiving that the affair had been somehow
injuriously blown to her—Mrs. Van Cortlandt's—ears,
he would have turned back with a word of explanation.
The widow knew that this sober second-thought would
have been sure to come to the man, and to have brought
him back, whatever his pride, and all the more because
of his pride, to speak with her again.   He had made no
such re-appearance, conclusive proof that he was in utter
ignorance of that passage in Miss Rivers's history.
What probability was there that she had told him even of
her engagement to Carroll De Lancey?   Let a knowledge
of that engagement first come to a man like Kenyon
Leigh from without; let the false story of that entangled
journey to New Orleans be sprung on his mind with no
knowledge of the true story there to correct it by—what
misunderstandings might not be stirred up?

Darkly these thoughts twined and untwined themselves
in the brain of the plotting woman, until they were
knotted into a firm web of action.   She would spread
before Kenyon Leigh, with all exactness of details, her
own lying version of that New-Orleans journey, and see
what would come of it.

Certainly there were numberless forces now which
might snap the cunningest snare she could lay for the
feet of Mr. Leigh's betrothed.   But every warfare was
waged against elements of uncertainty.   " When a great
general planned his strategy," she said to herself, " what
did he do about all those unknown movements which
would meet him from the opposite side?   He *dared* them."
She would dare.   Fate, as we have shown, permitted that
Mrs. Van Cortlandt should dare in this case with great
impunity.   And in the small hours of the night a letter
was written, which Tonson would carry to Mr. Leigh by

th2 morning light. Then the writer of the letter went to her late rest.

When a previously decorous life breaks out in some piece of atrocious wickedness, it is wont to be curiously asked, "Had this being always been a consummate hypocrite, doing other such deeds in secret, or did there come some complete moral turning-point, when he consciously sold his soul to Satan?" Probably an explanation far more commonplace, far nearer the level of our common human frailty, would generally be found the true one; viz., that this criminal kept himself all the while in very comfortable conscience by assuming that there were particular circumstances which quite took away from his particular act of crime all the criminal quality which such a deed would have in the abstract. Abstract murderers, it may be, even the murderer sees, — monsters who spill human blood for the mere pleasure of seeing it flow, diabolical creatures whom he in no wise resembles. He only stabbed his enemy, — the man who angered him, or who stood in his way.

That Mrs. Van Cortlandt could resolve to put her young rival out of the way by an injury so much worse than death, and sleep calmly after it, was not because she had been in the habit of lying away the characters of innocent girls; for this was her first act of the kind. This particular girl, against whom she had been planning one enormous lie ever since she first saw her standing beside Kenyon Leigh in the church-entry, she had a particular remorselessness in thus destroying. To begin with, she assumed this young ward of the lumber-merchant Slabwell to be a *parvenue*, and the kind of *parvenue* which roused her strongest animosity; viz., the feminine being who attained social distinction and the homage of men through her talents. These were the creatures — great opera-singers, actresses, and the like — who had been known to scale the social ladder by more audacious bounds than any other variety of mortal, passing, sometimes, from a peasant's cottage to a duke's palace.

This Rivers girl was such a *lusus naturæ*, getting herself into prospective alliance with so aristocratic a family as the De Lanceys when she was scarcely out of her pinafores, having such a class of introductions at Newport as enabled her to count beaux like Halstone Roosevelt in her train, and now drawing the famous Kenyon Leigh into the mad folly of marrying her, — a girl not only born beneath him, but one whose very gifts implied something unsound and erratic in the character: that he should choose a wife like this was only an example of the utterly wild fancies in love wont to seize upon mature men.

These were the widow's views: that they were mistaken enough in many directions did not prevent their adding a peculiar unrelentingness to her schemes.

CHAPTER XXIV.

THE next morning, before Mr. Leigh left his rooms, Susannah slipped under his door a letter which a messenger had just brought. Picking it up, and recognizing the handwriting of Mrs. Van Cortlandt, his first impulse was to send the note directly back unopened. But the next instant the fact that he was a minister took him by the throat. He was not wont to feel his profession throttle him, but it did now. He was the pastor of this lady who had offered him the one insult of his life, and it was his business to remember that she was under an intolerable but honest mistake. Without doubt this early note to him was a retraction, an apology. In this after-thought, which the writer of the note had secretly counted on for its being opened and read, it *was* finally opened and read; and these were the contents : —

"REV. KENYON LEIGH.

"*Dear Sir,* — If I could have conceived that Miss Rivers had another suitor within the circle of my acquaintance, naturally I should not have said to you what I did last night. But, as it cannot now be unsaid, I have no resource but to lay before you the plain facts which I thought it a duty of friendship to inform the Roosevelts of.

"Five years ago Miss Rivers, being then a pupil in a New-York boarding-school, became engaged to Carroll De Lancey of Baltimore. At the end of her school-term she made a runaway journey with this lover from New York to New Orleans, escaping from the city, at first, in the dress of a boy. In this disguise she travelled as far as Jackson, Miss., when, supposing, doubtless, that she was beyond the reach of recognition, she resumed feminine attire. In that city she staid all night at a hotel with Mr. De Lancey; the pair registering their names on the hotel-books as man and wife. In this character they then went on to New Orleans, in which part of their travels *I saw them myself* on the cars, where their infatuated behavior was such as might well draw general attention.

                "Respectfully yours,
                    "ADELAIDE VAN CORTLANDT."

Mr. Leigh tore this letter into fragments: but it had been read; that was all the writer wanted. And he answered it on the spot.

"*Madam,* — Received your note concerning some unknown young woman whom you have committed the extraordinary offence of confounding with the lady who is to be my wife. I have to answer, first, that Miss Rivers has never been engaged to any man but myself, and, second, that your persistence in this most odious chimera I shall never be able to pardon, save by remembering your total want of acquaintance with the young lady who will, I hope, in a very few weeks bear the name of

                    "KENYON LEIGH."

Giving this note to Tonson, he went down to breakfast.

Breakfast over, Mr. Leigh was again in his study, its door into the hall being left ajar, as it habitually was in these days, for a standing invitation to one young visitor to enter.

As he paced restlessly up and down the room now, waiting for Monny's appearance, he chanced to spy on the carpet a stray scrap of Mrs. Van Cortlandt's note, which had escaped from his destroying fingers. The very sight of this suggestive fragment, as he stooped to pick it up, brought a returning rush of anger which surprised himself. He sat down thrilling with a mysterious sense of exposure, as if he suddenly stood bare to some unknown wind, whose edge, among all the cutting airs that blow, he

had never felt before. It was the experience of living in
another's life, and that life not a man's, but a woman's.
He realized, for instance, that, if a slanderous tale had
been told him of some man whom he perfectly trusted, he
would merely have laughed at it, and, the more abominable
the slander, the more a sense of its absurditv would have
left small room for indignation. Or, if the ill tale had
really been set forth with all circumstantial details, he
would have gone at once to his friend, and said, "Here are
certain remarkable lies, which are so reported about you
that even honest people who do not personally know you
believe them. Tell me what are the true facts in your history that have been so perverted into these lying fables,
that I may be able to set you right before strangers."

No such simplicity of dealing could be thought of as to
the girl whose reputation was the sacredest to him on
earth. The most absolute trust that one could have in a
human being did not enable him, he found, to smile at
any calumny about Monny. And as for asking her to
explain, or even breathing to her one syllable of what he
had heard — nothing could have been more impossible to
him this morning. Yet he did not in the least question
that Mrs. Van Cortlandt was laboring under a sincere
delusion about Monny: not the faintest doubt of that
lady's integrity in all that she had done touched his mind.
He recognized, therefore, a certain quality of unreason in
the wrath which he felt against her, — against anybody
and everybody, who, whether they had ever heard Monny
speak, or even seen her face, dared to imagine evil of
her. Certainly Kenyon Leigh was not a man to strike a
woman, still less a lady guilty of nothing worse than a
mistake : nevertheless, he could not think of that note
without an impulse to deal a blow somewhere. He had
suddenly discovered that there were accusations in this

world not to be met by explanation, argument, words of
any kind, but by fighting.

All these blind heats of feeling, this perception that
man's sentiment for woman brought some peculiar, com-
plex modification into all mortal laws of action, were so
consciously new to Kenyon Leigh, he sat with the contem-
plative, half-wondering look of a man who suddenly sees
the old balances of things swimming round, and the new
level yet undetermined. And in the larger abstraction of
his mood mechanically came and went, as if they were
said over in his ear by rote, the words, the names, in Mrs.
Van Cortlandt's letter.

"Carroll De Lancey"—he had heard of him before: it
was in some talk of his father's, about a year previous.
Judge Leigh was still in the active exercise of his office
on the bench; and at that time his judicial opinion had
been privately sought by Mr. Carroll (who had revolved
round to America, for a season), as to whether certain
restrictions of Gen. Warwick's will could be set aside.
What the heir wanted was to make fly the whole of Gen.
Warwick's wealth as swiftly as he had already made fly
all of it that he could lay his hands on; and the testator
had prudently debarred him, for a long term of years yet,
from the former privilege. Judge Leigh had shown the
young spendthrift that his wish could not be granted in
law. And, as the Ieighs and De Lanceys had been somewhat acquainted in former generations, the judge had
chanced to speak with solicitude, in his son's presence, of
the wild courses followed by this last of the De Lanceys;
for Carroll's dissipations had become far more pronounced since those young years in which Monny had
known him. From what he recalled now of his father's
remarks, Kenyon Leigh could well imagine that Carroll
De Lancey had been involved in just such an intrigue as

Mrs. Van Cortlandt had described, and that the lady's account was perfectly correct, save her one monstrous mistake of having mistaken the young man's female companion.

In all these thoughts *about* Monny, Mr. Leigh became so lost as to be unaware of the girl herself when she presently appeared at his open door, he sitting by the farther window, his head somewhat turned away. ,She trod softly ; for her young heart was beating with a great timidity this morning, and it increased to a kind of fear as she stood arrested on the threshold by the very sight of her lover sitting there, so unaware of her, in that stirless attitude, as if the physical life was almost suspended by the intensity of the inner mental action. She meant to make the great confession to-day, before the sun should set ; and, with this trembling thought, her eyes took in, with some indescribable keenness of vision, the very breadth of the man's shoulders, the strong lines of his head as they came out against the light, the whole masculine unlikeness to herself : for the moment, the charm of that unlikeness was lost in the awe of it ; for the moment, her betrothed seemed to her an utterly unapproachable being. He stirred, perhaps he felt Monny in the air : turning his head, he rose up at once to his towering height.

Her mood of the moment was so strong on the girl, she involuntarily put out her hands, waving them, palms downward, with a suppliant gesture : — ·

" Oh, please stay down in your chair when I come in, and make yourself a little smaller ! "

" Rather a disrespectful way to receive a lady," said the mighty man, obediently reseating himself.

" No, no ! The usual etiquette shall be reversed in the case of giants. It shall be counted a sign of respect in them to remain seated, and let the small people stand."

"At least they may hold the small people up, then," said the lover, drawing the girl to his side.

It was still such a great and wonderful thing to put a lover's arm around Monny, to caress her, ever so lightly, the entrancing presence for the moment dimmed all other consciousness ; then he said, "And where are we going ?" — for Monny was dressed for walking.

"To the village, of an errand."

' And I am not to be invited to go too?"

"When have I ever invited you to go to the village with me of errands, — dressmaking errands?"

"Dressmaking in *this* village?" queried the man, a little surprised, but rashly fancying in the very word some hopeful suggestion of wedding-clothes.

"Not my own dressmaking," said Monny, "somebody's else, — Clara Macey's. She is having a new fall suit, and I am going down to see about it a little."

"I supposed dressmakers required their customers to come to them."

"No : it is only the very superior ones who can take on that dignity. Common dressmakers, like myself, work round from house to house."

"Ah! I cannot think what business, what friends, would take *me* abroad this morning," said the lover reproachfully.

"But there is nothing in the whole range of a man's duties so important as the proper looping of a polonaise," declared Monny. The foolish little words — she was mysteriously eased and happy at finding herself able to say them, just as of old, to this tremendous being. "Clara and her mother," she gossiped on, "have cut and made the suit very nicely by one of Mme. Demorest's patterns, which they sent for at my suggestion ; and now I am going in to loop up the drapery of the costume, give the final touches, the true urban fling. Clara is going to spend the winter in Boston, you see "

"How long time will this vanity take?" asked Mr. Leigh.

"It is according to how much vanity I put in. Clara Macey has very little vanity herself: so I shall put in a good deal. I must educate her by her clothes."

"Seriously, my darling, how long are you going to be away this morning?"

"Truly not much more than an hour."

"'Tis twenty years till then. What am I to do meanwhile?"

"Oh! you can go back to some of those deep, deep thoughts you were thinking just as I came in. If you sit apart in the inner court, that is to say your study, wearing that awful majesty of looks, when " —

"When we are married," promptly put in the lover.

"Then, in that state of life," the maid went on, "it will be necessary for you to keep by you a kind of sceptre, after the style of King Ahasuerus, — something to hold out, you know, when poor little trembling Esther comes in, as a sign that she may speak, or must be put to death on the spot for her intrusion. Only I do not exactly wish to call myself Esther; for I never liked her — hanging Haman's ten sons on the gallows! What had *they* done? And all those that she got slain on the fourteenth day of the month Adar! Do *you* believe in Esther?"

"I am thinking of that sceptre," replied the minister, not to commit himself in a point of Old Testament criticism too early in the morning, "wondering where I can obtain such an article in a republic."

"You might substitute a cane: or no — you do not carry a cane; then you can take an umbrella, and hold that out."

"Open, or shut?"

"Well, shut it could signify that all women are to flee on peril of their lives; open, that you are ready to endure for a while the rain of feminine speech." Still the foolish little words: she went on saying them from old habit of teasing this lover, and for the sweetness of seeing, by certain changing lines in his thoughtful face, that she pleased, that she was dear to him, even in her nonsense; yes, she had the assurance that he loved her — in some moods. But in his other moods, in that mood of high contemplation which so wrapped him a few moments ago, — how would she look to him then, with her faults, with that story which she must tell him to-day? With this inward question the playful sparkle died out of her eyes; and she said in a tone softly wistful, even sad, —

"Those thoughts you were thinking when I came in — they were far, far away from me, I am sure; far from all persons; gone into the world of pure ideas, where there is nothing to mar, where the soul *does* have its desire of perfection. Tell me, Kenyon Leigh, what nobler world were you dreaming of, just, just as I came in?"

"Darling," replied the man gently, for the girl's voice had grown strangely tremulous, "see who is the dreamer now. I sat here thinking only of Anemone Rivers, of this real world where she is: surely every thought I had, began and ended with her."

"And between the beginning and the ending where did the thoughts go?" persisted Monny, — "those long, long, parabolic curves they must have been making when I came in! Tell me this once: I wish to see into the construction of a man's mind, to know how he can be thinking so hard of a person, he does not know when the person has come, — it was so strange to me that you did not know I had come!" panted the girl, who had missed in her lover love's keen waiting, when every nerve listens for a footfall, and little guessed through what involved solicitude for her his mind had strayed out into those abstract reflections whose abstract quality Monny had instinctively recognized.

Well might Kenyon Leigh feel that woman brought a complexity into existence ; for, at this whimsical demand of his betrothed, he did what he had never done before in his life, what was more foreign to his nature, if possible, than downright lying, — he quibbled. He told the actual things which had passed through his mind, but transposed and changed all their connections.

"Thinking of the one person, I thought of — other persons — suggested by her," he began, not very fluently. "Of — my father, for instance. It crossed my mind, as I sat here, that the morning mail would soon be in, and that I might hear from him to-day — at home. He has been on a trip to the Yosemite, as I have told you, — started just before I arrived from Europe, — so that I have not seen him for more than a year. I naturally remember to-day, that I shall have the pride and joy of announcing to him the new daughter whom I hope very soon " —

Partly moved by some bashful little impulse to hasten over allusions to the new daughter, Monny interrupted here with, —

"And what *other* subjects and persons were in your head? You are to tell me every thing, you know. I shall see by your eyes when you have been truly candid," said the girl, her own bright eyebeams mischievously following and looking into her lover's optics, whichever way he turned his glance. And partly because he was so awkward in any *rôle* but the truly candid one, and partly because those brown eyes looking into the construction of

a man's mind made him more and more distractingly
helpless, he said, in his absolute belief that Monny could
never even have heard of the dissipated young Baltimo-
rean, who had lived nearly all his life abroad, —

"Thinking of my father, and of the last time I saw
him, I thought of a person he was concerned with just
then, — a very unhopeful young man whom you would
not care to hear about, — one Carroll De Lancey."

"Do you know *him?*" gasped the startled girl, withdrawing from the arm which encircled her.

"Why, do *you* know him?" rejoined Mr. Leigh, with
more composure than the dismayed Monny had shown in
her sudden outcry : still he was inwardly surprised, much
surprised.

"I knew him once," said the girl, "very long ago.
His sister went to school with me in New York : that was
how he came to be of my acquaintance. I knew him only
a little, — *very* little indeed. I must go now," starting
away with nervous flurry. "I promised Clara Maccy
that I would be there very soon after nine o'clock ; and
it is nine now. Good-by!" And she was gone to the
door. On its threshold she paused, fluttered uncertainly
for an instant, then suddenly flew back to her lover,
where he sat in his chair, held by the surprise which was
still on him.

"You will not think I am going to be so prying and
tiresome always, — asking people for their thoughts. I
hope I am not that jealous kind of tease. It was a silly
whim that took me this once, because — because I was
truly a little afraid when I came in, you looked so far
away. And I had things to say to you," she almost
sobbed, — "many things. I am coming back to say them
now, just as soon as I can. I am going to hurry. Good-
by, dear Kenyon Leigh!"

"Good-by, my darling, my one darling, whatever whims take you!" tenderly repeated the lover. "Good-by!" And this time Monny really went.

Certainly the emphasis with which she had declared the slightness of her acquaintance with a young man whom she was once engaged to marry had a very misleading sound. But those hurried words she had dropped, in the trepidation of finding that Mr. Leigh knew Carroll De Lancey, and knew ill of him, were all moved by the thing that came uppermost in her mind; viz., the plea she was going to make for herself, that, if she had known that young man better, she should never have fancied that she loved him. And the way in which she put this truth of her brief acquaintance with the young Southerner she did not pause to consider. It was one of those unfortunate gaps (unfortunate, if a man should ever come to weigh her statements in the balances of suspicion), which, in the feminine swiftness of her thoughts, were sometimes left between the thing in her mind and the words she spoke aloud.

Her lover certainly did not weigh any of her words with suspicion now. He put down all her startled manner to the fact that he himself had introduced young De Lancey's name with a stigma, — reason enough why the sensitive Monny would have blushed to own his acquaintance. Nor need that acquaintance have so surprised him, he reflected: Carroll De Lancey, as a young man of birth and fashion, had doubtless been decorous enough in his outside ways, especially a few years back. Altogether, he returned to his absorbing thoughts of the last hours, about hastening his marriage; and in the midst of these there was presently brought to the house, instead of the expected letter from his father, a telegram. Judge Leigh had just reached home, and was somewhat ill, not dangerously, but hoped his son Kenyon was at liberty to come at once for the visit that it had been understood he should make to his home when his father arrived. Reflecting now, that, the sooner he set out on this filial journey, the sooner he should be back, if there was nothing serious to detain him, he considered his telegram but a moment before deciding that he must take the next train up to Boston, which there was only just time to catch. So, leaving a farewell line for Mouny, Mr. Leigh ran by the shortest way to the station.

CHAPTER XXV.

THE lady who owned so efficient a spy as Tonson did not long remain in ignorance of this departure of Mr. Leigh, and she decided to improve his fortunate absence by making an entirely new move. She resolved to call on Miss Rivers.

Accordingly, about three P.M. of this same day, Mrs. Van Cortlandt appeared at Mrs. Doane's. Monny was in her studio; and, the lady sending up with her card a request that she might be allowed to come directly up to that room, Monny concealed her picture of the Knight-Templar, and then received the visitor.

" You have not called on me yet, Miss Rivers," began the latter, sinking gracefully into the offered chair. " But we do not wait for our minister's wife to call first: so, hearing that you are to stand in that relation to us of St. Ancient's, I present myself."

At this rather formidable address from " us of St. Ancient's," the maiden blushed a little, but replied quietly, " As I understood that you had come to Lonewater for retirement, I feared calls from a stranger, like myself, might be an intrusion."

The widow, perceiving that the girl was not going to be led into any babble about her lover, rejoined with her most charming manner, —

" You see that you were too modest. I have desired the pleasure of being acquainted both with yourself and your works. I had heard of your talent, but could not imagine seeing a gallery like this," she said, glancing around the room crowded with pictures. " May I look at all these lovely things?" she asked. And, rising, she made a queenly progress round the studio, surveying Monny's labors.

How did this woman manage to impress a girl like Monny Rivers as scarcely any woman had ever impressed her before? She certainly said nothing that was either brilliant or wise ; and the politeness, even of her introductory remarks to a young maiden whose engagement was not yet made public, was very questionable indeed, as the well-bred Monny would have felt if any other stranger had so addressed her. Yet, as she swept round that little chamber, she grew a more and more exalted being to Monny with every step. One sees such mysteriously superior personages among those who have long breathed the air of privilege. Their conversation has no illumination in it, either as to the life which now is or that which is to come : often, unlike Mrs. Van Cortlandt, they have no claims whatever to beauty, and it would be hard to say wherein their manners are really fine ; yet, being saturated with self-consciousness, of some refined instead of the vulgar sort, they impose almost their own estimate of themselves on all humbler souls.

Mrs. Van Cortlandt had not only her great beauty, but an eminent capacity for taking all that kind of social polish which seems like knowledge. Even her comments on the pictures, so reticent, so quietly dropped, had a certain effect of discrimination. Her own *rôle* in the world seemed that of *being* all perfections, — a dignity quite beyond that of *doing*, pictures, or aught else. The young girl did not think this cynically, but worshipfully, as this imposing lady reviewed her studio. The visitor certainly had some manner that enabled her to do things which in another

would have seemed altogether presuming. Thu; she offered herself as a subject for Monny's pencil. Mrs. Van
Cortlandt had very often been a sitter to artists, and her
self-suggested portrait now had naturally a deeper motive
than vanity. She wished to engage Monny in a special
conversation, and took this means to prolong her stay beyond the conventional limits of a call. The lady brought
about her proposal, of course, by the due degrees. Monny
was delighted to have the opportunity of sketching this
beautiful face, and Mrs. Van Cortlandt took off her bonnet
at once. The young artist posed her subject; and, when
she had become well absorbed with her sketch, the lady
remarked in a quietly careless way, —

"Do you know, Miss Rivers, that, while you are tracing
my face, I have traced yours at last? I had a strong
impression of having somewhere seen you before, when
Mr. Leigh first presented you to me in the little church
here; but until this moment I could not recollect where."

"I am sure I had never seen you before," said the
unsuspecting girl, looking up with her frank smile. "I
could never, never have forgotten your face, if I had once
seen it. I remember faces always," added Monny, lest
her involuntary tribute to Mrs. Van Cortlandt's beauty
should have sounded too broad a flattery.

"And I also, although I am not an artist, have a keen
memory for faces," replied the lady. "Yours, I am sure,
I saw once at New Orleans. Did you not spend a few
days at the St. Charles Hotel there five years ago last
spring?"

Monny had dropped her crayon in the start with
which she heard these words. Stooping to pick it up, she
said in a faint, reluctant voice, "Yes, I was in New
Orleans — at that time."

"I was sure of it. But stay — no, you could not have

been that young girl, after all," said Mrs. Van Cortlandt,
with well-feigned alternations of voice, as of one suddenly
pressed on by a crowd of confused recollections. "Now
that I remember, she was married, — an extremely youthful bride: still she was married.   I saw her not only in
the hotel, but in the cars, on her way to New Orleans.
She was with her young husband then.   Mr. and Mrs.
Carroll De Lancey — that was the name: I remember it
well, — an old Maryland family.   Pray, was it your married sister?   Have you such a sister so near your own
age, and marvellously like you?"

Monny Rivers could not lie; and now, although it
seemed to her that fate could not have ordained a more
appalling thing than that she must confess to this lady,
of all beings, her girlhood's wild adventure, she lifted
her young head, and said, with what steadiness she could
command, as she laid down her crayon, —

"I never had a sister, Mrs. Van Cortlandt.   And the
person — you remember at New Orleans — as Mrs. Carroll
De Lancey must have been — really — myself; for I
went there under that name.   It was an assumed name.
I was not married."

"Assumed name?   Not married?" repeated the lady
in a voice finely modulated to express unspeakable astonishment held in check by politeness.   "Pardon me; but,
as I have said, I saw the very young lady called Mrs.
Carroll De Lancey in the cars, and her husband with her
— surely her husband: it were to traduce her — you —
any young lady, to suppose that travelling-companion was
not her husband.   I do not understand.   I must beg you
to explain."

The entrapped Monny saw no escape: she must take
up the cross of that explaining.   Need we say how crush-
ing it was to her, how infinitely more scandalous sounded

in her own sensitive ears that entangled tale as she re-
hearsed it to the stately lady representative of Mr. Leigh's
parish than when comforting aunt Persy was the hearer?

Mrs. Van Cortlandt's double effort was to convince the
impressible girl, that, in her New-Orleans journey, she
had done something which society must needs regard as
perfectly heinous, but which she individually was moved
to condone and cover up, through regard for the young
betrothed of her minister. The accomplished woman of
the world was quite equal to this work : the art which she
put into her listening to Monny's story was something
entirely beyond the reach of the vulgar. No rudest
outcry of surprise at its surprising passages could have
been half so stingingly felt by poor Monny as the slight
lifting of those beautifully pencilled brows, the shocked
amaze that was allowed to gleam for an instant, as if
involuntarily, in the handsome gray eyes; to be quickly
veiled by courtesy, the restrained comment and question
interspersed from time to time without any air of curiosity, yet so contrived as to wring the last item of all that
history from the girl's lips. A part of it was really new
to Mrs. Van Cortlandt. All the intrigue about the will she
had never known a hint of before ; had never dreamed
that there was any deeper motive for the masquerade than
the madcap whim of Kate De Lancey, contriving the
disguise as a convenient one for two young girls to take a
long journey in unattended.

"Of course you have never mentioned a word of this
affair to Mr. Leigh," said Mrs. Van Cortlandt at last,
when she was satisfied that she had found out every thing
which was to be known.

"I meant to have told him to-day," replied Monny
quickly; " but he was called away very unexpectedly. I
had an errand to the village, and when I came back he

was gone. I shall tell him all about it just as soon as he returns."

"Surely," said Mrs. Van Cortlandt with her softly shocked manner, "you cannot repeat such a story as you have told me — to — a gentleman. Pardon me, my dear girl, if I take the liberty, since you have no mother, to suggest to you that Mr. Leigh is a very fastidious man — all men are so about what a young girl says and does."

The present young girl was one who could be imposed on by this miserable prudery of advice, as the widow had well discerned in the close study which this afternoon's long interview had enabled her to make of her victim. Monny colored painfully at being thus supposed to need reminders to modesty; then she broke out, —

"But I felt I *must* tell him, however trying it was. I do not like to have secrets from Mr. Leigh. It haunts me all the time. I have no peace."

"You have not reflected, I see, that this easing of your own mind may be at the cost of bringing Mr. Leigh into an extremely painful perplexity. Your secret is one which a man might feel that honor forbade him to keep."

Monny looked up blankly at these words.

"I mean," explained the widow, "all the deceit practised by your school-friend to get that will made in favor of herself and the brother whom you expected to marry. Such a fraud was a robbery of the nearer heirs, which a man like Mr. Leigh might feel himself bound to see rectified, even at this late day. You have not thought of all this?"

"Oh, no!" murmured Monny, growing pale with the utterly new dismay which these artful suggestions brought her.

"The property was divided between brother and sister, I

understand," quietly pursued Mrs. Van Cortlandt. ' Did Miss De Lancey leave any heirs?''

"Her baby. And the Italian nobleman whom Kate married, although he was in brilliant position, was not very rich, I believe. It would be too cruel — I could not bear to be instrumental in such a thing — to take away the inheritance of that child, — Kate's child. Surely that would be the robbery now ; for the Regdons, Gen. Warwick's nearest heirs, were very rich themselves, Kate said, and had no natural claim on him at all, and he did not intend them to touch his money. Oh ! I cannot believe Mr. Leigh would think it necessary to move in such a tangled affair, to go back of that will, when Gen. Warwick cannot come out of his grave now to make another."

" Precisely because it is so tangled an affair," smoothly replied the artful woman, " it should not, in my judgment, be imparted to a man. Men like to move, and are expected to move, on straight lines. A woman is not so rigorously held to account — in business matters. Thus the world might, perhaps, grant that a young woman, a girl so juvenile as you were when this deed was done, did not realize all the grave thing it is to tamper with property interests. But a man would be allowed no such ignorance of affairs ; and if he were made acquainted with such an act, however long after, he might feel himself a kind of accomplice in the fraud, if he did not reveal it. Being a woman myself, I agree with you, that the wrong in the making of that will was one of those wrongs which would probably become a worse wrong by any attempt to right it now. Clearly, so long as Mr. Leigh is left in ignorance of the affair, he has no duty about it whatever. Why, then, trouble him with this painful knowledge?''

The girl sat for a moment in stark bewilderment at this specious reasoning ; then she made a small clutch after her common sense once more. She began slowly, —

"It is something I have never thought of before, that there could be two kinds of right, — one for a man, and another for a woman. If it is so, Mrs. Bingham, who knew all about Kate's affair, is the one to tell me what I should do. I will write and ask her. I have thought a little of writing her before, for myself; but now there is a new cause, I will write instantly. You say she is in Europe: do you know just where she is?"

"I have no idea," replied the widow evasively.

"But surely," urged Monny in her eagerness, "a lady so distinguished in society as Mrs. Bingham — there must be those in New York who know her present address. Would you do me the great kindness to help me a little in this — to help me find out where she can be written to?"

"I will try: leave all that to me," said Mrs. Van Cortland, who, if this correspondence was to be, determined to keep it in her own hands.

"Thank you very much indeed," said Monny warmly.

"And let me suggest to you," continued Mrs. Van Cortlandt, "that there are other much more important inquiries for you to make immediately. That trunk which you mentioned, the trunk which you lost in Jackson," said the widow, who had extracted from Monny this afternoon all the minutiæ of her Southern journey, and seized at once on the incident of the lost trunk as something which she could weave usefully into her schemes, — "you say it was left behind on the depot platform?"

"Yes, it was of so little consequence," replied Monny.

"It is of the utmost consequence to you that it should not fall into other hands," answered the widow with the gravest emphasis. "After a certain lapse of time (once in seven years is, I believe, the stated period) all baggage thus abandoned at depots, and never claimed, is set up at public auction, and sold. After a trunk is sold in that way, it is opened, of course, by the buyer. Are there not things in your trunk which would identify it, your name, for instance?"

"Why, yes, it may be. There was a little underclothing in the trunk, I believe, — things that would be marked, of course. Oh, yes! my name was probably there," repeated Monny in a bewildered way, beginning to feel as if detectives were already on her track, with the formidable tone which Mrs. Van Cortlandt had assumed in her talk about the will, and now about the lost trunk.

"The trunk may still be locked up in the Jackson depot, since it is but five years since it was left there," said the widow. "I advise you to send on at once, and ascertain. Send a full description of the trunk and its contents, and, if it is there, you cannot fail to identify it. Then, of course, as soon as the depot officials are satisfied that you are the owner, they will send it right on wherever you direct. I will help you arrange all the details of this. Perhaps we had better inquire by letter first, and then use the telegraph to expedite matters."

"You are very good," murmured Monny.

"I feel that such a tell-tale piece of property as that trunk, with a masculine suit of clothes in it, ought to be got safely back into your own possession: otherwise no one knows into whose hands it might eventually fall, to be traced to you, and stir up strange stories. A clergyman's wife cannot be too careful of her reputation," said the mentor, with an emphasis which tingled to Monny's very soul. "It will be desirable for me to see you again soon,"·added the visitor, rising at last to go. The sketch of her head had, of course, been long ago dropped in the agitating talk into which the artist had been led. "Where shall we meet? You take long walks on the seashore, I hear. Who accompanies you?"

"I go alone with Duke George."

The lady made a movement of her brows, as if asking what manner of Cape-Cod nobleman that might be.

"He is my dog," explained Monny. "I mean aunt Persy's dog. He really belongs to the house; but he seems mine, because·he always goes about with me."

"Is — the keeper of this house your relative?" asked the visitor, again with her politely shocked manner.

"Mrs. Doane? — oh, no! I formed the habit of calling her aunt when I was a child, and used to come here with my nurse," said Monny, feeling that the lady of St. Ancient's was thinking her very pitiably a child still, falling into this strange rusticity of quoting the names of the household, human and· canine, as if all the world must needs know them.

In much more serious ways than these did this discomposing visitor drive Monny completely out of herself, skilfully managing through all this long interview to make herself at once dreaded and relied on by the young girl, who was easily led to exaggerate into a monstrous offence and disgrace that fact in her life of having worn male attire. For, like all thoroughly modest women, Monny was thoroughly conventional in every thing that concerned the proprieties of her sex. It is doubtful, by the way, whether the best girls are at all apt to go back of the convention in these things to inquire its why and wherefore, — extremely doubtful if it is really a sign of the most innocent mind among maidens to be much given to original views and positions as to what is modest or immodest in social observances. Blindly, and with innocent thoughtlessness, a young girl dances such dances, for instance, and wears such dresses to dance in, as she sees other reputable ladies do: usage, the practice of the best persons, is to her the sole law in these matters, within

which she is perfectly unconscious and serene, outside
of which she has a horror to be found. So, while a more
forward-thinking young woman might have re-assured
herself by reflecting that there was but small difference
between a modern pull-back and those cadet's trousers,
Monny, who could wear the former, while it was the
fashion, without a thought of impropriety, had seen herself in the latter, to use her own words, as a character to
be taken up by the police. And a torturing sense that
Mr. Leigh's lady parishioner thought her, at the best, a
very hoidenish, underbred girl, made Monny submit herself with the more passive obedience to whatever course
of proceeding the widow marked out for her.

The parish had got hold of the minister's wife, even
before she bore his name.

CHAPTER XXVI.

MR. LEIGH returned to the Cape after a four-days' absence, having left Judge Leigh recovering from his illness, and well rejoiced to learn the intended marriage of his only yet unwedded son.

It was past sunset when the eager traveller came riding over the familiar stage-road from the village station to Mrs. Doane's ; and, lo ! he met Monny on the way. Jumping from the vehicle to greet the surprised girl (she did not expect him until the morrow), he bade the driver go on to Mrs. Doane's with only his portmanteau, perceiving that Monny was not inclined to step into the stage, and ride home with him.

"I am so surprised at your coming to-night !" repeated the girl, with some strange fluttering. "I did not imagine meeting you on the stage. I had started for the village, and " — she faltered, "I really think I must go on. I had a most important errand."

"Then I will go with you," said the lover, turning promptly about.

"Oh, no ! I had started alone, and I can go on so just as well. You must be tired."

"Tired ? How *tired* must a man be to allow the dearest being to go over this desolate road alone in the gloaming ? "

"No, no, please ! I had *rather* you would not go," urged Monny in a tone of entreaty that there was no mistaking. "You know it has been a little understood that we should not walk about together yet in public. And

my errand is to your friend Mrs. Van Cort.andt. She
has called on me since you have been away: she shows
me much friendship."

Mr. Leigh stood astounded: then his amaze began to
clear a little, through a rapid inward process of conjecture and conclusion; and the end of it all was that he
said quietly, —

"Go on, then: I will wait for you here. Surely I
shall wait for you, and come to meet you. Where is the
dog?" he asked, looking round, and missing Monny's
invariable protector.

"I left him at home to-night. I thought I had better
not have great dogs with me, calling on — ladies who
have lived so much in Europe," said poor Monny, who
had left Duke George behind, from a feeling that Mrs.
Van Cortlandt considered it a piece of Bohemian wildness
for her to go about thus accompanied.

The inevitable thought that "ladies who had lived so
much in Europe" would think it far queerer for a girl to
be taking lonely evening walks without any escort at all,
naturally crossed Mr. Leigh's mind; but of course he did
not speak it aloud.

"The sun sets so deceivingly quick now, I did not
think it was quite so late," said the girl apologetically,
perceiving that Mr. Leigh was not altogether satisfied;
then she hurried swiftly away.

From the little group of pine-trees where they had
halted (it was at a point about two-thirds of the way
from Mrs. Doane's house to the village), the man stood
looking after the maiden with a sense that it was a most
extraordinary contingency that he should be forced to
stand helpless in the highway, and see his darling walk
straight to a woman who had believed such monstrous
things of her. True, when the first amaze with which he

had heard where Monny was going was past, he felt that this mysterious visit of hers to Mrs. Van Cortlandt ought to be pleasing to him. Evidently the lady had become disabused of her gross error, either through his own statement, or something which she had learned ; and she had hastened to atone for her offence by calling on Monny, and, as it appeared, establishing intimacy at once. In this idea he had allowed the maiden to go on : still the situation disturbed him ; and he soon emerged from the belt of pine-trees to keep the girlish figure in sight as it rose and sank, like a little shallop on a wave, with the undulations of the way. Then, as it grew to a nebulous shade in the twilight, and vanished in the hollow where lay the village, he walked on forthwith to do his waiting at the nearest point. Just outside the village he halted, lingering about there : over the endless stretching levels of sand and sea the wind began to boom desolately ; a gray night was setting in, and he could not disguise from himself that some chill had fallen on the meeting he had been anticipating all day over so many rolling miles. Meanwhile Monny arrived at Mrs. Van Cortlandt's.

"You sent for me, I am here," said the girl.

"Yes, another telegram has just come through from Jackson, about the trunk. They have found it at last ; and I sent for you, that you might forward an order for it in your own name. Sit right down here and write the telegram, and I will see it sent to the office."

"Is there no letter from New York yet about Mrs. Bingham's European address?" asked Monny, always more anxious about this matter than about the lost trunk.

"No : I do not learn that yet," replied the widow, who had no idea of learning at all where Mrs. Bingham was. "When is Mr. Leigh expected?" she added.

"Oh ! he has just come. He met me on the way here."

"And did you tell him where you were going?" cried the widow.

"Why, certainly. I did not dare go back, lest there was some very important reason for you to see me. Oh, it is all very distressing!"

"There *was* an important reason," replied the intriguer, whose first alarm at Monny's accidental meeting with Mr. Leigh subsided in the second thought, that, after all, this accident was not an unfortunate one for her schemes. "It is most necessary for that telegram to go immediately, and in your own name, for the trunk." And Monny wrote the despatch to the plotter's dictation. Then the latter let her victim go, trusting for herself to that fortune which favors the bold.

Only a bold and deeply-laid plot, in truth, could have prevented these lovers from coming to confidence. Even to-night, when Monny came outside the village to find Mr. Leigh waiting for her there in the falling darkness, the very weight on her young heart, an indefeasible rising sense that he was her true refuge, made her run with such impetuous abandon into his arms, he thought it a puerility in himself to have fancied something strange and disappointing in his first reception.

What need to chronicle in detail the days that followed? It was always the same history, — alternations of reserve and effusion, of melancholy, and anon a forced, wild gayety, as the troubled girl perceived that her depression of spirits weighed on her lover. She flew from one to another of these moods with some feverish unrest utterly unlike the sweet beguiling of her old changeful ways; for be sure that the girl "whom nobody ever got tired of, morning, noon, nor night," did not normally diffuse that sense of commotion which makes some iridescent feminine natures, for all their charm, a little fatiguing at last in too intimate intercourse.

No, Monny's lover recognized well that she was in some unwonted state. He supposed it a matter of nerves ; and certainly, for a man who had reached thirty-four all inexperienced in feminine nerves, he had now a tolerably severe initiation.

Now, while affairs were hanging thus, and Monny still putting off with peculiar evasion the fixing of her marriage-day, although the time for Mr. Leigh's permanent departure from the Cape was close at hand, he was passing, one afternoon, through the family sitting-room, and stopped to turn over a file of his newspapers (strewn on a table, for Mrs. Doane's reading), to see if his "New-York Times" of four days back might still be there. As it was understood that the dailies might be drawn on for fire-kindling before they reached that age, the desired journal had disappeared ; and Monny stepped out into the kitchen to see if, by chance, it might still be extant in the waste-box.

"It has gone up the chimney," she said, returning. "Did you wish to see it for something important?"

"To look over again the list of 'The Etolia's' passengers. It is not given in full in the later papers. Friends of mine, Gen. Bingham and his family, were on that steamer." Mr. Leigh was about to say that he wished to see if any other of his friends were there ; but Monny cried out breathlessly, "The Binghams on that steamer?—homeward bound? When is it due?"

"It was due several days before I left New York," replied Mr. Leigh, rather puzzled by Monny's tone, which, though agitated, had an expression of relief in it which seemed singular to him ; for the Atlantic steamer in question was so late, that serious fears had begun to be entertained for its safety. Mr. Leigh assumed that Monny knew this, as the papers every day now made some reference to the missing ship. But the girl had been so absorbed by her personal anxieties, she had scarce looked in the papers for several days past, and was all unaware of this alarm about "The Etolia." And now, as Jenny Hines came running in from the kitchen with a torn page or two of the destroyed journal, which she had chanced to use for wrapping-paper, Monny slipped out of the room and up-stairs, while Mr. Leigh was looking over the rescued fragment of newspaper, where was found the shipping-news and a list of "The Etolia's" passengers. Not finding Monny when he glanced up from this reading, he went to his study, where he presently heard the girl's door cautiously opened, her soft, swift flight down the stairs ; and anon, from his window, he saw her flitting away like the wind, in the direction of the village.

Her manner of leaving the house so plainly denoted a wish to be unobserved, the lover made no signal to her ; but musing afresh on the impracticable state into which his betrothed had fallen, when a half-hour or so had passed, he put on his hat, and went out by the same road which she had taken. Not wishing to pursue Monny quite into the village, remembering how shy she was of his escort there the night of his return, he loitered along the way, making little excursions into the waste on either side the road, to pass the time till she should appear.

Rambling thus, his feet making no echo in the soft, sliding sand, he came to a spot some rods from the highway, where he was startled to hear feminine voices close by, those of Monny and — Mrs. Van Cortlandt! They were sitting on the ground, behind a dense little clump of shrub-oaks, over whose roots and stems the blowing sand had curiously heaped itself and hardened, forming on one side quite a solid wall several feet high. Mr. Leigh knew the place well. He stood astonished at finding these two together again, feeling that Mrs. Van Cortlandt was very remiss in not having written him a straight apology, a square taking-back of all her charges against Monny, instead of familiarizing with her in this private way. He did not like it; and, with an instinctive impulse to take before the widow's eyes the attitude of Monny's betrothed, he was about to step forward, when some words from the girl's own lips transfixed him. She was speaking in reply to Mrs. Van Cortlandt. What the latter had said was not audible; but Monny's soft voice had some penetrating quality which made her speech so distinct, Mr. Leigh could but hear.

"Mrs. Bingham was the only living being who knew all about the affair from beginning to end. She knew that I was engaged to marry him, and that every thing came from that."

The desert reeled around the man as he heard these words; then, as Mrs. Van Cortlandt's voice went indistinctly murmuring on again, he was forced to collect himself so far as to know that this was the last place on earth for him to ask explanation of Monny in, and to retreat unobserved.

The two women, all unaware of the chance listener who had been so near, soon rose up from the ground where they had sat down in their talk, and moved slowly on towards the highway, which they had been approaching by a cross-cut straight over the sandy wastes from Capt. Gawthrop's; for Monny's sudden run to the village had been to carry to Mrs. Van Cortlandt, who had assumed the personal charge of sending all such letters, a letter which she had hastened to write to Mrs. Bingham so soon as she caught from Mr. Leigh's remarks the glad news that the lady was on a steamer already due at New York. The intriguer's task was simplifying wonderfully; for she knew, and perceived with joy, that Monny did *not* yet know that "The Etolia," with Mrs. Bingham on board, was very possibly lost at sea. She walked part of the way home with the girl, exerting herself to the utmost to appear Monny's best friend, quite abstracting from her manner to-night all that element of criticism which she had thought expedient to mingle in it at various times before.

Fate had marvellously favored this plotting woman from the beginning, but in nothing more than in giving her just such types of character to dupe as the great preacher and the artist-girl. The proverbial simplicity with which the gifted fall into traps which the average mortal would instantly suspect, does not necessarily imply that the former are such dullards in human nature. But an habitual pre-occupation of the mind with other than personal objects probably does not tend to develop a certain small kind of acuteness in detecting character, which may far more abound in people with whom even that involuntary mental current which runs on all day in the head, is chiefly concerned with persons and things visible. And a man like Mr. Leigh, whom man or woman could not approach with detracting little gossip about his friends or acquaintances, undoubtedly loses — such as the loss is — some of those side-lights upon character which gossip throws. In short, the minister had never discerned aught in the widow to enable him even to imagine that she was capable of playing a false part : still less could the trusting Monny imagine this of the beautiful woman whom she saw always as standing herself in the shadow of an irremediable woe, and sacredly moved, by the memory of her own lost mate, to help a girl in a strange embarrassment about a lover.

Nevertheless, this very night, when Mrs. Van Cortlandt

had left her, and the girl came alone to that little belt of
pine-trees by the roadway, where she had met Mr. Leigh
on his return to the Cape a few nights before, a singular re-action came over her.   It is always possible that
bare instinct will suddenly rescue a thoroughly truthful nature from whatever snares of false reasoning have
been cast around it, and thus it was now with Monny.
The experience was so new, so hateful, to her, of having
things to hide, secrets which obliged her to steal clan-
destinely out of the house where her lover was, and think
how she could creep back into it again unobserved by
him, — the mere situation was so intolerable, she suddenly
rose up against it as something which she could not bear
another day.   And with this strong uprising of her heart
came a new illumination to her brain.   All at once, like
a discovery, the idea flashed on her, that she could tell
Mr. Leigh the secret which so burdened her, separate
from that part of it which Mrs. Van Cortlandt had so
frightened her from telling; viz., Kate De Lancey's
operations about Gen. Warwick's will.

   "I will tell him every thing else," she said to herself, —
"how I was engaged to Carroll De Lancey, and just how
I went with Kate to New Orleans, and about the lost
trunk I have sent for: whatever shame and misery it is
to me to confess it all, this hiding and concealing is a
worse misery.   And I will tell him truly that there is
something more which I cannot tell him ; that is, the
reason why Kate went to New Orleans dressed as a man.
I will tell Mr. Leigh I cannot explain that till I have seen
Mrs. Bingham, and know if I have a right to tell it, even
to him.   Mr. Leigh would never pry in such a case: he
would not be like me, that silly, silly morning, when I
asked him for his thoughts.   But the whole story that
concerns myself I will tell him from beginning to end:

whatever they all say, I *will* tell him, I will." And with
a force of resolve which she had never had before she flew
over the homeward way.

Arrived at the house, she was hurrying over the stairs,
going straight for Mr. Leigh's study, when the door of
that study opened, and he spoke from its threshold,
" Monny, I wish to see you in this room immediately."

The mere word " Monny," aside from the strange tone
of command in which it was uttered, sent the warm blood
back upon the girl's heart. Never had Mr. Leigh called
her by that name before ; for, so soon as he had a right to
call her by any name more familiar than Miss Rivers, he
had begun to call her by that diminutive of his own inven-
tion, Ana. And now, as she passed through the study-
door, he closed it instantly behind her, demanding still, in
that strange voice which she seemed not to know, —

" Were you ever engaged to marry any man before
myself? Answer me yes or no."

" Y-yes — I was once — engaged — a little," gasped
the girl ; all the story that had been ready to rush so full
and free from her lips choked back before the startling
change which had come over her betrothed.

" The man was your lover? " hoarsely interrogated Mr.
Leigh. "I mean you engaged yourself to him, he was
your personal choice?" he repeated ; for he was clinging
to so desperate a possibility as that an American girl had
been affianced by any will but her own.

" He — he was — then. I was not quite seventeen."

As if these words were bayonet-thrusts, the man fell
back before them, — back to the very opposite wall of the
room. Monny dropped into a chair by the door, for her
very limbs failed her for trembling. Mechanically Mr.
Leigh followed her movement, sitting down where he was.
The width of the room was now between them : oh the

impassable gulf it seemed to Monny when he spoke again !

"And you told me solemnly, with your own lips, but a week ago, — that moonlight night when we went together to the beach, — that you had never promised yourself to any man before me."

"No, no! I could never have told you quite that," insisted the girl. "I always was careful *not* to say *exactly* that; for I remembered the other. I remembered him that night you speak of. He was in my mind when I said — what I said was, I had never cared for any man before so — so much as — for you."

All the tenets of mental reservation, that Jesuitism, that doctrine of devils, Kenyon Leigh found in these words; and his voice, his very face, seemed to freeze as he rejoined, —

"This man in your mind whom you so shaped your words to cover — what was his name?"

"Carroll De Lancey."

A perceptible shudder shook the questioner at this name; but he went on with the tense, iron tone of a man forcing himself to be deliberate, —

"The same man, who, on the morning after that night, in this very room, you told me that you had only the slightest accidental acquaintance with, that you knew him scarcely at all. You said this of a man whose promised wife you once were. Is this true? Are there two Carroll De Lanceys? Did you say those words to me that morning of the selfsame man who, you now confess, once held your plighted word to marry him?" Still, in a last agonized reluctance to believe, the man thus iterated and reiterated the same question. He would be answered; and the frightened girl could only answer by a silent affirmative sign.

At that sign a terrible silence fell in the room, broken at last by Monny, with one more struggling effort to explain, "I — it was all a romantic fancy, which many things helped on : I painted his picture unknown to him."

So she had painted another man's picture, even as she had painted his. That sacredest ineffable memory of his life was but a rehearsal. So thought the lover who had been the original of the Knight-Templar's picture ; and, with some inarticulate sound as of one suffocating, he rose, and was gone from the room.

CHAPTER XXVII.

MAN, naturalists tell us, is the only animal in the entire range of creation which abuses the female of its species. Might we dare suggest, as one possible cause of this bad eminence, that man is the only reasoning animal, and that reason in the masculine and the feminine head follows such opposite lines, there is a chance of more exasperating collision between the human male and female than Mr. and Mrs. Wildcat in spotted skins are ever tried with?

Seriously, from that lower strata of society where man verily behaves himself, to the wife who angers him, worse than any tiger in his den, maltreating her with a violence which he shows to no other creature (as is pointed out by some English writers of the day, speaking especially of the performances of the British "rough" in this line), — from these deeps up to the highest social air, does the peculiar intensity which marks the conjugal quarrel arise wholly, as our indignant English reviewers declare, from man's inherent idea of woman as his bond-slave? Or is it not partly due, at least, to this cause, — that the two sexes, once brought into any disputing attitude, have a genuine difficulty in understanding each other?

Certainly, as to the betrothed lovers whose tale we tell, the man had now come to abuse in his mind, to do a great injustice there to the maiden who had been his idol; and this state of things Mrs. Van Cortlandt, with all her plots, would have been utterly powerless to bring about,

but for the fact that the pair had as man and woman some
very unlike ways of looking at things. Yet this was a
pair united by so many affinities of taste and character, it
would be said, at least by the progressives of our day,
that the disturbing element which there is in difference of
sex would be sure to disappear. But, lo! on the very first
question of importance which arose between them (and
that a question so elemental to human conduct as speaking the truth), the man took an intensely masculine view,
the woman an intensely feminine one; and the two were in
the blindest collision. For the shock with which Kenyon
Leigh had gone out from the presence of his young betrothed had all fallen on him with that first discovery that
she had concealed from him a matter which he could not
conceive how any truthful being, man or woman, could
conceal; viz., the fact of an old betrothal on making a
new one. He knew that if he himself had ever, in any
sort of outward way, stood as a suitor to Mrs. Van Cortlandt, or any other woman, he would have told Monny of
it at once. And while he had had no disposition to be
over-prying into the question of the young girl's "little
fancies" among her numerous adorers of the past, if any
such fancy of hers had ever gone so far into the region of
actualities as a marriage engagement, he would have considered it her absolute duty to tell him of it unasked.
This tenacity of his feeling that an engagement had some
claim to be reported beyond any unacknowledged love-
affair, was certainly not because as a lover he placed the
mere effigy before the life of sentiment (no lover ever
did that): but he had that masculine respect for facts
which we have spoken of in a former chapter; and an
engagement was a kind of fact to him, — a positive stage,
as it were, in affairs of the heart. That is, he unconsciously reasoned about a promise to marry as about any

other contract or bargain ; to wit, that it had external liabilities, — had, therefore, by the very constitution of the
actual world, a necessity to be understood. These truths,
self-evident to the man, were a class of truths so unper-
ceived by the girl, that the merely prudential reason which
there was for confessing every thing to Mr. Leigh, that is,
the likelihood of these strange adventures of hers coming
to his knowledge from without, had never once occurred to
her.   No, the only reasons she had ever seen for telling
Mr. Leigh about Carroll De Lancey at all were very sublimated ones, — a wish to be utterly true, not to keep back
even a passing fancy that she had once had for another
man.   Naturally, reasons of this strain could only act on
her in very exalted moments, and even then not with that
steadfast compelling which would have been in a clear
mental conviction of duty.

Now the man, having no stronger mental conviction on
earth than that it was a folly, as well as a wrong, to attempt
to hide the actualities of one's history, inevitably assumed
that guilt of some sort was behind Monny's concealment.
Indeed, when a man makes elaborate efforts to hide any
thing he has done, he has generally done something which
he means to lie about through thick and thin, aware that
it will take all the resources of lying successfully to cover
up facts in this world. So, although all that terrible story
which Mrs. Van Cortlandt had set coiled like a serpent
in Kenyon Leigh's consciousness, to bide its time there,
could not fasten itself yet on a lover's belief, one deadly
fang of doubt in Monny was planted in his breast the very
moment those few overheard words of hers in the desert
revealed to him that she had been engaged before, and
had not told him of it.

If the man placed an exaggerated emphasis on this
matter, so, also, on the girl's side, it was all an exaggera-

tion of womanly sensibility which had caused her concealment; and probably neither of these beings could have
been quite the man and woman that they were without
being liable to such exaggerations, which were in the direction of their best, their most distinctive, virtues as man
and woman. That soul of integrity in affairs, trustworthi-
ness like a rock, which belonged to the man, probably
could not have so distinguished him but for the fact that
certain principles of action were so ingrain with him he
did not consciously reason about them at all, — did not
conceive that any right-intentioned being could be blind
to those principles. But the most right-intentioned Monny
was blind to them, *did* have another point of view:
while the man's vision took in the outwardness of things,
she saw only their inwardness. Integrity towards a lover
was to her all a matter of the *heart;* and conscious that
her heart was not less, but even more, whole towards Mr.
Leigh because of the man that was before him, she did
not see that her old bond to that man, righteously broken
and long outworn as it was, still *had been*, and, like other
facts, had made positive waymarks in her history, that
her future husband needed to understand.

The feminine way of looking at things, as we have before suggested, has, we think, its own great worth in life
and society; but the masculine way would certainly seem
the one best adapted for the management of business, of
public affairs. And, if education might somewhat approximate these differences, it still remains, as women
suffragists seem to forget, that the essential force and
value of every being lies never in the line of its bor-
rowed qualities, but always in that of its primary, its most
instinctive ones.

Well, to return to our lovers : that unlikeness of nature
which had been their mutual attraction had certainly

become their dark division now. The morrow came before Mr. Leigh again saw his betrothed; then, knowing of course, that the rending subject which had come between them could not be dropped there, he knocked at the door of her studio.

Ah! when she opened it, he knew that gone forever was that morning when he could turn his back on this girl at the voice of reason. Reason told him to-day that she had lied to him; yet, at the first sight of her troubled young face, every thing went down before the one need to be reconciled to her, — his darling.

But Monny would not take the woman's advantage. She saw that there was one thing in the world which the strong man before her was not strong enough to bear: he could not bear her tears. And, whether it was that old feeling of hers, that she would not have his love without his approval, she choked back the tears, and so restrained her trembling that to the eye she seemed suddenly to take the coldness, and almost the immobility, of a statue. This forced calm looked to the man like the putting-on of a mask of impenetrability; and his melting mood so far congealed, that he began, with a touch of the imperative in his voice, —

"That young man whom you were once to marry — Carroll De Lancey — is somewhat known to me by reputation. Stories have come to my ears about — him" (he could not bring himself to say to Monny's face "about you") "which give me a reason, a right, to ask where, in what places, you were ever with him. Did he visit you at your home, your uncle's house?"

"No: my uncle and aunt were in Europe then. I was at school in New York. That is the only place where I ever saw him — except in West Point, at a ball there. That was where I first met him. He was very handsome — he was *wonderful* for beauty. You noticed it your-self: you said, 'What a handsome young *caballero!*' when you first saw his picture. That was his picture which you found in my old school portfolio. And he was so accomplished besides: even the young men at West Point admired him immensely. He spoke foreign lan-guages so perfectly, and danced and sang beautifully. He sang to me the night after the ball, when we went in a moonlight party on the river: he sang, 'Drink to me only with thine eyes.'"

Every syllable of that beautiful old song, thrilling with love's divine exaggerations, shot through the heart of the man who heard these praises of his predecessor which poor Monny poured forth in her simplicity, striving to show some cause for that early infatuation of hers, fear-ing always, that, to those who knew him only of late years, perhaps the dissolute Carroll De Lancey showed no traces of that young splendor which had attracted her; and what, then, could Mr. Leigh think of her standards about suitors?

Mr. Leigh's thoughts were a whirlwind; but supremest of all rose some nameless, passionate torture of the lover's jealousy. Yes, with the intolerable sense of one belated, who has overslept the hour, the mature man sud-denly saw all the years behind him — saw all knowledge, duties, all labors that are done under the sun — burn up as the mere stubble of life in one consuming desire to have been beforehand with that dancing, singing strip-ling, into whose lot and nature the great preacher could wish this moment to have been born. Even Monny's little jest of the other day, "Stay down in your chair, and make yourself a little smaller, when I come in," came back now to this least self-conscious of men with the stabbing thought that she saw him as an ungainly

Behemoth beside the splendid young Antinous whose praises she could not forbear to his own very face.

Why had she ever broken with that lover? This inward question he at length put aloud, in some shape, to Monny.

"I—I found that he did not truly love me. And I grew tired of him myself before—right there in New Orleans."

"New Orleans?" Mr. Leigh repeated the fatal words with a sharp passionateness of outbreak. "And just now New York and West Point were the only places where you ever saw Carroll De Lancey! In one grain of mercy to me, or prudence for yourself, will you *begin* to speak the truth to me?"

To hear words, tones, like these, from Mr. Leigh's lips, so shook his young betrothed, she could only gasp, "I— I had forgotten about New Orleans— There is—some one coming into the yard to see you." Monny was standing now by the window.

And directly, indeed, a member of the household came up the stairs to summon Mr. Leigh below, and the interview was for a moment interrupted.

Returning to the studio as soon as his caller had left, he was astounded to find that Monny had snatched the occasion to quit the room and the house.

CHAPTER XXVIII.

THE man's way of looking at things, the mere pressure of her lover's mind on her own the moment it
ceased to be sympathetic, inevitably frightened the girl
whose bewildered fluctuations we trace. She did not
even know the point where his wrath began, did not yet
perceive that it was her concealment which angered him :
it was still her idea that the bare fact of her having been
engaged to a young man like Carroll De Lancey shocked
him as a blemish on her delicacy. How ever, then, could
she find face to tell him of that indelicate journey to New
Orleans? She fled.

Mrs. Van Cortlandt saw her rushing past the Gawthrop
house in the briefest time after the events of the last
chapter, and hurried into the street to intercept her with,
" Where are you going? "

" Home — to my uncle and aunt."

" Not directly, surely? " replied the widow ; for on
foot, and in her delicate morning-dress, the girl scarcely
suggested a railway-traveller.

" No. I knew the train had gone. But I am going
to the station to telegraph, to find out just where my
aunt is, that 1 may join her at once. I cannot wait for
letters — I cannot wait for any thing."

" Come to my room. and tell me what is the matter,"
said the widow ; and she drew the excited girl into the
house.

" What is the matter? " she repeated there.

"Oh! Mr. Leigh has heard in some way about my engagement to Carroll De Lancey—I don't know how —it seems to be in the air," moaned Monny. "And he takes it so—so hard, I dare not tell him the rest with my own lips. And I was going to tell him the whole of it last night, even without his asking me, even against your advice, Mrs. Van Cortlandt. But I dare not tell him now myself; and I shall ask my uncle and aunt to tell him. That is why I want to go to them right away, —to my own blood and kin," said the wounded girl, quivering with a strange, agonized sense of wanting home protection — and — against *him*.

"You say your friends are travelling?" quietly asked Mrs. Van Cortlandt.

"Yes, just now. They have been at Lenox for weeks; but aunt Helen's last letter, a day or two ago, said they were just starting for a trip in the Middle States."

"You would not wish to alarm your friends, to bring them suddenly here?" suggested the plotter.

"I mean to go to them, not to bring them here. Aunt Helen mentioned several places where they were to stop. I can certainly find out, by telegraphing to all of them, just where they are now."

The widow's swift thought, electrized by the consciousness that this one day probably held all her chances of success or failure, traversed an intricate maze of strategy, before she said, —

"I will go right over to the telegraph-office with you, my dear."

Hither Mrs. Van Cortlandt went, and easily enough prolonged through the entire day the business of finding out by the telegraph-wires that the Slabwells were at a mountain-house in the Catskills. She was careful not only to keep Monny with her in the village, out to send word to the Doane house where she was, well aware that nothing could look more suspicious to Mr. Leigh now than that the girl should be thus closeted with her accuser.

Then, as the hours of the afternoon wore on, she made two deeply-planned moves. First she despatched by Tonson, all unknown to Monny, a letter to Mr. Leigh, and, directly in wake of this letter, sent to Mrs. Doane's house the lost trunk, which had arrived that morning at the Cape-Cod depot, from Jackson, Miss.

Thus, to the appalled man waiting in the Doane house —appalled first by Monny's deliberate flight from his inquiries, and then by the still greater shock of learning that she had gone to Mrs. Van Cortlandt— came a letter like the following, which, with the fierce eagerness of the long day's suspense, he tore open and read : —

"REV. KENYON LEIGH, — Notwithstanding the tone of your last letter to me, it becomes my difficult duty to write to you again; for I must state, that, during your recent absence, Miss Rivers confessed to me with her own lips her identity with that young girl of the New-Orleans scandal, — a fact absolutely certain to me before beyond all human possibility of mistake.

"There is now one especial item connected with that journey which I must refer to. When Miss Rivers fled from her New-York boarding-school in male attire, she cut off her hair (to perfect her disguise), and threw it into a trunk, which was lost on her journey; that is, left, forgotten, at the depot in Jackson, Miss., —the place where the runaway pair openly took the names of Mr. and Mrs. Carroll De Lancey. As this trunk contained not only the hair, but her male disguise (a cadet's uniform), and other fatal proofs of her misadventure, she has been endeavoring during the past week to get it back into her possession, and to-day it has arrived in this very town. I hope that there are no more quite such ruinous witnesses as this trunk scattered abroad against her. But some one surely should look after this unfortunate girl in her present excited state, that she do not compromise nerself unnecessarily. In this view of duty I have kept her with me to-day, having found her going in wild agitation to the tele-graph-office, in the idea of communicating with her uncle and aunt about this past disgrace of hers, which to this day she has kept a profound secret from them. Nevertheless, with these extraordinary talents for concealment, there is blended such a vein of childish heedlessness, I feared, as I have said, to leave her to herself to-day.

"I hope that I may lay down here this most unhappy part towards yourself, which fate has so strangely thrust me into. Of course, could I have known in the beginning that it was yourself, and not the Roosevelts, who needed to be informed of Miss Rivers's wild past, I should have felt it impossible to discharge myself the duty of informer; but, knowing what I did of the girl, it was naturally inconceivable to me, either that a clergyman should think of her as a wife, or that she herself should desire such a position. Although now, when I reflect that a clergyman, being ruined in his profession as no other man is by a domestic scandal, can never afford to repudiate the guiltiest wife, I can see that powerful considerations of policy and prudence might impel Miss Rivers to marry a minister, aware, as she must have been, that the dark secret in her history was always liable to be dis-covered sooner or later by a husband.

"Respectfully yours,

"ADELAIDE VAN CORTLANDT."

Decidedly Mrs. Van Cortlandt knew where to strike. The last words of this horrible letter did more than any thing else in it to nail into the man's breast a conviction of the possible truth of it all. He had never ceased to wonder, with love's own humility, — we might add, with that especial humility of the man who loves a woman much younger than himself, — that he had been able to win this young heart for his own. This was the secret of it all, then : she had found it *prudent* to marry a minister.

And need we say that corroborative memories had rushed hideously on his mind at every point in this letter? The cut-off hair lost in a trunk when she was travelling —

could he forget how he had heard of that from Monny's
own lips? That morning when he had pulled out before
her very face Caroll De Lancey's picture, the statue-like
calm which fell on her, the winsome little appeal to him
with which she broke out of it, "I have learned lately a
little to cook"—was that her talent for concealment,
mixed with childishness? Yea, that sacred midnight when
she had flung herself sobbing on his breast, and cried,
"Take me into your church!"—was that a childish
burst of repenting? Heavens! had not the minister seen
transgressors before trying to shrive themselves, in some
more or less fantastic way, for their unconfessed sins—
to join the church on the stairs?

"And I saw woman, that she is like a snare, or some
such other object:" these words of old Gregory Thau-
maturgus, or some such other object among those anchorite priests whom he had hidden from Monny's reading,
dinned through his brain now as he stood paralyzed with
a sense of some craft in the girl which the falsest of male
beings could never attain to,—some fathomless duplicity
which only a creature who so mixed her very guile with
grace could show.

And now, in the wild whirl of these thoughts, he was
aware of a wagon driven up to the house, a noise about
the front door; and, feverishly expectant at every sound
from without, he stepped to the head of the front staircase. A man, admitted by Jenny Hines, was hoisting a
trunk up the stairs: it was the familiar driver of the
depot baggage-wagon.

"Miss Rivers's trunk," he said, doffing his hat to Mr.
Leigh as he reached the upper landing of the stairs, where
he paused, resting the trunk endwise, waiting for this
inmate of the house to suggest the precise spot where it
should be left. Mr. Leigh replied to this tacit inquiry by

pusl ing open the door of Monny's studio; and the man, depositing the trunk in the middle of that room, departed.

The much tossed-about piece of baggage was scrawled all over with railroad hieroglyphics; but one crimson card, printed with the picture of a hotel, and the words, "Harcourt House, Jackson, Miss.," — this hotel-card had kept its place through every thing, and glared on the minister now like a blood-red stain.

He walked round and round the thing as if spell-bound, never imagining that any deeper agency than acci dent had so timed the arrival of this fatal witness against Monny. No: that she should dig this trunk up from its five-years' hiding in the State of Mississippi, especially to destroy that black testimony against herself which Mrs. Van Cortlandt had declared it to contain, and then allow chance to tumble it down at his very feet, — this would be only another specimen of that infantile heedlessness and far-reaching secrecy which had so marked all the girl's course.

While the man was torn on the rack of these thoughts, the intriguer in the Gawthrop House was addressing herself to the most critical step of all; that is, directly after her secret sending-off of the trunk, she turned her conversation with Monny into an entirely new channel. First she informed the girl, what as yet the latter had heard no rumor of, that "The Etolia," with the Binghams on board, was believed to be lost at sea.

This was too great a tragedy for Monny to remember its bearings upon her own personal fate, until Mrs. Van Cortlandt said, with a singular accent, —

"Most unfortunate for you, Miss Rivers, that the only original witness to the truth of your account of the New-Orleans journey should be cut off in this way. It leaves you so sadly exposed to the world's suspicion, it is necessary, of course, for you to confess every thing to your aunt and uncle. But if you had only confessed to them at the time of the affair, five years ago! How very singular that you did not do it! If you had only told them every thing then, it would have been counted as a considerable proof of your honesty."

"Honesty?" repeated Monny in a dazed way, — "considerable proof? I — I think I do not quite understand you."

"I mean," deliberately replied the intriguer, "that your own story of that journey to New Orleans will be pronounced by the world too extremely wild and improbable to be true, — a quite impossible fable, in short. It will be said that the probable thing is that you made that journey alone with Carroll De Lancey."

"Probable that I — travelled alone like that with a young man? Who will say that was probable of me?" slowly repeated the astounded girl, a red flame beginning to burn up in her pure cheek. Still it was too impossible for her yet to conceive just all that these insinuations meant.

"Every one who knows life will say it," coolly replied the widow. "Carroll De Lancey's repute as a young man of pleasure, the fact that he was your *fiancé*, every circumstance, the world will say, points to the conclusion that it was a runaway love-affair."

"Why, there was not an atom of love-affair about it," Monny burst in. "Carroll De Lancey never stirred out of West Point till Kate and I got to New Orleans: he had not the slightest thing to do with our going there — *everybody* knew it."

"Will you name the persons who make up this everybody?" calmly rejoined Mrs. Van Cortlandt.

"Mrs. Bingham, she knew it well, and her maid Jane, and Kate — and all of us," cried Monny breathlessly.

"Miss De Lancey having died years ago, as you tell me, and the maid Jane dying at the very time of the affair," continued the widow with an iron accent, "and Mrs. Bingham now dead in all human probability, what being is alive to confirm your tale? I wish myself, Miss Rivers, to believe in you and to befriend you. But I am speaking to you of the outside world; and very strange stories, to which the witnesses are all dead, are not credited by that."

"Carroll De Lancey is not dead! — he — the chief witness," almost shrieked the girl, as she began to see at last the situation which this wily enemy would show her as her own. "He will swear to the truth of every syllable I have said about that journey; and his word can be taken by the whole world, — the word of a gentleman. He had no morals; but he *was* a gentleman, he would not lie."

"Precisely, if he is a gentleman," responded the widow, in her quiet, steely tones, "he *would* lie in your case, — the case which the world will believe to be yours. Do you not know that the one exceptional case in which a gentleman is allowed, nay, commanded, to lie, is to save (before the public) the honor of a woman who has lost her honor for *him?* Carroll De Lancey is worse than no witness for you; since, if he were to swear to the truth of your tale, the world would only believe he was ingeniously lying to screen you, as the code of a gentleman would oblige him to lie."

The woman of the world shook her over the abyss at last, — this Puritan girl, bred up in modesty from her cradle. The one virtue in which that unvirtuous lover of her girlhood stood immaculate — the word of a gentleman — would only beat her down the deeper, if she grasped at it to save her! The victim of this last terrible argument

on woman's peculiar position in life sat as if death-struck
for a space; then at last, stretching out her hands with a
blind, sick movement, she gasped faintly, "I must go
back—back to him. Why have you let me waste the
time so," she murmured helplessly, "to-day and all the
days gone by, without explaining to me before? When I
have ro cause to see my uncle and aunt, or anybody on
earth, except *him*."

"What are you going to say to him?" said the intriguer, laying a quick hand on the girl's arm, startled by
something in the white intensity of her face.

"That I release him forever — what else? Do you
suppose that I would marry *him*, — join to a name like
his my name, if the most outside being in all the outside
world could ever whisper that it was not a good name?
Let me go!" The widow strove yet to detain her: but
it was as if she had seized a whirlwind; the desperate
maiden broke from her grasp, and ran out of the house.

"The only correct actions are those which require no
explanation and no apology:" these words out of Auer-
bach rang in the ears of this hunted girl on her fugitive
way with that sound of absolute and awful truth with
which mere half-truths uttered in an aphoristic way
impose on a young mind. She felt banned for ever and
ever from marrying Mr. Leigh, although her worst con-
jectures, as she sped back over the old road to tell him so,
still stopped far short of any such horror as that he was
believing, or ever would believe, what Mrs. Van Cortlandt
had just told her the general world would believe, about
her connection with Carroll De Lancey.

How she reached Mrs. Doane's she did not know, only
that, climbing again the old stairs, her heart once more
stood still at Mr. Leigh's voice calling peremptorily to her,
this time from her own threshold, "Come in — here!"

Like a blown leaf she fluttered into the studio to see and recognize the lost trunk standing there in the middle of the room. With a low, frightened cry, as feeling herself pursued by fate, she stood motionless, turning deathly pale.

It seemed the very aspect of mortal guilt; and every emotion of the lover was swamped in the primal wrath of man deceived by woman with the last deceit. He drew her up to the trunk with such a grasp on her arm, — the strong man in his agony, — that she would have cried out in the flesh, if in the flesh she had any longer had the power to feel.

"Open that trunk, and show me what is in it!"

Her shaking hands made some helpless sign that she had no key, and with a thrust or two of the man's foot, the lid of the trunk (it was a slight packing-trunk) flew in pieces, and the contents fell out. They fell out, the long-severed golden curls, the cadet's uniform, the crumpled, yellowed ball-dress.

He plunged his hand into the heap of shining tresses, and felt them twine round his fingers as he held them on high. "You cut this hair from your head for a certain journey to New Orleans, five years ago, when you wore — these things?" he said, indicating the suit of male clothes with a shudder. He paused, compelling an answer; and the quivering lips shaped some inarticulate "Yes."

"In this disguise of a boy you travelled from New York to Jackson, Miss., where you threw these clothes into this trunk," he reiterated, "and took openly the name of a wife — of Mrs. Carroll De Lancey?" Again he paused, forcing an answer. And what could she answer but that helpless "Yes."

"And you intended to hide this, and marry me! Great God!".

She reeled heavily backward at these words — oi did he fling her from him like an outcast creature, while his fiery reproaches, like some deadly hail, went beating on her head? A moment longer the white terror of her face was still uplifted, with wild, asking eyes fixed on his; then, with some indescribable action of a slain thing, she fell forward, her head dropped upon the wall-table piled with the old school portfolios, her face hidden from sight; nor did she speak, or stir, or make one sign, until he left her.

All had passed in a few swift moments; and in a few moments more Kenyon Leigh left the house, and the evening train carried him from Cape Cod.

CHAPTER XXIX.

WOMEN, in judging of character, rely supremely on their intuitions : when these speak strongly, all contradictory evidence of a merely external kind goes with them for nought. Thus the utmost ingenuity of calumny would have been powerless to make Monny Rivers believe evil of Kenyon Leigh : there was no weapon in the whole arsenal of lies which could ever have slain her faith in him as his had been slain in her. She knew this : hence she did not ask how overwhelming might have been the evidence on which he had come to believe her a fallen girl, — that he could believe it on any evidence which mortal lips could bring was a blow under which she fell dumb as death. As to those perfectly automatic answers which she had made to his fierce inquiries over the trunk, if she remembered them at all, it was to remember that belief in her guilt had gone beforehand with him, or he would never have put those questions to her as he did.

This, alas ! was true. And, before accusing her of mad folly in allowing her lover to depart with that monstrous lie which had been forced on his belief all uncontradicted, it must be remembered, that, as women see things, she had no proof of her innocence to offer him ; for he had been able to reject what to her was the most infallible of all proofs, viz., the witness that should have been in his own heart that the things she was accused of were impossible to her. To find that this inner witness was not there was a discovery for which nothing of all that had passed between Mr. Leigh and herself since their misunderstanding began, had in the least prepared her. It meant something more to her than the destruction of all her personal happiness on earth: she could have faced that doom. She knew that human beings had been entangled before in dark nets of circumstantial evidence from which they could not free themselves, so that they had suffered, even unto death, for crimes of which they were innocent as angels. If the lot had fallen on her to be one of those hapless victims (and she believed that it had, when she came back to free Mr. Leigh from his engagement to her), it would only be one of the terrible mysteries of this earth, —mysteries which did not necessarily reach beyond it. Such a fate could conceivably be borne, hoping for the eternity which would show the innocence that could not be proved in time. But the horror which froze her soul when she found that not the hearsay world, but her own lover, could believe that unspeakable ill of 'her, was no such finite thing: it blackened beyond the gates of death, into all worlds, all lives which could conceivably be lived by the spirits of men and women. They were not alike: all her love-story had run its varying round to end at last in this most awful confirmation of the fear which had vaguely shadowed its beginning.

Night fell in the little room; but the crushed girl had no sense of time save that once she grew aware of some stir below stairs, which reached up to her with the tidings that one of Mrs. Doane's sick grandchildren (in the family where Susannah was gone) was dead, and that the old lady would like to go back with the messenger who brought the news (he came in a wagon); the bereaved family living only about fifteen miles away. Menay, whose only remaining consciousness was a desire to be alone, and to be asked no questions about Mr. Leigh.

roused herself to go down, and urge Mrs. Doane to take this journey to her daughter. So Mrs. Doane, feeling more free to go because of Mr. Leigh's departure, — she was not in the house when he went, and supposed that he had been suddenly called to New York for affairs connected with his parish, — made some hasty arrangements for the. care of the house in her absence, and was driven off in the wagon. Then Monny was alone.

The minister rode night and day on his search for Carroll De Lancey. To find that young man, and marry him to Monny, was the sole objective point remaining to him in existence. Beyond that, nothing was defined, except that he had done with preaching. As a minister he had but one more word to say, and it was, "I give up my commission : the problem of evil is deeper than I can fathom." If there was no truth in woman, there was no hope for man, — no hope in all the life of humanity. He was right in this conviction.

He went to New York to find that Carroll De Lancey was in Baltimore, and to Baltimore to learn that he was back again in New York. But in the latter city he at last laid hands on the young man. He found him in elegant hotel apartments, and at an hour of the night when Mr. Carroll (who had just returned to his rooms after some revel) was wont to be, as of old, and much oftener than of old, flown with wine. The splendid beauty of this Southern Antinous, the singular grace of his bearing, was only marred, not obliterated yet, by his reckless life ; and, recognizing at once the original of Monny's romantic picture, the visitor's first sensation was a devouring impulse to spring on the young man, and strangle him as his rival — the natural man was far from dead in this minister.

On his side, young De Lancey stood staring, through his mist of inebriety, at the imperious stranger who made such a volcanic irruption into his rooms past midnight.

"Deused if he doesn't look like his Eminence of St. Ancient's! — Protestant Eminence, with no toggery," he began to mutter to himself. Mr. Carroll's education abroad had all been in Catholic schools; and the imposing rector of St. Ancient's, who was too distinguished a man not to be known by sight to young De Lancey, suggested to the latter's drink-befogged brain a Romish cardinal. "What will your Grace have of me?" he asked, with a salute of the politest deference.

"Such miserable reparation as you can make, robber and villain!" thundered the accuser. "The fulfilment of the marriage-promise you made years ago to " —

He paused; for he could not bring himself to utter Monny's name here.

"Marriage-promises — are — not — my style," brokenly answered the young Bacchant, steadying himself by the mantel. A veritable Bacchant of old fable he looked to the minister, — some vision out of those days when conscienceless creatures laughed in an endless sunshine, took untroubled the things which seemed to them good; when scruples were not, nor right and wrong yet named; when nought was honor or dishonor; "when yet there was no fear of Jove."

"Never promised to marry but one girl in my life," the young man went on; "and she broke it off, not I " —

"Liar!" hoarsely interrupted the accuser.

The young Southerner's face, through all his intoxication, flushed angrily as he cried, —

"Don't give that word to me, — Eminence, or no Eminence! I tell you, never was engaged but once; and 'twas to a Puritan girl, by Jove! And her confounded relations broke it off. She had a *bourgeois* uncle, — none of her blood, but a kind of guardian uncle by marriage, — a regular Yankee peddler, psalm-singer," declared the young aristocrat, his lively memory of the plebeian style of Mr. Slabwell, and the furious moral drubbing which he had administered to him, leading to this rather mixed description of a man in whom the psalm-singing quality had decidedly died out. "The *bourgeois* Puritan! To suppose, because I took my little fling here and there, that I shouldn't know what was due to Monny Rivers — shouldn't treat her as a gentleman treats his " —

"Did you treat her like a gentleman, — that motherless school-girl?" cried the other; and in a storm of indignation he poured out that runaway story as he had heard it.

Staring with amazement, the young reveller heard, his potations beginning to clear a little from his brain with the successive shocks of surprise which this astounding visitor caused him.

"Liar yourself!" he found breath to retort at last — "or whatever villain got up such an abominable slander as that! Confounded fool he must be about women to try that sort of lie on a name like Monny Rivers. A girl," he said, with some aerial motions of the hand which indescribably recalled Monny and her ways, — "a girl that you can be about as familiar with as you can with a bird on a tree. That's what a man wants for his wife, by Jove! whosoever he may go larking with. She was to have been my wife," Mr. De Lancey broke out afresh, and with more soberness than he had yet spoken; "and, by Jove! no man shall insult her in my presence by asking whether she travelled alone with me day and night, putting up at hotels. I'll have a gentleman's satisfaction for that insult to the innocentest girl that ever lived. Stand off, and defend yourself, sir!" And the last of the cavaliers pulled out a brace of revolvers.

There was a genuineness in this outbreak, an unmistakable accent of respect in all the tone in which the Southerner spoke Monny's name, which thrilled to the soul of Kenyon Leigh. He seized his fiery challenger by the arm, not wishing at this moment to have his own brains blown out, or even to blow out Carroll De Lancey's brains, till he should extract more speech from him.

"Unhand me!" shouted the latter. "Miss Rivers went that journey to New Orleans with my sister, — not another living soul with her, — my sister Kate, dressed up in my clothes for a lark. Not a lark that I should have recommended beforehand; but, by Heaven! I'll defend them in it now, both those ladies, — Miss Rivers and my dead sister. Choose your paces, like a man! Stand off, I say!" furiously roared the would-be duellist. But Mr. Leigh succeeded in wrenching both pistols from his grasp, and hurling them across the room, where they exploded with no murder. Then he took Mr. Carroll by both arms with such a grip as mortal man has seldom laid upon his fellow.

"Speak, speak the *sober* truth to me!" he cried; "nor dare, on your life, to speak one syllable of any thing else!" And the mighty grasp which pinioned him, and those fierce eyes of the suspense-tortured man fixing his, so far magnetized the tipsy youth out of his tipsiness, that he did speak soberly enough at last to impart in some intelligible sort the true story of the two runaway school-girls.

As the listener heard it all, some strange convulsion passed over his face; then, letting go the young man with a suddenness which nearly threw him to the floor, he was gone from the room.

Mr. Carroll De Lancey stood long agaze at the door by
which the visitor had departed, as if he had seen a vision.
Then, gathering himself up, he strove to bring all his
confused faculties to bear on the amazing interview which
had just passed. Who had sent that churchman to drag
him, as by the hair of the head, to marry Monny Rivers?
The idea of the Church as the champion of the indissolu-
bility of marriage was familiar to the youth: had the
ecclesiastical ægis begun to extend also over engagements
to marry? He concluded so. The figure that had just
vanished had powerfully suggested to him Richelieu
launching the curse of Rome, only that the rector of St.
Ancient's, in his wrath, was infinitely more overwhelming than any player of the great Richelieu that Mr. De
Lancey had ever seen. Yes, the churchman had doubtless
descended on him in his official fury, rather mixing up his
business (priests were apt to do that) ; but one thing was
clear, that Monny's early engagement to himself had
somehow turned up unpleasantly for her. Perhaps, too,
all the surroundings of her life had been getting unpleasant these years. She lived with a guardian. Mr. Carroll
considered guardians a naturally pestiferous race ; and he
could well imagine the *bourgeois* Puritan a most tiresome
fellow, and his roof the dullest of places. Had all Monny's Puritan lovers of that cold North been growing
tiresome to her perhaps, and had she turned back to him
at last, whom she had cruelly rejected?

Mr. De Lancey was not a young man to die of heart-
break over any one disappointment in so gay a world ; but
he had been really disappointed in the loss of Monny
Rivers. He had never forgotten that rosebud girl of the
ballroom, who had remained, in truth, the only girl for
whom he had ever yet been willing to put on the serious
yoke of matrimony. He found himself fervently willing

to put it right ou for her now. Richelieu need not have made such a powwow. He would marry Monny Rivers to-morrow.

It was his place as a gentleman, he maturely decided, to communicate now with the young lady herself. Having reached this conclusion, he wisely decided, that, as a first preliminary in the new prospects before him, he should try to compose the present severe jumble of his thoughts by the restorative of sleep ; and, dropping on the nearest sofa, he slept accordingly.

Carroll De Lancey could sleep off yet, very heavy bumpers ; and when he awoke next day he was in fair condition to write a letter to Monny Rivers, whose present address he had learned through the churchman's fiery summons to him to go to Cape Cod and marry her. He wrote the young lady a very ardent but entirely respectful love-letter, re-offering himself to her, heart and hand. This letter he mailed her as a kind of herald, deciding, with a prudent remembrance of the *bourgeois* uncle, that he should wait an answer to the same, before presenting himself in person.

In that tolerably sober tale which Mr. Leigh had conjured out of Carroll De Lancey, the latter had naturally referred to Mrs. Bingham as authority. That lady, as Mr. Leigh knew, and as Mrs. Van Cortlandt very well knew at the time of her last interview with Monny, had arrived safely in New-York harbor, after all the alarming delay of "The Etolia."

Mrs. Bingham was a very old friend of Mr. Leigh's, and he sought and ascertained her whereabouts at once. She had gone to her out-of-town place on the Hudson, where Mr. Leigh saw her the very next day ; and how many words did it require from this lady to bring him up, out of the horrible pit of false belief into which he had fallen, into the sunlight of day?

Divine as was that sense of transition from hell to heaven in which Kenyon Leigh journeyed back to Cape Cod, it was pierced with a remorse which it seemed to him would go with him through life, and cleave to him in his shroud, — remorse for having ever doubted Monny.

Contrary to Mrs. Van Cortlandt's belief, Mrs. Bingham was in possession of data which enabled her absolutely to know and prove that Mrs. Van Cortlandt had knowingly and deliberately lied from the beginning. These proofs she naturally laid before Mr. Leigh, ere their interview ended. But even his indignation over the false woman who had so infamously betrayed them both occupied him but little, so absorbed was he in his own self-reproach, in forever asking himself what tenderness he had failed of towards Monny, that she should have so feared to tell him that poor little folly of her schooldays, which he would have forgotten with a kiss.

Well, Kenyon Leigh had not failed as a lover : he had merely failed, as a man, to comprehend a woman.

CHAPTER XXX.

THE despair of the forsaken girl on the Cape-Cod shore was a despair from which, in its nature, there could be no re-action : with every hour she only sank the deeper. Sleep never touched her eyelids, nor food her lips ; although she had sense enough left to disguise this from the villager who was housekeeper in Mrs. Doane's absence, and who regularly brought her meals to the studio. Any suspicions of this woman were easily enough quieted ; for, being almost stone deaf, she went about her duties like an automaton, and, sharing the village understanding that Miss Rivers was a genius, she concluded that the young lady's strange prisoning of herself in her own room was only one of the peculiarities of genius. Even Jenny Hines had flitted home from the abode which had suddenly grown so dull, and where there was nothing to do : so the solitary girl was all unwatched and alone in the darkness which was pressing upon her life and brain. She had no longer a thought of seeking her relatives : aunt Helen had no plummet to sound her sufferings now. These were not assuaged by a letter which came back to her from Mr. Leigh, — he had written it on the cars, when the first storm of his emotions left him space to reflect on one last service that could be done the girl.

"Miss Rivers, — You must marry Carroll De Lancey. I shall find him, wherever he is, and bring him to you, and perform the ceremony myself.

"KENYON LEIGH."

The man's intent thus to officiate was only moved by his instinctive impulse to make sure that the thing was done; but to Monny there was an iron hardness, even a terrible mockery, in the laconic note.

Mrs. Van Cortlandt also received a letter from Mr. Leigh about the same time. Yes, the proud man humbled himself to write to the widow, in a blind sense that the aid of some woman would be necessary to get Monny married to Carroll De Lancey quietly and without scandal; and Mrs. Van Cortlandt, as knowing the whole history, and having the tact of a woman of the world, seemed to him the one to accomplish this. His note to her was brief and formal enough, but the intriguer clutched it with wild exultation. Once get Monny married to Carroll De Lancey, and Mrs. Bingham would rise from the dead in vain to undo the bond.

She knew, as we have said, that Mrs. Bingham had thus risen, — that she had landed safe in New York. It would be a desperate race with time now; but she had already won many desperate chances in this contest, and, suppressing a fierce excitement under her wonted calm manner, the widow sped to the house of her victim. The first sight of the latter alone in her studio strengthened the hopes of the traitress; for she saw that the crushed girl had sunk down without a thought of doing battle for her name and fame. No: Monny's was not a spirit to have fallen helplessly under any other kind of false accusation. If she had been charged with theft, murder, any crime in the calendar save this which she had been accused of, she would have summoned all her clear young faculties to set the facts of her innocence in such a light that they should be evidence to others. But to know that the purity of a pure maiden could be a debatable thing, that belief in her could turn on such a question as the

proving of an *alibi*, — this, as we know, had unhinged
existence to her. The only response she made to Mrs.
Van Cortlandt's salute was to indicate that she had given
orders to admit no one.

"Yes, I know," replied the intruder. "But I come
from Mr. Leigh. He has written me a letter," and she
displayed the missive. "He sees, as the whole world
would, that your only salvation is in marrying Carroll De
Lancey, that marriage with any other man is forever impossible to you. And, since the engagement with Mr.
De Lancey was broken off by yourself, doubtless the
young man can be induced to renew it. Mr. Leigh will,
I am sure, accomplish this. He wrote me, asking me to
see you at once, to arrange things; for, of course, the
sooner you change your maiden name, the better."

While all these words were said, Monny's eyes, lifted
in their strange, still agony, to the speaker's face, grew
wide and wider with an utterly new insight. She saw
— at last — HER RIVAL. Stunned by the revelation, she
sat for a space; then she rose slowly to her feet, with
some strange, strange exaltation in her bearing, which
made her slight figure seem to fill the room, even to the
effacing of the tall woman, — so little has mere altitude
to do with the presence. Self in its last and dearest
stronghold was being conquered in the girl by a mightier
solicitude.

"When you are married to Mr. Leigh," she began in
a thrilling voice (the startled intriguer changed color, but
did not deny the impeachment), "there is something I
should wish you to have." And, turning, she took a canvas which was leaned face towards the wall, and set it in
open view on an easel. It was the resplendent head of
the Knight-Templar, — *his* in every line and feature. For
the moment, even Mrs. Van Cortlandt quailed before the

living glory of that face, the solemn, ringing voice of the girl who had painted it for love's sake, as she said, —

"There came a power upon me, when I painted that picture, to make it true, to show him for the wonderful being he is : therefore I wish you now to have it, — kept away somewhere where he will not see it (he will not wish to see *my* works) ; but keep the picture where you can study it daily, that it may help *you* to know him rightly, to understand him as he is. How else can you make him happy as his wife?" murmured the girl with a voice of anguished yearning, divining in this clairvoyant moment, if never before, the woman's alien spirit, and comprehending what it would be to Kenyon Leigh to have in his married life at once all the loneliness of solitude, and all the *ennui*, the obstruction, which there is in intimacy without companionship.

"I came to speak of the other affair, — of *your* marriage," began the widow, restless under that soul-piercing gaze which her young victim bent on her face.

"There needs no talk about that," said Monny, recalling herself with a shiver, while that stony veil of apathetic despair which had been lifted a little by her questioning throes over Kenyon Leigh's fate settled again upon her face. "I shall make no trouble. I shall obey Mr. Leigh. Until he comes, leave me, leave me, madam! *Leave me!*" and there was an imperative passion in the girl's voice which at last the persistent widow dared not disobey: she went.

Death-like was the low moan with which Monny turned then to the picture of her lost lover: the sobbings of her broken heart made a cruel sound in the little room. By and by she went searching for that sketch she had made of Mrs. Van Cortlandt's head : when it was found, she set it up beside his. Terrible hours went over her while she gazed on the twain. They were to be one, and she was to be delivered over to Carroll De Lancey: the whole plan of earthly things, the very sense of her own being, grew confused and lost to her, save as consciousness lived round these two events, which she saw fate, like an iron wheel, swiftly rolling on to bring to pass.

It was, perhaps, from her deep habit of loyalty to Mr. Leigh's direction, that her mind had made no active resistance to the idea of marrying Carroll De Lancey; or, indeed, the fact that the young Southerner was the one being in the world to whom she would never have to say, "I am innocent," may even, at least, for the first moment, have given his name a sound of refuge to Monny.

But there came a violent awakening out of this passive acquiescence. This was when Carroll De Lancey's own letter reached her (it came some twenty-four hours after Mrs. Van Cortlandt's visit to her room). Mr. Carroll's letter was a very proper love-letter; for when he was himself that young man had an admirable sense of the proprieties. But that any man in the universe should dare address love-words to her, save Mr. Leigh, thrilled her with a sense of mortal insult: she felt as an outraged wife might feel. Heretofore shame had fallen on her name only; now, with this marriage to another man, it would reach her very self, would burn into her own soul forever. This degradation she could not bear, and live; and out into the wild night she fled, distraught. Her insomnia of so many nights and days had become at last a self-begetting disease: to the fierce throbbing brain-cells there was no longer any possibility of rest. Only one idea was seized by her reeling faculties. It was that Heaven had always allowed women the right to choose death rather than dishonor, and that the hour of that last alternative had come to her. Out of a world where mistakes were

far more surely punished than crimes, a world which had
some terrible necessity to keep social forms inviolate at
any and every cost, she must go — and go to-night. She
felt the pursuers close on her track, — that strangest trio
of pursuers, — coming with that dreadful swiftness with
which all the crises of her fate had crowded on each
other; and deliriously she started for the sea. In the
deserted house, with only the deaf woman in the kitchen,
there was none to stay her: only a faithful, four-footed
creature sprang out and followed her as she ran from the
house.

"Go home!" she bade him. But Duke George, usually obedient to a word from his young mistress, found
something too strange about this lonely *sortie;* and, disappearing for a moment only, he was presently rushing
again by her side.

"Go home! go home!" she cried. But he only
wagged his tail deprecatingly : he would not leave her.

She fell on her knees, clinging desperately round his
neck, and sobbing, "Mind poor, poor Monny, and go
home."

As if the wail of human anguish pierced to the com-
prehension of the brute creature, this time the dog did go
back; and the panting fugitive went on her wild flight
alone.

All the stark immensity of sand and sea and sky lay
'n that kind of spectral gloom made by a moon shining
behind one uniform, thick veil of cloud ; only in the west
there was a long belt of livid light where the sun had
gone down, momently darkening, and, like a lonely speck
in the awful universe, the girl felt herself flying on and
on, with a blind terror in her crazing brain, lest that
sullen, vanishing light would not last long enough for her
to find her grave by. But the fire of fever in her veins

bore her up and on with such speed and strength, incredibly soon she reached the bluff, the beach, and that sound of the surge which told her that the tide — was not in, but coming. She fled on towards the sound; but her feet sank in the briny ooze: the belt of tide-mud was impassible. At this she turned, and rushed away for Roaring Ledge, — a broken chain of rocks which began a short distance above her, and extended far out into the deep sea. She had just reached this ledge when a shaggy form pushed against her — yes — Duke George. He had only made a feint of going back: at a little distance behind her he had stealthily followed all her flight. Many and many a time, at low water, had he gone out on Roaring Ledge with his young mistress (its farthest seaward rock was a favorite sketching-place with her), her light foot springing safely enough over the sea-channels between the rocks, when these were shallow, and the sun was shining. But now, in the slippery darkness, and with the hoarse tide coming in, the creature knew it was a place of death, and tugged at her dress to ask what wild business she had there. She thrust him off: but he would not leave her; and, as she still plunged wildly on, he flew after, beginning finally to bark aloud.

With a last, cruel sense that her very dog was turned her foe, the delirious girl leaped only the more desperately from point to point, catching foothold by that miraculous sense with which the somnambulist walks where the waking could not tread, — the tide was rushing in to meet her only a few rods beyond, and she could jump from the rocks into depths where the sea devoured its dead, and never rolled them in shore to trouble the eyes of the living. With this one idea in her burning brain, she bounded on, until in a desperate struggle with the dog, — who, as if comprehending at last that his mistress had

gone daft, seized her garments to detain her by force, —
she caught her foot, whirled, and fell headlong: her
temples struck with sharp concussion on the rock and
she knew no more.

Then, indeed, the dog, with no conflicting instinct of
obedience, lifted up his wild cry for help over that silent
form. Setting his teeth in the girl's garments, he dragged
her to the higher levels of the rock ; but even around
these the waves were rising with frightful rapidity, and a
bark that grew human in its anguish rang afar through
the shrouding darkness and over the beating seas.

———

A man who had ridden early and late rode up to the
Doane house not very long after Monny fled from it.
Mrs. Doane was with him. She had come home by rail
from the next station above Lonewater. To the first
inquiry made by both, the deaf housekeeper replied that
the young lady was quiet in her own rooms. These being
forthwith explored by Mrs. Doane, and found empty, she
said to Mr. Leigh, "She has gone to the village, of
course ; probably to the Widow Macey's. Some one will
be coming home with her presently."

Waiting being impossible to the man's mood, he was
rushing out of the door to go to the village, when Bobby
Hines, small member of the very large Hines family,
came running up the yard, calling out, "Where's Miss
Monny Rivers?"

At this echo of everybody's cry, Mr. Leigh stood still,
while the child panted on, — .

"The tide hev' got her dog out on Roaring Ledge, and
he's barking dreadful! And mother said I must come
and tell Miss Rivers, cos she'd take on so if he was
drownded. Mother said maybe he'd hurt hisself out

torment you a good deal more. But what could anybody
do about it?"

"It was a very bad business," said the general.

"Was it a business to be told of? Was that story, in
any of its features, a story for general circulation? Of
course, I expected Miss Rivers would tell her husband,
when she came to have one. But, at the time, was it not
the part of wisdom, so far as human wisdom can foresee
any thing, to hush the whole thing up?"

Gen. Bingham here did finally make some concessions
to his wife's view of things; but, perhaps because it hurt
him so much to make them, he presently turned to another
phase of the subject.

"Pretty, you say she is, this bride of so many perils?
What is her style?"

"Round and dimpled," replied the lady, "dark eyes,
and the most beautiful fair hair and complexion in the
world."

"How charming! There shall be a reception in her
honor, to which none but men shall be admitted, especially
the unhappily married men like myself (Gen. Bingham
worshipped his wife). Do you suppose, that, after suffering the oblations of women to Kenyon Leigh, the men
of this parish are not going to take it out now in adoring
his wife?"

"You know that you worship Mr. Leigh yourself," put
in the lady; "only, being a man, nobody misunderstands
your sentiments."

"Well, the feminine worshippers will have the same
'mmunity, now that he is to be married, and married to a
being who has inspired him with a veritable *grande pas
sion*, as it seems the golden-haired young person has. I
find that exactly as it should be. The rockiest heart that
is walled up around emptiness will tempt the artillery of

the daring; but the one fortress of that kind which the most roving sentimentalist leaves in peace is the one that is occupied already by a supreme conqueror. Yes," concluded the general, "we secular men may worry along as we can with our imperfect mates; but to a 'magnetic' minister Heaven should send his absolute affinity. Of a pulpit genius you should always be able to say in one and the same breath, 'He's a great preacher, and very much in love with his wife.'"

If doubts still trouble the mind of readers as to the fitness of Monny Rivers for a minister's wife, it is certain that she would meet the case as defined by Gen. Bingham; and, the general being a chief warden of Mr. Leigh's own church, it will be seen that the *parish* was satisfied. That is enough.

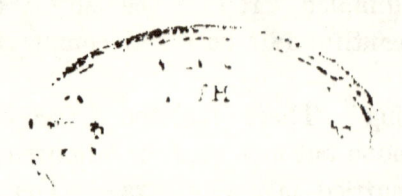

of the strange events which had attended his courtship),
"one mystery, which, as a man, I humbly ask you to
explain to me, my dear. Why, why, *why*, did you ever
advise Miss Rivers to secrecy in the first place, when
an open disclosure at the time of all the facts, just as
they were, about that New-Orleans journey, would have
shown everybody how absolutely innocent the girl was of
any fault whatever?"

"Spoken like a man," replied the lady; "when, after
two or three repetitions, all the facts would infallibly have
been told just as they were not. Once let out such an
adventure as that about a young girl, and 'Enter Rumor.
painted full of tongues.'"

"Oh, if we must hide facts, because liars will pervert
them!" said the general.

"You know, Arthur, you *must* acknowledge, that men
can afford to have facts told, when women cannot. At
the very best, that story would have given Miss Rivers's
name a dashing, adventurous sound, — a kind of name
that no girl ever deserved less."

"And if rescue had come to her a little later that
drowning night, and she had died there, as the end of all
that mad tangle of lies that she had been wound up in by
concealment, would not that have been rather more serious
than to have had a wrong sound given to her name half a
dozen years before? Young members of the sensitive
sex have drowned themselves, and never been brought to
life again, either, for considerably less cause than she had
after Mrs. Van Cortlandt got hold of her and her story.
You see, that story was not completely hidden, with all
your pains. There was Mrs. Van Cortlandt knowing it
all the while. Somebody always *does* know things that
have really occurred," persisted the man.

"Now, Arthur, could any mortal foresee the criminal

The boat came up, and took in the three,—the man, the dog, and the maiden; but her they lifted as we lift the dead.

———

"Is she dead?" a tall, proud woman came stealing up to Mrs. Doane's door to ask, an hour or more after the unconscious young form had been borne through it.

Susannah lifted high the lamp, and glared fiercely into the speaker's face. "If she *is* dead, an' you want to 'scape the gallows, go buy yourself a dose of sure pison, and drink it quick! For Mr. Leigh hab found out all your wickedness,—tellin' lies on dat pore drowned chile; an' if she never open her innercent eyes again, he'll hab you hung for her murderer!"

From these lowly lips Mrs. Van Cortlandt knew her doom; and the poor, guilty sinner slunk away in the darkness, hastening to put the breadth of a hemisphere between herself and the place where she had played a satanic game, and lost it.

———

The rescued victim did open her eyes again, but not with any knowledge of what they looked on, for many long nights and days. It was through the very gates of death that she came back to life, and oft was the passage terribly uncertain.

But youth at last conquered, and the love that watched her with superhuman watch-care.

———

"There's one thing," said Gen. Bingham to his wife (Kenyon Leigh's wedding-cards were just out, and had moved a new rehearsal, by this deeply interested fireside,

www.ingramcontent.com/pod-product-compliance
Lightning Source LLC
Chambersburg PA
CBHW031050110726
47900CB00003B/874